BEHIND DISTANT STARS

Book Two in the Chronicles of Fid

David H. Reiss

Behind Distant Stars Copyright © 2018 by David H. Reiss. All Rights Reserved.

All rights reserved. No part of this book may be reproduced in any form or by any electronic or mechanical means including information storage and retrieval systems, without permission in writing from the author. The only exception is by a reviewer, who may quote short excerpts in a review.

Cover designed by David H. Reiss

This book is a work of fiction. Names, characters, places, and incidents either are products of the author's imagination or are used fictitiously. Any resemblance to actual persons, living or dead, events, or locales is entirely coincidental.

David H. Reiss
Visit my website at www.davidhreiss.com

Printed in the United States of America

First Printing: Sept 2018
Atian Press

ISBN: 9781718081536

Dedicated to Freya.
(Farewell, little huntress. You were loved. You are missed.)

Also, to Drew.
A more patient, supportive and loving spouse has never lived.

To Mom and Dad,
for so many reasons that I can't count.

And to David, Jeremy and John,
who have once more been essential in helping to bring a book to fruition by serving in the roles of pre-readers, assistant editors, and (most importantly) friends.

CHAPTER ONE

THE FIRST STRIKE TOOK ME BY SURPRISE, A BLAST of cerulean energies that splattered harmlessly off the back of my helm. Alarm shocked through my system and my heart pounded in my chest; the suit's sensors should have detected and prioritized any threats before so near an approach. Their failure indicated the possibility of a dangerously competent enemy. Long-ingrained reflex guided my quick spin and energy-weapons activation, instantaneously ready to counterattack with deadly force.

My disbelieving gaze was still focused upon my opponent when the second ineffective beam reflected off my chest.

"Surrender, Doctor Fid," my assailant demanded. "You won't escape this time!"

I was floating a few inches above the ground and encased within what is often described as the most fearsome and technically-advanced powered armor in human history. Faceless, emotionless; the suit's surface did not reflect light at all. Within the black were displayed the stars, distant pricks of light and nebulae, the night sky held within my person. Were it not for the crimson glow that seeped from the armor's joints, Doctor Fid would have appeared an imposing man-shaped rift into deep space.

The silence stretched uncomfortably long.

"...Do your parents know that you're out fighting crime at this hour?" I finally asked. "It's a school night."

Evidently, that was a poor choice of phrasing if my goal was to dissuade a rebellious teen-aged superhero from attacking.

The young hero scowled, flying a low circle around me and launching blast after blast of his blue-tinted energy beams. I was compelled to admit that (when sufficiently motivated by childish pique) the boy was capable of generating a fair bit of power. If I'd been wearing a version of my armor only a generation or three prior, I would have been forced to evade. Currently, however, I was safely cocooned within the upgraded Mk 36b: my latest medium-duty model, with frame and armor-plates upgraded to the remarkable orichalcum alloy. Only my now-legendary 14-foot-tall Mk 35 heavy-combat armor was mightier. The new force-fields held, and the hero's glowing streams of power poured off of me and boiled into the air.

Cherenkov was a relative newcomer to the superhero scene; a Manhattan-local social-media superstar who mimicked the melodramatic style of speech favored by many of the more publicity-savvy champions, he used recordings of his battles to build his brand. He'd been trending very high on the Internet recently and had used his popularity to crowdfund the purchase of his new admittedly-quite-professional-looking costume: A black bodysuit with white stripes and cobalt trim, constructed excellently from the highest-end of the skin-tight protective materials. His belt had a series of utility pouches and a simple domino mask hid his identity; when his powers were active, his eyes, eyebrows and close-cropped hair all glowed the same color as the energy blasts that he was so thoughtlessly throwing.

(The youth's superheroic alias, at least, was worthy of approval; it had been Russian physicist Pavel Cherenkov who'd first identified the specific effect of radiation that caused certain forms of nuclear reactors to glow the same color as the boy's energies. A proper reverence for luminaries in the scientific fields was admirable.)

I identified his nearby camera drones and began circumventing their electronic security, then floated higher off the ground to limit the chance that the boy's missed attacks would accidentally start a fire; he'd located me near some Hudson River docks and there were wood-framed buildings nearby.

"You should re-think your choices, child," I sighed, though the Mk 36b's vocoder that disguised my voice also struck much of my weariness from my tone. "This cannot possibly end well for you."

"I'm NOT a child!" he grunted, gathering himself and aiming his most impressive burst yet.

"Then stop acting childish. You literally cannot harm me," I said as the pale-blue beam dissolved against my force-fields.

"I have to do something! You're a villain, and I'm a superhero," he called back. "It's not rocket science!"

I'd been younger than Cherenkov the first time that I'd plotted an orbital re-entry as an amusing hobby-project; rocket science was no mystery to me. Why the boy continued to press his useless attacks, however, remained a conundrum. While I was certain that the young man was competent against lesser threats, I was Doctor Fid! For more than two decades, I'd left a trail of violence and destruction in my wake.

Just in case the child's intent was to delay me until reinforcements could arrive, I ordered a small fleet of my microdrones to keep their sensors configured to watch for the approach of additional heroes. A remote-hack of the cellular phone that Cherenkov kept in one of his belt-pouches indicated that he hadn't sent any recent messages, but it never hurt to be careful. Buried amongst his private messages, however, was an e-mail from one of his fans that suggested a possible explanation for his continued aggression.

"You were a hero," I objected, blocking his next blast with the palm of my hand. "At the beginning, when you first started your video channel. You stood up to bullies, took down local drug dealers, tried to make your school safe. But now you're just another glory-seeking fool, chasing ratings so desperately that you'd start a fight you have no chance of winning." The email had suggested that fighting the infamous Doctor Fid would attract additional viewers and offered guidance as to where I might be found. How that knowledge had been acquired would be an issue to research at a later date. "You can have your footage, but I'm leaving."

I aimed a pulse of kinetic energy at the flying teen, insufficient to cause damage but adequate to knock him back a few feet. Cherenkov's eyes widened and he crossed his arms over his chest to soften the blow as it struck. He looked surprised, as though the idea that he might be hit was somehow unexpected.

I have, in the past, swatted Peregrine from the sky and targeted Haste mid-sprint; Cherenkov was swift, but not nearly so quick as some of his older brethren. Had he never viewed footage of my prior battles? In any case, the lack of damage seemed to embolden him and he wasted several more blasts of his pale-blue energy attack upon my shields as I slowly drifted higher into the night.

"Do not attempt to follow." From the information that I'd gleaned online, the young hero's flight power was limited in altitude. It would be a simple thing, to climb to the clouds and then make my exit.

"Hah! Run away, then," he taunted, and I could hear the elation in his voice. "The forums are right, you have gone soft!"

"That," I said, my departure halting as I slowly spun to face the superpowered social media celebrity, "was a phenomenally stupid thing to say aloud."

"What are you going to do about it, old man?" he challenged, though I could see the frightened realization dawn in his eyes. There must have been some method to his madness, some specific drama that he'd intended to film; he was, however, suddenly realizing that I wasn't following the same script. Cherenkov began to float backward reflexively, putting more distance between us.

The few paltry meters would in no way be sufficient.

"I'm going to give you some advice, Corey," I chuckled darkly, the Mk 36b's vocoder altering my voice such that it dripped with menace. "You don't mind if I call you Corey, do you?"

"Wh-what?" The high-school-aged boy yelped and was shocked into stopping his slow retreat. "How did you...?"

"You activated your camera drones using your mother's credit card," I explained. "Also, your first costume was constructed of SpectraMax Duraweave #112, and the only order for that color in this region was paid for from the same account."

"You can't do that," he blustered. "You can't just steal credit card information and unmask people!"

"I'm a villain, Corey, and this isn't a game." I slowly floated closer. "But you needn't be concerned about your identity being revealed; I've shut off your camera drones' audio."

For two decades, the world's mightiest heroes have stepped back nervously when I appeared ready for battle. If those same heroes discovered how many secret identities I had divined through via data-mining algorithms, the mass apoplexy would shake the world. In general, though, the information I'd gathered had been used only for research and planning purposes during the process of choosing which so-called 'superhero' would be my next target. Cherenkov was only the second to whom I'd revealed such knowledge, and I wasn't certain that doing so now was a wise choice. Still, he'd irked me; I wanted the teenager cowed.

"Wh-what," the young hero stammered nervously, looking very much out of his depth. "What are you going to do to me?"

"Advice, Corey. As I said. I'm going to give you some advice." I summoned my ruby-pommeled scepter (one of Doctor Fid's more well-known implements of terror) to my hand and Cherenkov visibly flinched. At a mental command, the starfield pattern displayed within my armor began to slowly swirl. "And you are going to pay attention!"

"Okay! I get it." He bit his lower lip, gaze occasionally flicking from side to side as though looking for assistance or escape. Neither was immediately forthcoming. "I'm listening."

"Very well." I aimed the tip of my scepter at the flying, glowing teen and he cringed. The boy's shift in demeanor made me smile behind my faceless mask, but the armor's vocoder removed all amusement from Doctor Fid's threatening voice. "If you intend on being a social media star, I wish you well of it. You've developed the skill set to market yourself effectively, I'm sure that you'll be successful.

"But if you truly intend to be a hero," I continued, "then you need additional training and significantly more backup. The 'lone avenger' act may play well to romantic archetypes, but it's far too easy to be caught off guard when you are alone. If you had four or five companions and stumbled across a threat too dangerous for you to manage, you might have been able to cover each other's escape. But right now, your fate is entirely mine to decide."

He gulped.

"My suggestion is that you reach out to one of the local hero teams; they have contact information for all the training facilities. Tuition is often waived for promising students, but even if not...I'm certain that your crowdfunding talents could be put to use."

"...Uhh..."

"Training with one of the major schools will help when you need to be licensed and will make you eligible for lower insurance premiums. Being an uninsured vigilante right now may seem like fun, but the moment you turn eighteen the vultures will begin to circle."

"...Okay."

"Finally, and I can't stress this enough...think before you act. Sometimes, discretion really is the better part of valor! Justice is often better served by making a phone call to the authorities rather than intervening yourself."

"Okay," the now sullen teenager repeated, looking subdued. "Yeah, I get it. I will."

"Good," I stated evenly. "Very good."

"Thanks, I guess."

"You're welcome," I laughed softly. "And now, you can help me with a problem of my own."

"Um. Okay...?"

"Apparently, some members of online forums have been saying that Doctor Fid has gone soft." I swung my scepter experimentally, as though warming up my arm. "You and your cameras are going to help disabuse them of that notion."

"What?" He looked surprised. "How?"

"As an object lesson." It took a moment for the statement to sink in, and his eyes widened in fear. "But don't worry...I've already called for an ambulance and verified that you're covered by your mother's medical insurance."

Cherenkov tried to flee, then tried to fight. Neither solution worked in his favor.

❦ ❦ ❦

An adorable little android was glaring at me.

"What?" I asked finally, setting down my soldering iron. This secret laboratory was isolated deep in the mountains, but since the new and much-safer teleportation platforms had been installed...this location was just as convenient as any other. Also, it was just as easy for my artificially-intelligent ward to find and surprise me here as it would have been at our home.

"You hurt him!" she complained, crossing her arms across her chest. This was her second body: a delicate child-like frame with no hair and skin too perfectly smooth to be human. Her expressive eyes, now narrowed accusingly, glowed robin-egg blue. "You were supposed to just let him go!"

"Supposed to?" I chuckled, "Whisper, Cherenkov attacked me, not the other way around."

"Ok. Um," the elfin android looked embarrassed. "I **thought** you'd just let him go. 'cause he's harmless, I mean."

"I'd planned on it." I stood and slowly stretched; the

medical nanites that suffused my system did much to relieve the infirmities of middle-age and the wear-and-tear that a violent lifestyle inflicted upon my body, but for some reason did nothing to eliminate tension when I'd been slouching over a desk too long. I'd need to reevaluate their programming. "He pressed the issue and was in need of instruction."

"He's in the hospital, Terry!" Whisper objected.

"Some lessons are painful," I frowned, reminiscing. "The important lessons, even more so."

"I just...didn't think that you'd hurt him, is all. He's not much older than me."

Technically, I supposed that she was older than the high-school hero. Her creator had started work on her program two decades prior, but she'd only gained sentience after a few years of work...and her emotional development had been stalled for several years due to hardware limitations. When I freed her from isolation, I'd granted her access to significantly more computing power and she'd since begun to slowly mature; the child psychologists who had been consulted all concurred that Whisper's psyche seemed to be that of a perfectly healthy, albeit extraordinary, eleven-year-old girl.

"He's a teenager, almost an adult," I replied, although in retrospect I was possibly the worst person in the world to be judgmental about emotional development relative to one's own age. I'd completed my doctorate by Corey Pierson's age, and yet I'd been far older before I'd truly begun to understand responsibility; feeling more than a bit hypocritical, I smiled softly to the android that I considered to be my little sister.

I may have thought of her a sibling, but our actual relationship was more complicated. The first wholly artificial being recognized under the Synthetic Americans' Rights law, Whisper was my civilian identity's ward. There could be no replacing her deceased father/creator, so adoption hadn't been an option. And besides, I didn't know how to be a parent.

I'd been a big brother once before. I'd been a failure, then; this time would be different.

"You're right," I acknowledged. "I should have shown more restraint."

"Mm!" she agreed.

"I'll send a card, and make sure that no one else can trace his identity the way I did," I sighed. "Fortunately, I did no permanent damage; he'll be fine. He's just lucky that he ran into Doctor Fid! There are villains in that neighborhood who would have done far worse."

"Um. Yeah," Whisper giggled nervously. "Lucky."

"Whisper," I spoke slowly, "have you been lurking on Cherenkov's fan forums?"

"...maybe...?"

"And did you feed Cherenkov information about how to find me?" I'd been on my way back from a visit to the Lassiter's Den, a secretive bar and restaurant that catered to supervillains. If the boy had confronted me only a few blocks earlier, other villains would have joined the battle to try and make certain that the location of their favorite watering hole was not compromised; it would have been a bloodbath.

(An odd thought occurred to me; I happened to know for a fact that the current leader of the New York Shield - one of the most powerful superhero teams in the United States - was aware of Lassiter's Den, but there had been no raids or attacks. Another mystery added to the queue, something to investigate further another time.)

"His eyes glow the same color as mine!" she defended, apropos of nothing.

What did his appearance have to do with whether or not she'd sent- Ah. It was beginning to sound as though Whisper had a minor crush on the young hero that I'd just finished pummeling. Oops.

"I just thought his videos would be more popular if he showed that he could fight Doctor Fid," she finished, looking embarrassed.

Oh, sweetheart, I'm sorry. I shifted to mental contact so that she could sense my self-reproach. The neural interface through which I controlled Doctor Fid's armor had long since been upgraded such that we could communicate instantly via quantum-tunneled network, even if I were as distant as high Earth orbit. The capability to transmit deeper emotional content was an unexpected benefit. **You should have said something!**

I was asleep. She looked away, flustered. The updated programming and new body that I'd provided for her allowed for her to rest and dream; Whisper was still getting used to experiencing altered states of consciousness.

I checked my system's log files to verify another

suspicion. Cherenkov had been able to approach unnoticed because he'd been specifically designated as a non-threat to my automated systems. Whisper had been thorough.

He seems like a good kid, I comforted, then switched back to speaking aloud. "I'm sure that he'll be back up and posting videos in no time."

"Are you sure?" she asked, nibbling at her lower lip.

"I'm not positive, but I think it very likely. Anything else happen while I was out?"

"Not really." Her expression looked absent while she parsed through thousands of media feeds. "Nothing worth mentioning."

"In that case, I think I should get some rest, too." I made certain that my tools were stored away properly then began moving towards the teleport platform. "Let's go home."

" 'kay."

❧ ❧ ❧

When my current house had been purchased, it had been larger than I'd needed; the property had been a status symbol appropriate for my civilian identity's position as CEO of a growing biotechnology company, a well-furnished mansion in which to grant interviews or impress investors. I hosted dinners for AH Biotech's executive staff, too; inviting them into my 'home' improved morale.

My true refuge had been in my labs and manufacturing facilities, separate installations hidden throughout the northeastern United States. Every lab had a cot and a refrigerator; for years, I'd barely spent any time at all in Terry Markham's estate.

That pattern had changed when I'd invited Whisper into my life. We played at the domicile, visited with her friends. The house was still larger than was necessary but it no longer felt empty.

The smell of frying bacon lured me to the kitchen.

"You're up early," I yawned. "What's the occasion?"

"Dinah got another puppy!" Whisper was standing on a step-stool at the stove, making pancakes. Also, making a mess that I would need to clean up later. "You're going to take me to her Dad's house, so I can meet it."

"I am, am I?" I couldn't help but smile.

"Mm!"

"As you wish." I poured myself a mug of coffee and sat down at the kitchen table; soon, a plate-full of lopsided pancakes and only-slightly-burned bacon was set before me. "Thank you."

She set no plate for herself; when we'd begun designing her current body, we hadn't considered adding the capability to eat. She seemed to enjoy cooking, though, so further research and testing were on the list of action items.

"Yum!" I told her; she smiled cheerfully and hacked my brain to borrow the sensory data. "What time is Aaron expecting us?"

Aaron Schwartz was the CIO of AH Biotech; he'd been with the company for years, and his daughter was Whisper's best friend. Terry Markham had, as CEO, long maintained the appearance of amiable camaraderie with his subordinate; the illusion had crystallized over the course of the prior year, and Aaron was as close to a genuine friend as I currently had.

"At ten!"

"I'll finish eating and get ready."

"Yay! Oh. Um...and you have to promise not to be mad at Cherenkov."

And suddenly, the breakfast bribe made more sense.

"I was only asleep for a few hours," I complained. "What did he do?"

"He was trying to be nice," she insisted. "He said that he was out of line, and thanked Doctor Fid for taking it easy on him."

"Oh, for the love of Tesla..."

"He may have also mentioned that you gave him good advice on how to be a better hero."

My hands covered my face. "I'm guessing that the online communities took notice?"

The android giggled prettily.

"Doctor Fid was the most feared supervillain on the planet," I complained tiredly. "I fought Valiant for twenty-two and a half minutes!"

"And then you saved the world," Whisper sang merrily.

"I was taking vengeance against Sphinx and the Legion!" I threw up my hands dramatically. If my ward-slash-adopted sister wanted to make this argument into a game, I was willing to play along. "Saving the world was just a side effect. Besides, I live here too! It was selfish, really."

"And you saved that kitten..."

"It was falling off a window ledge," I defended weakly.

"That was just reflex."

"Don't be mad at Cherenkov," she insisted. "The kitten video has more downloads, by far."

In retrospect, that kitten had been the beginning of the real public-perception shift. Prior to that damned calico, the media hadn't known which way to jump. Cloner, the new leader of the New York Shield, had been publicly declaring that I had averted an alien invasion and freed dozens of worlds from horrific oppression...but most remembered my vicious battle with Valiant, and the image of Doctor Fid's fearsome armor facing down one of the largest forces of heroes ever assembled. They remembered footage of brutal beating after brutal beating, two decades of pain and destruction left in my wake.

But then I was soaring over downtown Boston and heard a little boy crying for his mother's help. Somehow, his kitten had squeezed out of his apartment window onto the building's slim ledge, well out of his reach. The earlier rain had left the concrete wet and cold, and the poor thing was shivering and mewling helplessly. The child was begging, weeping, calling for Mason (the kitten's name, presumably) to come back...but the unfortunate feline was too scared, too confused.

And then there was a gust of wind, and tiny Mason stumbled and began to fall. The child shrieked like his heart was breaking and I dove from the sky like an ebon comet.

"Thank you, Mister Fid!" the boy whispers as I carefully hand the squirming kitten back through the window. His focus is on

Mason, not on the armored horror floating outside his apartment, and his fingers tremble as he strokes the beloved pet.

"It's Doctor, actually," I reply, the armor's vocoder stripping the embarrassed relief from my voice.

"Thank you, Mister Doctor!"

I made sure that the window was safely closed and continued my errands, then ended up in one of my laboratories performing tests. It was hours before I discovered that the incident had been captured on film and gone viral.

"I haven't gone soft," I grumbled. "I just haven't found anyone worth mauling in a while."

"Can we get a puppy, Mister Doctor?" my sister teased.

"Sure. Fid will drown it on camera."

"No, he won't!" Whisper looked scandalized.

"No. But this is getting out of hand, Whisper. I know you think that it's funny, but it's not. I spent more than two decades building Doctor Fid's reputation. The work is important."

"The heroes are all still afraid of you," she assured me, though there was a hint of reproof in her voice. "It's just the media. Blow something up, beat up someone popular, they'll remember who you are."

"I just live streamed the cudgeling of a teenager." I sighed and used my neural interface to mentally scan through recent comment threads on the KNN CapeWatch forums, and other news commentary. "They're treating it as evidence that Doctor Fid is a hero."

"Then maybe Doctor Fid should become a hero."

"You know," I smiled slowly. "That might not be a bad idea."

"Really?" She perked up, expression one of surprise and wonder.

"It could work marvelously!" I grinned and swept the little android up in a brief hug. "No matter what the pundits are currently saying, though, it will take some time to convince the world that Doctor Fid has really changed. This would be a long-term plan."

"I can help!" she chirped enthusiastically, "I can watch the news feeds and online forums to analyze public opinions, and we could plan and make Doctor Fid the best hero ever!"

"Your assistance would be very much appreciated."

"Yay!"

I closed my eyes, envisioning the way it might play out. Right now, the media only toyed with the idea that Doctor Fid was a hero, that one of the world's most feared supervillains had reformed; over time, that could be shaped and built upon...what would at first be only a faint hope would swell until the populace was firmly—finally—convinced. The idea of redemption was powerful; eventually, Doctor Fid would be welcomed.

Some heroes would never truly be persuaded, but in public they'd be forced to play along. I imagined Doctor Fid standing alongside local heroes, cameras flashing as the former villain reached out to the leader of the Boston Guardians to symbolize a new alliance. Titan's jaw would clench so hard that the veins at his temples throbbed, but he'd force a smile and accept the handshake.

"When I finally return to normal," I murmured, hand closing as though responding to the imaginary Titan's grasp. "When I finally return to being Doctor Fid, they'll be crushed. A betrayal like that...people will hate me like never before."

"...what?"

"It's a brilliant idea, Whisper. Thank you!" Using my neural link to contact my primary computer systems, I opened several new project files and started gathering resources to begin constructing a proper plan.

The media's current treatment of Doctor Fid was unacceptable; this new scheme would take significant amounts of time and effort to implement, but the narrative would, in the end, be under my control. I could return to my crusade and punish the unworthy. Even better, I would serve as an example that the public granted trust to their heroes far too easily. The next time one of their champions betrayed the people's confidence, the hero might actually be held accountable. It would be glorious.

Whisper was staring at me with an indecipherable expression on her face, so I grinned reassuringly. "If Aaron is expecting us at ten, I should probably start getting ready. We can wait to begin work until afterward."

"Okay," she responded quietly.

Feeling brighter for having decided upon a plan of action, I hurried off to shower, shave and otherwise prepare myself for the day.

CHAPTER TWO

Aaron handed me a beer; it was a generic brand, not one of the craft brews that I'd become snobbish about lately. It was, however, cold in my hand.

"Thank you." I took a grateful swallow. It was a hot day and both of us were too close to the grill, poking at burgers while watching the children run with the playful dogs; Whisper had been oddly quiet for the drive, but her mood had brightened after only a few moments of exposure to the new puppy. "I'm glad that we got a chance to visit before you left."

"Me too," he smiled, waving to his daughter. "We're only going to be gone for a month, but Dinah's definitely going to miss Whisper."

"They'll text and video-chat," I replied dryly. "Whisper is good about that."

"It's not the same."

"No, I suppose that it isn't." I was only guessing. My own youth had not been characterized by a thriving social life; I'd been too mentally advanced to develop friendships with children my own age, and too emotionally immature to connect with my intellectual peers. I had my books, and eventually my coworkers...but I was already of age when I first developed true friendships. As an adult, I'd gained sufficient perspective that a few weeks of absence had not felt so overwhelming. I was, however, observant enough to notice Whisper's growing sadness as her friend's departure date neared. "Still, when you get back, Dinah will have interesting stories to tell."

"It's gonna be a great trip!" Aaron agreed. "My first road trip in ages. Finally get a chance to see the country a bit."

"I've driven cross-country a few times now," I noted, and swiped a pair of tongs to check my burger for done-ness. "Every trip's been worth the effort. You're bringing the dogs?"

"Only for the first part. We're leaving them with my parents in Shenandoah."

"In that case, make sure to bring books or movies for Dinah." I'd only been on one road trip with Whisper and she was extraordinarily patient for a creature her mental age. Decades ago, before my younger brother Bobby had been murdered...those road trips had been exercises in boredom management. Books, movies, toys, snacks...We'd cycled through them all, and even then frequent stops had been the norm.

"We will," he nodded, then smiled teasingly. "You going to be able to hold down the fort while I'm gone?"

"I'll do my best to make sure the company's still standing when you get back," I replied; truth be told, I didn't expect a tremendous change in my own workload. Aaron had trained his subordinates well, and any problems would likely be handled long before they landed on the CEO's desk. "You're taking the northern route?"

"No, there're a bunch of big wildfires, don't want to get cut off."

"Yeah...I heard about that," I lied, as I used my neural tap to browse through news reports and hacked internal memos from the U.S. Department of the Interior and the Federal Emergency Management Agency. It looked as though this year was particularly bad, with six large blazes currently burning and fire departments working around the clock to contain the damage. "I just hadn't realized that the roads would be closed."

"It's been a particularly bad year, this year," he lamented.

"And a hot summer."

We toasted to the pleasant heat and drank from our still-ice-cold beers.

I started a program to perform detailed analysis of firefighting techniques; if Doctor Fid were to be seen a hero, then saving firefighters and combating the conflagration would be a good place to start. Professional heroes rarely intervened in wildfires; they may receive some protection from good Samaritan laws, but the liability insurance policies that most heroes operated under was almost always limited to specific locales. There were several volumes worth of fine-print and exceptions but as a general rule...if a hero was outside their contracted region and happened to witness an event where superheroic intervention would be a boon, their insurance would cover liability. If a government official specifically asked for assistance, their insurance would cover liability even if they had to travel to arrive on site. But involving oneself in a distant emergency without an invitation could be professionally ruinous.

Of course, a villain like Doctor Fid was not concerned about liability issues. Perhaps embarking upon a public works project to improve upon existing firebreaks would make for useful publicity…

Disaster assistance - and, perhaps, more kitten-rescue - seemed as though it would be a preferred first step; with sufficient publicity, it would be inevitable that the media become enamored with the desired narrative: that Doctor Fid had turned over a new leaf.

(Interrupting crime would be more dramatic, but also much more likely to end in confusion. If I were present when a hero responded to a bank robbery, the actually-guilty villain might get away while I was busy subduing the spandex-wearing do-gooder.)

"You're leaving on Monday?" I asked to confirm.

"Yup. It'll take that long just to get packed."

I continued to make small talk but was distracted by planning. Over sixty-seven thousand acres of currently active conflagration…even with the vast technological resources available to Doctor Fid, it would be almost impossible to quell the fires before my company's CIO began his journey.

There was nothing quite so invigorating as a proper

challenge.

❦ ❦ ❦

In the towering Mk 35 powered armor, I soared over devastation; the ground was black with char, smoke swirled and sparks climbed through the rippling heat. Soot-covered tree trunks, denuded by the hungry flames that had already devoured this region, stabbed into the air like irregularly spaced still-hot spikes.

My research had indicated that wildfires were a natural part of the ecological lifecycle. Even so, flying over mile after mile of destruction was sobering.

A dozen heavy-combat drones formed a wide circle around the Mk 35; with weaponry and walking-legs retracted, the automatons appeared to be naught but massive star-field patterned columns floating through the air. The horizon glowed, muted by billowing black smoke, and I sped towards the blaze's front. Emergency-radio broadcasts had indicated a team of firefighters had been cut off by shifting wind patterns.

Help was en route, but I was closer.

A fire is, when viewed objectively, a fairly simple system consisting of three components: Heat, fuel, and oxygen. Remove any one of those components and the flame is extinguished. Theoretically, I could devise a force-field that selectively filtered atmospheric oxygen, and any fire within that field's boundaries would be extinguished; I would need to maintain that field until the region had cooled, else heat and fuel could cause reignition, but approaching the triangle from that corner was at least hypothetically plausible.

On the macro-scale, removing the fuel was the simplest solution: carefully placed blasts from Doctor Fid's (and from the drones') weaponry to clear grass and trees from the wildfire's path, and the flames would burn themselves out when they had finished consuming the fuel at one edge of the destruction. It was only a matter of creating a broad enough firebreak that wind could not carry sufficient sparks to restart the blaze. Even with the wind kicked to a chaotic roar by the fire's rising heat, it would be a relatively simple task to create a broad enough gap. Unfortunately, the process would be sufficiently destructive that the method would be too dangerous to use when there are civilians to be rescued on the ground.

Eliminating the heat was the most technically intriguing problem. One of the most important defensive inventions within my arsenal has been my inertial displacement device, a method of creating a bounded energy field linked to an artificially-created pocket-dimension; the actual functionality was complicated, but the end result was that the field allowed for kinetic energy to be shunted from the normal world into the pocket-dimension. This limited the effect of impacts or sudden accelerations upon whatever is inside the field. A punch from the extraordinarily-powerful Valiant was painful even through armor and displacement-field, but at least my head was not rattled to jelly inside my armor.

(The Red Ghost and I had formed a secret partnership to

bring similar devices to the public, creating safer automobiles. The first generation of protected vehicles had recently arrived at dealerships around the world.)

Heat is just an expression of molecular vibration; it had taken seven and a half hours of study and testing, but I'd now refined a method of re-directing said energy from the physical world into a pocket-dimension as well. The process was too slow to be used as the primary means of firefighting. Even with all twelve heavy drones assisting, it would only be able to affect a few thousand square feet at a time. Over sixty thousand acres were currently engulfed in flames, so attacking so vast a swathe of land a few hundred feet at a time would be a fool's errand. It would, however, be the safer option when attempting to perform a rescue.

As I neared the trapped firemen, my drones deployed their spider-like walking legs and dropped to the forest floor and I landed among them; the thermal-redirection field was fiddly; anti-gravity and flight capabilities would have interfered with the new feature's functionality.

Beyond the circle formed by the combat-drones, the world was aflame. Tendrils of every conceivable shade of yellow and orange swirled, crackling and rumbling, devouring everything in its path and rendering the ground barely visible through the churning blaze. The canopy carried the flames higher, towering more than a hundred feet into the air and making the thick smoke glow. It was an illusion, I knew, but the inferno seemed alive...seductively beautiful and yet terribly hungry.

Within the circle, the flames perished; charred husks cast

smoke only for a moment before settling into a chilled and silent tableau. This was a forest's gravesite, grim and still. I marched forward, carrying an island of cool and forbidding safety with me as I moved.

I found them, a twenty-man crew, huddled in emergency fire shelters: a line of side-by-side silvered cocoons. With chainsaw, adze, and shovel, they had hewn a circular firebreak around their makeshift camp, but the roaring flames had lit the canopy above and cast embers among them. The flames were too close, too hot, and oxygen was being sucked away to feed the greedy blaze. The shelters' mirrored surface did much to reflect radiant heat and to trap at least a little bit of breathable air within, but the unfortunate firefighters would not have survived much longer without assistance.

My approach was inaudible over the wildfire's crackling roar; the sudden chill, however, would have been immediately noticeable when the drones encircled the camp. Even so, it was nearly thirty seconds before they began to stir. The delay was a reasonable precaution; opening one of those emergency shelters too soon could be a deadly mistake. With the metallic-skinned pods still enclosed, they began to talk among themselves.

("Is it over?" "What the hell…" "Quiet, everyone! Count off! Barton, you ok?" "I'm fine." "Eric?" "All good." The foreman continued asking after his men, and the relief in their voices was plain as it became clear that none were injured.)

I cleared my throat; the Mk 35's vocoder made the sound

loud enough to pierce the roar of flames that still surged beyond the circle of cold my drones provided. "We are in no real rush, but the fire continues to advance," I commented evenly. "I was hoping to create a firebreak before the Grey Mountain Vineyards are consumed."

Emergency shelters exploded open with the frenzied efforts of the men trapped within, soot-covered and weary firefighters emerging like pupae from a chrysalis. The foreman stilled and grabbed the man next to him by one shoulder, but the others swore and scrambled away. One or two looked towards the flames, eyes wide as they considered trying their luck within the conflagration rather than confronting the notorious villain that somehow stood among them.

I couldn't help but feel a moment of vindication; the media's ongoing attempts to paint me as a hero had not yet been so successful that those who met me were unafraid. Even brave men would risk the pyre rather than face Doctor Fid! Twenty years of villainy was not so easily erased from hearts and minds. Sadly, today's plan was to scratch away at that reputation rather than to reinforce it.

"Do not be alarmed!" I ordered. "I'm here to help."

They didn't look at all reassured, but the foreman was quickest to realize that their options were limited.

"Thank you," he smiled unsteadily. "It was getting a bit toasty."

"I have water for you." A panel opened on one of my drones, displaying a supply of sealed water-pouches. "You can drink as we walk."

"Where are you taking us?" One of the other men (Barton?) asked.

"Due West, to a region that's already been burned and starting to cool. Your rescue crews can meet you there."

They looked at each other helplessly, then moved to quickly distribute the water pouches. I approved of their pragmatism.

"Let's be off." I took the lead, near the edge of the circle created by my drones; their odd, frighteningly insect-like gait gathered many a nervous look from the rescued workers, but the drones were able to keep pace as the group began to march through the conflagration. Wherever we traveled, flames guttered and died.

At first the firemen were reluctant, but (when it became apparent that no immediate harm was awaiting them) they began to pick up their pace. Fear was beginning to fade, replaced instead by a mix of confusion and gratitude. We walked in silence, a grim mobile island of blackened chill in the midst of a roiling blaze.

It was a hard hike for those who were not wearing powered armor; the ground was uneven, but we forged ahead as fast as we were able. I had further plans, and the workers were as eager to be free of me as they were to be free of the wildfire. It would have been easier (and faster) to have my drones go airborne and lift them to safety...but I hadn't thought to rig any safe method to carry so many. A broad, horizontal force-field, perhaps, that passengers could stand on like an invisible platform? The drones could already create fields of that size and shape, but the current implementation was frictionless. That could lead to tragic consequences when accelerating at height. A project for another time!

We pushed on. The flames became sparse - most vegetation here had already been consumed - and heat-driven winds didn't howl quite so loud. Eventually, we reached a safe zone and my drones turned off their heat-redirection field.

"I've kept your rescuers apprised of your current location," I told the bewildered firefighters as I lifted off the ground. "Good luck."

And then I was soaring east, back towards the wild roar and boiling haze and hellish glow. Behind my faceless mask, I could feel my lips pull up in a mad grin as my warstaff was summoned into the Mk 35's massive hands. Visual data was useless as I dove into the smoke; sonar, radar, and global-positioning-satellite data guided me as I arced south towards the inferno's border. Through fire and chaos, I was untouched.

Escaping the riotous wildfire felt like entering into another world: behind me was a hellish inferno, and before me an open forest, untouched and green. The sudden transition was jarring, and I had half a mind to swim back into the blaze simply to repeat the experience. I chose against indulging; I was here for a purpose.

I climbed higher while my drones descended towards the ground. A hundred feet aloft, I aimed the warstaff and unleashed a slim cone of white-hot plasma. Lesser vegetation was instantly carburized under the onslaught, and trees detonated thunderously as the moisture in their trunks flashed to steam. There was nothing left within the beam's path, not a blade of grass or even a twig; the superheated, highly ionized gas had left only charred, slightly-shimmering earth in its wake. My drones hastened to extinguish any blazes started on the edge facing away from the wildfire.

I soared forward, carving a fifty-foot wide path of empty devastation to serve as a firebreak.

☙ ☙ ☙

The second conflagration was in western Indiana, about eighty miles south of Lafayette; technically speaking, this fire was not endangering any of the cross-country routes that Aaron had been considering, but it was threatening residential areas of the state. Creating the narrative for Doctor Fid's supposed 'redemption' was at least of equal importance to saving a friend's road trip. Saving farms and houses and towns was a worthy diversion. And besides…attending to emergencies outside of my CIO's path would further limit any chance that these acts be identified to benefit a specific journey.

Years prior, I'd been driving a moving truck full of munitions along Interstate 70 and taken a detour through this region. Sadly, the campsite in which I'd enjoyed a pleasant evening under the stars had now been turned to ash.

I hadn't thought about that trip in a long while; it had been intended as a staging mission while preparing an attack upon the Denver-based hero Windstormer…but then Gamma had done something egregiously stupid, and I'd decided that the giant Atlanta-based 'hero' was more deserving of Doctor Fid's attentions. Again.

(It occurred to me that I still had a few million dollars' worth of high-energy weaponry stashed in the Mile-High-City. Those arms were hopelessly outdated now, of course, but I made a note to retrieve them anyway. Perhaps they could be disassembled for useful components.)

When I arrived near the wildfire's front, local news-station camera-drones were waiting for me. Some, no doubt, had already been tasked with gathering footage of the uncontrolled blaze that was greedily devouring the Owen-Putnam State Forest; more cameras had been dispatched, I was certain, upon the spreading news that Doctor Fid had contained the Allegheny wildfire.

It was only four AM but the flames lit up the horizon like a bloody, crimson-tinged sunrise; I circled once to evaluate where the firefighters were currently working to fight back the blaze, and where my assistance would be useful.

A known hero, invited by the local authorities, would have taken the time to consult with the workers below to coordinate efforts and raise morale. That option was made more complicated by my historic villainous reputation; without the immediate threat of immolation to spur on cooperation, the sudden appearance of Doctor Fid could create more distress than the approaching inferno.

With planning, effort, and many more sleepless nights like this one, that effect would be mitigated. My socio-statistical projections indicated that I would soon be able to interact with disaster-relief crews without causing unnecessary friction. For a while, at least...until some 'hero' did something so foolish as to require Doctor Fid's more malicious attentions, and the wheel of public opinion turned against me once more. As it should! I was as unworthy of accolades as those I punished. In a better world, the beaten throngs would join me among the scorned; instead, they merely acquired a hospital stay at my hands. It wasn't much, but it was something. My own simple effort to improve the pool of superheroes that children might look up to.

Speaking of which...my sensors indicated a man-sized object flying from the direction of nearby Spencer. The omnipresent smoke limited the effectiveness of long-distance visual enhancement, but I quickly realized that 'woman-sized' was a more appropriate label for the approaching superheroine. She was wearing a black and tan costume with an abbreviated dark cape; her tawny mask wrapped around her head and was shaped to offer a distinctly feline impression. I didn't recognize the outfit.

She was flying straight towards me, so I decided to wait rather than begin creating the firebreak. Unless this newcomer was secretly more powerful than the mighty Valiant, I had little to fear while wearing the Mk 35 and was surrounded by a dozen heavy-combat drones.

Her speed wasn't particularly impressive; I had time to run two separate simulations of the wildfire's progress before she arrived.

"Doctor Fid," she acknowledged. The woman looked tense and haggard; from the soot that marred her costume, I imagined that she'd been running herself ragged aiding the work crews all day. "I've been watching the news. Are you here to help?"

"I am," I replied simply.

"Well, thank God." She exhaled slowly, and her apprehension faded into weary hope. "What can I do?"

It took a moment to calibrate my response. There'd been a calculated risk that the men I'd rescued earlier would have required additional persuasion before accepting my assistance, but my career has included a great deal of practice at disrupting civilian resistance; long experience, however, had led me to expect more stubborn recalcitrance from anyone wearing a mask. It was disappointing to realize that the intimidating monologue that I'd prepared would go unspoken.

"Liaise with the firefighting teams; they know you, I assume?"

"I can do that. You going to do the same thing you did in Pennsylvania?"

"Similar." I brought up a holographic map with several locations marked off. "There are work crews currently active here, here and here. I don't want to get too close to them."

"I'll talk to them, see how they want to split the labor."

I nodded to indicate agreement and she floated towards what I assumed to be the firefighters' mobile headquarters. It occurred to me that I hadn't gotten her name, but it didn't seem particularly relevant. So long as the work proceeded safely (and I wasn't required to subdue the feline-themed newcomer), I supposed that exchanging pleasantries was unnecessary.

I had time to optimize one of the sub-unit interfaces within my warstaff before the heroine returned, carrying a map.

"Skip these areas for now, then come back and finish off the work." She pointed at areas clearly delineated on the unfolded paper. "I'll be running messages and making sure that everyone is evacuated safely."

"I understand," I stated gravely, then turned my back on the heroine to fly towards my soon-to-exist trench's origin point.

"Hey," she said, interrupting my departure. "I don't know why you're doing this, but...thank you."

I didn't respond verbally...I simply nodded in acknowledgment and then accelerated to maximum speed so abruptly that my inertial-dampeners were barely able to keep up.

The tan-and-black clad heroine's identity was still a mystery to me and an image search performed upon the relevant authorities' databases had offered no clue; she wasn't contracted through any of the local government that I could find and was not insured by any of the major companies. An amateur, then.

I had no idea if she were one of the few genuinely good heroes, or if she was one of the selfish, dangerously arrogant lot who made up the bulk of Doctor Fid's victims. If she were within the latter category, accepting her gratitude now might make future beatings awkward.

I summoned my warstaff and began the process of carving my mark into the earth. The constantly-flowing stream of white plasma lit the forest like day, and my drones settled into the laborious task of making sure that no smaller fires were set when a tree exploded during the moment of incineration.

✥ ✥ ✥

By the time that I returned home, the sun was high in the sky and even the impressive regimen of neurochemical and pharmacological alterants within my system was having a difficult time keeping me awake; I'd stashed the Mk 35 in the deep-sea lab and (after making sure that Whisper did not have any guests) used the teleportation platform to travel back to my house.

"Hi, Terry," my android sister called cheerfully, then her glowing blue eyes widened. "You look exhausted."

"I *am* exhausted," I chuckled. "I'm going to get some rest; I'm hoping to go back out in a few hours."

"Mm!" she agreed.

"Anything interesting going on?" I trudged towards my room.

"Not really. The internet's going insane about Doctor Fid's 'heroism', of course, but we expected that." She skipped along beside me. "Villains on the dark web are nervous."

"Anything worth mentioning?"

"Mm. Not really. Skullface called you mean things, but he always does whenever Doctor Fid is headline news. The FTW and a few people from Lassiter's are defending you."

I wasn't worried about the opinions of the members of the

FTW; that organization—created by my unfortunately deceased friend Starnyx—was a collection of non-violent hackers and social activists, and I was on decent social terms with several prominent members. They would not think less of me for the ruse that I was undertaking. The villains who socialized at Lassiter's Den, however, were a more complicated issue. It is true that none among them were close friends, but I'd spent a long time cultivating my reputation in those circles. These next few months were likely to be uncomfortable for those with whom Doctor Fid had shared drinks.

No matter. When the plan was done, I would be welcomed back like a king.

"Oh!" Whisper perked up, "Phantom Puma wrote nice things about you on social media."

"Who?"

"The heroine you helped in Indiana!"

"That's an odd choice in names," I commented tiredly. "Mountain lions aren't even native to that region."

"She has kitty powers!" Whisper seemed far too cheerful for this hour. "Maybe she was bitten by a radioactive cougar?"

A Chesapeake-based heroine named Lynx used to joke that she got her powers after being bitten by a glowing eponymous feline; I suspected that she'd actually made a deal with an extradimensional entity, a cat-god from another world. Who could know for certain? Heroes led odd lives.

"Well, keep an eye on the news. If you need anything, don't hesitate to wake me up." I was tired, but not so tired that I was willing to let my sister down.

"Okay. Sleep well!"

I dreamed about deep water, rain, lush greenery, the sounds of waterfalls, and a world untouched by flame.

CHAPTER THREE

By Monday morning, weariness had become my boon companion. I wanted nothing more than to bury myself in blankets and hide from the world; sadly, Terrance Markham was expected to appear at his day job. I considered calling in ill but demurred; due to the very many modifications that I'd made to my body, I'd never actually taken a sick day because I felt unwell. Faking a cough to pursue Doctor Fid's villainous tasks had occurred more than once, but allowing actual physical weakness to control my actions? Never. My level of exhaustion made that pride more difficult to justify; nevertheless, I struggled on. Greeting coworkers with a professionally-friendly smile took all of my focus, but I managed to successfully navigate to my office.

From AH Biotech's origin, I had established myself as the sort of CEO who arrived early and stayed late; given that my neural interface allowed me to digest information at high-speed, and also given the existence of the very many programs that I'd written to assist in the day-to-day tasks of a chief executive officer...only a fraction of my time at the office was spent upon work-related efforts. A more significant percentage of my day-time hours were secretly spent upon Doctor Fid's research and simulations. With a quantum-tunnel mental link to the computers in my labs, I did not even need to touch my work-computer to accomplish the tasks; I could control the test equipment or robotic drones in any of my lairs from half a planet away to continue working to uncover the mysteries of the universe.

Today, I strained even to keep up with Terry Markham's work. There were personnel issues that needed sorting, raises and letters of condemnation that required my research and sign-off, financial reports from multiple departments, information about public markets and competitors...Not to mention meeting after interminable meeting. The work that AH Biotech did was important (proving that it's possible to save the world without spandex or flashy powers!) but I was having trouble focusing, and the day's labor would not be up to my usual standard of excellence.

Also, I had developed significant regret for the existence of the open-door policy that I had long-ago implemented.

"-so we need to re-think our approach in MEA," Kimberly said earnestly. "We've been hitting roadblocks increasing sales there."

"So are our competitors," I reassured her, struggling to maintain my even tone. "The market is soft in that region."

"At the last earnings call, I got dinged pretty hard." She shifted uncomfortably. "I don't want to get surprised again."

There was an ongoing feud between myself and the chairman of the board of directors. We had a fundamental philosophical disagreement, Henry Collins and I: I felt that the company that I founded should have the creation and marketing of life-saving biotechnological marvels as its primary focus, whereas he felt that the company's primary focus should be funneling vast sums of money into his pocket. He'd issued several ultimatums over the last year, demanding that I cease investing so heavily in the infrastructure necessary for long-term growth; he also seemed to resent every penny spent on research and development instead of marketing.

Every once in a while, Henry Collins initiated an attempt to have me removed as CEO and to have me replaced by a more tractable executive; most of the harshest questions and comments at our investor meetings were placed by individuals from his camp. Thus far, I'd rebuffed his attempts by making the company so wildly successful that few felt the need to rock the boat. He and his supporters were being made wealthy by my hatred, but I let that rage simmer without acting upon it; the company's goals were more important than my personal feelings.

Doctor Fid's nemesis was the Red Ghost, but Terry Markham's was Henry Collins. The Ghost once shredded my intestines with a gauss cannon, but I still maintained that Doctor Fid was the luckier of my two identities.

"Kim, you're doing fine. I'm not going to tell you not to push in MEA, because I'm sure that you'll grow our business there...But don't worry so much."

"My people are worried," she countered, looking frayed. "I had to talk one of my best salesmen from jumping ship. When the financial news picks up a bad enough quote, it doesn't matter what the truth is. People are nervous."

"Ok." I took a deep breath and tried to concentrate. "So, what were you hoping to change?"

"We should revisit working through a reseller in –"

"No," I interrupted. "We shouldn't."

"Terry, they have business contacts that we don't." She wouldn't meet my eyes.

"They have business contacts we don't want." My hands clenched into fists, hidden under my desk. "Warlords and dictators…we don't need their money!"

Over the course of his long career, Doctor Fid had traded with many devils; my civilian guise, on the other hand, dared not do the same. AH Biotech needed to be beyond reproach.

Kimberly was silent for a while. Truthfully, she looked more relieved than upset; Kim was a compulsively good person, and the idea of approaching unethical resellers would never have sat well with her. The only reason she would ever have considered it was, I was certain, the external pressure being thrust upon her by the board of directors.

Straining against seemingly impossible odds could make good people make bad concessions. They think to themselves that the dark path is the only one available, or that if they don't bend, then they will be broken. I broke, long ago; I created Fid and every horror that followed was by my own choice. My employees didn't need to suffer the same destruction.

When AH Biotech had been founded, I'd been afflicted with sociopathic traits that were remnants of the many open-brain surgeries that I'd performed upon myself as part of my efforts to shape Terry Markham into a villain sufficient to fill Doctor Fid's armor. My goals for the company had been logical and my methodology Machiavellian; it had only been enlightened self-interest that had guided me to seek out dreamers and idealists to make up my early employees. I was still constantly surprised by how remarkably effective that choice had been. Also, grateful for my brain-damaged-self's foresight.

"We're going to get beaten up again," Kim said quietly.

"Then take the punches with a clear conscience," I responded grimly. "As long as I'm in this office, you and your people won't need to make that sort of compromise. If you need me to rally the troops, let me know!"

"I will." She looked grateful, then tilted her head curiously. "Are you okay?"

"I have a headache," I forced a comforting tone into my voice. "It's nothing."

It was one of my rare actual headaches rather than one of the migraines that accompanied Whisper hacking into my brain to alter my memories. Really, those incidents had been my own fault for failing to place safeguards before allowing her consciousness direct access to the same network of supercomputers that my neural link was connected to; her father/creator had, after all, been a supervillain named Apotheosis. I should have known to be more careful. Whisper, on the other hand, was blameless for the directives buried within her code, and we'd long since dealt with the problem. I was in need of analgesics now rather than an improved firewall.

"Well, you should get some rest," she frowned. "You look terrible."

"Thanks," I chuckled wryly. "That's definitely good for my ego."

"I'm sorry, I didn't mean-"

"Don't worry about it, I know what you meant," I smiled, now more genuinely amused. "I'll catch up on sleep tonight."

We made small talk for a while, and it was a much-relieved Director of Sales that eventually left my office. I closed my eyes and slowly inhaled, light-headed and strangely dizzy. I was motionless but felt as though I was drifting backwards, a slow and endless fall.

"Hey, boss-man. You got a moment?"

I opened my eyes and affected a pleasant smile. "William. Of course, I have time. Come in."

When I eventually returned home, I fell into my bed and fell asleep almost immediately.

And then, due to a malfunction in its guidance system, an oil tanker struck a reef off the shore of the Alaska coast. There were a limited number of individuals who could have responded quickly to a disaster on that scale; even fewer who had the technical expertise or equipment to safely contain the hazardous spill. I injected an adrenalin cocktail into my heart and slowly clawed my way from slumber's grasp.

It took three hours of focused and intense labor, but Doctor Fid's Mk 36b and an army of light-duty drones were able to avert ecological catastrophe. And then I fell unconscious in my armor and slept through the entire journey back to my deep-ocean lab.

Maintaining a secret identity was easier as a villain, I decided, when I woke up and called in sick; a supervillain had the option of choosing when to commit a crime or perform an assault. Heroes, on the other hand, are forced to be reactive, and thus on-call at inconvenient moments. I didn't think that I would enjoy this aspect of the 'Fid pretends to be a hero' charade.

Feeling empathy for a struggle that superheroes faced left a bitter taste in my mouth. I would need to bring this deception to a close before pity or compassion arose; I was undeserving and so were they.

※ ※ ※

"Are you awake?" Whisper poked me on the shoulder gently. She'd given me twelve hours to catch up on my rest, at least.

"No." I yawned and twisted to lay face-down on my pillow.

How about now? She poked me in my brain.

"Ok, I'm awake." I rubbed at my eyes. Over the years, I've experimented with using psychoactive drugs or electrical stimuli or adrenalin to keep myself alert, with varying levels of success; I'd managed nearly four days without a significant period of uninterrupted rest this time, for example. When it came to recovery, however, I'd discovered nothing that worked more effectively than a comfortable bed. "I'm awake."

"Yay!"

I didn't bother looking at the alarm clock; my neural link provided nanosecond-accurate time. Sleep had claimed most of the day, but I had to admit that I felt much improved now. Mentally spooling through my news and email notifications found nothing that required my immediate attention. "Hey, we still have a few hours of sunlight...Want to go out to the park?"

"Mm!" she affirmed, smiling cheerfully.

"Then git. I need to shower and shave." I rubbed at my chin. "I'll be ready in about twenty minutes."

The little android giggled and scampered out of the room while I attended to my much-belated morning ablutions.

Oh! Whisper's mental voice snaked into my head. **Terry, the Boston Guardians are going to be on KNN CapeWatch tonight; I think they're going to be talking about Doctor Fid.**

We'll be home in time to watch the broadcast, I assured her as I brushed my teeth. Even though we could both stream media directly into our consciousnesses via network connection, she still preferred actually sitting in front of the television for entertaining broadcasts. Watching together was a social experience and one that I was happy to share with her.

Which park do you want to go do?

Oooh. Can we go to Carson Beach?

I winced but forced cheer into my mental voice. **Sure, we can do that.**

Yay!

I didn't mind the ocean. The Mk 35 and 36b had both been tested in the dark, deepest depths, and I often soared over the waves when en-route to one location or another. My adopted little sister, too, had become completely enthralled with the seemingly-endless expanse of blue-green water; one of her most treasured belongings was a glass statue of a leaping dolphin, and it was a genuine joy to watch Whisper splashing at the tide's edge, giddy and enthusiastic.

But beaches held other memories for me: moments of bittersweet joy and heart-wrenching terror, of blood and pain and tears and hatred so strong that my chest ached just thinking on it.

Sadly, my traditional coping mechanism for dealing with mixed feelings—donning my armor and locating an unlucky hero to batter—was currently unavailable to me. Yet another unforeseen negative consequence of the theatrical farce that I'd embarked upon! Ah, well. In the immortal words of the patron saint of supervillains: Don't plan the plan if you can't follow through.

The beatings would be delayed 'til another day.

❦ ❦ ❦

It had taken nearly a year of biofeedback training, intensive study and consultation with acting coaches before I felt comfortable pretending to be an extrovert. The curriculum had been necessary as I prepared to start AH Biotech; a CEO must project power and confidence, after all. I employed surgery, electromyostimulation, genetic alterations and a handful of other more esoteric methods to make myself taller and more aesthetically pleasing for the same purpose.

When the mask of corporate executive Doctor Terrance Markham came off, however, I quickly faded back to Terry Markham, awkward introverted academic.

Whisper, on the other hand, was a natural extrovert. We'd arrived at high tide when conditions were at their prime; Whisper approached a group of children her own age and convinced them all to join her as she made sandcastles. She only looked vaguely human, but still she was quickly able to insinuate herself into their group. Remarkable.

I stayed on the boardwalk and watched her play. It was good to see her happy. It was good to see her get out of the house and meet new friends. But every once in a while, the wind would shift and the fresh salt breeze would hit me just right and I was at a different beach building sandcastles with my brother Bobby, completely ignorant of what was to come.

※ ※ ※

The sun is high in the sky, and the heat beats down on me as the cool wind pauses. I use my forearm to brush at a bead of sweat on my brow, wincing only slightly at the feel of sand scraping at my face, and otherwise ignore the discomfort. I've consulted the relevant texts and performed some basic experimentation to confirm my initial calculations, but now that construction is before me my attention is riveted.

"It's not going to work," Bobby objects, but he's giddy with anticipation anyway.

It's very likely that Bobby is correct. I see now that there are many variables that I failed to account for: the breeze, the temperature...my preliminary calculations had been estimates only, but I'd built the forming tool anyway. And now, the sand-filled mold is at the center of our makeshift castle, a slim and high tower.

If I can successfully slide the mold up off the sand without destroying all of our work.

I'm careful, but my hands aren't perfectly steady. Every tremble and I can see flecks shift, a few grains fall. And then, disaster.

Bobby is laughing at me, and I'm holding a slender tube over the ruins of our castle. The tall tower has tumbled, knocking over the smaller parapets and destroying much of the detail that we'd worked so hard to add earlier. And now I'm laughing too, because it was just ridiculous and the day is too beautiful to be annoyed.

(In my head, I'm designing a simple and lightweight derrick to lift away future sandcastle molds. Or perhaps a coiled energy field, to drive away the plastic using static electricity. A mist generator, to keep the sand at the appropriate level of moistness. With proper compaction and the correct ratio of liquid, an eight-foot tower is theoretically possible; I've done the math! But those are future projects, and Bobby is here now.)

"It's your turn!" I grin, offering him a plastic shovel. "Show me what you can do."

"I can't," his smile slowly fades. "You have to go to work at two, right?"

I blinked, then twisted to find my wristwatch laying on our beach towel. Once again, I'd lost track of time. I'm lucky that Bobby is better at that sort of thing than I am, or else we'd have missed our appointment.

"Can you drop me at the hotel?" Bobby asks plaintively. "I can read my comics there."

"I wanted you to come with me for this one, kiddo," I try to suppress my grin. "The meeting won't be too long, I promise."

"Aw, c'mon, Terr. It's my birthday! I don't want to just sit around while you talk science stuff."

"It's not 'science stuff', Bobby." I don't laugh at his tragically disappointed expression, but it's a near thing. "It's a deep-sea tetherless submersible drone..."

"Booooring. C'mon, please? Just drop me off."

"We're going to see Paul Riley." I pause. "I really, really think that you want to meet him."

"Why?" he asks plaintively. "You got me new comics to read and a new Bronze figure! I wanna go back to the hotel. Please? As another birthday present?"

"Wait, wait." I motion for him to come closer. "I'm going to tell you a secret, something really important, but you have to be quiet, okay? You can't say anything until we're alone with Mr. Riley."

"Okay...?" Bobby looks confused. He knows me well enough that I'm sure he can see my anticipation but doesn't understand it yet.

"The superhero Bronze's secret identity is Paul Riley," I whisper, even though it's a loud beach and no one was likely to overhear a casual conversation.

"No way!" Bobby's eyes widen. "For real?"

"For real! I figured it out, and I wanted to introduce him to you on your birthday. We're going to surprise him."

He leaps across the ruined sandcastle and hugs me around my waist. The sand grinds into my sunburned back but I don't care because I'm laughing too hard and everything is perfect.

"C'mon, let's get going." I carefully peel out of the hug and start collecting the plastic buckets, shovels, and molds. "We don't want to *be late!"*

"This is going to be the best birthday," Bobby declares. "Ever!"

In forty-seven minutes, Bronze is going to let my brother die...but I don't know that, so I grin goofily in response. Bobby's hand is small and warm inside my own, and there is a giddy bounce in his step as we walk back towards our rented van.

❧ ❧ ❧

Whisper waved to me and I waved back, forcing a cheerful expression. The bulk of my attention, however, was upon the kidnappers.

I'd noticed the grey panel-van following us as we drove but hadn't considered it to be a threat. Paparazzi, I'd thought, or perhaps a reporter looking for shots of the recently-acknowledged-as-a-U.S.-citizen little android; there had been a fair amount of media coverage when I'd sued the state of Massachusetts on her behalf after her citizenship hearing had been canceled. Also, we'd both been present when Senator McClelland's Synthetic Americans' Rights bill was signed into law.

Senator McClelland's own grandson was a square-jawed military hero, his consciousness re-created after death from an extensive brain-taping experiment performed by a DARPA research project. His miraculous resurrection made for a feel-good story. Whisper, on the other hand, was adorable and tremendously photogenic; of course the reporters focused on her when writing their opinion pieces and editorials!

The van's passenger had been carrying an expensive

camera, so I'd dismissed them as no threat. Now, however, I noticed that driver and passenger had separated to opposite sides of the beach, and that the camera had been left behind. I used my neural link to activate and summon a small group of stealthed combat-drones, just in case; they would take nearly a minute to arrive.

Whisper, sweetheart? I sent a mental message.

Mm? she replied, not the least bit distracted from her focused efforts to place a found stick atop her sand castle like a flagpole. Her multi-tasking capabilities were truly remarkable.

I don't mean to alarm you, but I think that there are some bad men here at the beach.

Oh, her mental touch felt disappointed. **Do we have to go?**

I think that it would be a good idea.

If we were together, the kidnappers would likely retreat and seek another opportunity. Kidnapping a child right out of a parent's arms might create a visceral fear, but it was dangerously risky. There is no threat in the world so deadly that a parent would reliably be cowed when their child is in danger; it didn't matter if the kidnappers were hulking brutes, bristling with guns and blades...when some parent heard that shrill, terror-filled cry for Mommy or Daddy, they run to attack no matter what. And if the kidnappers had to injure the parent in order to get away, well, who was going to pay the ransom? Professionals wait for an opportunity to isolate their target.

Doctor Fid had never been involved in a kidnapping. He

did, however, occasionally drink at a bar where other villains discuss their careers. Powerful microphones and targeted recordings often made for darkly educational evenings.

This particular pair of prospective kidnappers had hoped, no doubt, that Whisper would stray further from her guardian. If so, their plan had been foiled; I was attentive and not so distant that they could get to her before I arrived to interrupt; I was certain that they would back off and return to their van to wait for another opportunity. And once Whisper was no longer in immediate danger, I could annihilate them at my whim.

Preferably in a manner that did not arouse suspicion that Terry Markham was in some way connected to Doctor Fid.

And so, Whisper started making her apologies and saying goodbye to her new friends while I surreptitiously kept my attention upon the two potential kidnappers; they did not appear to be making a move towards the beach.

Embarrassingly, I was completely surprised by the third attacker: a jogger on the Harborwalk that came up behind me and injected a fast-acting sedative into the side of my neck.

CHAPTER FOUR

A FAIR NUMBER OF ALTERATIONS HAD BEEN performed upon my body in order to improve effectiveness in my villainous career. The neural interface and the aesthetic changes barely scratched the surface; muscle and bone structure had been enhanced to make me stronger and more durable than a normal human. Microsensors provided medical telemetry data, and nanites coursed through my veins to significantly hasten my healing. Surgical robots had cut into my own brain for various (now mostly repaired) purposes. And most of my internal organs had been replaced with highly efficient cloned versions, to free up space within my ribcage to install other technological devices.

My digestive and cardiovascular systems could metabolize most sedatives faster than they could be pumped into my body; a single syringe could effectively be ignored, no matter what the contents. I was, however, in a very public place and I didn't want my civilian identity to be exposed...so I feigned going limp, eyes drifting closed, and was caught by the 'jogger'.

Terry! Whisper yelped, and I heard her calling my name aloud as well.

Stay where you are! I implored, staying slack as my assailant dragged me towards his van. Other voices raised alarms, but the van's driver and passenger had run over as well, lifting me up and manhandling me towards the parking lot before any resistance could be mounted. **I'm fine. I just want to make sure that I'm away from public view before I free myself.**

But-

When I'm gone, go back to the car and lock yourself inside. If anyone asks, just say that we had a plan for this sort of thing. Really, I thought, we ought to make a plan for this sort of thing. **Activate the self-driving feature to get home, okay?**

("Christ, what the hell is this guy made of, lead?" One of my kidnappers complained.)

'kay. I could hear the whimper in her mental voice.

I have combat-drones en route, I'm not in any real danger, I assured her as my body was thrown roughly into the running van. The door slammed shut with an authoritative thud. **The beach wasn't very crowded...Do you see anyone calling the police?**

Mm.

Ah, well. An officer may come to interview you before I get home. Just tell them that you're not supposed to talk to them without a lawyer or guardian present, ok? The van's wheels squealed as we tore out of the parking lot. **Remember to sound scared when they talk to you!**

I am scared, She admitted.

Everything will be fine, I repeated. Someone was stepping on the side of my head to hold my body still while another pair of hands searched my pockets for my cel-phone. Whoever was wearing size-thirteen military boots, I decided, was going to be hurt the most.

I heard a crunch, then the sound of a window rolling back up. No one would be able to follow my cellular phone's GPS in order to rescue me, I supposed. I wasn't worried; the subcutaneous trackers within my body were more accurate than my phone's GPS.

"That went smooth," the driver said. "Barry, good job with the hypo."

"No names!" Barry grunted irritably.

"This guy is out," said Military Boots, as he roughly nudged the side of my head with his toe. "Don' worry 'bout it."

"It's a bad habit," Barry glowered. "If you want to stay on this team, you maintain protocol."

"You're not the boss," The driver griped. "You can't kick me out."

"I know the boss," Barry countered. "And I'm not trying to kick you out. You did fine; I'm just telling you what you need to do if you want to keep on after this job."

Whisper...? I asked silently, **Did you happen to get a good look at the jogger who injected the sedatives into my neck?**

Mm! She uploaded the image into my thoughts; Barry was apparently a tall, athletic man with dark skin, a shaved head, and a salt-and-pepper van-dyke beard. **I haven't identified him, yet.**

Add the first name of 'Barry' to your search, I suggested. **That might help.**

She sent a mental hug as well as the distinct impression that she'd made her way back to our car.

Clever girl. It took effort to keep my lips from twitching into a smile. **Keep in contact, let me know if you need anything; I'm going to let these gentlemen bring me to their employer.**

I summoned a few more combat drones to join the small swarm that was now following high in the sky above. Doctor Fid generally never involved himself with the doings of non-costumed criminals, but it seemed to me that requiring professionalism in one's crew implied an experienced leader; a neophyte would lack the knowledge necessary in order to be so particular. Preparing a bit of extra firepower seemed a reasonable precaution.

"The police just announced a BOLO for a gray van." From the voice's location, I guessed that it was the man who'd had the expensive camera, the one that I'd dismissed as a paparazzo. I dubbed him 'Passenger' for ease of reference. "No license plates."

"No worries…We're here," Driver piped up cheerfully, and the van hit a solid bump as it turned up a ramp. Tires screeched on smoothed concrete as the vehicle wound its way up a series of inclines and then came to a halt. Even with my eyes closed, I knew that we were in a parking garage; the echoes were quite distinctive. "You three take sleeping beauty to the SUV, I'll burn the van and meet you at the warehouse."

Military Boots 'accidentally' kicked my face again before

rolling me to one side so that he could get a good grip on under my shoulder. I feigned being insensate and mentally updated my plans for the man. Pliers would be involved. Also, fire ants.

I was aware that fire ant stings rank relatively low on the Schmidt Sting Pain Index; they were, however, simple to acquire and easy to manipulate into swarming behavior. A villain named the Ancient published a treatise on the subject several decades ago; to the best of my knowledge, no minion ever betrayed him after the article appeared in print.

Barry grabbed under my other shoulder, and Passenger grabbed my ankles. When the van door slammed open, it was a matter of seconds before I was manhandled into the back of an SUV and concealed under a wool blanket. After a moment or two of jostling, we were again underway.

🕷 🕷 🕷

"Sometimes I wish I wasn't smart," I confide.

"You're not just 'smart'. You're extraordinary." Dad pauses and then points to the socket wrench.

"Sometimes I wish I wasn't extraordinary, then." I sigh, but obediently hand the tool up into his waiting hand. He's repairing the garage door; it makes weird noises and isn't quite closing correctly on the right side. I have a dozen ideas as to how functionality can be improved, but all require resources that are currently unavailable.

"That's too bad," my father grunts and fumbles to align a bolt. "I kinda like you the way you are. I'm proud of you, kid."

"I know," I grimace. "But it's hard."

"You can figure out things in seconds that take me hours," he smiles affectionately. "Being smart makes some things easier."

"Not everything."

An intelligent child is perceptive enough to identify defects in the world around them, as well as to correctly identify how intensely helpless children are to correct those problems. A more gifted child is able to create complex plans that circumvent youthful limitations to overcome specific issues. The truly exceptional are cursed to look deeper, to analyze the system as a whole and come to the realization that individual problems are often symptoms of greater societal flaws that are so deeply ingrained that they simply cannot be resolved in a timely manner.

Sometimes, the skill to construct algorithmic models to predict the actions of one's peers doesn't help one to avoid adversity. It just means you can see the punch coming from further away.

Tomorrow isn't going to be a good day at school. I've done the math.

🙦 🙦 🙦

ature to Terry? Whisper sent a mental query; she sounded calmer now. **I found the identities of the three men I saw.**

Thank you, Whisper. Everything is going smoothly here. So I now had names and faces for Driver, Passenger, and Barry. I supposed that I didn't really need to know Military Boots' name since he was soon to be deceased. **As soon as I find out why I was taken, I'll take care of this and find my way back to the house. Have the police called yet?**

Not yet. I'm not even home.

Well, keep me in the loop. I took a few moments to reprogram the stealthed combat drones that were still following overhead; four peeled off to go follow Whisper, just in case there were any problems. The rest remained above, silent and unseen. **And don't worry, everything will be fine.**

You're not Doctor Fid right now. You're my brother Terry, she whispered quietly. **Be careful.**

I will. I checked my GPS coordinates and tapped the aerial footage from my drones, and settled in for the possibility of a long drive; the interstate we were on headed south and the vehicle was now in the passing lane. In retrospect, I decided that the parking garage would have been a more favorable location to make my escape; that these professional kidnappers had felt comfortable using the location to swap vehicles implied that there had been no cameras present. The interstate was far too public and I dared not risk any action which would draw undue attention upon my civilian identity. Whatever our final destination, though, it was certain that the intent was to bring me someplace well out of the public eye. Whatever they intended, they surely would not want to be observed. All the better for me.

Mostly, I was annoyed that it seemed increasingly likely that I'd miss the opportunity to view this evening's episode of CapeWatch with Whisper.

"So, why's the boss got such a hardon for this guy?" Military Boots broke the silence.

"I don't know," Barry replied, after a moment's hesitation. I guessed that he was operating the vehicle; he sounded like he was in the driver's seat. "Probably something this guy made. He's the CEO of a medical company."

Not precisely true; AH Biotech had a wide range of products, the vast majority of which were aimed towards solving ecological disasters. Our medical department had recently made several major high-publicity breakthroughs, true, but the corporation had a much broader focus. On the other hand, it seemed remarkably unlikely that anyone would kidnap the CEO of a growing company for access to a genetically engineered bacterium designed to safely metabolize plastic waste from within ocean water.

"Is the boss sick?" asked Passenger—Andy Marsden, according to the bio that Whisper had uploaded into my brain; a career hoodlum, though he'd never been charged with kidnapping. Andy had been a suspect in two murders but had never been charged, and had no known affiliations with any gangs or criminal organizations. "He didn't look sick."

"How would you tell?" Military Boots laughed. "Maybe he looks paler when he has a fever?"

"Stow it!" Barry growled. (Barry Smith, formerly associated with a New York heist crew that had gone defunct. He had an extensive rap sheet for youthful violent acts but had apparently grown out of that tendency after a stint in the military.) "Don't talk about the Boss while we're still in Boston."

"You're kidding, right?" Military Boots sounded aggrieved. "Look, I get why you don't want to use names in the field, but we all work for the same guy."

"The boss is paranoid about this city," Barry explained

patiently, as though to a five-year-old. "It doesn't matter if you agree with him or not. If you accept his cash, humor him on the little stuff."

"Yeah, yeah, sure." I imagined that Military Boots was rolling his eyes; it certainly sounded like it from the petulance in his voice. "Whatever."

And that seemed to confirm that my kidnappers intended to take me out of the Boston area. Ah, well. According to my medical telemetry, the sedative that they'd dosed me with would have been sufficient to put out a normal person of my height and build for two to three hours. Even with weekday early-evening commute traffic, a journey of that length could have brought me all the way to Providence or Plymouth.

I hoped not; that would be a long and rather boring drive. I was curious as to who had ordered my kidnapping, but not so curious that I'd be willing to pretend unconsciousness through several hours of stop-and-go rush-hour traffic. If we looked to be heading in that direction, I would try to make an earlier escape.

"Why's the boss so paranoid about this place?" Passenger asked. "It was an easy job."

"Fid owns Boston," Barry stated evenly.

"What the hell would Doctor Fid care 'bout a random kidnapping?" Military Boots scoffed. "Besides, everyone says Fid's lost his balls 'n gone hero."

I reconsidered my position on fire ants. How hard would it be, really, to import a non-breeding population of tarantula hawk wasps?

"The boss doesn't believe it," Barry dismissed. I was

beginning to like him. "Besides...Even if Doctor Fid's gone white-cape, the boss still doesn't want to get caught operating in Boston. It's a thing the big names do."

Well, that narrowed the field dramatically! Traditional criminals and minor-league supervillains usually didn't pay too much attention to the territories claimed by major villains. The most famous and most feared, however, were more jealous of significant intrusions into their domain. When Imperator Rex decided to steal a music box from the John F. Kennedy Presidential Museum in Boston, he'd contacted Doctor Fid first to negotiate terms.

(At the time, Imperator Rex had been attempting to acquire every piece of artwork suspected to have been created by the Ancient; a scavenger hunt of sorts, attempting to find clues as to the whereabouts of the Ancient's hidden fortune. Sadly, Imperator Rex's quest was left unfinished when he was captured by the San Francisco Paragons. If ever I had a few weeks free, I ought to chase down those leads. One more task for the queue.)

So...CEO Terrance Markham's kidnappers were in the employ of a supervillain of sufficient notoriety that he (Military Boots had used the male pronoun) feared being caught intruding upon Doctor Fid's domain. Many feared Doctor Fid's raw might, but fewer were paranoid about what surveillance capabilities I maintained in Boston; a few comments had been made one night when I'd been visiting my friend Starnyx at Lassiter's Den, but I was reasonably certain that the stories had not spread to become general knowledge.

Skullface had been a regular at Lassiter's Den and could easily have overheard whispered rumors. Given the telling comment Military Boots had made regarding their boss' pallor, he seemed the most likely suspect.

Seven years ago, Skullface had made a deal with an extra-dimensional demonic entity to gain power and had since quickly risen to prominence. The now-skeletal creature leveraged his magical abilities to gather a significant force of mercenaries and followers. The dangerously mad scientist Dr. Anthony Chaise was among his most trusted devotees, and while I knew my work was superior...I had to admit a grudging respect for the destructive capability of the man's devices. Using Chaise' weaponry, Skullface had caused dozens of dimensional breaches during his assault upon the United Nations building; the cadaverous villain had been incarcerated after that debacle.

(For more than two decades, Doctor Fid has avoided capture. Sometimes, I wondered why I put forth so much effort! The skeletal villainous sorcerer was strong and tough, but he wasn't terribly bright; if he could escape imprisonment after only a year or two, then surely Doctor Fid would have been able to slip from confinement before the first meal was served. Were it not for the importance of Terry Markham's role at AH Biotech, I'd have been tempted to allow myself to be captured by heroes just so I could enjoy the effort of puzzling my way free.)

In addition to his raw physical capabilities, Skullface employed magical attacks that were sufficiently dangerous that I was wary. His cruelty, too, was reason enough to be on my guard; captives had been rescued from his clutches, but never willingly released. Any unfortunates that the heroes failed to locate in time inevitably were retrieved post-mortem. My plan to gather information by waiting to confront my kidnapper was seeming less enticing by the moment. If a confrontation with Skullface were inevitable, being safely encased within the Mk 35 Heavy Combat armor would be much preferred.

Fortunately, I had my abductors outnumbered one against three.

Military Boots and Passenger continued to talk amongst themselves, and Barry's attention was on the road. No one was watching the vehicle's cargo. Very slowly, I began shifting underneath the wool blanket until my questing fingers found a fire extinguisher. Heavy, but not so large as to be unwieldy; it would make an effective hand-to-hand weapon.

Doctor Fid was a veteran of hundreds of battles. The person I was when outside of my powered armor, however, was not. I'd learned to take a punch and grit my teeth through pain long before adulthood—the benefit of near-constant childhood bullying—but I'd known better than to fight back. As an adult, when Bobby was murdered, when I started the process of becoming Fid...I'd taken martial-arts classes and studied combat with the same devotion that I'd once applied towards applied mathematics or quantum physics. Beyond the sparring that took place during my lessons, however, there had never been an occasion for my civilian identity ever to become involved in a physical dispute.

My lips pulled back into a fierce anticipatory grin. It felt as though my birthday and Christmas had both come at once! I needed only to wait for an opportune moment in which to enjoy the present that fate had offered me. Sensor data and live footage from my overhead drones was streamed to my neural interface; it would take careful planning and precision timing to initiate my offense at a moment when no other drivers on the busy interstate highway were endangered.

Even when I had been at my villainous worst, I'd endeavored to avoid allowing innocent bystanders to become collateral damage. My civilian identity would need to be even more careful; even minor casualties would increase attention. While the secret identity of Doctor Fid was well insulated from Dr. Terrance Markham, it was never truly safe to relax under the media's scrutiny.

The best-case scenario would be to escape without witnesses and to return home without explanation. The police would assume that I'd somehow paid off my kidnappers, and a threatening letter from my lawyer would ensure that no information was released into the public eye. Given that my company worked with genetically engineered viruses, bacteria, and other biotechnological marvels, it was likely that certain three-lettered federal agencies would eventually be informed; there would be questions as to the nature of the compensation that I'd offered my abductors, but that could be handled easily enough. Moving a sizeable sum of money to an anonymous offshore account would add authenticity to my replies; while waiting for my escape opportunity, I hacked a bank in the Cayman Islands to begin preparations.

Despite all my training and plans, I could not wholly suppress an annoyed growl when my aerial drones detected unexpected company. Fortunately, road noise muffled the sound such that none of the vehicle's occupants turned to check on their supposedly-unconscious cargo.

Whisper, do you know if tonight's episode of CapeWatch is supposed to be a live-presentation or pre-recorded?

It was recorded this afternoon, Whisper replied. **Why do you ask?**

Oh, no reason. I mentally sighed, resigned. **I'll be home soon.**

And then the car was flipping end over end, a chaotic roar of impact and shrieking metal and shattering glass.

"Fuuuuuuuu-" Military Boots shouted; he, Barry and Passenger had all been wearing their seatbelts but were still jerked about wildly as the vehicle caught the edge of the road and tumbled off the road. Unsecured, I bounced forward into the passenger compartment, smashing face-first into the back of the driver seat and then sideways into an already-broken window. And then we were spinning chaotically and, dazed, I could not keep track of every impact. Something heavy struck the side of my skull and the world contracted to a single point of light, and then nothingness.

❧ ❧ ❧

"Oh, honey. What happened?" *My mother clucks disappointedly and gathers me up into a hug. The embrace is warm and gentle, but her fingers are dry and scratchy from over-exposure to paint* thinner; she's been in her studio again this afternoon. A wildlife painting, I know; a noble stag silhouetted against the moon. The sketches are beautiful.

"I tripped," I say. My lip is bloodied and I have abrasions on my forehead, one elbow and one knee. My shirt – an orange, yellow and brown striped polo shirt that I'm fond of – is ripped near the collar and I'm smudged everywhere with mud. My backpack, dropped near the front door, was still dripping. Reluctantly, I try to pull away; Mom shouldn't need to get dirty. Not for me.

"Uh-huh." She doesn't let me escape. "And what really happened?"

"You know what really happened," I whisper; my voice is so quiet that even I have trouble making out the words. I relent and return her hug.

"Was it that Bryant boy again?" she asks, pulling away only far enough so that she could look me in the eyes.

"I don't remember."

"You've never forgotten anything in your life," she frowns. "Not even from when you were a baby. Was it Kenny Bryant?"

"Yes. No. Not really," I nibble at my lower lip, suckling at the salty and metallic taste of blood. "He was there."

"I'm going to call his mother again," Mom tells me. "He needs to stop this."

"No. It won't help," I inform her seriously. "Last time, he just stopped when the teachers were watching. Except for science class, 'cause Mr. Phalen pretends not to notice no matter what anyone does."

"You should stop correcting Mr. Phalen in class," she chides.

"He should stop being wrong in class," I riposte. "It doesn't matter."

"Honey, of course it matters. They're hurting you!"

"This is just the way it is. It won't last." My studies indicate that violence is likely inevitable; in media and in academic papers, records of bullying within school-age populations were ubiquitous. I generally avoided the soft sciences, but in this case there had existed a broad enough range of sociological studies that I'd been able to construct useful mathematical models: aggressive, bullying behavior towards smaller and vulnerable individuals was within the range of normal behavior for children of this age. I was the statistical outlier, not them. I was the freak. "It'll be better once I get into college."

She hugs me again but doesn't look convinced.

"It's all right." It feels odd, having to comfort my own mother. "If I don't react, they get bored after a while."

"After hurting you for a while, you mean," she bites out. "If it wasn't that Bryant boy, who was it this time?"

"Louis," I admit.

"Louis Nguyen?" She blinks. "I thought he was your friend?"

"I don't have friends," I state matter-of-factly. "They all hate me."

"They don't hate you," Mom sighs, wrapping her arms around me in another hug. "They don't know you well enough to hate you."

I know that she is wrong; I don't really understand hatred, but I'm fairly certain that knowledge is not a prerequisite. Correcting her, however, seems like it would be counter-productive.

"Don't worry, Mom," I murmur. "I'm getting used to this."

She breaks into tears, and I can't figure out why.

❦ ❦ ❦

Grass was pressed against my cheek and I hurt everywhere.

There was a moment of terrifying panic when my reflexive attempt to poll my armor's system-telemetry failed; it took a few groggy seconds to remember who I currently was and what had occurred. I must have been thrown clear of the wreckage because I could see the SUV's smoking remains behind me.

And there was Titan, standing victorious at the side of the road over my now-handcuffed kidnappers.

Groaning in pain, I tried rolling to my side and pushing up to a kneeling position. Medical telemetry from one of the devices embedded within my ribcage confirmed that I had no broken bones, but I still felt as though I'd been fed through an industrial shredder. Pain had never been a stranger to me; the sheer abundance of injuries, however, marked this occasional as exceptional.

"You shouldn't move." The Red Ghost was at my side, a gentle hand trying to keep me still. "An ambulance is already on its way."

I shook away his hand and forced myself upright, mentally replaying video gathered by my drones: the seven-foot-tall, muscular form of the silver-clad Titan barreling from concealment to strike the speeding SUV's rear driver-side wheel with enough force to whip the vehicle into a spin; the SUV had slid sideways off the side of the road, hit a ditch and flipped, shedding debris and glass as it tumbled over a hundred feet. I hadn't been ejected until the vehicle had nearly come to a halt. I couldn't help but wince at the image; in the video, I looked limp and lifeless.

I'm fine! I quickly assured Whisper, knowing that she had surely been monitoring all of my drones' feeds. **No permanent damage done at all.**

Mm, Whisper acknowledged, but she didn't sound convinced.

"What…" I rasped, then coughed up a bit of blood; I'd bitten my tongue while being rattled about in the crash. I spit out shards of glass as well. "What's going on?"

"You were kidnapped." The Red Ghost spoke evenly and professionally, but I'd spent enough time watching him as Doctor Fid that I could recognize the anger warring with worry in his voice. "We've captured the men responsible."

Most of his attention was upon me, cataloging my wounds and attempting to determine what emergency treatment might be needed. The Red Ghost did, however, spare a moment to glare at the leader of the Boston Guardians; he had not, I gathered, approved of the method Titan had used to stop the car. While he was distracted, I ordered my medical nanites and other internal devices to keep myself alive but otherwise mimic normal human response; I didn't want Doctor Fid's nemesis to notice anything unusual about my civilian identity. Instantly, the painkillers that had kept my discomfort manageable faded and I began to shake.

"Stay still," the Red Ghost directed, helping me to lay down again. From this close, I could see that the Hispanic hero looked exhausted; his deceptively-simple cowl hid most of his face, but I could see the hollow under his eyes.

"What...happened?" I asked

"There was a car accident." He made a face as though the word 'accident' tasted sour on his tongue. "Titan rescued you. You know who we are?"

"The Guardians." I managed a brief, trembling smile. "I recognize you."

"Well, you're safe now," he assured me.

The other Guardians – Aeon, Regrowth, and Veridian – had gathered around Titan as he began interrogating the injured-but-still-conscious trio of kidnappers. If I'd been in my armor, my sensors and auditory enhancement algorithms would have easily been sufficient to listen in; instead, one of my well-concealed high-altitude drones used a non-visible laser-interferometer as a microphone to record the conversation.

"Are you well?" Red Ghost asked, brows furrowed in concern. I'd turned a strangled laugh into a hacking cough when Titan had accused my abductors of working for Doctor Fid.

"Water," I croaked. "Please."

A straw was placed against my lips and I sipped carefully, thoughts swirling. My original plans were now in disarray, but the afternoon was not a total loss. I'd be able to gather useful information about my captors by listening in on the interrogation, at least. Passenger had already broken, telling

Titan about how Skullface had contacted him and how long the operation had been planned. Military Boots was grunting irritably, answering questions in monosyllables, and Barry was stoically silent.

The ambulance would perform basic tests and bring me to the nearest hospital, but I could refuse treatment in favor of promising to see my private physician; there were security and financial considerations when a CEO is incapacitated, after all. The Guardians' media machine would work to keep this incident out of the news since it would inevitably become apparent that my injuries had occurred as a direct result of Titan's actions. So...aside from the crick in my neck and the myriads of contusions and lacerations that now covered my body...this result was objectively superior to many possible outcomes.

My subjective experience was less favorable.

Sirens were audible in the distance and I groaned, aching and annoyed. When I eventually returned home, at least, I could use the systems in my armor to reprogram my pain response. For now, I just closed my eyes and concentrated on my breathing. And debating if it would be worth the efforts necessary to get tarantula-hawk hornets into Military Boots' prison cell. Probably not; according to the audio I was recording, Military Boots had just accidentally told Titan where Skullface' current lair was located, which meant that Skullface was likely to get to the poor bastard before I did.

"So," I rasped. "My sister and I were supposed to see CapeWatch this evening. Did I miss anything interesting?"

The Red Ghost didn't answer at first, so I let my eyes

flutter open to see if he was still here. He was staring down at me in amused disbelief, looking from my wounded state to the cataclysmically wrecked SUV and back again. Finally, he began to laugh.

CHAPTER FIVE

THE HEROES ABANDONED ME TO THE EMERGENCY medical team's care and sped off, presumably in an attempt to catch Skullface unawares. I wished them well of it but didn't hold out much hope. The planning of this crime had implied a level of paranoia that would not easily be overcome.

Sadly, my certainty that the Guardians would want to suppress news of my kidnapping (and subsequent injury) proved to be unfounded. There were reporters already present when I arrived at the hospital; 'rescuing' a local entrepreneur was apparently just the sort of publicity that Titan wanted for his team. Fortunately, a helpful EMT assisted me to make a phone call to AH Biotech's legal office before I departed the ambulance. It would have been unfortunate were AHBT's staff surprised by a sudden blitz of questions.

The ghouls had their cameras ready but were unable to get much footage of my gurney before the emergency-room personnel swarmed and rolled me into the hospital. I could tell from the technicians' expressions that I looked a fright; biometric telemetry indicated that I was positively covered in contusions, abrasions, and lacerations.

"Can you tell me your name?" asked one doctor, shining a light in one eye then the other to check for an uneven response. He was a balding African-American man, slim and tired looking, but clearly focused upon his work.

"Terrance Markham," I replied calmly. The sensors spread throughout my body reported that I'd suffered a concussion in the initial accident and that medical nanites had already repaired the bulk of the damage. The microscopic devices had, however, now been reprogrammed to ignore any externally visible injuries; there had been too many witnesses who'd seen me now, and an unnaturally-fast healing rate might inspire unwelcome attention. The tiny machines' only current focus was upon deep-tissue repair and internal swelling while ignoring the superficial issues like blood loss from my many cuts.

Hospitals have a unique smell to them. There is the strong presence of disinfectant, of course, but that can never quite cover the scent of human suffering. Of sweat and blood and vomit and urine and defecation. I've always admired emergency room staff; maintaining their will to do good in this environment must take phenomenal resolve. They were, I thought, truer heroes than anyone who wore spandex.

"And do you know what today's date is, Terrance?"

I told him the date but had to bite my lip to keep from continuing on to speak the millisecond-accurate time; my neural tap allowed me to retrieve chronometric data from atomic clocks in orbiting satellites. The remnants of the head injury must have still been inflicting minor difficulties—I'd never made that mistake before, revealing information from my neural interface out loud.

"Excellent!" the doctor smiled. "And can you tell me what happened to you?"

"I could," I began, "but I thought that would be a matter for the police?"

"This is just for diagnostic purposes." His brows furrowed curiously.

"Very well," I exhaled slowly. "I was kidnapped by a villain named Skullface, and my life was saved by the Boston Guardians. My injuries are the result of a car accident that occurred during the rescue attempt."

The doctor looked up at the EMT to confirm my story, then turned to a nurse. "Patient is aware of his surroundings and is exhibiting no slurring or delayed speech. No evidence of vomiting or imbalance and pupils are normal. Mark down that there's no evidence of a concussion."

"No stiffness in my neck, tingling or numbness in my extremities, or loss of bladder or bowel control." I grimaced only slightly to avoid straining the skin around my split lip. "I'm not a medical doctor, but I am First Aid/CPR/AED certified."

"Well, I'm going to run some more tests anyway. Can you feel this? How about this?" He used a probe to check for areas of numbness and checked my pulse at my extremities. He and his technicians took notes of my blood pressure as well. "No evidence of spinal injuries or internal bleeding, but we'll know more once we take x-rays and an MRI."

"No," I interrupted calmly. "If there's no indication of

immediately life-threatening injuries, I'm refusing treatment beyond bandages and stitches."

"The tests are perfectly safe," the doctor insisted.

"I know." I forced a wider and more comforting smile, despite the discomfort. "I'm the CEO of a major corporation and there are security concerns. My private physician has already been notified and is standing by."

"Sir, I really do believe that it's in your best interests to—"

"I am aware of my rights," I informed him, apologetic but firm. "You haven't mentioned any injury that requires you to render immediate treatment, and I'm of sound mind."

He stared at me intently, judging if there was a case to be made for diminished capacity. He frowned but nodded anyway. "Stitches and bandages only. We'll need you to sign a release form."

"Of course."

"If we find any life-threatening injuries, we're keeping you anyway," the Doctor informed me, seriously.

"I'd expect nothing less," I chuckled. "Thank you."

"Don't thank me," he grunted, annoyed. "You're being an idiot."

By any objective measure, I counted as one of the most intelligent people on the planet. I was, however, quite cognizant of the fact that being intelligent did not necessarily imply that one always made intelligent choices. Case in point: My first five years as Doctor Fid.

"If there are any complications, I'll accept your 'I told you so'."

Refusing advanced medical care may not have been wise, but it was necessary. Any detailed testing would certainly discover the physical and chemical alterations my body has undergone. Explaining away those changes would be challenging; I could claim self-experimentation for the marvels that AH Biotech creates, but that would be calamitous for the company's future.

And besides, even if concealing my dual identity was not an issue…maintaining secrecy regarding health issues was a valid concern for someone in my position. When the CEO of AstraTech was diagnosed with cancer, his company's stock price plummeted. His prognosis had been good and there'd been no risk that the company would be left leaderless. The business, however, never truly recovered.

The doctors and nurses provided stitches and bandages, and I maintained polite cheer through all of their efforts. It was dark by the time that I arrived home to meet with Whisper but the hug was worth the wait.

At the end of the day, bearing this discomfort was a required sacrifice; the actions of heroes had stolen more options from me than had my kidnappers. Unsurprising.

※ ※ ※

There's an orchard near my Mom and Dad's house with apple trees that grow near to the sidewalk; it's fenced off with signs to let the public know that the trees and their fruit are privately owned but that does little to discourage opportunistic harvesting. Low hanging fruit along the sidewalk's edge can be plucked by every person passing by, so the rate at which the trees are depleted is predictable.

Apples that grow higher into the canopy are left alone...until a particularly adventurous fruit thief decides that he or she really wants that snack. Then trees are climbed, or rocks thrown, or branches shook to dislodge the less-easily obtained bounty.

Sooner or later every apple falls; the only question is, how much injury is done to the tree beforehand? More damage occurs during the acquisition of that final apple than during the process of completely denuding the lower branches. The behavior patterns of a casual scrounger are different from those of a determined plunderer. If trees were intelligent, then surely they would produce all their fruit within easy reach.

If I run, some of my pursuers might give up their efforts. I'm skinny and awkward, but also fast; only the most tenacious will catch me. But those stubborn predators will be more vicious as punishment for making them work. I could fight, I could tattle or let my Mom call the school again...all these strategies would deter many assailants, but not all. The ones who aren't afraid or the ones who have something to prove will find a way. They won't be gentle. The only aspect of control within my grasp, then, is influencing how and when the violence occurs.

"Hi, Kenny," I say, and I think that I'm beginning to understand hatred after all. "Did you have a question about the physics test?"

Kenny is four years older than me and isn't scholastically inclined. I'm not the only 'nerd' he picks on; I'm just the smallest and weakest, with the fewest friends to protect me. He looks at me and scowls, hands clenching into fists.

It's safer to be the low hanging fruit. More predictable. Deciding to dangle within reach is a choice, and the opportunity to make one's own choices are rare. And if you know you're going to lose, make the loss as painless as possible.

❧ ❧ ❧

After Whisper had been settled in her room, I used the teleportation platform hidden in my home office to visit the lab where the Mk 36b was stored; inside the armor, I could use my neural tap to completely turn off my pain receptors. There were chores to be done and perhaps a rescue or two to be performed before I turned in for the night.

Already, AH Biotech's senior staff had been consulted and our press department posted a brief announcement—and statement of gratitude—to the Boston Guardians. Dealing with the now-very-public nature of my injury would be annoying, but it was the latter aspect of the press release that truly rankled.

I didn't understand it. I'd faced Titan in dozens of battles, fought him for years. The man had always been arrogant and obnoxious but also professional. If he'd been incompetent, I would have seen to his final defeat long ago. This rescue, however, had been intensely reckless. Terry Markham had escaped with relatively minor trauma, but that was more due to hidden upgrades than to the heroes' efforts.

Had it been an accident, I wondered? Titan's second in command was thorough and meticulous; he would have identified the possibility that the kidnapper's victim was unsecured in the vehicle. Titan must have disregarded the

Red Ghost's warnings and attacked anyway.

Being overruled would have explained the Red Ghost's discontent; he'd obviously been frustrated by his leader's actions while he was seeing to my injuries.

The botched 'rescue' could have been a mistake, but I worried that it may hint at a more serious issue. If Titan had honestly initiated the assault with the assumption that an innocent victim was an acceptable loss, then he'd fallen too far. Accounts with the heroine Sphinx had been settled only a few months prior; in the name of what she perceived as being the greater good, she'd committed horrors. Nothing was so deadly as misplaced righteousness...nor was anything quite so repugnant.

I initiated a few experiments and performed a few maintenance tasks before slipping out of the laboratory to launch myself into the sky. A radio-monitoring program notified me that there was a fishing boat in distress a few dozen miles off from Rockport, and the Mk 36b would be able to reach the sinking vessel faster than the coast guard.

Skullface's kidnapping attempt had forged a discomfiting link between my two personas. If Doctor Fid's philanthropic efforts continued without pause despite Terrance Markham's injuries, one more wedge would form to separate the two identities in the eyes of any investigators.

With shaped force-fields and anti-grav, I was able to keep the boat afloat long enough to tow the ship into harbor and then finally disappeared into the night. I dared not push my system too hard; all eyes would be upon Terrance Markham on the next day.

※ ※ ※

The door to my office was open, but my visitor still knocked politely before leaning in.

"Hey, boss-man," Willy Natchez greeted; he was tall, dark-skinned and slim without appearing skinny; he had the angular, solid build of a long-distance runner. "You got a moment?"

I couldn't help but chuckle. Willy was one of our newer full-time employees. He'd come to the company as a postdoctoral student working on a project co-sponsored by MIT, but we'd snapped him up as soon as the opportunity presented itself. He was bright. All my own advanced degrees were in the physical sciences, mathematics, and engineering; even so, I'd studied enough of the life-sciences to identify true innovators. William would, I knew, eventually grow into being a valuable asset to AH Biotech.

He was also refreshingly informal when dealing with upper management. Sometimes, he took advantage of my open-door policy to chat about interesting academic articles that could have bearing upon our own research or product lines. Other times, he dropped by to discuss local restaurants or obscure science fiction films that he'd recently watched.

"William. Come in."

"Ouch," he grimaced. "Should you be here today? You don't look great."

"It's mostly superficial damage," I reassured him.

"I saw some pics on the news. Thank God for Titan, yeah?" He grinned in supportive commiseration. "You were damned lucky to walk out of that wreck."

"Yes," I forced a smile. "Lucky."

Already, this had been the sixth time in one morning that I'd been forced to express gratitude towards the Guardians, and Titan in particular. It was going to be a long day.

"So, I wrote up a bunch of movies for you." Willy grinned helpfully and handed me a few sheets of lined paper. "I labeled the ones that'll be good for kids, too. Whisper 'll like 'em."

"Thank you," my brows furrowed in confusion. His handwriting was small, but fortunately quite legible; this was not a short list. He'd included brief reviews on each entry and had even recommended viewing order.

"I figured, if you're going to have some time...it'd be good to catch up, y'know?" He shrugged as though embarrassed. "Most of these are in my library, I can drop off discs anytime. Just call!"

"I appreciate the thought. I'm fairly busy these days, though, so it might take some time." I moved to set the paper in my inbox to be sorted later.

"Huh? I thought...oh. Yeah, never mind," his smile grew tight. "I should probably get going."

"No reason to rush off," I looked at him intently. "What's going on?"

Willy Natchez was a truly talented microbiologist or else I wouldn't have pushed to poach him away from his career in academia. He also had secondary traits to recommend him:

William was calm in the face of stressful circumstances, and his generosity and pleasantly irreverent manner had made him an important social part of his work environment. Also, he possessed a genuinely supernatural talent for being in the right place to discover useful information for his friends.

Willy didn't seem to be aware of this mystic ability; he just wandered through life helping the people around him and smiling a lot. I'd yet to determine when or how he'd acquired this power, but I took advantage of it shamelessly.

"Oh...My fiance's best friend works for Pierce Kennelly?" the American-Indian man looked sheepish. "She overheard him 'n Collins talking. I thought you'd have heard."

Pierce Kennelly and Henry Collins were executives at the same investment firm, and both were on AH Biotech's board of directors. If Henry Collins were gathering the BOD, I could imagine only one reason: to appoint an 'interim CEO' while I recovered from this 'trauma'.

As Doctor Fid, I had drowned my sorrows alongside genuinely psychopathic mass-murderers who were less predictable about taking advantage of others' misfortune.

"I haven't checked my email in a while," I smiled reassuringly. "It's no big deal. Thank you again."

"No problem, boss-man." His natural cheer quickly reasserted itself. "Heal up quick, yeah?"

"I will."

He left, and my mind swirled as I used my neural tap to gather information. I hacked the email accounts of members of the board, checked their travel plans and scoured their social media accounts...It took several minutes before I'd gathered enough data to understand my circumstances.

I had several days before the board convened. Henry Collins was lobbying heavily to bring the other members to his side and opinions were currently split. Collins was trying to portray his decision as a humanitarian effort, but that effort had backfired; none who knew him believed him capable of humanity. The bulk of the board was awaiting confirmation that I was negatively affected by my ordeal.

The problem was non-trivial. The board was familiar with my history of success but didn't know me on a personal level. As the chairman, Henry Collins had made an effort to keep me from interacting with other board members directly. The directors would no doubt be heavily influenced by appearance...And I looked like a giant walking bruise.

Again, I resisted the urge to reprogram the medical nanites coursing through my veins. The Red Ghost had seen my wounds up close; given his anger at his own team leader, it was exceedingly likely that the Ghost would follow up on the case to reassure himself that no further harm had been done. The man was, unfortunately, far too observant to take for granted. He would notice if even a single bandage was out of place. Every wince or stagger was an absolutely necessary sacrifice, yet also risked sabotaging my position with the board.

Henry Collins could not have chosen a more advantageous moment to attempt his *coup d'état*. But I was no longer a child, and neither Doctor Fid nor Terrance Markham would ever be considered easy prey. Never again.

※ ※ ※

I slam the door behind me and sit on my bed, features pulled tight with the effort not to burst into tears. My room is a chaotic mess of notebooks and texts; a calculus book falls to the floor and falls open on a problem I solved four months ago. There are notes in the margin for a separate project, something that I'd set aside for another time. An intriguing solution springs to mind, another approach that might yield a more elegant proof.

I kick the book closed in a fit of pique.

"Terry?" My Dad knocks on the door but doesn't open it. His voice is muffled only slightly by the thin wood. "You ok in there?"

"You don't trust me!" I call back, and saying it aloud hurts.

"Now, that's just not true," he chuckles softly, and I can imagine him shaking his head.

"You don't trust my math," I accuse. "That's the same thing."

"Disagreeing isn't the same as distrusting, Terr."

"How can you disagree with math?" I ask, confused. "It's...Math!"

"Ok, I've been thinking about how to explain this," my dad pauses. "In a vacuum, what variables do you need to account for to calculate a ballistic trajectory?"

"What does that have to do with anything?"

"Bear with me, Terr. This is probably the only time in my entire life that I'm going to get to use math to win an argument against you, let me enjoy it."

"Fiiiine." Irritated, I walk to the door and open it. Dad's

expression is playful, but I can see sadness too. He doesn't like fighting with me. I don't like fighting with him, either. "Initial height, initial velocity and initial angle."

"But if it isn't a vacuum, there are a lot more variables to consider, right?"

"Uh-huh." Calculating the theoretical atmospheric drag upon different household objects had become something of a hobby of mine.

"So, that was the problem that your Mom and I had with your math." He hugged me a bit tighter. "You had all these graphs and proofs to show that there're bullies everywhere, 'n that the most predictable thing to do was to maintain the status quo. I'm sure your logic was internally sound...but you forgot that you don't live in a vacuum, Terry."

"...there were other variables I should have taken into account?" I shifted into the hug.

"You forgot about us. We love you, kid. It doesn't matter what the math says, it makes us sad if you get hurt."

Mathematically, it was a poor argument. The existence of additional variables doesn't automatically imply that those variables are statistically relevant. Even so, my chest aches with gratitude and love.

"...Kenny is really gone?"

"Expelled and moving to Colorado with his Mother." Dad sounds satisfied.

"I'm scared," I admit. "I hate him, but I know what to expect when he's around. He's...consistent. What's going to happen tomorrow?"

"I don't know. But I know you'll be able to figure it out. Stop *worrying about how to manage your losses."* Dad ruffles my hair and I pretend to be upset. *"You don't have to lose, kid. You've got the biggest brain I've ever heard of. Maybe you can't change the entire world, but you can fix your little part of it. Find a way to win."*

❦ ❦ ❦

"Welcome to KNN CapeWatch. I'm your host, Stan Morrow." The aging journalist's smile was gentle, supportive and friendly. He'd occupied that comfortable-looking leather-upholstered chair for more than a decade now, commenting upon current events related to the superpowered community; he'd had a long career in which to learn the best methods to put his guests at ease.

"And I'm Pamela Green." While Pamela had had no reporting background prior to acquiring her current role, she'd grown into her position admirably; over the years, she had developed a tremendous talent for asking insightful questions in a manner that drew out thoughtful responses from her interviewees. She was a team-player that often accepted a supporting function to her cohost, but even a casual study of the pair's effectiveness highlighted her importance to the show's success.

"Joining us today is AH Biotech's CEO, Dr. Terrance Markham. Welcome!"

"Thank you, Stan. Pamela." I donned professional CEO smile #3. My still-healing lip stung, but conveying the proper image was of the utmost importance. I needed to appear strained but not beaten, controlled and upbeat about my situation. "It's wonderful to be here."

"We're lucky to have you," Pam commented, smiling tightly. "From what we understand, it was a very near thing."

"My co-host is referring to Dr. Markham's recent ordeal. You were kidnapped, were you not?" Stan leaned forward, brows furrowed in concern.

"I was." I grimaced as though pained by the memory. "I was at the beach with my ward when I was attacked from behind and sedated. I don't remember much about the ordeal, I'm afraid."

"As a reminder to our viewers, Dr. Markham's ward is the first completely artificial sentience recognized as a United States Citizen after the Synthetic American's Rights Act was signed into law." Stanley's voice was warm and supportive, as though personally proud that his country had passed the legislation. I wasn't surprised; one of his first professional interviews had been with the A.I. superhero known as Cuboid.

A few months back I'd had the opportunity to destroy Cuboid's body, shattering it into at least seven separate distinct parts. Good times.

"Her name is Whisper," I grinned. "Mostly, I'm just relieved that she wasn't hurt."

"Still, it must have been terrible," Pam sympathized. "Watching you be taken, I mean."

"I've talked to her about it, of course. She's a strong girl, though, and I wasn't held for long." I nodded, looking at the female co-host approvingly. "It's good of you to ask after her! She loves this show, I'm sure she'll be ecstatic."

"She likes superheroes?" There was pleasant interest clearly visible in Stan's warm smile.

"She does, but I think that she likes you two more," I laughed. "Whisper thinks you ask entertaining questions."

"We do try!" Pamela looked positively delighted.

"Who's Whisper's favorite hero?" Stanley asked.

"It used to be the Red Ghost, but it may have changed to Titan." I maintained my pleasant smile as I lied, despite the sour taste in my mouth. "It was Titan that saved me from the kidnappers."

"I was expecting you to say Cuboid," Mr. Morrow shrugged sheepishly. "I shouldn't assume."

Tell him Cuboid is mean! Whisper transmitted via my neural tap. She'd never forgiven the older artificial intelligence for ignoring her friendly greetings, months before.

"She's expressed pride in Cuboid's accomplishments. He is, after all, the world's most famous artificial intelligence." Whisper blew a raspberry directly into my skull, but I persevered. "But the Guardians are a local hero team and the Red Ghost was her favorite."

"But Titan saved your life?" Pamela queried.

"That's why I'm here," I feigned an earnest expression. "I wanted to tell my story, and offer my gratitude to Titan and all the rest of the Guardians for their efforts to keep the peace here in my hometown."

"You should re-think your praise," boomed Doctor Fid, his terrifying voice seeming to come from everywhere and nowhere all at once. Stanley, Pamela and I jerked in surprise.

(My own startle was simulated; I'd reprogrammed my nervous system to make my reactions seem realistic. For the duration of the broadcast, my autonomous response would be carefully augmented to overcome any unnatural hesitation on my own part.)

Pam turned wide, startled eyes towards her co-host. "Is...is that...?"

I was looking to the left, so I missed the moment when the Mk 36b strode from shadow into the studio. The reaction from the camera crew was immediate; furniture and equipment were bowled over as the staff scrambled for cover. Someone screamed briefly and then was quickly shushed.

I spun immediately, then froze.

There stood Doctor Fid. The armor's surface absorbed light, so thoroughly non-reflective that the villain seemed almost a silhouette...an imposing, six-and-a-half-foot tall and vaguely man-shaped hole in the world. There were stars visible within that blackness, pinpricks of light and color as though I was staring into the deepest and clearest night sky imaginable. There was no sense of contour, no sense of solidity; instead, there was only the disorienting certainty that I could reach into the infamous villain and touch the cold vacuum of space. Only at the joints were hints offered as to the powered armor's three-dimensional shape; smoldering lines of crimson bled from the seams, an angry glow as though something infernal was encased within. The helm itself was faceless, featureless and disturbing in its lack of humanity.

Modifying the Mk 36b for autonomous movement had taken only a few hours. The suit was being piloted remotely via neural interface; combat effectiveness would suffer if I attempted to multitask, but the armor was certainly still capable of being used for intimidation purposes.

No one dared move, lest they attract the monster's attention.

"Do not attempt to contact the authorities," I had Doctor Fid intone. "I intend no harm towards anyone present, and I will not be here long."

"Ladies and gentlemen," the aging host was pale but rallied gamely. "We appear to have been joined by Doctor Fid. Doctor, welcome to CapeWatch."

For a moment, the armor held stationary: the world's most heavily-armed statue. Finally, Fid nodded graciously. "Thank you, Mr. Morrow. It's a pleasure to be here."

"Why are you here?" I asked Doctor Fid and the faceless, implacable helm turned to face me.

I had designed that armor. I'd built the Mk 36b with my own hands, and I was controlling the suit myself via neural interface; even so, I felt a shiver along my spine when under that intense, emotionless gaze. I steadied my nerves and straightened my back; the motion was calculated: strong enough to imply bravery but not so tense as to imply insolence.

"I come bearing truth," Doctor Fid replied.

"Truth about the Guardians?" Pamela probed. "You mentioned that Dr. Markham should reconsider his appreciation…"

"I did," Fid's deep voice rumbled. "Footage of your 'rescue' has been uploaded to the Internet, and will be shown here as well."

The video-screen behind Pamela and Stanley powered on suddenly to display an aerial view of a familiar SUV driving southwards away from Boston. We all turned to watch. The camera crew, too, seemed to regain some semblance of professionalism now that their initial terror had faded. They spread out to right any fallen equipment and made certain that their footage was well-framed.

"Are those the kidnappers...?" Stan asked curiously.

"Yes. My drones were flying high above and Dr. Markham was in no immediate danger," the fearsome armor waved towards me, and the screen shifted to display a backscatter x-ray view of the vehicle's interior. "As you can see, your captors were all secured safely in their seats. You were resting loose within the storage area, unconscious. What occurred next was no accident."

The image shifted again, a standard full-color view but now in very slow motion. Pamela gasped wordlessly as Titan darted from one side, striking the SUV with what looked to be the force of a speeding locomotive. Metal crumpled and the vehicle was launched off the road, hitting a ditch and tumbling ferociously.

I couldn't help but cringe at how limp I appeared in the video when centrifugal force flung me through a side window to land face-first in the grass.

"As you can see, Titan acted with blatant disregard for a civilian's safety. You are a lucky man," Doctor Fid told me with grave certainty. "The odds of surviving such an impact were not in your favor."

I could only nod, briefly.

"Why were you following the kidnappers?" Pamela pressed, curiously.

"I was hoping to trail the abductors to their employer," Doctor Fid replied. There was a finality his tone that dissuaded any follow-up questions about what fate was intended for Skullface.

"If it's all right, I would like to return focus to Titan's actions." Stanley began, "I'd like to remind our viewers that—at the Mercer-Talon Incident—Doctor Fid revealed terrible crimes that had been committed by two formerly-well-regarded members of the New York Shield. A few weeks ago, Doctor Fid confronted the young hero Cherenkov and offered advice on how to be a better hero. And now, with this video...Doctor Fid, is it safe to say that you are working to hold heroes accountable for their mistakes?"

Under my mental direction, the empty armor turned its attention upon the show's host.

"You already have a guest," Fid rumbled. "Invite me back another time."

And then the fearsome villain nodded in something akin to respect and acknowledgment to the three of us assembled, and silently returned from whence he'd come: floating silently into the shadows and out of the studio.

(A temporary teleportation platform had been constructed in a rarely used stairwell; once the Mk 36b had 'ported back to the laboratory, the drones would make quick work of disassembling the platform and flying off unseen.)

"...Aaaand I think that now would be a good time to break for commercials and a new pair of trousers," Stan joked. "After these words from our sponsors, we'll return to speak with Dr. Terrance Markham about these new revelations. I'm Stanley Morrow, and this is KNN CapeWatch."

The two co-hosts were invigorated when filming resumed; our interview was delightful, ranging from the philosophy of heroism, to the history of my company, to proposing humorous suggestions as to what the initials in AH Biotech's name stood for.

("Apocalyptic Horrors." I joked, deadpan. "Because I'm secretly a supervillain. Bwahahahah.")

We discussed the Synthetic Americans Rights Act, the tribulations of dealing with medical insurance bureaucracies and a host of other topics. And if I still looked the part of an injured, bruised man...I also displayed Terry Markham to be self-controlled, alert, thoughtful and capable despite his hardships.

The board of directors decided against my 'temporary' replacement.

CHAPTER SIX

Cherenkov shared a link.
1 hr. - Public
Week Two of training with the Junior Shield…Who knew being a superhero would involve so much homework? :(Cloner is a taskmaster, but I'm learning a lot. Tomorrow, we're going on a field trip to train in the Simulation Chamber upstate!
    Comments:
        Janet Hine: Good luck!
        TallBrian43: Homework lol. That sucks ballz.
            - **Cherenkov**: It's not that bad, really. It's mostly learning laws and procedures for working alongside different organizations. How to gather evidence, how to perform a citizen's arrest, etc. We're learning about forensics too, it's awesome! nothing like on tv, though. :/
            - **TallBrian43**: Sounds cool
        Triumph: I remember my first time at the Chamber. You're gonna have a blast! And

don't worry, they never put the newbies through a Kobayashi Maru sim. :)
- **Cherenkov**: What's a Kobayashi Maru sim?
- **Brute**: An unwinnable sim, just to test how you deal with adversity. It's a reference to a really old movie.
- **Majestic**: 'Really old' :(I saw that in the theater!
- **Brute**: Did they have theaters when you were a kid? I thought it was all just cave paintings and shadow puppets around the campfire.
- **Majestic**: Ouch!
- **Jason Green**: A no-win scenario.

BlueEyedGirl: Good luck in the Simulation Chamber!
- **Cherenkov**: Blue Eyes! Hey there, I haven't heard from you in a while. Thanks!

BlueEyedGirl (Private message): After you got hurt, I wasn't sure if you wanted to hear from me.

Cherenkov (Private message): No worries. You told me where I could find Doctor Fid, I'm the idiot who shot him in the back. My fault!

BlueEyedGirl (Private message): Still, I'm glad you're all right.

Cherenkov (Private message): I'm doing great. If it wasn't for you, I wouldn't be working with the Junior Shield now! Don't feel guilty.

BlueEyedGirl (Private message): Yay!

Cherenkov (Private message): So, how've you been doing?

BlueEyedGirl (Private message): Ok, I guess. I was sort of angry with my brother about something, but then he got hurt and I feel guilty about being angry with him.

Cherenkov (Private message): Is he okay?

BlueEyedGirl (Private message): Yeah, he'll be fine.

Cherenkov (Private message): I'm glad. What were you angry about?

BlueEyedGirl (Private message): His, um, career. I was hoping that he'd make a change because I asked him, but he doesn't seem to want to. It's hard. I don't want to grow up and live like he does.

Cherenkov (Private message): He's trying to convince you to follow in his footsteps?

BlueEyedGirl (Private message): No! Kind of the

opposite.

Cherenkov (Private message): Then don't worry about it. Don't give up your dreams for him, but he shouldn't have to give up his goals for you either.

BlueEyedGirl (Private message): I guess. I just worry…his job isn't safe.

Cherenkov (Private message): Neither is mine! I was put in the hospital by Doctor Fid only a few weeks ago. Some careers are worth the risk, y'know?

BlueEyedGirl (Private message): Yeah. Sorry…

Cherenkov (Private message): Nothing to be sorry about. Hey, you've talked about your brother before and it sounds like he's a good guy. If this is really bothering you, you should talk to him about it.

BlueEyedGirl (Private message): Thanks. I'll do that soon! For now, I have to go…I think we're about to have company.

🙞 🙞 🙞

Um. Terry? Whisper called, her mental voice sounding strangely tentative. ***You should probably come home.***

Can it wait about forty-five minutes? I asked. It was only a bit after supper; I was currently working from my

deep-ocean manufacturing facility while wearing Doctor Fid's mostly-obsolete Mk 31 light-duty armor for its pain-relieving benefits. I'd just finished laying out a prototype circuit-board, an experiment to improve myoelectric control of simulated muscle-fibers. If it functioned as predicted, I could think of applications for prosthetics and ultra-lightweight strength-enhancing suits. Also—once Terry Markham had publicly recovered and could afford to take vacation time—some more surgical self-modification. For what I had in mind, a week-long medically-induced coma would be required for neurosynaptic remodeling to be completed.

Not really. I noticed on satellite footage—we have a visitor approaching the front gate.

I used my neural tap to stream video from the home security cameras that surrounded Terry Markham's property, blinked in surprise, then signaled the Mk 31's emergency speed-release. The armor fell away in chunks as I staggered towards the teleportation platform. **I'll be right there. Thank you!**

You're welcome, she chirped cheerfully. **You have to introduce me!**

"We'll see," I said aloud, dizzy from the rushed teleportation and the sudden return of bone-deep aches and pains. I'd managed to get back to my home-office before our guest arrived; Whisper was waiting for me and I gave her a brief hug.

The front gate's intercom buzzed.

Technically speaking, I didn't need to press the reply

button on my home-office desk, nor did I need to lean towards the microphone. The security system was linked to the home's private network, and that was at my complete mental control. In this case, I did reach for the panel if only to reassure myself that my hands were steady. There were no indications of trouble, but even so...this was not a meeting that I could have predicted.

"Yes?" I asked politely. "Can I help you?"

"Dr. Markham? I'm the Red Ghost of the Boston Guardians," the costumed Latino man replied, looking straight into the visible camera. "I have more information about the kidnapping attempt and was hoping that we could talk."

"I'm afraid your mask makes that difficult to prove," I lied; my security system's hidden sensors took very detailed scans. "Could you demonstrate your powers to verify your identity?"

"Of course." His crimson cowl did nothing to hide the brief approving smile that touched his features before he dissolved into a red mist.

I buzzed the gate open when he re-solidified.

The Red Ghost had arrived riding a sporty, powerful-looking electric motorcycle that matched the color of his cowl and long, flowing cloak; the bike looked custom and was likely the work of Professor Paradigm. One of the few currently-active genius-inventor heroes, Professor Paradigm worked on the west coast and supported himself by selling vehicles and communication equipment to other superhero teams. Grudgingly, I had to admit that his aesthetic sense was exquisite. I'd never been particularly enamored with motorcycles in the past, but even a screenshot of the Red Ghost's bike made me wonder about how the wind would feel on my face as I hugged corners on twisty mountain roads.

"Welcome." I met the hero at the front door and paused only a moment to spare a lustful glance at the two-wheeled masterpiece parked at the driveway's end. "Please, come in."

"Thank you," he grimaced, "I wasn't certain that you would allow me onto your property."

"Until the lawsuit is resolved, I don't think that Titan would be welcome," I admitted, "but I don't hold you responsible for your superior's actions."

AH Biotech's lawyers had insisted on pursuing a claim against the parent corporation that supported the Guardians. I didn't expect that we would win—the modified 'good Samaritan' laws that heroes operated under protected their legal interests unless malicious intent could be proved—but it was very possible that there would be an out-of-court settlement.

"Again, thank you." His frown deepened. "And I'm sorry."

"For what?"

"For not stepping forward, myself." He looked away, plainly embarrassed. "I should have told you of Titan's mistake."

"Why didn't you?" I asked. I'd certainly come to expect better from him.

"Honestly? Emotional whiplash. I was as angry as I have

ever been." He closed his eyes before continuing, "When I saw that you were alive, I was too grateful to think."

And this was why I considered the Red Ghost to be my nemesis. Not his powers, nor his talent for combat, nor even his annoyingly effective detective skills...but rather because he was a genuinely good man. His remorse was sincere and I could not hate him for his part in this particular debacle. Doctor Fid's purpose was to punish heroes for their missteps; the Red Ghost made few, and yet he still opposed Doctor Fid.

Also, he'd once used one of my own re-engineered gauss cannons to blow a two-inch hole through my small intestines. The ghost had an admirably efficient approach to combat when properly provoked. Damn the man.

"Well, for my part, I forgive you."

"I don't deserve that," he shook his head. "I'm sorry."

"Deserve's got nothing to do with it," I rasped in imitation of a famous actor's line, and then hid my wince at the Red Ghost's startle; the sudden return of my aches and pains must have been making me loopy.

"I said that to someone else, relatively recently." Red Ghost barked in short laughter. "Strange the way the world works."

Doctor Fid had been more than a little bit drunk when he'd sought out his long-time nemesis at two-forty-seven AM to have a heart-to-heart; during that conversation, the Red Ghost had delivered that line in much the same manner. I still wasn't certain that the business deal that we'd eventually embarked upon was the wisest choice, but (under the false guise that he'd reverse-engineered Doctor Fid's inventions) the crimson-clad hero had begun the efforts to release some of my safety-related technologies to the public. Unsurprisingly, the Ghost was donating the majority of his profits to charity.

"You mentioned that you had news?" I changed the subject, not-at-all-subtly.

"I do," the masked man nodded. "Did you want your head of security here?"

"I have a consultant that I work with, but he's not here at the moment."

He frowned, "You should have a team on-site."

"I hardly think that would be necessary…The people who tried to take me are in jail."

"The man who hired them is not," Red Ghost insisted. "He might try again."

"Is Skullface even still a threat? I thought that he'd be avoiding Boston after…"

"After Doctor Fid implied a threat on national television?" The Red Ghost smiled wryly. "It's unlikely, but Skullface has made foolish decisions in the past."

"I'll talk to my consultant," I nodded. "Have you found out why Skullface targeted me?"

"Actually, yes." He sounded apologetic, as though somehow disappointed that the motivation was so base. "Last year, you won an auction for a piece of artwork that he wanted."

The only item that I'd acquired via auction had been a piece formerly owned by the governor, reputedly received as a gift from the supervillain known as the Ancient. Though beautiful, it was not terribly prized among collectors. Its only real value lay in the legend behind it: that some few of the Ancient's gifts had contained clues as to the whereabouts of his lost hoard of wealth and knowledge.

Skullface was on a treasure hunt, and he'd targeted Terry Markham in Doctor Fid's city to begin his search. The sheer gall was remarkable. I couldn't think of an easy way to retaliate without compromising my plan to pretend at heroism; under most circumstances, Doctor Fid's response would be apocalyptic.

"All this for a vase," I sighed. "Ah, well. Thanks for bringing this to my attention, at least."

"You're welcome. Oh," his expression once again grew serious. "I do have some more information about Skullface and his employees; hopefully, it will be helpful for your security consultant."

"That would be very much appreciated," I chuckled softly. "First, though, can we take a break? My ward was hoping to meet you."

"I'd be delighted." And now his smile returned, broader and more genuine.

Yay! Whisper cheered into my head.

※ ※ ※

Gratitude wars with jealousy.

The infant—my brother—looks up at me with wide and curious eyes. He's in the small crib, though he doesn't crawl very well yet. Even without the off-white vertical wooden bars, he wouldn't get far before Mom or Dad could scoop him up and bring him back to safety.

I can lift him. Mom lets me hold him, sometimes. I'm good at being gentle.

I reach between the bars and touch Bobby's palm; he closes his fist around my finger and answers my delighted laugh with his own. His hands are soft and warm, and his fingernails are like needles.

I smile and Bobby lights up, grinning toothlessly with an expression that is more pure than I have words to describe. He squirms and waves his free hand and kicks his feet. Bobby doesn't want to let go of his big brother's finger.

Repeating an earlier experiment, I tap on the edge of the crib gently to form a simple sequence: one tap, then two taps, then three, then four. I repeat this several times and then added a change. One tap, two taps, three taps, six taps.

Nothing.

He doesn't squeeze my finger, doesn't change expression…He just smiles that giddy smile up at me, ecstatic at the attention.

"Hey, kiddo. Whatcha doing?"

I start in surprise and twist to look up at my father; he's standing right behind me and I hadn't heard him approach. Bobby doesn't let go of my finger; his grip is surprisingly firm for hands so small. He's tiny, though. I could pull away if I really wanted.

I don't want.

"I was just testing Bobby's pattern recognition skills."

"I think that you're going to have to wait a while for Bobby to start counting with you." Dad chuckles softly and gives my shoulder a gentle squeeze. "He's just a baby."

"Just a normal baby," I reply wistfully.

"Yup...He has ten fingers and ten toes." He kneels next to me. "I checked at the hospital."

"You know what I mean."

"You have ten fingers and ten toes, too."

"But I'm not normal," I don't cry. I have more control than that.

"You're special."

I lower my gaze.

"Bobby is special too," Dad says.

"How?" I lift my hand slightly, enjoying how Bobby tugs even tighter on my finger.

"He's my son. He's your brother. He's special to both of us."

"That's not what I meant when I was talking about being normal, and you know it."

"I know what you meant, Terry," he makes a disappointed clucking noise with his tongue. "But you're my firstborn son. You'd be special to me, no matter what."

"I..." The words feel heavy in my throat, "I just was hoping that Bobby was like me. So I wouldn't be alone."

"You're not alone, kiddo." Again, the hand squeezes comfortingly at my shoulder. "You have a Mom, a Dad, and a little brother. And you'll have more friends, too."

It's not the same, *I'm about to say. I'm too strange for people to care!* But then Bobby makes an odd giggly noise and kicks his legs and I feel suddenly dazed.

He's a baby. His brain isn't freakish like mine is. He's a decade younger than I am and I can think of a thousand ways that we're different from each other...but Bobby doesn't want to let go of my finger.

"Hey, Dad?"

"Yeah?" he smiles, but not in my direction; both of us are looking down at the baby.

"I just figured out something important."

"And what's that?"

"Being a genius doesn't mean that I'm not being an idiot."

He snorts in laughter and leans against me. We find some squeaky toy that is (I think) supposed to be a cartoonish representation of a bluebird and play peek-a-boo with my brother.

Maybe being different doesn't mean being alone, after all.

※ ※ ※

As he turned onto the main road, the hero's long crimson cloak snaked sinuously behind him; it seemed almost alive, willful and hungry. Given what I knew of the Red Ghost, I imagined that the material had been carefully chosen to enhance the effect. It didn't seem the sort of detail that he would leave to chance.

I tasked a sensor array to take careful measurements and recordings of the Red Ghost's beautiful motorcycle as he sped away. I had no need of a cape, but the bike...that was a wonder.

Thus far, the evening had been equal parts exhilarating and exhausting.

If there were any superhero whose investigative skills I genuinely admired, it would have been the Red Ghost. He was observant, open-minded and methodical. Even casual interactions with him felt like a sparring session, jabs and holds gentled lest too much be revealed and an entire defense collapse. Enclosed safely within the Mk 35 heavy-combat armor, I would still be wary if he stood in opposition. The Red Ghost had never been known to employ a weapon that might scratch the Mk 35's surface, but still I'd be more comfortable battling Gamma or Titan any day. Resourcefulness and raw will made for a danger far greater than the ability to throw cars or shrug off plasma-blasts that might liquefy solid stone.

The man hidden behind that red cowl, Miguel Espinoza, was the single greatest threat to my plans, my identity and the life that I'd built for myself. Given a thread to tug at, a hint of impropriety, and he could tear my world apart.

You like him too, Whisper noted mentally. She sounded tired; she didn't experience weariness the way a biological being might, but her quantum psyche did experience highs and lows.

I do, I admitted. ***He's the exception that proves the rule: a good person, wearing a hero's mask. If there were more heroes like him Doctor Fid would never have existed.***

She paused, and I heard her feet in the hall as the little android approached physically.

"He's not the only one," she said quietly. "Valiant is good. And Regrowth. And maybe Shrike and the rest of the Brooklyn Knights."

"This is true," I grimaced. "And others. I made a list after the battle at the Mercer-Talon building."

That had been one of the largest assemblages of superheroes in the modern age; when it became clear that the heroes were outmatched, many scattered or retreated from the field...A surprising number, however, stayed to rescue civilians or to protect the wounded. I hadn't expected to see so many, rising above themselves and risking true sacrifice for their fellow man. It was humbling. It was awe-inspiring.

It was intensely annoying.

Punishing the unworthy had always been among Doctor Fid's highest goals; that task was easier when I could assume that choosing to wear spandex and a mask was—by itself—evidence of a moral failing. Maintaining that assumption was more difficult now that medical nanites had repaired the last of my neural scarring. The self-inflicted surgically-induced sociopathy that I'd once inflicted upon myself had now faded, and it was becoming increasingly difficult to choose targets worthy of discipline.

Not impossible, of course. Titan had thoroughly earned his place on my docket! And there were so many others, too many, enough still to make my blood boil with rage.

I shook away my anger and looked down to face my ward, brows furrowed curiously. "Why mention them, sweetheart? The good ones, I mean. Where are you going with this?"

"You work with the Red Ghost and contribute to Valiant's charities and help others without them even knowing...but you still talk about the heroes as though they're all bad," she lowers her eyes. "And I don't think it's fair. Cherenkov is a hero. And Doctor Fid's a hero now, too."

"Doctor Fid is not a hero," my back stiffened. "It's just pretend."

"It's not pretend to the people you saved," she replied

quietly.

I pulled the little android into a gentle hug. "They'll hate me again, soon enough."

"The day you saved me, you told me you were a bad man," she pressed the side of her head to my chest. "But you were my hero, too. Maybe you can be both."

"No!" I growled, and then winced and softened my tone when I felt Whisper squirm uncomfortably. I let her go. "I'm sorry, but no. Bad people can't be heroes. Bad people aren't worthy."

"I don't want to be a bad girl." Whisper looked up and her glowing-blue gaze met my own; she sounded forlorn, and I heard a slight tinge of fear that broke my heart.

"Then don't. Be a good girl," I tried to comfort her with a gentle grin. "You can be a hero for both of us."

"What about Doctor Fid?"

"I can be a bad man who does good things," I decided. "Is that enough for you?"

"Yeah," she smiled tremulously. "Yeah. It is."

I gave her another hug, then returned to my work when she scampered back towards her room. There was much to do: Stanley Morrow from Capewatch had reached out to Doctor Fid hoping for an interview, and an affirmative response would require careful planning. I needed to put more thought into the means by which a functional brain-tape technology would be introduced to the public. And more wildfires had erupted in California that Doctor Fid could work to contain.

There was little rest for the wicked, and even less for the

sort-of-kind-of wickedly benevolent.

❧ ❧ ❧

Tired, reeking of soot and ash, I was making one final patrol circling downtown Boston when a tree waved for my attention. It was not quite so late that I was willing to be rude towards one who had earned my respect; to the best of my knowledge, only Regrowth had such fine biokinetic control over plant life. Doctor Fid's Mk 36b medium-duty armor slowed in its flight, hovering silently while the oak's branches creaked and groaned. A bough pointed west, and other trees along that route echoed the movement.

I flew west.

Regrowth was a heroine and a member of the Guardians but I had no reason to expect an ambush. She'd been present when I first contacted her paramour (the Red Ghost) for the late-night discussion which resulted in the secret business dealings that allowed his new company to market my inertial displacement devices to car manufacturers, potentially saving hundreds of thousands of lives. Also, Regrowth was aware that I had uncovered her civilian identity.

Even so, I summoned medium-combat drones to soar high overhead—just in case. Heroes can be unpredictable.

The helpful trees guided me to the south-west corner of the Boston Public Garden. I floated lower, where Regrowth appeared to be meditating cross-legged on a park bench. She was wearing her traditional green-and-brown, close-fitting full-body uniform, and didn't seem at all bothered by the evening's chill. A sensor reading confirmed that she'd had temperature-regulating functionality added to her deceptively-simple-appearing costume. There was padding and light armor sewn within as well. The design was elegant and clever; I approved.

"You wished to speak with me?" I asked, the armor's vocoder stripping weary curiosity from my tone.

Regrowth opened her eyes. "I do."

"So." I settled to the ground. This location was well-chosen; we were surrounded by sufficient greenery to conceal our meeting from prying eyes. Also—should hostilities arise—Regrowth was at her most powerful when surrounded by a wide variety of flora. Here, she could have fought off even the notorious Doctor Fid until reinforcements arrived. Behind my helm's featureless face-plate, I could not help but smile. "What can I do for you?"

"You can tell me what the hell you're up to," she stated evenly. There was no anger in her voice, but the bushes and trees surrounding us shivered with tension.

I'd gotten used to heroes treating me with a wary respect; Regrowth's straightforward demands were a pleasant change. If conversing with her lover was a sparring match, then a confrontation with Regrowth was being stalked by a powerful predator: there were no tentative jabs or attempts to feel out her opponent—there was only measured analysis followed by a pounce for the throat. When dealing with supervillains, at least, she tended to get to the heart of issues without indulging in the usual banter.

"Is it so hard to imagine," I began carefully, "that I might be looking to make amends for my misdeeds?"

"No," she quirked a smile. "Remember, I was there when you spoke to Red Ghost. I know that there's a human being under that armor. It's very easy to imagine you choosing to make amends."

I paused before replying, taken aback; Regrowth's response wasn't at all what I'd expected. Given that she'd opened with the accusation that my recent actions were part of a larger plot, I'd anticipated only scoffing dismissal. Also, I was surprisingly touched by her high opinion of me. I'd acted a monster for so long that being acknowledged as 'human' was high praise, indeed.

"Then, why do you think that I'm up to something?"

"If you were serious about turning over a new leaf," she explained, "You wouldn't do it with theatrical heroics. You'd build something extraordinary, something to improve the world."

"I did that," I raised my hands defensively. "Or have you already forgotten the battle against the Legion?"

"You saved the Earth," she shook her head, and I could hear amused gratitude in her voice. "But I think that'd have only been the start if you were really seeking redemption."

"Perhaps I have projects in the works, machines that are not yet ready for public consumption?"

"No. You're Doctor Fid." Her lips twisted into an appreciative smirk. "You'd wait until the new technology was ready and lead with that. It's your greatest strength, but you've always been too proud of your toys."

I tried to think of a counter-example from my long career

but was unable to do so. After every setback, Doctor Fid had returned to his labs and only emerged when a new and improved suit or drone had been designed. It was, I supposed, a reasonably predictable pattern. Damn it.

"What would you say," I asked quietly, "If I told you that this wasn't an act and that I was serious about trying to become a hero?"

"I'd tell Miguel, and he'd believe you," Regrowth replied, equally gentle. "And he'd be very disappointed if you were lying."

Ouch.

"It's an act," I admitted. "A temporary diversion to manipulate public opinion. I...don't expect to ever again become the creature I was two decades ago, but I'm still Doctor Fid."

"Why?" The heroine didn't seem surprised, and she didn't seem annoyed. I'd been expecting at least a judgmental glare, but instead the only expression that I could read on her face was acceptance....as though I'd merely confirmed her prediction.

"There were several reasons." Behind my opaque faceplate, I was smiling wryly. "But if I'm being truly honest with myself? Because I thought it would drive Titan mad."

"Excellent," Regrowth's smile was delightfully wicked. "How can I help?"

CHAPTER SEVEN

Whatever his faults, Skullface was an experienced villain and thus did not skimp when it came to outfitting even a temporary lair. Somehow, he'd acquired a ranch on the western edge of Brockton; this was, I felt certain, where CEO Terrance Markham would have been brought instead of the obvious decoy location that the Guardians had raided after the 'rescue'. The building was well-shielded from casual scans, but a drone-based visual inspection through a cellar window showed a room well-appointed for torture and interrogation. There were two outbuildings housing well-armed mercenaries, and there was every indication that the main ranch-house contained some sort of advanced power generator. Doctor Chaise's doing, I presumed.

It had taken hours for my new microdrones to walk on-site. Flight might have tripped sensors hidden on the property; the anti-gravitics normally used in my drones were difficult to detect but not impossible—and Skullface certainly had cause to be paranoid. He was operating only an hour south of Doctor Fid's city.

The estate's means of defeating remote surveillance were subtle and wholly unlike my own stealth technologies. Effective, as well; for the first time in a very long while, I was limited solely to the drone's visible spectrum cameras when attempting to gather information. I looked forward to studying whatever remnants of the technology remained undamaged once this operation concluded.

Floating two-hundred-thousand feet above, the Mk 35 Heavy Combat armor's onboard cameras lacked the resolution to do better than count the number of cars present.

"Are you ready?" I queried via a very secure tight-beam laser radio connection.

"Whenever you are." Regrowth sounded calm, focused and professional. Capturing a high-profile supervillain had been her idea, a way to create a news cycle certain to drive Titan insane. I'd been reluctant, at first; I did not intend to play-act at being a hero forever, after all, and it would be inefficient to create enemies on both sides of the costumed divide. Serendipitously, I'd unearthed evidence of Skullface's location. I may have been hesitant to cause unnecessary friction within the villainous community, but Skullface had thoroughly earned my ire. The last of my objections drifted away like smoke, and the heroine's plan moved forward.

"I'm on my way." I performed final calculations and then cut my flight systems. With a low-powered forcefield configured to create a near-frictionless cocoon around me, the acceleration was remarkably smooth. I estimated slightly less than two minutes until impact.

It was a moment of perfect beauty. The highest clouds—

wispy chaotic white puffs strung in lines from the collision of warm and cool fronts along the coast, or gray intimidating masses gathered by the mountains to the west—were miles beneath my feet, and the Earth's gentle curve was framed by a thin cloak of blue. I could see vast swaths of untouched wilderness and interconnected hives of humanity along the eastern seaboard, and the grand celestial expanse stretched overhead in fathomless black broken by countless flecks of delicate brilliance.

There was ugliness down there, too: scars from industry and greed, stains of sprawling inequality, sullied regions of blight and decay. Descending from the stratosphere, however, those blemishes seemed small and manageable. The flaws were tiny compared to the surrounding grandeur.

This world deserved saving.

"How are your efforts proceeding?" I asked via radio. At just under thirty-five seconds, gravity had accelerated my fall past the speed of sound.

"On schedule," she replied, though she sounded distracted. From what I understood, exercising her power in the current manner required intense concentration. Controlling existing plants was relatively simple; causing large-scale growth took time, and a significant array of tree-roots would need to extend under the expected battleground for the heroine to be most effective. Much of the work had been done the prior evening, but the critical last few dozen feet might have caused enough disruption below the surface to cause damage to the sidewalk or driveway.

So...She toiled while I dropped, and we both trusted that

any sudden crack appearing in the pavement would not be noticed during the remaining minute of my fall.

The ground was getting closer; the air was less thin, and cotton-like high-altitude clouds passed so swiftly that I barely had time to identify them before they were gone. I was nearer to humanity now, no longer separate from the Earth...I was coming home.

This world deserved heroes; real ones rather than frauds like Titan! Someday, perhaps Whisper would take on that role. She would be extraordinary. For now, though, a monster could do a hero's work.

"Incoming," I warned, "In ten, nine, eight..."

I pulsed a massive amount of energy into my defenses: structural integrity, inertial displacement and force fields all operating at such intensity that I imagined that I could see the haze. Alarms would be tripped by Doctor Chaise's sensors, I was certain, but my speed was too rapid for the alert to be useful. I struck the ground directly in front of the ranch house at nearly three times the speed of sound.

The resulting explosion and shock-wave was glorious.

The protections that Doctor Chaise had placed on the house were instantaneously overwhelmed. Kinetic energy equivalent to more than two tons of TNT shattered wood and stone and glass into scrap, the front of the structure blown backwards as though punched by a giant fist. Even smoke and dust were thrust from the point of impact, leaving me standing in a shallow thirty-some-odd foot wide crater of perfect destruction.

The Mk 35 heavy-combat armor towered fourteen feet tall

with an intimidatingly broad frame. As with all of Doctor Fid's armors, the surface did not reflect light; if not for the traces of angry red that leaked from the suit's seams, it would appear a giant, man-shaped hole in reality that led into deep space. The night sky, shaped into a deadly and fearsome threat. In this orichalcum-framed armor, I'd faced Valiant in hand to hand combat for more than twenty minutes. In this armor, I was invincible.

"SKULLFACE!" The armor's vocoder made my shout into a roar, a shriek promising unimaginable violence. I imagined that what remained of the foundations shook from my voice alone. "You trespassed in my domain. Face me, if you dare!"

Seconds passed. Sensitive micro-parabolic microphones detected shouting and the sound of movement within the building, but no movement was visible.

"Oh, for the love of God," Regrowth groaned over our communicator link. "Please tell me that we got the right house."

"The anti-surveillance measures are still in place, and the protections were definitely Doctor Chaise's work," I replied tersely. My explosive entrance would have leveled an unmodified house rather than simply damaging the face of it. "I can hear movement insi-"

And that's when an eldritch blast from somewhere inside the damaged building put a three-inch hole straight through the Mk 35's faceless helm.

❧ ❧ ❧

"You're a freak," Louis whispers over my shoulder, but he doesn't hit me. I made sure that he got caught last time, and the time before. The second event had occurred in Mr. Phalen's class; I like the temp teacher that is replacing him, sort of. She doesn't talk to me, but she doesn't turn a blind eye to bullying, either. That's not until fourth period, though, still hours away.

I'm winning.

On my left, Missy avoids looking me in the eyes as she takes her seat. Of all the students that participate in this class, she's the most studious. I tried offering help with her homework once, but Kenny overheard and made a joke. Everyone laughed, and Missy doesn't acknowledge me anymore. Wayne—on my right—waves to her as though I'm invisible.

"Good morning, class." Ms. McSorrel greets us. "Did everyone have a nice weekend?"

"Yes, Ms. McSorrel," some of us reply. Chairs scrape across ceramic tile as the last students take their seats.

"That's wonderful to hear!" She smiles pleasantly. "Did anyone have any questions about the project due on Thursday?"

I do, but I don't raise my hand; Ms. McSorrel doesn't like it when I take classroom time away from the other students. Some primary documentation I found conflicts with the information in our history texts; it's not even important stuff, just differing accounts about who was in a room while a treaty was being signed. But the assigned book might be wrong. Maybe. First-hand accounts can lie, *too. Or be misremembered. I don't know what to do.*

Maybe Mom will help. Ms. McSorrel looks busy; she's answering Ian's questions now about how to format an in-text citation, and it sounds as though that discussion is going to take a while.

"Freeeeak," Louis murmurs softly, and someone else smothers a laugh. *I don't turn to see who. It doesn't matter. Technically, I suppose that he's correct—I exhibit traits that are abnormal. Historically, though, the word was usually employed to refer to individuals with unusual physical features. I don't like the person I see when I look in a mirror, but I don't think that my appearance is outside of statistical norms.*

I wonder what my brain looks like. If I open up my skull, would I appear human? Perhaps I'm only monstrous on the inside. A neural malformity might explain why I'm the only person who can't see what everyone else sees. It must be hereditary; Mom and Dad don't seem to be able to see it, either.

I'm winning. This is what winning feels like.

No one has hit me for weeks; instead, an invisible and impermeable barrier has sprung up around me. Everyone knows that it's my fault that Kenny moved away. Everyone knows that it's my fault that Louis was suspended for a week and that Mr. Phalen was fired. Crowds of students part like the red sea when I move down the hall; no one wants to get too close lest they be next.

Ms. McSorrel smiles, "Are there any more questions?"

Why am I like this, I don't ask. What's wrong with me? If someone would just tell me, I could fix it!

I open my textbook to the appropriate page and prepare to take notes. This isn't math; I actually need to study history to make sense of it.

Ms. McSorrel begins her lecture.

※ ※ ※

In a heartbeat, my warstaff was summoned to my hands and I was pouring plasma-blast after plasma-blast into the house's wreckage. There must have been a hardened bunker somewhere within, beyond my drones' field of view. I tasked my robots to explore while I darted to one side to seek out cover.

"Are you okay?" Regrowth called over the radio, sounding worried.

"I'm fine," I gritted out, frantically remodulating my forcefields in real-time as additional magical attacks were emitted from within what remained of the ranch house. I'd originally calculated that the orichalcum alloy invented by Whisper's creator would be defense enough against even strong magical attacks; apparently, I'd been incorrect. "Keep an eye on the outbuildings, I hear movement."

"I'm on it," she replied, and thick tree-roots uprooted themselves to wrap around the first armed mercenary that ran out one of the doors. "How are you fine? There's a hole in your head!"

"The Mk 35 is fourteen feet tall. I'm not."

"So your real head isn't in the armor's head. Good. Whew!" Four more mercenaries followed the first, training their fire in my direction before being swept back in a wave of wood and bark. "Why put a humanoid head on the armor at all?"

"So that someone like Skullface has an obvious target to waste his first shot on," I laughed harshly, aiming a few kinetic energy blasts at the ground between myself and my attacker to throw up an instantaneous cloud of dust behind which to hide.

"Fair point."

In an organized effort to avoid a bottleneck at the outbuilding's doors, a dozen mercenaries in beige body-armor had simultaneously dived out the windows and broken into teams of three. Another wave swiftly followed. How many employees had Skullface kept on site? There'd only been four cars on the property.

Less than a third of the fire-teams directed their weapons towards me…the rest sprinted east, toward's Regrowth's hiding spot.

I blamed Doctor Chaise. He must have set sensors around the property that had evaded my detection.

"Incoming!" I warned.

"I see them. Don't worry about me," I could hear her smug smile over the radio. "I've had twelve hours to grow defenses under that field."

"Have fun," I grunted, gathering myself for an assault. "I'm going to go kill Skullface."

"You mispronounced 'capture'. Again." There was steel in her voice.

During the process of re-engineering Terry Markham into a creature that could fill Doctor Fid's armor, no small amount of training was put towards training my dramatic skills. Fulfilling expectations drove public response: an intimidating monologue was more likely to be replayed on the evening news, and menacing laughter from the shadows was more effective at demoralizing one's victims than any simple display of power. Creating a persona that fulfilled many of the expected tropes had been a useful tool when clawing my way to power.

"Oh, right." Banter was a less frequently used skill, but it was disturbing how easily I fell into the rhythm. "I forgot that I'm supposed to be a hero now. We'll call it an accidental decapitation when the suspect resisted arrest."

"Doctor..."

"My body camera mysteriously stopped functioning just before the suspect reached for my weapon..."

"You're less amusing than you think you are." She sounded distracted, coordinating plant-based attacks upon dozens of mercenaries at once.

I just triggered my maniacal laughter generator and dove into the breach, accelerating so hard that my inertial displacement devices made an audible whine. A series of magical attacks launched towards me, but I was prepared; two blasts were dodged, and the third swatted from the air by a swing of my staff.

As I passed over the threshold, the world twisted and stretched; the walls faded into the distance, hidden by a dull mustard-colored haze and syrupy red light that oozed from glowing noxious pools. The ceiling fled completely, and I could see the night sky but the stars were wrong. I could feel their hatred as they glared down upon me. And every breath I took scorched at my throat, tasting painfully of blood and sulfur.

It was that latter effect that impressed me the most; the Mk 35's air supply was wholly self-contained. Despite any damage that the suit had suffered, I knew that only pure and clean air was reaching my lungs. But still, each wheezing gasp through clenched teeth ached.

Magic. Bah.

"Can you hear me, Regrowth?"

There was no response.

Whisper?

Nothing.

The neural link communicated via quantum tunnel; mere distance would not have cut off communication so completely. I hadn't been teleported, nor was this an illusion. Fortunately, the scenario did seem to resemble something that I'd read once. The reprehensible Ancient had—more than two decades ago—written a monograph on projected realities of sorcerous origin. In order to dispel the working, I would need to find and destroy a series of runes and I would need to render the caster unconscious.

The former task seemed as though it would be tedious without access to my normal sensor capabilities, but I found myself very much looking forward to the latter.

Time and space twisted vertiginously, and Skullface was excreted into visibility. In this place—this world of his making—he stood thirty feet tall and blazed with power; a hideously gothic gun-metal gray armor surrounded his skeletal form, and magic symbols that hurt to look at were etched into the suit's surface.

"Well, thank Tesla," I boomed, my lips pulling back into a feral grin. "I worried that this fight was going to be boring!"

The abomination roared in challenge, and hellfire poured from its bleached-bone jaws and empty eye sockets; my own wild laughter was projected loud enough to compete. There were no more words between us—only hatred and anticipated violence.

As though triggered by some unheard signal, we both charged.

※ ※ ※

Exhausted and sore, I stumbled through the ruins in front of the ranch house. Skullface had fled, but I could not count his retreat as a victory.

In that strange, magically-created sub-dimension, he'd had near as much raw strength as Valiant as well as access to mystical attacks that my force-fields were ill-equipped to defend against. If Skullface had also owned the skill to judge the level of damage my technological protections had suffered, the battle would have ended in his favor.

I'd bluffed 'til the end and he'd withdrawn to see to the many wounds I'd left upon his person. Skullface, perhaps, would see the conflict as a draw. I knew better; I'd been unprepared for this particular opponent and nearly paid a permanent price.

The realization rankled.

Ideas and designs for numerous improvements warred for my attention, ranging from boosts in efficiency to strategically-placed increases in armor thickness. For now, though, the idea of lab-work held limited appeal. A warm shower and a comfortable bed were much more enticing.

A quick ping of GPS satellites confirmed that some time-dilation shenanigans had occurred; we'd traded blows for nearly half an hour...but atomic clocks confirmed that only a few minutes had passed in the real world.

"I'm afraid that I lost our target," I transmitted to Regrowth, glad for the vocoder that altered my voice and removed any trace of my weariness. "Any difficulties on your end?"

"Oh God. God. Thank God," she sobbed in a strange and manic tone that made my back stiffen in alarm. Over the communicator, I could hear her take a shallow breath to steady herself. "Things got, um, interesting when you disappeared. I could use a bit of help!"

"Are you injured?" I shot into the air; Dr. Chaise's technology was still interfering with some of my scanning technology, but as I gained altitude the effect began to fade.

She took too long to answer. "A bit, yeah. Also, buried and running out of air. Hurry. Please!"

I issued a command to summon a triage-capable medical drone from a warehouse in Boston and sped to Regrowth's last-known location. She'd made her stand in the forested edge of a clearing.

The grove had been verdant, once; lush and beautiful, a gently sloped field lined with sturdy English oaks that she could put towards her own defense. There'd been low bushes for cover and a plethora of flowers and vines for the heroine to control. Even against an army of mercenaries, she should have been safe.

Some remnants of green remained, but anything larger than a blade of grass had been shredded to kindling and charred. My sensors identified Regrowth's position and I dropped to the ground so that I could begin digging, using the Mk 35's massive hands to tear up volumes of dirt and pieces of shattered tree roots. My powered armor might not have been ready to go one-on-one with Valiant at the moment, but it could still move earth quickly.

"What happened?"

"I had everything under control, and then Chaise showed up with an honest-to-God flying saucer," she grunted uncomfortably. "I used a tree to bury myself to get out of his line of fire, but his stupid ray gun destroyed too much of the root system for me to dig myself out."

She may not have been able to dig, but Regrowth had been using her power to stabilize the earth. Roots from small grasses and weeds had stretched into a net, binding great clods of soil together and keeping the ground from collapsing as I tore into it. In moments, I was able to free a path to the trapped heroine; she'd been packed in tight, with only a few inches of space free around her upper body.

I had never considered myself to be particularly claustrophobic, but I shivered at the mere thought of being constricted similarly. That Regrowth had maintained her wits was remarkable.

With delicate care, I managed to lift away enough debris to lift the coughing woman out from under the earth. Even through the thick layer of dirt, I could tell that she wasn't bleeding heavily. One of her arms was, however, badly broken; it looked as though she'd gained an extra elbow mid-bicep and I couldn't help but wince in sympathy.

"I have a medical automaton en-route, but I can dose you with painkillers right now."

"Oh, God yes!"

The Mk 35's life-support systems include a wide array of medications and narcotics useful for keeping my body functional during the rigors of combat; I routed an appropriate dosage to an external hypospray spray injector.

"Whoo, that's the stuff." The change in Regrowth's expression was almost instantaneous, and tension bled from her shoulders. "Damn…Why are you a supervillain, again? If you market this, you'd be able to take over the world legally."

"That particular cocktail was made possible only by ignoring copyright and patent protections to an egregious degree," I chuckled, relieved that she felt well enough to jest. "One of the benefits of being a villain."

"Put a bottle of that in a 'to-go' bag, I may consider changing sides," she joked, then took a deep shuddering breath. The tension seemed to bleed out of her shoulders. "Thank you. God. I didn't think I was getting out of that."

"I had no choice," I replied, and I altered the programming on the armor's vocoder to allow some of my relief and humor to slide into Doctor Fid's modulated speaking voice. "The Red Ghost would have killed me."

"He still might. I didn't tell him that we were doing this," she half-smiled apologetically.

I stilled, motionless like a goliath statue. "...Why not?"

"Miguel's angry at Titan, but not angry enough to gaslight him," she shook her head. "It's not the way he thinks. He'd quit, or maybe even turn on Titan publicly...but he wouldn't help you with this."

"That is unfortunate."

"I called him when you disappeared. He's on his way now," she shivered, sounding strangely vulnerable.

It occurred to me that—though his motorcycle was undoubtedly lovely—The Red Ghost probably couldn't manage more than a hundred miles per hour on surface streets...and that there hadn't been terribly much air in the hole in which I'd found Regrowth. "You've told him that you're safe?"

She averted her gaze and didn't answer.

"Call him," I instructed. "I won't go far until we know for sure that Skullface and his minions are gone."

I secluded myself so as to give Regrowth some privacy for her call, and also to hide my own injuries. I hated fighting magic users; far too many of their attacks bypassed physical defenses. Even with my nanites working at full capacity, it would be hours before I stopped bleeding internally.

The flying medical automaton arrived before Regrowth waved for me to return. It hovered twenty feet overhead, waiting patiently until I called it down.

"You should go," Regrowth told me. "The entire team is on its way; Titan and Veridian 'll find an excuse to start a fight if you're still here."

"Let my drone fix your arm first," I suggested. "If you're

willing to accept more of my illegally obtained medical assistance, I can have your arm back in working order in two days or so."

She nibbled at her lower lip and nodded, and I gently helped position her for the medical robot to have easy access. A half-dozen arms, bristling with surgical equipment, extended from within the floating device.

"You're probably going to want to close your eyes for this next part," I informed her. "It won't hurt, but watching the process is exceedingly disconcerting."

She did so, the automaton began its bloody work. I hacked her home computer remotely and played a song from her collection; the music drowned out the disturbingly wet noises caused by the quick and precise surgery underway. Watching the apparatus work from this angle was a new experience. Until this moment, I'd been the robot's only patient.

The nerves in her broken arm were temporarily severed, allowing the robot to smoothly reposition the limb and set the bone. The process of lifting away muscle fiber and fascia so that dissolvable mesh bracing could be installed was messy but swift.

Idly, I searched through the rest of her playlists. Regrowth had an interestingly eclectic taste in music. Not all of it was to my personal taste, but I took note of a few bands and albums to investigate at a later date.

"You should release this medbot to the public," Regrowth suggested, raising her voice to be heard over the music. "You could work something out with Miguel, like you did with the inertial displacement fields."

I'd conspired with Miguel Espinoza—the Red Ghost—so that he could claim that he'd reverse engineered the inertial displacement technology from equipment that he'd taken from me during our battles. The rules regarding profiting from a supervillain's work were complicated but were generally structured to discourage villains from profiting from their crimes. Heroes were granted a significant benefit of the doubt, but that charity was not limitless.

"I'm open to discussing the issue," I conceded. "However, the laws concerning introducing medical technology are very complex."

"I'm just saying...I have a shattered humerus, and you just told me that I'll be healed in time for Friday's tennis lesson. That could help a lot of people."

"Had."

"What?"

"Had a shattered humerus. The drone is finishing weaving a temporary cast, and you'll get feeling back in your arm right about...now."

Regrowth blinked her eyes open just as the medical automaton retracted the last of its tools. Her right arm was now immobilized, slightly bent at the elbow, and wrapped in a near-skin-tight weave of hardened silk fiber. "It doesn't hurt much at all."

"You still have my painkillers in your system. It will ache later this evening."

"Well, damn. I'm only giving this service two stars on Yip." She grinned, then her expression turned serious. "You should get going...The rest of the Guardians will be here soon."

I nodded. "There is a stand of pine over there, still alive. If I bring you to it, will you be able to use them to maintain defenses long enough for help to arrive?"

"Yeah."

"Very well. Thank you for your assistance, and I'm sorry that you were injured. I should have planned for aerial support."

"You pulled me out of the dirt, there is absolutely nothing you can say that will make me place blame on those metal shoulders. Now git."

I got.

CHAPTER EIGHT

A THOROUGH DIGITAL SEARCH THROUGH THE secretive (and supposedly 'unhackable'. Hah!) darkweb forums used by many ne'er-do-wells to conduct their online business confirmed that Skullface had been building up a small army of mercenaries. The efforts had been slow and careful to avoid casual detection; my own monitoring programs hadn't noticed anything awry, and it had only been by expanding upon information that I'd been able to find about Barry, Military Boots and the rest of my abductors that a pattern began to emerge. Building up these forces had been the work of several months, begun long before I'd begun my heroic charade.

Successfully stealing technology from Doctor Fid's domain would be a direct attack upon Doctor Fid's reputation. The attempted kidnapping of a corporate officer hadn't been a mere heist intended to gather up one of the Ancient's relics; it was also an attempt to destabilize my preeminence in the New England area. It was an insult and it was a challenge! The skeletal supervillain—perhaps thinking me a weakened target after the battle at Mercer-Tallon—had been looking to uproot me from my domain.

Gaining one vase would be a coup but gaining control of New England would be a triumph. The Ancient had, after all, been based in Rhode Island—well within the region I had claimed. The greatest density of the Ancient's belongings (and the most likely location of his hidden trove) was under Doctor Fid's control.

Skullface had gone to ground, and Dr. Chaise's technological savvy had somehow allowed him to do so thoroughly enough that even Whisper and I working together were unable to find a trace. If Skullface was moving resources into my domain, however, then those resources would be unearthed and decimated. If he wanted the Ancient's artifacts then I would find them first. Whatever he desired, I would see him denied!

The Ancient had been a terrifying villain: a powerful sorcerer and a gifted scientist, he'd created horrors with which to plague the superpowered community. He rarely faced his foes directly; instead, he'd created monsters or empowered minions to fight in his place. And although he'd been captured six times, no one had ever been able to determine from whence he'd come; it was as if he had simply appeared fully formed—menacing and dangerous—to begin his reign of terror.

Twice, he'd escaped while awaiting trial, and four more times he sat through his time in court, smiling calmly as his crimes were recounted. No prison had held him for long.

The Ancient had disappeared before I'd finished building the first of Doctor Fid's armors. According to rumor, he'd shown up at Lassiter's Den, quiet and thoughtful, and ordered a Sazerac cocktail; upon finishing his drink he had wept and disappeared into the night...never to be heard from again. To this day, ordering a Sazerac at Lassiter's Den was as good as announcing one's retirement among the villainous community.

The Ancient was gone, but his legacy lived on. Young upstarts occasionally rose up—claiming to be the Ancient's heir or lost disciple—and the heroes gathered in force to combat the new threat. A number of heroes and villains were still active who'd been granted their abilities during the Ancient's terrible experiments. And rumors spread of a vast abandoned treasure trove.

Supposedly, clues had been left as to the location of the Ancient's hidden trove in works of art, jewelry and literature that he'd spread throughout the world. He'd been a generous patron to many very-uncomfortable academics; given his reputation, even the most dedicated of scholars had nervously accepted their tribute. Other pieces, he'd given away as tokens of respect to rulers and kings, to lawmakers and businessmen and community leaders and humanitarians.

It was difficult to say what had motivated the villain's largess; only a small percentage of the offerings appeared to be at all connected to the Ancient's villainous goals. The distribution seemed random...and that, perhaps, was the point. Over the course of twelve years, the Ancient had dispersed a wealth of possibly relevant items evenly across the Earth's surface.

When the Ancient had disappeared, there'd been a mad

scramble to acquire these objects. Many had been traded or sold to private collectors, more had gone to auction, and others had simply been stolen. Forging certificates of authenticity had been a lucrative business for those who were willing to risk the wrath of an unhappy (possibly superpowered) client.

The villains who'd known the Ancient best had been firm believers in the rumor of a hidden trove; Imperator Rex, in particular, had spent years seeking out items that he'd believed might hold clues. When one such item had been located in a Boston museum, the feared supervillain had come to ask my permission to rob an institution within my territory….as Skullface should have done, had he desired to avoid my wrath.

The means by which some of this knowledge had been gathered sickened even me, but information itself is neither good nor evil. Even if I never uncovered a path to find the Ancient's lost fortune, there was value to be gleaned from any research I uncovered along the way.

Whatever inborn ability allowed some to babble incantations and thus reshape reality, I had none of it. Magecraft itself was beyond me. The science, though, was intriguing. I had suspicions regarding the nature of so-called 'magic' that would be easier to confirm with access to the Ancient's meticulous notes. Also, I wished for my defenses to be better prepared when next I faced Skullface in battle. The Ancient's knowledge would certainly help in that regard.

It would, however, be several days before I could devote myself fully to this new scavenger hunt. An opportunity related to my current heroic ruse had arisen and my attention was riveted.

❈ ❈ ❈

"Welcome to KNN CapeWatch," The speaker's voice was warm and unhurried. "I'm your host, Stan Morrow."

"And I'm Pamela Green." A slight tremor in her introduction betrayed her own tension, but she smiled pleasantly nonetheless.

"Today's special show is being recorded in an undisclosed location with no audience and limited staff on site, so please bear with us if there are any technical difficulties."

"These precautions are necessary because today we've managed to wrangle some time with a man who has never been interviewed, despite spending decades in the public eye," Pam continued professionally. "Our guest tonight has a long and violent history, but his recent actions have caused many to speculate that he's had a change of heart."

"Doctor Fid," Stan's voice grew serious. "Welcome to our studio."

The invitation to appear on this show had represented an intriguing opportunity, but also a significant risk. Answering questions in a manner that was beneficial to the current scheme—pretending at heroism—while not disrupting other long-term goals would make for a complicated balancing act.

"Thank you both," I acknowledged, taking a seat in a reinforced easy chair and trusting in the Mk 36b's vocoder to alter my voice and to strip any nerves from my tone. "I appreciate the efforts that you've put forth to make certain that this interview could occur."

"You are one of the world's most well-known individuals on the planet, and yet you are also one of the most mysterious." Ms. Green gestured towards me appreciatively. "As journalists, how could we resist?"

"Even so, I'm grateful."

"You're very welcome," Stan assured. "A bit of background for our viewers today: Doctor Fid's first public appearance occurred more than twenty-two years ago, and he quickly became one of the world's most feared villains. He's fought countless battles and faced the Earth's mightiest heroes, yet has never been captured or unmasked."

"It is more recent news, however, that has created the most controversy. Eighteen months ago, a video surfaced in which Doctor Fid renounced violence and joined the anti-corporate hacker collective known as the FTW. Doctor, would you care to comment on that decision?"

"The leader of the FTW—Starnyx—may have been a villain, but he was also a good man and a respected friend. When he died, I...I was inspired to follow his example."

"How did that work out for you?"

"Well, Stan, I'm afraid that I wasn't a good fit for the FTW's culture," I shrugged the Mk 36b's shoulders expressively. "You have to understand, the FTW is made up of idealists who use illegal but non-violent means to combat social injustice; my reputation, on the other hand..."

"Is brutal," Pam supplied.

"Yes."

"How long were you able to stay with the FTW?" the older man asked, gently.

"Only for four months," I said. "At that point, I was framed for a murder and the organization disavowed me."

"The murder of the Red Ghost," Pam supplied.

"Yes. Fortunately, the reports of his death were greatly exaggerated."

They both laughed, gentle and appreciative.

"And only a few months later," Stan continued," You exposed the heroes Sphinx and Peregrine for their crimes against humanity and saved the world from an alien invasion."

"It was a busy year."

"Now, I fully intend to grill you for details about your long career." Pam leaned forward seriously. "But it is recent events that have generated the most speculation. You've worked to mitigate the effects of natural disasters and rescued emergency personnel. You once again unearthed evidence of a hero's immoral actions. You recently assisted local heroine Regrowth in an attempt to capture one of the most dangerous villains in America."

"And you rescued a kitten," Stan interjected, amused.

"I did."

"Many have begun to wonder if the most feared supervillain of our generation has undergone a moral transformation. They wonder if Doctor Fid should, in fact, be regarded as a hero. What do you have to say in response to that speculation?

"Nothing. Or rather...I don't feel that I have the right to

offer an opinion as to how I should be perceived."

"And how do you perceive yourself?" Pamela asked.

I paused before answering. "As a work in progress."

"More than two decades in armor and you're still figuring things out?"

"I've lived an eventful life," I explained. "It would be more strange, I'd think, if I failed to be affected."

"Can we talk about your eventful life, then?" Whatever fear or reticence had gripped Pamela earlier, she was over it now. She'd caught the edge of a story and her eyes blazed with interest.

She'd been a fashion model, once upon a time. A lovely face, hired more as an appeal to certain demographics than her skill as an interviewer. Under Stanley Morrow's tutelage, however, she'd blossomed into quite the investigative force.

Her smile made me genuinely apprehensive. Impressive.

"When I agreed to appear on CapeWatch, I did think it likely that my history would be mentioned."

Pamela looked to Stan and he took over so smoothly that I suspected that the interchange had been practiced; where her expression was almost predatory, his was all warmth and acceptance. It seemed that the role of 'good cop' was being played by an affable, paternalistic academic, and 'bad cop' by the fiercely intelligent brunette.

"We've mentioned the twenty-two years that have passed since your debut," Stanley began, "but we haven't discussed the six years in which you disappeared from public view."

"Your first five years were characterized by continuously escalating violence," Ms. Green asserted, "culminating in a battle against Valiant himself on the White House lawn."

"For our younger viewers, I'd like to take a moment to discuss what it felt like to watch that battle on television. We'd grown up with the absolute certainty that Valiant was indestructible. He's vulnerable to magic attacks, of course, but when it came to a physical fight...all of us would just sigh with relief when Valiant appeared. We knew that we were safe, that everything would be all right...And then Doctor Fid landed in D.C., his robots blackening the sky to deny the entirety of the United States Air Force."

"I remember," Pamela said quietly. "My mother and I were watching the news in the kitchen, and the battle seemed to last forever. Dan Rather was narrating, a constant flow of up-to-date information about evacuation efforts, military response, etc. And then he just fell silent for a while..."

"...Because it was confirmed that Valiant was injured." Stan finished. "That was unthinkable! It felt as though the breath had been crushed from my lungs. In that moment, everyone on the planet was afraid of Doctor Fid."

That had been one of the most exhilarating moments in my entire life. I did not, however, think that gloating would set the desired tone.

"I remember," I stated quietly.

"After that battle," Stanley continued, "Doctor Fid disappeared."

"Years later, when a more-powerful-than-ever Doctor Fid reappeared, his tactics and choice of targets changed," Pamela said. "This led many to suspect that the original Doctor died of wounds suffered in that battle against Valiant and that it is a different man wearing Fid's armor today. Would you care to comment?"

"No matter what reply I give, you could only take me at my word."

"Give us your word then," Pam said.

"Responsibility for Doctor Fid's actions—past, present, and future—rests solely upon my shoulders," I declared evenly.

"That is...a surprisingly evasive answer," Stanley frowned. "Accepting accountability is not the same thing as confirming identity."

"Identity is a more complicated question. Are you familiar with Theseus's paradox?"

"No." Stanley Morrow tilted his head, puzzled. "I'm afraid not."

"It's a thought experiment from the ancient Greek biographer, Plutarch. He wrote, 'The ship on which Theseus sailed with the youths and returned in safety, the thirty-oared galley, was preserved by the Athenians down to the time of Demetrius Phalerius. They took away the old timbers from time to time, and put new and sound ones in their places, so that the vessel became a standing illustration for the philosophers in the mooted question of growth, some declaring that it remained the same, others that it was not the same vessel'."

"You think that you're a different person because you replaced your arm and cloned a few organs?" Pamela scoffed in surprised disbelief.

"More than a few," I answered calmly. "The work was

performed little by little, but I'm fairly certain that not a single untouched piece remains of the man who fought Valiant sixteen years ago."

Neither host had anything to say in response to that; I could see in both their expressions that they were envisioning a scarred patchwork horror hidden within the Mk 36b armor: an aged Frankenstein's monster. If that image propagated and drew attention further from the objectively-attractive CEO Terrance Markham, so much the better.

"I usually feel as though I'm the same person," I confided. "I have all of Doctor Fid's memories and all of his knowledge and skills...and yet, I can also say that the person I am now would make different choices than the person who wore Doctor Fid's armor twenty-two years ago. As I said previously, the question of identity is more complicated than the question of responsibility."

"I know that I'd make different decisions now than I did when I was young. That's just being changed by experience," Stan said slowly. "I think most people would agree with that."

"Most people haven't performed fourteen neurosurgeries upon themselves, several of which were designed specifically to alter core moral decision-making processes."

"I think I asked the wrong question," Pam shook her head. "I shouldn't have asked who is under that armor. I should have asked *what* is under your armor."

"I am Doctor Fid."

※ ※ ※

"Welcome back to a special episode of KNN CapeWatch. I'm your host, Stan Morrow."

"And I'm Pamela Green."

"Our guest today," Stan continued, "is the notorious Doctor Fid."

"Greetings."

"Before the break…" Pam began, "we'd been discussing one of your early battles against Gamma."

"Yes," I acknowledged. "I've faced Gamma several times."

"I was wondering if we could discuss a different battle," she continued, wearing an expression of predatory anticipation that gave me pause. "In particular, your battle with the now-retired superhero Clash."

"Ah." Hidden within my faceless and expressionless helm, I winced. "That fight was…unfortunate."

"For viewers who may not recall, the event in question took place at Axiom Laboratories in New Jersey, eleven years ago." Stanley looked a bit surprised at the topic shift, but he rallied gamely. "There was a demonstration only a few blocks away, so there were several camera crews nearby…That incident was one of the most well-documented conflicts in Doctor Fid's history."

"And also, one of the most vicious," Pamela added, and I

was lost.

❦ ❦ ❦

"Screw you," the metallic hero growls as he struggles to his feet. Clash is ankle-deep in rubble; our free-for-all had migrated to the campus' main parking lot, and the pavement is now pocked with craters of pulverized concrete. His costume—a simple red wrestling singlet with black trim—is torn and ripped in several places, revealing deep scrapes carved into his normally mirror-polished steel-like body. His chest heaves with every breath, gleaming teeth bared in a defiant snarl.

I wait, honestly impressed, while he visibly shakes off his weariness. The man's fighting skills can use some improvement, but he is able to soak up a beating like few that I've ever encountered. Clash might be superhumanly durable, but I'm beginning to think that his will is stronger even than his biometallic flesh. He lifts his fists into a boxer's guard and stumbles towards me.

I slip a left-hook to his body. Even through the Mk 17's inertial compensators, the shock of impact travels up my arm. He drops his elbow to guard his ribs, and I take advantage with a straight punch to his chrome-like face.

Clash doesn't fall.

I am so tired right now. Three days, I've been awake! If I'd had time, I would have completed the Mk 18 and this fight would already have been over. I know that I'm upright only due to the stimulants being poured into my body by the Mk 17's internal medical system. But today is the anniversary and I need a fight. It would have taken another week for the newer armor be fully functional.

I grab Clash by the face and throw him through a parked car.

It takes a few seconds for the last of the debris to settle, and then all goes still. In the distance I hear sirens and anxious shouts but here there is silence. I can go home, lick my wounds, get drunk. Mourn.

Clash isn't really an enemy...just a convenient foe. A hero I knew I could isolate, to lure here with the threat of blowing up Axiom Labs. It's been twelve years exactly since a different hero let my brother die, and it's been helpful to have someone to punch.

The violence has been genuinely therapeutic. But now, Clash is down and I finally feel empty.

There are news cameras nearby: unmanned drones, a helicopter and even a brave camera crew on foot. This is an opportunity. The public needs to be shown that heroes will let them down. Children need to know...heroes can't be trusted to keep them safe! Wearily, I step forward to recover Clash's unconscious body. The media needs to see him at my mercy.

Something strikes my chin and the world goes white. I feel like I'm flying, flowing away as though pulled by the tide, but the armor's telemetry says that I'm still. Was he just feigning unconsciousness? Something explodes and I'm on my knees. My perception of time is strange; it seems to take hours for the Mk 17's visual systems to reboot, and yet I don't have enough time to take even a single breath. I look up and the universe tilts dangerously; someone is standing over me, glistening orange and yellow as the fire reflects of his metallic skin.

BRONZE!

And now I'm on top of him, bearing him down with the raw force of my madness. Every night for more than a decade, I've dreamed of this, of ash and blood and tears. I have him!

Bobby died heartbroken. He was in my arms, I was watching his eyes! I could see which wound hurt him most. Bobby knew himself betrayed, and that pierced someplace deeper where the bullet could not reach. My baby brother died with an injured soul, and the culprit responsible is finally—finally!—in my grasp.

I'm weeping with relief even as I brush aside my victim's final, weak defense. His guard is down and I have him! It feels even better than I'd hoped. I'm free. I'm whole. My hatred pours out of me like a physical force, a tsunami of rage that follows every punch to its target.

My arms are like pistons that deliver punishment one strike at a time. Until the fog lifts and it isn't Bronze at all. That particular 'hero' died years ago, before I was able to confront him. Bronze is now—and will forever be—beyond my reach.

I'm standing over Clash's prone, unconscious form and I've done something horrible.

🙝 🙝 🙝

"I'm sorry," I told Pamela; she'd been talking and I hadn't been paying attention. "Can you repeat the question?"

"I asked if you have regrets."

"I have an ocean of regrets," I replied. "And yes, my treatment of Clash is among them."

"If you could talk to him—talk to any of the people you've hurt—what would you say?" Stanley asked. He still looked a bit puzzled by the direction that Pam had taken the interview, whereas she looked like a cat that had found a saucer of cream.

"I think...it would depend." I laughed ruefully, brief and bitter. "There are many for whom an apology can never be enough."

"Well...as luck would have it, you have an opportunity to make amends." Looking unbearably smug, Pam motioned to one of the studio technicians. "Caller one, you're on the air."

As ambushes go, I had to admit that this one was elegant. I was beginning to think that I ought to tell Pamela about Lassiter's Den so that she could enjoy a drink among her peers.

"My name is Edward Prewitt," the caller began. "My father worked at Tyrion Solar in Chicago."

"Your father is Abraham Prewitt?" I asked.

"Yes, I...you remember?"

"I do. The area had been evacuated when I set off the explosion, but your father ran back into a burning building because he believed one of his interns was still inside. He is very brave."

"He was," Mr. Prewitt choked. "He passed away two weeks ago."

"I am very sorry for your loss," I said

"It was your fault!" Edward spat. "He never had problems with his lungs until after that fire!"

I used my neural tap to hack a few hospital records and relied heavily upon the diplomatic training that I'd suffered through while recreating Terry Markham. It felt odd, using those skills from within Doctor Fid's armor. "Emphysema can have many root causes, and the Tyrion Solar theft occurred seventeen years ago; there is even a well-documented genetic link, you ought to be tested. Regardless, I apologize for any part that I may have had in your father's illness. I know that it doesn't help, but you should know that the devices that saved the Earth from alien invaders used technology evolved from his work."

There was more. I accepted his recriminations and offered condolences; it felt like walking a minefield, naked save for a blindfold.

Now that I knew what to look for, I was able to remotely hack the studio technicians' switchboard; there were more than two dozen calls waiting on hold. I was able to fall into a rhythm: accept, sympathize, offer anecdotes or vague explanations where appropriate. It was a performance and the creature inside the Mk 36b was experienced at pretending. This twist was unexpected, but it could still be finessed into a positive outcome.

Taking advantage of this, I thought smugly, would be no difficulty at all.

※ ※ ※

When I eventually arrived home, I found Whisper in her room. I couldn't look at her; instead, I sat at the edge of her bed, supported my elbows on my knees, and slowly lowered my head into my palms. Behind me, I heard her sit up and snake out from under her covers. When a gentle, comforting hand came to rest on my shoulder, I almost wept.

"I was fine," I said, "until Melissa Halden called. She'd been in the crowd at my second bank robbery. A little ponytailed girl—younger than you. Smaller, too."

"You've mentioned her," Whisper replied softly.

"I just...It wasn't a hostage situation. I never threatened them! I told the civilians to get down while I gathered the cash and ripped a dozen safe-deposit boxes from the vault. I didn't hurt anyone, but this little girl just kept crying. Screaming."

Whisper didn't say anything; she just let me talk. I wondered if her Father had done this after a crime gone wrong. By all accounts, he'd been a decent man despite his villainous occupation.

"I kept track of Melissa; it's been two decades, but I checked on her. When she applied for college, I manipulated a few records to make sure she got a scholarship. She has friends, she's even engaged. I thought she was fine! I didn't hurt her! But then she was on the phone..."

"I heard."

"She started crying, and I just kept remembering what it was like, twenty years ago. I kept hearing that high pitched scream..."

"I'm sorry."

"Thank you." I took a deep breath, straightened to sit upright, and turned to face my ward. Her glowing blue eyes were wide with concern, so I forced a comforting smile. "How bad do you think it will be?"

"Mmm? The response to the show, you mean?" her brows

furrowed confusedly. "It won't be bad at all. It will all work out, even better than planned."

"I cut the interview short and ran away." I lowered my eyes again, embarrassed.

"You didn't run," Whisper giggled teasingly, and some of the tension in my chest began to fade.

Technically, that was true; I hadn't run. I'd stammered out an apology and flown straight through the studio ceiling. Fortunately, no one had been injured by falling debris.

I'd been focused solely upon the shame at my loss of control. Now, I worked through the numbers and began to believe that Whisper's assessment was correct: my lapse might—in the end—work to Doctor Fid's benefit. The entire show, I'd been working to portray Doctor Fid as a tragic figure looking to atone for his dark past. That role, that narrative...that was a story that the public would be willing to accept.

I knew better, of course. Doctor Fid's dark past wasn't something that could be atoned for; it was something to be endured.

I hadn't seen the CapeWatch program's final edit yet, but I expected that their portrayal would linger upon my abrupt exit. It was useful drama, certain to earn them ratings and awards. Stanley and Pamela would reach out to profilers and heroes, asking for comments. The public might empathize with the flawed, hurting Doctor Fid that they imagined. It could only aid the current endeavor. And once all this was completed—once Doctor Fid was returned to his proper villainous role—judiciously applied violence would erase the memory of any momentary weakness.

"I'm sorry," I sighed, "It's been a long day. I shouldn't be bothering you with this."

"It's all right," she smiled. "I wasn't asleep."

Technically, she didn't need sleep at all. Allowing her subconscious to make emotional linkages to the vast amount of data that she accessed every day, to collate between actual and virtual experiences, did seem to assist in her ongoing process of assimilating new hardware. Her emotional matrix—stored in quantum state across multiple data centers—was maturing beautifully.

"Waiting up for me?" I smiled.

"Not exactly. I was doing research! Um. You know, KNN producers reached out to several hero teams before agreeing to let CapeWatch set up your program? Just to get opinions and things?"

"I assumed that they would."

"I read the studio execs' email; the Red Ghost convinced them." Whisper looked uncomfortable. "He, um, wrote a pretty nice essay about you. Here, you should read this."

She inserted the files into my brain and I absorbed it quickly.

"This is...lovely." A frown formed at the corners of my lips. "Kind, supportive and hopeful."

"Mm," she agreed.

"He thinks I could be a hero," I whispered, uncertain if I should feel pleased by his regard, or angered that someone I respected understood me so poorly. The dissonance was dizzying. "This is...worrisome."

"Mm? Why?"

"We're in business together, he and I," I explained. "I'd rather not disrupt our professional relationship when the plan is done and the ruse discarded."

"You like him," she admonished. "You don't want to lose his respect."

"That is true as well."

"Don't worry," Whisper consoled. "Even when you aren't pretending to be a hero anymore, you'll still be a bad man who does good things. The Red Ghost 'll understand."

Was I particularly fortunate, or was that simply an inherent trait that younger siblings be more wise than their elder? Given the way my luck usually trended, I was tempted to believe the latter. Whichever case was true, I was humbled and grateful.

CHAPTER NINE

"LIFT EIGHTEEN INCHES," I TOLD VALIANT. "AND STOP. Good."

It was remarkably quiet despite the size of the gathered crowd. The onlookers kept their distance—the work site was dangerously unstable—and had concentrated around the hastily strung-up barricade tape perimeter. There were news crews, fiercely intent but speaking in almost reverent tones; there were also desperate parents and worried relatives and throngs of hopeful well-wishers. I'd anticipated shouting and wailing, furious anger and thrown bottles. Instead, there was only the pressure of their gaze and the weight of their longing.

I orchestrated an invasion.

Forty-one of my smaller construction-drones crawled into the wreck like a swarm of metallic cockroaches escaping from the light, joining the hundreds of microdrones that were already present below. Some of the newly arrived robots sacrificed themselves, attaching permanently to twisted i-beams so that their structural integrity fields could shore up the groaning steel. Others deployed manipulating arms to shift fragments, to quickly cut away dangerous scrap and to weld supports into place. The remainder were tasked with exploration and monitoring, feeding mountains of data for me to sift through and analyze.

"Ok, good. You can let go."

And he did, carefully. His hands weren't shaking; Valiant's strength was legendary. Lifting a few thousand pounds of debris was no stretch of his abilities. In a different situation, he might have dived into the wreckage, tossing steel and concrete aside as though it weighed nothing. Now, however, he took a deep breath and waited slowly for my next order.

"That one next. It can stand a three-foot lift, but move slowly."

The afternoon sun was sweltering and I was grateful for the climate control systems in the Mk 35 heavy-combat armor. There were no birds and few clouds; just the open blue sky, beautiful and clear and offering no escape from the oppressive heat. Even Valiant had sweat beading at his brow, and I'd seen footage of the massive African-American hero diving into the mouth of an active volcano.

He stood at seven and a half feet yet always felt taller. There was a density to him, a presence…an instinctive awareness of his raw power that tugged at some long-forgotten instinct and told one's subconscious to be wary. I'd faced him in battle three times and that sensation never dissipated. His sky-blue and white costume had gathered red-brown stains from rust and dirt as we'd worked; we'd been here for more than an hour already, delicately lifting and shifting and shaping the mass of what would have been an enormous office-complex had the construction been completed.

The recently repaired Mk 35 stood fourteen feet tall and yet I somehow felt as though Valiant towered over me.

"How are they doing?" he asked, the hint of a worried smile touching the corners of his lips.

I consulted my sensors.

"Stable," I replied. "Scared, but holding up; they have fresh air now, and my drones are providing light. I have a supply train bringing in fresh water and snacks. One of the teachers is having them sing."

"Can I hear?"

I routed audio to my armor's external speakers; I'd been focusing on the maths—the calculations necessary to forge a safe path through chaos—so I hadn't really listened. It had been just one more data stream, less pressing than updating models for metal fatigue or shifting stresses.

Only half the children were singing, I thought, and their voices were untrained. I wasn't fluent enough in Chilean Spanish to catch all the words; it was a slow and hopeful song with a catchy chorus, something about a spider that was lost and alone but climbing towards the sun. Some of the voices were thready and weak while others were enthusiastic. I'd been able to explain that the mighty Valiant was here to save them, and that had been enough to stop the majority of tears. Many of the voices, too, were off-key or missed the song's beat.

It was one of the most beautiful things that I'd ever heard.

"Let them hear, too." The hero nodded towards the gathered onlookers, his eyes wet with unshed tears. "Play it for them."

"If this doesn't work, it would be cruel."

"Then we'd damned well better make sure this works."

After a moment's consideration, I nodded; my larger construction automatons were gathered along the edges of the disaster site, waiting for my orders to converge. For now, I made use of their speakers as I relayed the signal.

If I'd thought the crowd silent before, then I'd been mistaken. A hush descended and it felt as though the entire planet were holding its breath. There were a few choked sobs, a few prayers, and then one by one the gathered crowd joined to sing along. Rusty voices, throats tight from too much time spent weeping, slowly gained in strength until I imagined that I could feel the chorus in my chest even through my armor.

With my face hidden behind the Mk 35's featureless mask, I could not wipe away my tears. So instead I turned to Valiant, voice gruff only to my own ears. "Good. We're ready for the next lift. That large chunk of concrete can be lifted free; the shifting weight won't cause any problems."

This couldn't go wrong. I wouldn't allow it.

The sinkhole had opened after the tremors faded. What must it have been like in that school? To the frightened children, and to the brave teachers reassuring their charges and trying to keep them calm? There must have been a moment when the shaking stopped, when they all exhaled and believed themselves safe. And then the world tilted horribly, betraying their trust.

It was positively astonishing that so few died in the initial fall; the ground had dropped away in a consistent cascade, providing just enough support that the small building was almost entirely intact when it settled into the depths. Rescue crews had begun their assessment and the news broadcasts were calling it a marvel.

The aftershocks hit and the sinkhole widened to reach a nearby construction site. Onlookers could only watch in horror as a quarter million tons of steel and concrete poured on top of the schoolhouse below. The roar of the collapse had been phenomenal but it hadn't been loud enough to drown out the screams of the families who had already been gathered at the perimeter.

Again, the hapless children had defied the odds; the skyscraper's skeleton twisted and complained as it crumpled, wedging itself to form a precarious framework of creaking spars resting against the school's rooftop. The majority of the debris was still held back by that imbalanced obstacle. Once again, the number of deaths had been minimal.

A miracle, the reporters said breathlessly. While they thanked God, I only wished that I was sufficiently religious to believe that I might earn a few moments in God's presence; even a second would be time enough to fully charge my warstaff's main weapon. My sensors had been able to confirm that there were at least nine young voices missing from that chorus, and nine families who would flinch every time the word 'miracle' was spoken in their presence.

It was up to Valiant and myself to ensure that there would

not be a tenth child silenced.

"Okay," I told the taller man, "my drones are in place. This next one is going to be an eight-foot lift, and you'll need to take a half-step to your right as you reach max height. That section right there."

When the Earth's mightiest hero had arrived with the intent to save the day, the local heroes had stood aside. Valiant was renowned worldwide for his rescue work, and yet he'd been able to shift only two girders before the entire structure had creaked and begun to settle...threatening to crush the survivors below. A camera had been focused on the hero's face; I'd been watching the television from home with Whisper at my side. In that moment, Valiant had looked so lost that my own chest had ached in sympathy. My ward-slash-adopted-sister met my eyes and I'd nodded; within seconds, I'd hacked a few radios that were within range of Valiant's hearing to relay four words in Doctor Fid's modified voice: "I'm on my way."

"Good," I said, when the lift had been completed and my automatons had welded further supports in place. "We'll have a path cleared in no time. That I-beam next..."

※ ※ ※

"Terry!" Bobby's eyes light up and he launches himself at me like a pouncing leopard. If the six-year-old lacks the agile coordination of the feline that he's emulating, then he makes up for it in enthusiasm; he crashes into my legs and wraps his arms around me in a tight hug. "You're home!"

"Mmm-hm! I just got here." I muss his hair and he twists away to pat it back into place with both hands. I can't help but laugh; he looks exactly the way that I imagine I must look when Dad does it to me. He utters the same indignant whine while hiding a secretly pleased smile.

"Are you here all summer?" Bobby grabs my hand and tugs me towards his play area.

"That's the plan!"

My schedule has become more flexible since I completed my bachelor's degree. Much more of my research and coursework is self-guided now, and arrangements have been made for me to keep in contact with my supervisor over the holiday. I fully expect to take advantage of my time here. I want to finish designing a high-efficiency internal combustion engine design for sale to an oil company. They'll bury the patent, of course—a more efficient engine meant less gasoline sold—but the sale would still be lucrative.

I'd had to forge a false identity to arrange the sale; even my reputation at MIT isn't enough to convince a large company to purchase technology from a teenager. So, I used a name similar to my Dad's and the bank lets him deposit the checks because they think it's just a misspelling. Neither of my parents like the skulduggery, but they can't argue with the results; sales like this one help cover unexpected scholastic expenses like Michael.

My parents wouldn't let me—sixteen now—attend college alone; they'd located a responsible masters student to be my dorm-mate. The proceeds from my sales help pay his tuition, and in return he watches out for me. Mike takes the work seriously and I rarely find solitude while on-campus.

I don't begrudge him for his scrupulous nature; my parents need the reassurance that I'm safe. I also have to admit that I've certainly benefited from his advice and assistance. Even so, I'm definitely looking forward to quiet isolation while at home. When my little brother is done with me, of course.

"We're playing heroes," Bobby tells me, holding up an action figure. "I'm Defender. Who're you?"

I study the terrain. Bobby has taken over this section of the living room; some toys and books are spread haphazardly across the floor, but the majority are collected into painted wooden bins. Dad makes them; I'm sure that the colorful boxes that he'd once made for me are stored safely in the garage. Much of the remaining floor space has been transformed into a battleground.

Villains have taken the high ground atop a cushion stolen from the couch. I see Metalstorm and the Ancient there, surrounded by a palisade of foam building-blocks. I don't recognize the other two figures in the villains' lair, but that isn't surprising. My studies have taken up the larger portion of my schedule these last few years, and I've had precious little time available to follow the careers of new heroes or villains.

Heroes litter the field below. Resolute lies prone with his arms bent at odd angles, and the Gray Dragon has a toy car resting on his chest. Bantam is face-down at the foot of the cushion plateau; I imagine that the diminutive hero must have tried rushing the evildoers' base and been taken down by Metalstorm's attacks.

"I'll be Bronze," I say, looking for Bobby's favorite action figure.

"No, you can't," he objects. "Bronze controls metal with his mind. He can't fight Metalstorm, it wouldn't be a good story!"

"But Defender and Bronze are friends. Wouldn't Defender call his friend to help if he knew he was fighting someone like Metalstorm?"

"Nuh-uh. 'Cause Metalstorm would run away instead of getting beaten up, and Defender wants to get Metalstorm for beating up Blue Bandit."

"Why'd Metalstorm beat up the Blue Bandit?" I ask, still looking over the throng of figures to decide on a which hero I will choose. "Aren't they partners?"

"Nuh-uh," Bobby repeats. "Blue Bandit's a hero now, he helped Defender save New York."

I'd overheard a few of my fellow college students talking about a recent threat to Manhattan but hadn't investigated further. The Blue Bandit was more of a super-powered burglar than a villain; if he truly had helped save the city, then I can understand why he might have been granted a pardon and been allowed to join a superhero team.

Although high-school was less traumatic than middle-school and college is less painful still, my understanding of friendship is still largely academic. Being hurt by betrayal, on the other hand—that I can comprehend fully. More than one of my fellow students has attempted to 'befriend' me with the sole intent to take advantage of my work. All in all, I think that I would have preferred physical bullying. It makes sense that Metalstorm would seek revenge against his former colleague.

"So, maybe Defender would call his friend in secret?" I find a metallic action figure where it is placed carefully in the corner. "Then Bronze could sneak up on Metalstorm and Metalstorm wouldn't know to run away. Then Bronze and Defender can work together to fight the Ancient and the other villains!"

"You're playing it wrong," Bobby whines. "It has to be a good story, and Defender has to beat Metalstorm himself 'cause Blue Bandit is HIS friend now."

I choose an action figure that depicts the lioness-headed heroine Chimera; Bobby's smile lights up when I try to imitate her famous roar.

"She hates the Ancient," the six-year-old explains. "It'll be a good fight!"

Chimera is right to hate the Ancient, I know. I've stumbled across a few of his scholarly works (no publication would dare refuse his submissions; not after what he did to the editorial staff of the American Journal of Clinical Nutrition) and I have to admit that his logic and scientific rigor is sound. His methodology, however, is often horrific.

Now that I think about it, one of the papers discusses using magic and science to create animal-human hybrids that (at least superficially) resemble Chimera. None of the kidnapped test-subjects had survived more than a few weeks after the study was completed, and I can see why the heroine might hold a grudge.

"Dyefendyer," I growled, trying to mimic the heroine's odd, throaty speech pattern. "De Ancient has tyoo many henchmen! I'm going tyoo fly around deir base and draw dem out."

"I'll be ready to help!" Bobby replies, moving his action-figure into position. Defender can't fly, but he can cover ground with remarkable speed by leaping tens of yards at a time. While Chimera circles high above the villains' lair, Defender will follow and take potshots at any goons who try to shoot her.

"Rarrrr!" Chimera begins her diversion, and battle is joined.

The actual assault takes more than an hour to adjudicate; I

portray the minions when Defender attacks and Bobby plays the villains. The fight goes back and forth, but in the end Metalstorm is captured and the Ancient escapes while the heroes are busy rescuing hostages.

"So, was that a good story?" I ask while I begin putting away some of the toys.

"Uh-huh!"

"Even though one of the villains got away?"

"Being a hero isn't about winning every fight," Bobby informs me, uncharacteristically serious. "It's about being a good guy! They had to save everyone! Defender 'n Chimera 'll catch the Ancient next time."

"They will, huh?" It seems increasingly likely that I'm going to be playing Chimera tomorrow, too. I'm going to practice imitating her roar just in case.

"Uh-huh," Bobby says with the same level of certainty that I use when defending a mathematical proof. "The good guys always win eventually."

"Always?"

"Always. They HAVE to, 'cause they're superheroes!"

I'm not certain that statement is accurate, but Bobby obviously believes it with all his heart. And if there's any statement that I know I can hold as axiomatic, it is this: my brother has a good heart.

I muss his hair again then dodge away from his playfully irritable retaliatory swat. Together, we run to find Mom and find out when dinner will be ready.

※ ※ ※

Valiant reached into the blue plastic bucket, stretching out his massive hands to cup as much ice and water as he could manage; a chuffing sigh of pleasure escaped barely parted lips as he splashed the frigid mixture upon his face and head. He stood there, wet and tired, and took a deep, slow breath. In through the nose, out through the mouth. A contented expression spread across his broad features, and then he bent to grab two ice-cold beers from the pail.

He offered me one, but I shook the Mk 35's faceless head. He shrugged and dropped the beer back into the bucket. It clinked and rattled off another bottle, and the entire contents sloshed as the ice settled. After popping the cap with a practiced twist of his fingers, he took a slow swallow and then grinned.

We didn't speak; we just stood and watched as a rescue-worker carried the first child out from the pit. The crowd's murmurs increased in volume, but the cheering didn't really start until the dust-covered little girl was passed into the arms of her parents. I didn't need to know the language to understand what was said. The sound of a child calling out to her mother is universal. Her father tried to be stoic, to be reassuring, but when the little girl's fingers touched his face he bawled so hard he choked. His hands were shaking when he reached to touch the little girl's hair.

Then the next child was lifted up, and the ovation grew

louder.

"You should be there," I told Valiant.

"Nah. This moment belongs to them." He nodded briefly towards the children and the rescuers and the eager parents crowding towards the now-stabilized disaster site's entrance. "We did the part that only we could do. This part is theirs."

"The children will want to meet you. You saved them."

He motioned with the bottle, "You did too."

"I'm not their hero," I replied, monotone. "You are. That means something to them."

"I'll come again next week to make sure they know I remember them." He waved and smiled to the children as they were reunited with their families but he made no move to join them. "Look at them. Right now, they don't need a hero; they have everything they want. I'm not going to interfere and neither are you."

I looked, and I saw that he was correct. One boy was carried up, his thin arms wrapped tight around his rescuer's neck. He too was covered in gray and brown dust, but tears had carved clean trails down his face. He blinked as he came up into the sunlight and his gaze traversed the entirety of his surroundings. His eyes paused briefly upon Valiant—still smiling and waving—but then his gaze fell upon an aged man with dark eyes and a white, bushy mustache. For the boy, the rest of the world ceased to exist as he leapt into his grandfather's embrace.

I turned my head away. "I should go."

"Don't." He shook his head, and I couldn't read the emotion in his eyes. "This moment is theirs. But getting to watch it? To know you made it possible? You earned that...so stay."

Watching the love and relief of the reunions made me feel like a fraud and a voyeur, but I stayed nonetheless; it was heart-breakingly beautiful. I was happy for them. Of course I was! I was also so filled with rage and jealousy that I could feel my heart pounding in my chest. The urge to lash out, to punch someone—to turn my emotional torment into physical pain and inflict it upon a deserving target—was overwhelming, and I was intensely aware that Valiant was only a few feet away. I could strike him with all of my strength and he would stand up and be ready for me to hit again. But my gaze turned towards the nine families that had been pulled aside by the rescue workers and their vacant, grief-stricken expressions as the trauma counselors tried to console them. There'd been enough bloodshed here. There'd been enough agony.

"Are you all right?" Valiant asked.

I must have made a sound or motion, offered some hint that had gotten past the Mk 35's algorithms that stripped emotion from my voice and made my body language inscrutable. I didn't know what it was and made a note to review my suit's recorded telemetry at a later date. But the massive hero's concern felt intensely genuine; at that moment I couldn't keep myself from replying.

"I wish it had been you," I told him, "when it was my family in danger. You would have saved my brother."

Valiant's eyes widened slightly, and I realized that more information about Doctor Fid's origins had just been revealed than I'd let slip for more than two decades and a television interview.

I wasn't particularly worried that the information could be used to betray my civilian identity; I'd long since corrupted just about every digital trail that would connect Dr. Terrance Markham to the superheroic violence that had taken Bobby's life. The databases for every news organization in the country had incorrect names for Bobby and I listed among the victims of Locust's attack, connected to an old and unassailable false identity that I rarely used anymore; the one I'd used to sell patents when I was a teenager. Any reporter who might remember more accurately than what was in the official transcripts had long since retired.

What terrified me was the pity in Valiant's eyes. That, I didn't know how to deal with.

"I can't promise that," he replied sadly. "I haven't been able to save everyone."

"You would have tried. You would have cared. Perhaps that would have been enough."

There was silence between us. The Earth's mightiest hero kept waving to the children and to their families, kept smiling for them, but to me he just offered brief worried glances. I somehow got the impression that he was considering offering sympathy for my loss. If he did, I wasn't certain that I could restrain myself from violence.

"Can I ask who it was?" he finally asked, tentatively.

"Hm?"

"You didn't say you wished I was there," he explained. "You said you wished it was me that was there. That implies there was someone else and you wish it was me instead."

"I'd rather not discuss this matter any further."

"Was it Clash?" he mused out loud. "That'd explain a lot."

"It wasn't Clash," I bit out. "And I'd rather change the subject if you don't mind."

"It couldn't have been Lycan. He didn't even have his powers when you first showed up."

"It wasn't anyone I've fought." I shook my head slowly. "It was someone else, someone long dead. Not by my hand. And if you continue this line of questioning, my response will involve summoning my warstaff and doing my best to recreate last year's most-viewed video on the Internet."

During the incident at the Mercer-Talon campus—when I'd saved this planet and dozens of others from a star-faring empire's oppression—Valiant had been possessed by telepathic alien invaders. There had been moments of terrible carnage and extraordinary heroism during that battle, with almost all of it immortalized by the news-camera drones that had circled the combat zone. I'd combed through that footage for information about the heroes that participated: their strengths, their weaknesses, their actions in the face of unbeatable odds. Despite all of that, the scene that got the most views was the moment when I'd sought to neutralize the mind-controlled Valiant with a full force swing of my staff...that landed squarely between his legs.

Some of the humorous sound effects edited into the video by amateur comedians were actually quite clever.

"I'm sorry," Valiant apologized, though he seemed more amused by the threat than wary. "I won't pry anymore. I've just always been curious why you do the things you do."

"I suppose that I understand. I've often wondered what motivated you as well."

"You want to know why I keep at it? This. This is why." He smiled broadly and returned to waving as another dust-covered boy was lifted out of darkness and into the light. The crowd cheered once more.

"I see," I replied, forced to concede that his argument was a strong one. So I reached into the bucket to retrieve an ice-cold beverage and said nothing further until the last child was retrieved.

≈ ≈ ≈

"Terry, wake up!" Bobby nudges at my shoulder insistently. "It's just like we played! You have to come!"

The previous night had been spent improving the maths used in algorithms to simulate airflow over twisting airfoils; it was part of a project suggested by my doctoral adviser and I'd gotten carried away. The sun had already been warming the horizon before I'd finally succumbed to sleep.

"What time is it?" I grumble, eyes still closed.

"It's almost lunch," Bobby grabs at my shoulder and tugs. "Get uuuuup."

I blink myself awake and find Bobby's eyes only inches from my own. In my weariness, I hadn't felt him climb on the edge of my bed.

"Ok, I'm up."

"You have to hurry," my little brother insists and then dashes

towards the door. "It's on TV! Hurry!"

I'd fallen asleep fully clothed, so I roll to my feet and stagger after Bobby. "What's on TV?"

"Chimera's fighting the Ancient!"

I'm not as much of a superhero fan as Bobby is but his enthusiasm is contagious. I shamble faster.

The big television is in the living room, already tuned to a program that focuses on superhero news. There's another TV in the kitchen and I kind of want something to drink, but I'm captivated by the images on the screen. Bobby is bouncing in his seat and I join him on the weathered faux leather couch.

Chimera isn't fighting alone; there are three other heroes that I don't recognize on site. They've broken into pairs so that they can alternate defense and attack, and—exactly the way my game with Bobby had predicted—the winged and lioness-headed heroine joined forces with a dark-costumed strongman who travels by leaping and seems to fight primarily hand-to-hand supplemented by occasional long-distance attacks using a generic blaster rifle.

The heroes are being swarmed by black-scaled bipedal lizard creatures, red-eyed and vicious. There is something hypnotic about the way the creatures move, their long tails twisting sinuously to maintain balance as they slither smoothly over and around each other to claw at their prey. Their scales, I see now, aren't true black; there is an iridescence there and every explosion makes the lizards flash in purple and green.

Chimera alternates between flying low overhead to rain energy blasts down upon the horde and dropping to the ground to help defend her partner. The heroes are making progress; the battleground is already littered with downed enemies and they'd worked their way closer to the dais from which the Ancient was monitoring the battle.

"They found his secret hideout," Bobby says helpfully. "It's near a lighthouse on the cliffs."

Another camera is focused on the Ancient himself. The slim, white-haired man is frowning—apparently disappointed at his creations' performance—but does not seem terribly concerned. He occasionally issues orders but most of his time is spent jotting careful notes as the assault continues. When the image pulls back, I can see the lighthouse Bobby referred to; it's an old, heavy stone structure but still looks to be in working order. There's a secondary building near the tower's base and it is from atop that building that the Ancient is overseeing his minions.

Where had he housed the scaled beasts, I wonder? Even if they were stacked like cord-wood, there isn't enough room for an army inside the outbuilding. My question is answered when reinforcement monsters scramble up from over the cliff-face. The true base must be below where the camera cannot reveal.

All it takes is a momentary stumble, but Chimera's partner is overrun; he disappears under a writhing, biting mass of iridescent black scales. The felinoid champion dives into the chaos without hesitation, roaring in angry challenge. I can't see what's going on. Broken lizardlike bodies are thrown into the air, bludgeoned into painful shapes or rent by the heroine's claws. The camera focuses on one such creature, the glow in its red eyes fading; its long fangs are still extended and look to be coated in fresh blood.

Bobby is wrong. This isn't just like the way we played at all.

And then Chimera explodes from under the crush, shedding reptilian attackers like water. She's carrying her injured friend over her shoulder, a frenzied effort that obviously strains her power; she's carried civilians to safety before, I've seen it, but the hero in her arms looks to be at least twice her mass. She dips low and a lizard-thing stretches to open a painful looking gash in her leg. Fiercely determined, the lioness-headed heroine ignores her injury and speeds towards the building where the Ancient awaits.

The villain has picked up a staff, twisted and gnarled and covered in mud-colored runes that pulse like a giant creature's slow heart. Even on a television screen, it hurts to look too closely at the eerie glow. Despite his advanced age, the Ancient is still fit; he twirls the rod in a practiced motion, smooth like something out of an action movie.

One of the heroes still fighting through the waves of reptiles shouts for Chimera to wait but she persists. The wounded, bloodied hero that she was carrying is set down atop the dais and she confronts the Ancient on her own.

The camera cannot capture what is said, but she bares her teeth in a feral snarl and attacks.

Chimera has the advantage. The Ancient is surprisingly adept at physical combat with his weapon of choice but the heroine is a truly ferocious brawler; she doesn't let up, doesn't give him a moment's pause. Even the lightest tap from that horrific staff hits like a truck, throwing the heroine back nearly to the edge of the platform...but she scrabbles to her feet and dives back into the fray before the Ancient can escape.

And then the elder villain shouts a word that sounds alien to a human throat and touches the staff to Chimera's chest.

The camera's telephoto lens catches her expression: anger shifting to wide-eyed surprise as her body locks up like a statue. The white-haired man smiles pleasantly and makes as though to topple Chimera's frozen form off the platform into the midst of the frenzied lizard creatures below. But he is too late: the other heroes have arrived and the aged villain is surrounded.

Bobby cheers excitedly as the Ancient surrenders. This is, I think, the fourth time that he's been taken into custody. Hopefully, this time it sticks.

"I told you she'd catch him," Bobby smiles. "I told you!"

"Yup, you're right," I agree, carefully ignoring the part of me that can't help but notice Chimera still standing rigid, expression locked in a rictus of terror.

"The good guys always win eventually," Bobby says, satisfied, and turns off the television.

❧ ❧ ❧

It was—once again—very late when I arrived home. Several million dollars' worth of equipment had been left behind, expended in the rescue efforts; the devices self-immolated when all danger had passed so as to ensure that no third party would attempt to reverse engineer any of my technology. I'd taken time to set my manufacturing facilities to begin the process of creating replacements before I finally used a teleport platform to travel from a deep-sea lab back to my study in the Markham estate.

My medical nanites and other internal systems made quick work of re-balancing my neurochemistry; a few good hours of sleep and I'd be ready to tackle whatever the morning threw at me. For the most part, I was expecting for my civilian persona to work through the usual pile of relatively simple administrative tasks required of a CEO. Responding to emails and letters, taking meetings, talking with investors. In a strange way, I was looking forward to the tedious but familiar routine.

There was a quiet knock as I was preparing for bed.

"Are you awake?" Whisper asked, opening the door just a crack and peeking through. In the dim light, her soft-blue glowing eyes seemed to blaze.

"For a little while, yet," I chuckled. "Come in."

She smiled, practically skipping as she came to sit on the edge of the bed. "I've been watching the news!"

"Nothing horrible, I take it?"

"Even the ultraconservative talk shows are saying nice things about you." She sounded smug. "And they HATED you just a few days ago."

"That's a shame," I smiled. "I was enjoying watching the mental contortions that they had to twist themselves through in order to denounce firefighting and rescuing fishing boats."

"My favorite was the cat," she giggled, and made her voice gruff to imitate a famous radio provocateur: "Red-blooded Americans love dogs! This is obviously part of the ongoing Liberal conspiracy to feminize America! Unbelievable! Cats! How obvious is Doctor Fid trying to be? He's a villain, folks, mark my words...next he's going to be rescuing ferrets or hamsters, instead of our God-given hunting companions, dogs!"

"...Did you practice that?"

"Maybe a little," the little android replied mischievously.

"It's funny!"

"So, since Alec Whats-his-name likes dogs, does that mean that you are rescinding your request for a puppy?"

"Fallacy of origins!" Whisper objected. "Just because a bad man likes dogs doesn't mean dogs are bad. Besides, puppies aren't dogs. Puppies are puppies!"

"Puppies grow up," I pointed out. "And puppies are a lot of responsibility. I keep odd hours, you know, and I get distracted when I'm in the lab…you'd need to be even more responsible than Dinah is."

"I could do it!" she insisted.

"And no stealing my drones and programming them to clean up pet messes," I ordered, then relented: "Or at least, not when we have company."

"I won't!"

I thought about nine families who had nothing left to them but mourning and regret. What would any of them give, I wondered, for a chance to turn back time and grant their child just one more smile?

"I'll see if I can get out of the office early, tomorrow. We can drive to some of the local shelters."

"Really…?" Her voice had dropped to a whisper, and the wonder and excitement in her eyes made me want to cry.

"Really."

She jumped into my arms and, for just a moment, I felt whole.

CHAPTER TEN

"-REPEAT, ELEVEN PEOPLE HAVE BEEN CONFIRMED dead and at least twenty-three injured, eight of whom are listed as being in critical condition. Boston Memorial hospital has declined to give more detailed information about the casualties until families have been notified. We bring you now to our reporter on site at the Museum of Fine Arts."

Skullface had successfully elevated himself from source of irritation to target of seething rage.

"Thank you, Jill." The reporter stood in the courtyard before what had once been the Huntington Avenue entrance to the Boston Museum of Fine Arts. One of the columns over the entrance had been shattered and another badly cratered. Debris littered the usually pristine plaza, police tape warded civilians away from dangerous areas, and investigators and construction workers could be seen swarming across the grounds. "As you can see, the police have released much of the area to building inspectors. No official estimates as to how expensive repairs will be have been made public, but some experts have suggested that tens of millions of dollars will be needed. And that, of course, doesn't take into account the priceless works of art or the incalculable loss felt by those whose loved ones were taken by this unexpected and horrifically violent attack."

Decades ago, Bobby had been to that museum on a school field trip. That had been before the remodel, but he'd still come home to tell me about the visit with breathless awe. My baby brother had passed through the entrance that was now scarred with twisted rebar, shattered granite and marble, and chalk human-shaped outlines. The cameraman had kept at a respectful distance, but still I'd seen one outline that looked terribly small. Only a few feet away was an overturned stroller with a missing wheel.

"Have investigators determined what Skullface was looking for?"

"I'm afraid not, Jill." The young reporter's grave tone dipped even further. "There was enough damage done to the Art of the Americas exhibit that it may be weeks before a full inventory can be performed."

Skullface would have had a quicker path to his target had he come through the Fenway entrance. Even easier would have been blasting a hole in the museum's eastern wall and striding directly to the desired prize. He'd chosen his means of entry and exit solely for dramatic purposes. Skullface had wanted a body-count. He'd wanted to send a message.

"Has there been any word on Veridian's condition?"

"Again, I'm afraid not. An EMT confirmed that the hero was treated for a broken arm on site and airlifted to a confidential location."

"Thank you, Brian. We're now viewing a bystander's

recorded footage of the Boston Guardians confronting Skullface's forces, and the moments leading up to Veridian's injury."

Skullface obviously hadn't desired a fight against Doctor Fid; he'd waited until it was confirmed that I was out of the country before he'd attacked the museum. Whisper had been wise to turn off the news notifications that would normally have been transmitted directly to my neural link; a distraction during the rescue could have proved disastrous.

On screen, shaky footage revealed four of Skullface's minions were carrying a heavy-looking crate using poles to form a litter. Five more spread out and took cover as the Guardians arrived, immediately opening fire with energy-rifles that surely must have been Dr. Chaise's invention. Skullface himself was unhurried and seemed more intent upon casting eldritch blasts at huddled bystanders than he was in seeing to his own defense.

Titan shouted an order and then Regrowth and the Red Ghost broke off to evacuate civilians; Aeon, Veridian, and Titan converged on Skullface in a frontal assault. The battle was chaotic. Skullface and his minions kept on the move, denying the three Guardians on offense the ability to surround their target. Dr. Chaise's weapons packed an obvious punch; Titan was repeatedly blown backwards and his two less-physically-powerful teammates were left to fend for themselves. Aeon's energy shields flickered into and out of existence, leaving her unable to remain on the offensive while cocooned within the milk-white protective spheres. Veridian darted overhead, flying in tight loops and twists to avoid enemy fire and occasionally respond with his own emerald force-blasts.

The four mercenaries carrying the crate finished loading their cargo into a nondescript white van and sped away.

For all the tumult, the heroes appeared to be making progress. With civilians evacuated from immediate danger, Red Ghost and Regrowth rejoined the attack by focusing on eliminating the criminal riflemen.

And then an armored transport dropped from the sky, bristling with energy weapons and laying waste to the front of the building. The attack must have been coordinated because all of Skullface's men had been ready to dive for cover. The vehicle looked to be of Professor Paradigm's design, but highly modified by Dr. Chaise and painted to match Skullface's black and dull mustard-yellow motif. In an instant, the battle's tenor shifted: Veridian was shot from the sky, and the trees Regrowth had been controlling to corral the henchmen were incinerated.

Losing the frayed control over his temper, Titan charged forward in a frontal assault upon Skullface. The villain was ready for him, and Titan was repelled by a purple-black blast of mystical energy that threw the Guardian's leader up into the pillars that stood over the Boston Museum of Fine Arts entrance. A massive chunk of stone was thrown clear, striking Veridian just as the green-clad hero was beginning to climb to his feet.

A stray blast from the flying transport's weapons was thrown towards the amateur cameraman and the footage ended.

"This is Jill Janson from WBZ news, thanking the Boston Guardians for their heroic efforts. Without their intervention, who knows how many lives would have been lost? We at WBZ wish Veridian a speedy recovery and look forward to seeing him flying over our streets again soon."

Skullface had been close enough to Boston that he'd been able to stage this attack less than an hour after I arrived in Santiago, Chile. He'd been waiting for me to leave town and yet none of my sensors and monitoring programs had been able to identify even a hint of his presence! I'd spent too much time playing hero and too little focusing upon my own realm's defense. That would need to change.

In the meantime, my hidden factories were tasked with rebuilding my supply of construction drones. I suspected that more would be needed before I could engineer my final confrontation with Skullface.

❦ ❦ ❦

The black lab puppy had an odd twist to her run as she bounded after a giggling android. It was awkward and adorable, as though the little dog's hind legs were trying to outrun her front. Her tail wagged furiously and her head was held high, attentive and joyous. Someday, I was sure, she would grow into those over-sized paws; for now, she bounced from stride to stride, occasionally tumbling and scrambling back to all fours without pause.

Whisper changed direction, still carrying the puppy's favorite chew toy as bait for the game. She zigged and zagged, eyes focused more on the pup behind her than her own path. And then she was down, rolling in the grass and almost immediately set upon by her pursuer. The black lab ignored the toy and instead darted to enthusiastically clean Whisper's synthetic ears. She squeaked and tried to cuddle the black bundle of fur and energy against her chest, but the puppy was having none of it; she squirmed free and continued her assault, licking eagerly at the side of Whisper's head.

The pair had been inseparable for the first five days and—true to her word—Whisper had taken to her responsibilities with remarkable zeal. Together, she and I had penned in a section of the den and set down puppy pads for her new pet to be paper trained; Whisper kept the area clean and had stayed just outside the penned area while the pup slept.

Android and canine had both found their feet and were running once more, this time in a wide circle. I knew that Whisper had access to power fed via quantum-tunnel from a Westler-Gray reactor; from whence the puppy got its energy, I had no idea.

"Stay close to the house," I called. My original intent had been to come outside to sit and brood while Whisper played, but I'd since discovered that it was impossible to languish in dark speculation while an elfin childlike android attempted to teach a puppy how to play tag. I smiled and waved to my little sister as she ran.

We'd visited four shelters before Whisper had made her choice; she'd wanted every puppy we saw but insisted that we keep looking anyway. When we'd found this puppy, the last of its litter, it had been love at first sight. Whisper had stumbled hesitantly to the chain-link cage, eyes wide. And the little black lab had looked up at her, sniffed at her offered fingers and then its tail began its hopeful, happy rhythm.

"I'm naming her Nyx." Whisper had told the cooing attendant at the animal shelter. "Because her fur is black, and Nyx was the Greek Goddess of the night." But across the neural link, her mental touch was filled with memories of a man who'd teased her and called her a shell-script, but also read to her and kept her company when I was in a medically induced coma. Who joked and played and treated her like a little girl instead of a science experiment, and who had been Doctor Fid's first true friend and one of her first friends as well.

Eric Guthrie, AKA Starnyx...taken from us both by violence. We'd seized our revenge, Whisper and I, but Starnyx's absence had still hurt. But now his namesake capered about our lawn and I knew my friend would have loved this.

To hell with Skullface's plotting; I had other priorities.

I clambered to my feet and joined the chase.

☙ ❧ ☙

```
THE EFFECTS OF TEMPORAL LEUCOTOMY ON SUPERNORMAL
                     ABILITIES
     Surgical Attempts to Alter Akashic Identity

                   THE ANCIENT
  Acknowledged Master of Mystic and Physical arts,
```

David H. Reiss

Rhode Island

Prior studies have demonstrated that the majority of extrahuman talents are connected to the affected individual at a level that cannot be explained by purely biological phenomenon. Abilities were shown to remain functional, though often weakened, after gross morphological changes have been inflicted upon a statistically relevant percentage of test subjects. Mystical analysis demonstrated that the experimental subjects maintained unique ethereal records throughout the procedure with full dissolution occurring only moments before termination.

In sixty-four percent of test subjects, there existed a measurable correspondence between the persistence of supernormal capabilities and the moment of akashic detachment. Means of termination were altered throughout the study, and a deeper analysis of the data revealed that the greatest variances were found when brain-death occurred in stages prior to the halting of other autonomic processes (table 1). With these anomalies in mind, further study was put towards the complex links between neural functionality, akashic identity and supernormal abilities.

Measured psychosurgical operations were performed upon the anatomically intact brains of powered test subjects, and the extirpation of sections of the frontal, parietal and occipital lobe showed limited but predictable effect upon retention of akashic identity. Leucotomy upon the temporal lobe, however, produced unexpectedly significant results, and complete temporal lobectomies induced immediate alterations to the subjects' connection to the akashic field, even when biological functions were maintained for significant periods after procedures were completed.

In layman's terms, sufficient damage to the temporal lobe re-shaped the body/soul gestalt so fundamentally that external connections were disrupted.

Given that this new evidence supported the theory that the loss of supernormal abilities corresponded with akashic detachment, further investigation was planned to determine if surgical methods could alter akashic identity without otherwise impairing cognitive capability. A focused study on transtemporal incisions followed, with desired regions marked on a grid (fig 1). Test subjects were secured in the standard fashion…

&&&

It had been decades, and no one had been able to crack the riddle of the Ancient's treasure. Most doubted that any hidden hoard existed at all; it was merely wishful thinking, they scoffed. The villain was gone and good riddance! What can be gained, they asked, by chasing after dusty horrors and lost riches? If you need to increase your fortune you should rob a bank, said the villains. The Ancient's legacy should remain buried, said everyone else.

I'd spent several evenings poring over the Ancient's published academic papers, reading them over and over to develop a feel for his thought process and style. I was bent towards this task, now. If there existed a hidden collection of the Ancient's writing and research, I wanted it. My reasons were threefold: First, to make complete my eventual victory over Skullface (and likely force him to step forward and confront me directly). Second, to understand and make use of the knowledge embedded within. Finally, to burn whatever were the most horrid discoveries that the brilliant, foul madman had unearthed.

Information might be neither good nor evil, but it could certainly be dangerous. For the greater good, some knowledge would best be excised from human understanding. Even in the published papers, spread throughout dozens of openly available periodicals, there had been hints of principles too perilous to be entrusted to the public.

Although the furor of those early treasure hunting expeditions had long since faded, some would still notice if a new player began acquiring relevant works. Through false identities, I was able to purchase a handful of items via online auctions. To do more would raise red flags.

And so began a massive and expensive effort to examine said items in place with their owners none the wiser. For the most part, this effort could be performed utilizing silent and camouflaged microdrones; occasionally, however, a more personal touch was needed. For that purpose, Doctor Fid's Mk 37 Stealth armor had been designed.

Whisper, I hate to be a bother, I sent my thoughts via

my neural tap's quantum-tunneled network link, **but I think that I am going to need your help with some research.**

Okay, she chirped. **How can I help?**

I've worked my way to the basement, but the layout doesn't match the filed floorplan. Could you check public records for unusual building material purchases in the region, between eleven and thirteen years ago?

The Trask estate that I was currently infiltrating had been reconstructed in that time frame; in addition to the new pool and hideous roman columns, it appeared that the drug-lord property owner had also added an underground refuge in which to wait out attacks from his competitors. I'd already checked the safe in the main estate and been disappointed, so I presumed that the painting I was here to examine was stored in the sanctuary below.

If the bunker had been constructed using modern technology, I would not have needed to come here on my own. My drones—properly controlled—could easily have defeated whatever defensive software Edward Trask's private security could have brought to bear, but this was all heavy vault doors, combination locks, and massive five-spoke safe handles. From what my scans could determine through the thick walls, even the currently-locked-closed hidden air vents were controlled by manual cranks.

And so I'd come here myself, practically invisible to the naked eye and to electronic scanning alike. The Trasks were hosting a fundraising party for local politicians, so the majority of security was focused upon the dining hall and the veranda where the guests had congregated. I'd simply floated in, a metal encased ghost, and worked my way towards the lower level.

Four thousand tons of concrete went missing from Trask Construction twelve and a half years ago, Whisper noted. **A lot of rebar, too. Their insurance paid out and everything.**

Assuming that the sixteen-inch-thick walls butting against the main property were maintained throughout the structure, I calculated that the shelter's overall size could not be more than six thousand square feet, which matched the readings that I'd taken earlier. I'd been worried that there might be more; given the depth and density of the construction, I'd been concerned that my sweep hadn't been able to reveal the hidden chamber in its entirety. The Mk 37 was impressively stealthy, but manual searches still ate valuable time. I wanted to be long gone before the security guards performed their rounds.

Thank you, I sent.

Mm!

I slaved my hands to my armor's programming as they worked to solve the vault combination lock.

The main portion of the estate had been decorated with the peculiar aesthetic of a creature who wished to display his wealth...but refused to trust in the judgment of a professional architect or interior designer. Individual items were all of superb quality: checkerboard marble floors in the halls, thick velvet drapes on the windows, beautifully restored hardwood furniture, and oil paintings with gilded and hand-carved frames. Taken together, however, they seemed a vulgar mishmash of styles and extravagances. The entrance to the underground sanctuary had been hidden behind a particularly gaudy tapestry.

Microdrones were monitoring the party at the other side of the estate; the guests did not seem disturbed by the decor. The fine catered food and an open bar had more than offset any poor impressions that the donors might have had of their host.

It was very likely that most of those gathered had no idea how the Trask family had earned its fortune. Two, in particular, would have been horrified: a husband-and-husband pair of actors, both intensely passionate activists for measures that combat the proliferation of illegal narcotics. That Edward Trask invited them here said much about his brutal sense of humor. It was tempting to inform the pair of their host's profession. It was tempting to burn this entire estate to the ground and salt the earth.

Another time, perhaps. For now, I had a mission.

The massive steel vault door shrieked as it swung open. I was glad for the thick walls and draperies, then, for their ability to muffle noise; even so, if there'd been anyone on this floor the cacophony would not have gone undetected. The stealth technologies that rendered this suit nearly invisible were incompatible with the layered forcefield emitters that the Mk 36b used to deaden sound. Fortunately, the security guards were occupied with the party and the metallic complaints were undetected.

I floated inside. Where the public areas of the estate were ostentatious, this hidden area was marked by an almost military austerity. There was an armory to one side of the vault door and emergency medical supplies to the other. Concrete walls were painted the tone of desert sand, and furniture had been chosen more for durability and comfort rather than appearance. There were no works of art or valuables present in this first room, but a slim hallway extended further and I could see doors on both sides.

There were several bedrooms (only one of which looked as though it had ever seen use), a restroom, and storage of various types—food, supplies, and pharmaceutical entertainment. Towards the end of the hall I found what I was seeking: a room that contained a collection of artworks, obtained illegally and thus not displayable on the walls of the estate above.

Behind the Mk 37's faceplate, I frowned. Two drunk party-goers had slipped away from the veranda and begun exploring the house. I tasked a microdrone to monitor their progress and alert me if their unguided tour took them too close to the basement. I'd left the vault door open to avoid making unnecessary noise; if they were caught by a drug lord's security near to an open vault, I couldn't imagine a pleasant end to their evening.

I found my objective: a stunningly beautiful impressionist painting reminiscent of the famous Luncheon of the Boating Party; the Ancient had composed this himself, mimicking Renoir's style with remarkable aplomb. His college friends, depicted at a picnic; with only a few strokes of a brush, trust and intimacy and friendship had been captured on the canvas. Towards the rear of the crowd, almost unnoticeable, a young woman was looking directly at the artist with an expression of merry acceptance so loving that it tore at my heart.

I think that it was at that moment that I realized that I hated the Ancient.

His intelligence marked him as being as inhumanly freakish as myself…and yet he'd had this! I'd been blessed with my parents, with my brother. The expressions in this painting, however, hinted that the Ancient had somehow managed to function smoothly within a much broader social circle. How had he managed it? What had his secret been?

I was so intensely jealous that had the Ancient appeared before me I would have incinerated him on the spot.

With hands steadied only by software algorithm, I began my inspection.

The pigments in the painting were a mix of classic methodology and modern improvements; there was a purple made from the mucus of a rare snail, a vibrant red from crushed beetles, and hints of ultramarine blue from a powdered semi-precious stone. Other colors were store-bought synthetic paints. I saw no immediate pattern to the Ancient's choice, modern or ancient technique, but noted the differences for later study. Analysis would come later. For now, I observed.

There were scuffs and nicks at the edges of the canvas. The spacing could have indicated a code, or else they might simply have been damages caused during one of the many times this artwork had been stolen.

Hyperspectral infrared reflectography revealed that the visible image had been painted atop another: a forested landscape with an unfamiliar tower in the distance. Of this, I took even more detailed scans. There was a code here, I was sure of it. The Ancient had alternated the use of old lead-based and modern titanium white pigments in intricate patterns.

There were other oddities, too: hints that solvents had been used to clean some sections of canvas but not others. Base-tones in the underpainting that did not match the final work. I felt as though I could examine this work for hours and still find new and intriguing quirks.

Sadly, I didn't have hours available; the two inebriated explorers had been noticed, and the guards began their rounds early to be certain that no one else had wandered away from the still-festive party above. Carefully, I set the painting back upon its easel then darted back to the underground bunker's entrance.

The guards were too close for comfort, but I swung the vault door shut nonetheless; leaving the passage open might have made it easier to fly out a window and escape unnoticed into the night, but I imagined that the drug-lord property owner would place unhealthy scrutiny upon his guests when the anomaly was discovered. So, I re-locked the door and positioned the tapestry into its normal state. When the guards rushed in to investigate the noise, I floated to the ceiling.

"What'd you hear?" asked thug number one.

"I dunno," replied thug two. "Something."

"You sure? I don't see nothing."

"Yeah. Maybe. I dunno. Check careful, the boss 's in a

mood."

"Yeah."

And so I stayed pressed against the ceiling as the two security guards checked every nook and corner of the basement. I dared not shift an inch; the Mk 37's stealth technology was remarkable, but it wasn't true invisibility. Every time they crossed beneath me or their flashlights swept past my location, I held my breath.

"I got nothing," thug two said, sounding annoyed.

"Same here."

"Maybe I heard something outside?"

"Yeah. Call it in."

And finally, I could relax; the two guards wandered to check other rooms and I was left alone. Part of me wanted to stay, to wait until the coast was clear and return to examining the Ancient's painting, but it was getting late and I'd already recorded all the scans that I'd intended to capture. Somewhat reluctantly, I floated up from the basement and made my way to the open sky.

Sometime over the next few weeks, I'd be sure to leave anonymous tips to the appropriate authorities. Seeing Edward Trask linked to his drug-running business would not be as satisfying as laying waste to his estate, but it would be vengeance enough to pacify the part of me still enraged by that damned painting.

CHAPTER ELEVEN

From: Cherenkov
To: BlueEyedGirl
Subject: THANK YOU!!

Thanks for the advice! Those articles were perfect, I aced the exam. Also, you were right about Brute: he totally drops his shoulder before throwing a haymaker; I beat him three times in open sparring before I told him how. Majestic was impressed! Brute was pissed off for a while until I told him how I was doing it. He's getting extra training now to lose the habit.
How do you get your info? This is the third time you've saved my butt.

From: BlueEyedGirl
To: Cherenkov
Subject: Re: THANK YOU!!

Yay! I'm glad that it helped.
I read a lot and do research myself, just for fun.

I also steal from my brother's archives. He studies heroes and has lots of useful information. Oh! You're going to be partnered with Exbow for patrols next week, right? Bring high-carb snacks! Like pretzels, I mean. She'll be your friend forever. Also, be careful not to fly out of her line of sight. She gave Whistler a lot of grief for that. Check these links.

From: Cherenkov
To: BlueEyedGirl
Subject: Re: Re: THANK YOU!!

Really? She doesn't eat much at the NY Shield cafeteria. I'll give pretzels a try, though. Thanks! Also, I'm getting better about not rushing ahead on my own. It's one of Cloner's pet peeves, he dinged me pretty hard last time we had patrols. Is your brother a former hero? Majestic says that the write-up you sent on Brute's fighting style was professional and used a lot of terminology that's only used in the main four training schools.

From: BlueEyedGirl
To: Cherenkov
Subject: Betrayal

You promised you wouldn't share it! I'm really

angry at you now.

From: Cherenkov
To: BlueEyedGirl
Subject: Re: Betrayal

I'm so sorry, Blue eyes. I totally forgot! I won't do it again.

From: Cherenkov
To: BlueEyedGirl
Subject: Re: Betrayal

Blue eyes? Are you here? I mean it, I was just talking with Majestic and Brute in training and I didn't want to take credit for myself, because it wasn't my work. I'll be more careful. Please?

From: Cherenkov
To: BlueEyedGirl
Subject: Re: Betrayal

Look, I understand if you don't want to send me any more stuff, that's totally cool. Just don't leave me hanging, okay? You were, like, my biggest fan when I was just getting started and I'll totally

miss talking with you. I'm really really really sorry!!
P.S. Also, you were totally right about the pretzels. Thank you!

From: BlueEyedGirl
To: Cherenkov
Subject: Apology accepted

Ok, fine. I'm still mad, but it's all right. You can be mad at people and still be friends.

From: Cherenkov
To: BlueEyedGirl
Subject: Re: Apology accepted

I really am sorry, and I'm glad you're my friend. Oh, you didn't answer my question. Is your brother a former hero? It'd be great if I could work with him sometime. I'm not supposed to do unsupervised patrols, but Cloner says it's cool if I'm partnered with someone licensed and insured. And maybe I could meet you, too!

From: BlueEyedGirl
To: Cherenkov

Subject: Re: Re: Apology accepted

I don't think it'd work out, my brother isn't exactly a hero. And I'm sorry, I don't travel to New York often. :(Oh, I noticed that the Junior Shield canceled their patrol schedule next week. Is everyone okay? Was someone hurt?

From: Cherenkov
To: BlueEyedGirl
Subject: Re: Re: Re: Apology accepted

No one was hurt; we're just closing ranks because the team leaders think Skullface is in town. The higher-ups don't want any of the junior team patrolling until he's caught. It sucks. We're stuck inside, and most of our teachers are running around in Brooklyn so we aren't really learning much. I'm getting caught up on schoolwork, I guess. :(

From: BlueEyedGirl
To: Cherenkov
Subject: No Patrols

I hadn't heard that Skullface was in NY. Stay safe!

From: Cherenkov
To: BlueEyedGirl
Subject: Re: No Patrols

Well, maybe he is and maybe he isn't. Nobody's seen him. Cloner says he is, though, and Cloner knows everything.

From: BlueEyedGirl
To: Cherenkov
Subject: Re: Re: No Patrols

I'm beginning to get that impression, yeah.

❧ ❧ ❧

Several years ago, I'd built a swarm of microdrones and unleashed them to construct a map of Manhattan's underground. The sheer number of unused tunnels and caverns was astounding. There were dilapidated subway stations, some decorated with graffiti and occupied by squatters, others completely lost to time. There were steam tunnels and maintenance shafts, long since abandoned. Dark and empty and foreboding, unused sewers and massive drainage pipes snaked under the city with tendrils stretching out under the neighboring boroughs like the roots of a great, invisible tree.

I'd also found the secret lairs of two active heroes, three

villains, and one of the Ancient's abandoned laboratories. After investing in a thorough cleaning, the latter was appropriated for my own purposes. I'd built a teleportation platform there and could use a secret door to enter into the subway tunnels. From there, a path to Lassiter's could be traced without ever stepping foot aboveground.

Years before the first superhuman had arisen, Lassiter's Den had already been a known sanctuary among the local underworld. On the border between the territories of two criminal organizations, the Den had become a place for members of each group to meet and negotiate. Over time, other gangs began to use the location for a similar purpose. Now, Lassiter's Truce was upheld by Lassiter's patrons, a tradition that traced back for the better part of a century. Committing violence here would earn the enmity of a large number of dangerous people.

Under most circumstances, I still chose to fly from Boston to New York City. The travel was calming, a ritual that gave me time to think and prepare for whatever task lay ahead. Once upon a time, I'd looked forward to those flights, basking in the knowledge that there was a friendly greeting awaiting me.

My truest friend—Starnyx, killed by the telepathic alien Legion officers whom I later annihilated—had haunted Lassiter's Den like an amiable ghost. And every time that I was so fortunate as to run into him, I left the region feeling just a little bit closer to being human.

With Nyx gone, my journeys to the City that Never Sleeps were now taken solely for professional reasons. Starnyx's compatriots (members of the social activist hacker collective that my friend had helped to create) treated me with respect, but the camaraderie was long gone.

On this evening, I used the teleportation platform. Even with my stealth technologies enabled, there was a chance that someone would see evidence of Doctor Fid flying through downtown. Word would spread, and I was sure that Dr. Chaise would at least be listening in on the police radio bands.

After working alongside Valiant in Santiago, I was even less sanguine of my chances to enter and exit Lassiter's Den without being forced to deal with a confrontation.

There would be no violence within the bar itself; that law was inviolable. On the street at the entrance, or in the alley behind the establishment—that was another story. The Mk 36b was powerful, yet the combined might of the bar's patrons could not be ignored. Arriving via the freight elevator from the tunnels below would allay the threat of attack until after I'd had the opportunity to make my case and gather what intelligence I could pry from reluctant lips.

So I hovered above the detritus, not bothering even to shine a light as I floated through over-sized pipes and drainage shafts. Relatively recently, I'd discovered a means for my forcefields to keep any form of refuse from touching the surface of my armor and to stave off even the slightest hint of odor. Several times, I needed to traverse sections of still-active subway tunnel; fortunately, gathering the current status of every train was simple and it was a trivial task to weave my way through without the slightest chance of accident or discovery.

Soon enough, I arrived at the freight elevator. Many of the larger and more inhuman patrons found entrance into Lassiter's Den via this route; a creature like Minotaur could not arrive at the front door without being observed. Their route through the subway tubes was less circuitous than mine, but also riskier; passengers speeding by occasionally caught glimpse of Bullwhip or Minotaur or the Lizard King on their way to Friday night drinks, creating all sorts of rumors about monsters living in the darkness below New York.

I was as much a monster as any of Lassiter's patrons. I did not fear their recrimination for my actions in Chile, nor did I fear their rejection. I didn't. If my hand paused before the button to call down the freight elevator was pressed, it was only because I was distracted by other weightier issues.

The lift brought me to the main floor, and from there I walked through the kitchens towards the bar area. None of the prep-cooks even looked up as I passed; they were used to the foot traffic, I supposed.

I'd never eaten at the restaurant attached to Lassiter's Den; every method that I'd devised thus far to take in solid food without removing my helmet has yielded messy or inadequate results, and I'd never felt that visiting in my civilian identity was worth the risk. For now, I pumped a sample of air from the kitchens into the confines of my normally completely-isolated suit. The room smelled delicious: there were the heavy, rich scents of pan-fried chicken, earthy aromas from roasted root vegetables, and competing bouquets from simmering soup stocks. I delayed (procrastinated, I finally admitted to myself) another few seconds to enjoy the breath's taste before stepping through the final door.

All eyes fell upon me and there was a moment of quiet.

Lassiter's Den had changed over the decades but still retained much of its old-fashioned charm. The bar area was dimly illuminated, old polished wood warmed by candles and an array of simulated gas lights. Intricately molded shelves held an impressive collection of expensive (and not-so-expensive) spirits and glassware, while the mirror behind the bar was smoked glass. The plastered walls were painted the color of age-yellowed ivory, though the lower third was protected by a cherry wood wainscot, matched in tone and polish to the bar top itself. The barstools, tables, and booths were simple, but sturdy and kept in good repair.

The clientele here was atypical; there were benches that would provide a comfortable rest for all sorts, from the most diminutive villain to the most hulking of brutes. When Doctor Fid—wearing the Mk 36b medium-duty combat armor—took a seat at the bar, there was no worry that the suit's great weight would overstrain the furniture. The stool had been designed for just such a purpose.

"Doctor Fid," William Wasserman nodded to me. "We just received another shipment of Starnyx' favorite."

"A pint, then."

The silence continued as the bartender poured my drink from the tap.

Though my back was turned to the room, my sensors

showed that several costumed patrons were coming to their feet; surely, I wondered, they would not dare attack me here? If they intended to break the Lassiter's truce, the building itself—one of the most important landmarks in the criminal world—would surely be damaged; any attack capable of even catching my attention would render the beautiful bar and the wood-faced columns into kindling. I shifted power to force-fields, just in case, and subtly shifted so that my body would protect William from any energy blasts. I turned slowly, carefully, so as not to provoke an early assault.

And then the applause began, followed by laughter and shouted congratulations.

I checked my sensors but was unable to detect any mood-altering chemicals in the air, and a more detailed scan confirmed that there had been no accidental transportation to an alternate universe where the heroes sported evil goatees.

"Most of them have families," William murmured from behind me. "And so do I. My grandson is the same age as the children you saved."

Not knowing what else to do or say, I raised my beer in salute. The cheers were confusing but gratifying nonetheless. I'd originally come here to ask after Skullface's location, but instead I found myself making small talk and shaking hands as the horde converged.

Even when unexpected circumstances trended in my favor, I found it irksome when events transpired in a manner that made a mockery of mathematical projections.

I'd studied the men and women who frequent Lassiter's Den. I knew them. Hardened criminals drank here, fiends who would not balk at committing horrors to achieve their goals. Some patrons were vicious and cruel, others were misfits trapped by circumstance or poor past choices. Over the decades, a culture had evolved that included a quiet acceptance of even the darkest of villains, and a deep-seated disdain of heroes.

This was not the reaction that I'd predicted. Fortunately, the facial recognition systems built into the Mk 36b identified someone in the crowd that might have indicated a possible explanation.

"I'm going to pose a hypothesis," I murmured, using directed speakers such that only William would hear. "I suspect that—when news of the events in Chile first broke—the patrons here were not inclined to laud my actions. I further suspect that at least one un-costumed civilian (and possibly more) argued in my favor, buying drinks to soften tempers and making speeches that emphasized the humanity beneath the villains' masks. Eventually, the crowd's views evolved."

"She didn't say anything that I wasn't already feeling, Doctor Fid."

I just chuckled, ordered a second beer, and then made my way through the crowd to find a short, stout civilian who was sitting alone and reading a book. I set the glass on his table and he looked up, eyes losing focus as he gazed at the stars within my armor's faceplate.

"I was thinking we should talk," I said to Cloner, and sat

across from him.

A microexpression of surprise flickered across his face followed quickly by amused resignation. "How'd you know?"

"My armor has very good scanners," I disambiguated; the truth was that I had yet to create a way to identify one of Cloner's bodies using technology. Every last method that I'd tried showed them to be an ordinary human, no different than any other person on the street. And yet Cloner had created and controlled hundreds—perhaps thousands—of unique bodies without any pattern to race, gender or appearance. This particular iteration I knew simply because I recognized it from two prior encounters: he'd been to Lassiter's at least once before to entertain the crowd with bad jokes and had also been the last surviving Cloner from the battle at Mercer-Talon.

Many years past, all of Cloner's duplicates had been identical and that had been thought to be the limit of his power. He'd used those replicas as cannon-fodder, swarming into battle with slapstick humor and suicidal abandon but always protecting his original body. When that body was murdered by a villain named Spiker, it was assumed that the clones would soon perish…but they did not. Instead, the clones learned to create clones of their own and he'd overcome the identical-duplicate limitation. As long as one body survived—somewhere—Cloner could likely live forever and repopulate planets.

"So," the dark-haired man smiled, "What'd you want to talk about?"

I used my forcefields to create an invisible semipermeable dome around our table; no one would overhear our conversation. "I want to know why."

"Uh, you're gonna need to be a bit more specific." He scratched at his neck, as though his collar were bothering him; I'd spent hours watching footage of his battles, his interviews. Every one of Cloner's bodies had its own unique nervous tics and reflexes, their own autonomic functions. The amount of processing power necessary to simply maintain his bodies at a ready state was remarkable; I reminded myself that he'd been an experienced veteran long before I'd built my first armor and that he was a hive-mind who could operate using the resources of hundreds of bodies at once. Despite his casual body language and informal language, his was an intellect worthy of respect.

"Why did you use one of your other bodies to convince the patrons here to accept my presence?" I asked, directly. Cloner's mental faculties might be a threat to be wary of, but not one to fear. I was Doctor Fid.

"You're a scary son of a bitch," he grinned, taking up the glass of beer that I'd set on his table. "You know that?"

"I do, yes." Hidden within my armor, my smile was smug.

"I meant scarily perceptive; I guess spine-chillingly creepy and intimidating fits too," Cloner chuckled and took a swallow from his beer.

"Thank you, on all counts," I nodded in acknowledgment. "I would, however, still appreciate an answer to my question."

"Partially because you saved my life," he replied, still

smiling as though he had not a single care in the world. "Which sounds kinda selfish considering how many billions of other sentient life forms you saved from the Legion, but there you go. Also, the Red Ghost found out something that convinced him, and he's my friend. You're terrifying...but he thinks you'd make a good hero."

Unable to detect any nefarious intent, I considered the hero before me. He'd been effective and manipulative, yes, but not malicious. If Cloner were telling the truth—and I had no evidence that he was not, though I dared not take his honesty for granted—then it seemed likely that his actions would prove no threat to my long-term plans. Finally, I asked: "Do you know why he's so certain?"

"That's not my story to tell. Ask Red Ghost."

"I'm asking you," I growled, turning down the emotion-dampening aspects of the vocoder that created Doctor Fid's voice.

"Okay, okay. Jeez." The overweight little man took a long drink, dark eyes still directed at my facemask. "You remember when you were accused of murdering him, 'cause he overstressed his power and everyone thought he was dead, when he'd really just accidentally jumped to another dimension?"

"I was there," I replied dryly. "Of course I remember."

"He held a press conference, told everyone he was on an uninhabited alternate Earth, yeah?"

"Yes." Though he'd been close-lipped when I attempted to discuss the event with him directly.

"Well, that was true...and it was months before he

figured out how to get off that Earth. Time dilation stuff, you prob'ly understand that better 'n me." Cloner shrugged. "The thing is, he dropped through a couple other alternate dimensions before he got back to this one."

Suddenly, the Red Ghost's reluctance to comment on his missing time made sense; he was wary of my technology's ability to recognize deception by analyzing body language, tone or biometric data. A lie of omission, however, was rarely caught. Damn the man.

"And in one of these alternate dimensions, he found information that led you to believe I would make a good hero?"

"Yeah. But like I said...it's not my story. Ask him for details."

I remained still, my thoughts swirling, and used the straw-like appendage that extended from my armor's forearm to take a slow drink from my own beer. I could press for more information; Cloner was a talkative sort, it probably wouldn't be overly difficult to lure out further information. On the other hand, I had the means to contact the Red Ghost...and I was painfully curious to hear the truth from his own lips. Rather than pushing the hero before me, I thought, it would be better to wait and receive my answers directly from the hero that I considered to be my nemesis.

"I am grateful for your efforts," I lied, "but you will stop now. Let me forge my own path."

"Sure, sure...if that's what you want." There was a playful glint in his eyes that made me doubt that he'd back off completely, but I believed that the overt manipulation would cease. If nothing else, I was certain that this confrontation would alter whatever game that Cloner was playing; he knew that I was aware now and would need to shift his tactics should he desire to continue his attempts to shape my choices.

I nodded, satisfied, then straightened my back to sit a bit taller. "I do have one other question."

"Yeah?" he tilted his head, brow furrowed curiously. "Okay, shoot."

"Where," I intoned, increasing the volume of Doctor Fid's highly-masked voice and adding a threatening bass rumble, "can I find Skullface?"

His grinned beatifically, "No idea. I was lying through my teeth when I spread the rumor. Red might think you're a hero, but I still wanted to know where you're getting your information. You have our internal notifications system hacked, yeah? The messages only went out a few hours ago, and here you are."

I chose not to confirm nor deny his assumption; Whisper had informed me that Skullface was in New York City so I assumed the hack must have been hers. I made a note to urge her to withdraw; the superheroic artificially intelligent being known as Cuboid may have been scarce since the battle at Mercer-Talon...but Cuboid was a member of the New York Shield. Interfering directly with their servers was dangerous.

"All this, simply to sate your curiosity? You play a dangerous game."

"That wasn't the only reason," he grinned merrily.

"And what, then, is your other reason?"

"Remember after Mercer-Talon? I told the world that I owed you a beer. I just got most of this bar to buy you one. You're welcome."

I couldn't help it; I laughed before I thought to turn off my armor's external speakers. Cloner looked annoyingly self-satisfied.

"So," he asked, "We done here, then?"

"We're done."

"Good, I gotta drain the lizard," he belched and stood up. "Great beer, by the way."

He wandered towards the restroom, and I was gone before he returned.

※ ※ ※

Less than eight hours after I'd left a message at one of our dead drops, the Red Ghost replied with coordinates for a meeting; either I'd gotten lucky, or else he'd been checking the location regularly. The possibility of the former made me nervous, for the flavor of luck that usually rained upon me was of the sour variety. The latter raised my consternation even higher.

If the Ghost was checking our dead-drop locations regularly, it was because he'd been hoping to see me. Why, then, hadn't he left a note of his own? My mind swirled with possibilities, each more damning than the last. Had Regrowth informed him that my heroic actions were merely an act? If so, what was his intended response?

In that scenario, I hoped that the Red Ghost chose

violence. If he instead merely looked at me with sad disappointment, I would be forced to flee in shame.

The codes within the missive were valid and indicated a late-night meeting in an abandoned warehouse near the docks; I knew the place. Technically, I owned it. It was nearby to one of the fake-bases to which I'd lured the Guardians and I'd snapped up several nearby properties through a complex web of holding companies. There was already a movement to renovate the region after the destruction caused by the battle, and I stood to make a hefty profit. Eventually. The Red Ghost had been a forensic accountant prior to gaining his superpowers, and I needed to be very careful before liquidating those assets. He and I may have been secret business partners, but he was also still a hero. If he uncovered even a thread of evidence, that thread would be tugged at until the entire tapestry unraveled. Greater care would be preferable so as to avoid conflict altogether.

It was dark and low clouds blocked any hint of the moon's light. There was some activity by the harbor; a shipment of furniture by the looks of it, with dockhands taking overtime pay to see the crates safely unloaded. My sensors spotted a few chartered boats in the bay; some were giving late night romantic tours, and others were seeking the bluefish schools that were currently in season. All in all, a quiet evening.

The warehouse skylights were open so I slipped through and landed gracefully at the appointed time.

The Red Ghost was waiting for me. In the shadows, his

long crimson cloak faded to black; the hood was folded back, though, and the eyes behind his mask were gravely serious as he stepped into a sliver of light.

"Doctor," he greeted. "It's good to see you."

"Is it?" I asked. "I wasn't certain what to expect. Regrowth nearly died while fighting at my side."

"She didn't die. You saved her life," his lips turned up in a bright and honest smile. "For that, you have my eternal gratitude."

"Regrowth wouldn't have been in that position if I hadn't accepted her offer for help," I shook my head, my shoulders hunched from the weight of my guilt. "I should have been more careful."

"Elaine is a strong, stubborn woman." There was worry in his eyes, but also fond exasperation. "She makes her own choices. She made a decision and events turned south. Sadly, that happens in our chosen profession. But my fiancee is still alive because you pulled her from the ground. I am not in the least bit angry at you."

"Fiancee?" I asked.

"Yes."

"Congratulations," I said, and he looked so smugly pleased that I almost laughed aloud.

"So," he coughed, now embarrassed. "Why did you want to talk?"

"I recently bumped into Cloner," I replied. "He mentioned that you might have a story for me."

"Ah." He looked away, "I wasn't certain that I should tell you. It is a sad tale."

"It may be important. Cloner told me that you'd been to more than one world, after the Legion officer's attack?"

"Yes. I hadn't known my mists could do that, to disperse myself so thin that I slipped between dimensions. That first world...I didn't know where I was. It was beautiful and green and lush. I thought that perhaps I was dead and that I'd somehow found my way to Regrowth's heaven where I could wait for her. Growing things are her domain. I quickly realized that wasn't the case; I was alive, but not on earth. The stars and the moon were all wrong."

While many of my inventions utilize artificially-created sub-dimensions, I'd never constructed a device to travel between naturally-formed dimensions. I was familiar with the math, however, and there were certain quantum variables that made accurate transmission difficult. The rifts were far too unstable for my comfort; whatever force granted the Red Ghost his powers, it must also have protected him from the possibility of being caught between.

"Still," he continued, "I expected rescue so I set up camp and waited. As the days turned to weeks, however, I knew that all must have believed me dead. I waited until my powers were recovered—it took several months—and then I turned to mist and pushed, attempting to repeat the experiment that had thrown me to the wrong world."

This newly discovered aspect of the Red Ghost's power simplified the maths for interdimensional transportation. In my head, I was beginning to design a mechanism that would have assisted in getting him home. Perhaps I could miniaturize it sufficiently that he could carry it on his person, just in case. Those months when we'd all thought him dead had been unpleasant.

"When I regained consciousness, I was somewhere else. Another uninhabited world. So I waited, survived, then tried again. Eventually, I thought that I'd found my way home. It was a world similar to this, but the heroes were different. And I found myself—another Miguel Espinoza—still working at H&H Global in New York."

There was a note of longing in his voice. Could he miss the tedium of a nine-to-five job so terribly? No, he was respected here, comfortably wealthy (in no small part due to his secret dealings with a supervillain, admittedly), and now engaged to an extraordinary woman. Perhaps that other Miguel had settled down and had a family. The life of a superhero was less stable than that of a forensic accountant, and I supposed that stability had a certain appeal all its own.

"I found that world's incarnation of Professor Paradigm and he offered to help me get home. Apparently, the device would only work for me because of a quirk of my powers—"

Hah!

"—but he was able to get something working. Just before I left, though, I'd made a joking comment that only Doctor Fid could have constructed it faster, and one of Paradigm's assistants startled. He mentioned that he used to call his brother by that title because his brother was a P-H-D Doctor..."

"...and 'P-H' is pronounced ffffff," I completed, feeling lightheaded. "What happened to his brother?"

"Sadly, his brother was killed in a supervillain attack

decades ago, protecting him. I think...I thought that was that world's version of you. That you were dead there. I'm sorry."

"Sorry?" He was talking about Bobby. An adult Bobby, alive! I always suspected that, somehow, Bobby's death had been my fault. That I'd failed him. Now I knew that somewhere in the multiverse, there had been a Terry Markham who'd been a better brother than I. Who'd moved faster, been luckier. That incarnation of Terry had somehow managed to save his little brother, and I was intensely jealous. "There is nothing to be sorry about."

"I just told you that I'd visited a world where you'd died, decades earlier. Mortality can be a hard thing to face."

"If that had been an alternate version of me, then that version had died while sacrificing himself for a loved one. There's no sadness in that, and no regret."

The Red Ghost smiled softly, "I was right. You would make a good hero."

No. It was a bittersweet comfort, though, to know that some other Terry would have been worthy.

"What was his name, Paradigm's assistant?"

"His first name was Robert," the hero frowned, disgruntled and embarrassed. "Relaying the story of his brother's...of your death left him distraught, and he excused himself. Paradigm activated the interdimensional matter transport device before I could press further."

I glared suspiciously, though I knew that he could not sense it through my armor's faceless helm. None of my data trawling programs had reported any unusual searches for information about Terrance or Bobby Markham, and there'd been no hint of recognition when the Red Ghost had met my civilian guise face to face. Given all the surgical and genetic alterations that I'd performed to change my appearance, I supposed that the CEO the Red Ghost had met wouldn't at all have resembled the other-dimension laboratory technician.

Generally speaking, I was skeptical of good fortune; whenever I encountered some, it seemed that there was sure to be a price extracted at a later date. If the Red Ghost was being truthful then the timing of his travel represented an instant of remarkable serendipity. I made a note to prepare a bunker for when the other shoe dropped.

If he were dissembling, then he either knew or would soon discover the connection between Doctor Fid and Dr. Terrance Markham. In which case, I made a second note to prepare for war.

"Are you all right?" the Red Ghost asked.

"I'm simply...digesting the information," I replied. "For the record, I'm glad that you were able to make your safe return. Also, I have an idea for a single-use cross-dimensional travel device that you could carry on your person should this happen again."

"Already?" He looked amused.

"It will require testing and fine-tuning before I construct an easily-carried prototype," I said, defensively.

He shook his head, chuckling, "I didn't mean to start a competition between you and Professor Paradigm."

I coughed dismissively. A competition between Paradigm and myself would not be much of a competition; the white-lab-coat wearing poseur would build a beautiful motorcycle, and I would build something to make motorcycles obsolete. Still, the alternate-universe Professor Paradigm had managed to return my nemesis, so I supposed that he wasn't wholly incompetent.

"Oh," the Ghost added, his expression suddenly solemn. "There was something else that I wanted to talk to you about."

"Go on," I prompted, strangely relieved that the source of my foreboding would finally be revealed.

"I'm sure that you've noticed that Titan has been…increasingly erratic."

I cut my armor's external speakers to keep from broadcasting my disbelieving snort.

"He has made some ill-advised choices of late," I finally replied, dryly. Terry Markham still sported remnants of bruising from Titan's 'rescue'; medical nanites had long since repaired all the internal damage, but the external persisted. I'd forgotten how slowly unmodified humans heal.

"It had gotten to the point where I was considering leaving the Guardians and moving back to New York. I could not, in good conscience, support him if he continued to lead the team in such a reckless manner."

Cloner's close contact with the Red Ghost suddenly made more sense.

Selfishly, I didn't want him to leave. The Red Ghost was my nemesis, my rival, and I didn't want to share him with New York City's villains! Someday, Doctor Fid would return to his chosen career, and I'd expected that the Red Ghost would be present to oppose me. Even with my teleportation platform located in the bowels of Manhattan, it would be inconvenient if I needed to travel every time I wanted a proper opponent.

Beating upon the remaining Guardians would become very boring, very quickly.

"I wish that you would reconsider," I said finally. "Without your presence to keep Titan in check, his actions might endanger this city's citizenry."

"I came to the same conclusion," he nodded. "Instead, I reached out to the Guardians' insurance company and expressed my concerns. Titan was brought in for psychiatric and medical treatment."

"I suppose that more congratulations are in order then," I bowed my head respectfully. "I assume that you've been granted leadership of the Boston Guardians?"

"It's only temporary, I hope," he grimaced. "Titan was a good man, once."

"I suppose..."

"It is only in the last few years that his control has wavered," the hero asserted loyally. "When he's recovered, I'll gladly hand his title back."

Grudgingly, I had to admit that there was some truth to his claim; Titan had been relentlessly dedicated when he'd first come to Boston. His tactics had been more nuanced then, and the early battles genuinely challenging.

"You know that I have no love for the man," I told the Red Ghost, "but for your sake, I wish Titan a speedy recovery."

"It's funny you should say that," the hero smiled, and I

felt as though I should check my surroundings for a trap. "You see, the hospital discovered that Titan has Chronic Traumatic Encephalopathy; it is—as I'm sure you're aware—a degenerative brain disease usually associated with concussions and traumatic injuries. The medical community does not know of any successful treatment or cure."

I groaned softly, knowing what he was about to say next.

"Fortunately," the Red Ghost continued, still smiling in a manner that made me think of a cat that had successfully dipped a canary in cream, "I just so happen to know a former villain who has the technology to repair damaged neurons and glial scarring."

Damn the man.

CHAPTER TWELVE

"YOU SHOULD SAY 'NO'," WHISPER INSISTED, ONE hand absently petting at her puppy's neck.

I wasn't terribly surprised; while the little android was usually unfailingly generous and kind, she also had something of an unforgiving streak. The monstrous part of me thought that to be adorable, but the portion of my soul that remembered being Bobby's older brother knew better. She'd grow out of it, I was certain...and when she did, I'd rather that she not have unnecessary regrets.

"I haven't made my final decision," I replied, "but there's no harm in at least examining the medical records."

"Titan's mean!" The tired black dog's chin was resting in Whisper's lap, his tail wagging slowly. They'd stolen a corner of my study, quietly (and sometimes not-so-quietly) playing while I worked. A conference call with a supplier in Bangalore had been thoroughly—though pleasantly—derailed earlier in the evening.

"He is, yes." I quirked an uneven smile. "But maybe he won't be after I fix him."

"By 'fix' do you mean 'replace his brain with a baked

potato'?"

I tried to be stern but couldn't help but chortle. "Whisper..."

"He's mean, and he hurt my big brother," she pouted. "And a baked potato would be an improvement, so he should be grateful!"

"He's ill," I corrected. "Is Titan mean, or is his disease mean?"

"I don't know."

"Neither do I," I admitted. "I'm beginning to think that it may be worth the effort to find out for sure."

"Mm," Whisper said, not sounding convinced.

"If I move ahead with this procedure," I added, "then Titan owes me his mental health and his career. I can hold that over him forever."

And besides...I was reasonably certain that I'd be able to sneak a few rice-grain sized high explosives into Titan's skull for future entertainment purposes. I doubted that I'd ever choose to activate them, but their presence would still make me smile behind Doctor Fid's faceplate every time Titan interfered with one of my future plans.

🙞 🙞 🙞

The terrible music made my skull feel too tight: pounding bass and distorted vocals, with the volume raised past the point where the audio component's fidelity suffers. I can fix that. I have an idea for a slim, picture-frame-like speaker. A tympanic membrane overlaid with an ultrafine copper mesh, stretched taut within the frame. Electromagnets strategically placed...It will be able to exceed the volume of the current equipment and the midrange fidelity will be clearer. Crisper.

"I can fix that," I try to say. The slurred words sound alien, as though someone else is using my mouth to speak. "I k'n fiiz thaa."

"Jeez," someone laughs. "The kid is wasted!"

"Nah, he's fine." A strong hand claps me on the shoulder. My lab partner for o-chem, Randy; I helped him study and he invited me to meet his fraternity brothers. "You're fine, right? Here, drink this."

A red plastic cup is pressed into my hand and I swallow a mouthful of the sickly-sweet tea. It's warm in here, with the loud music and the dancing and the boisterous crowd. The air is thick with smoke, too, stinking of pine and skunk. It's too hot and the drink is cold, so I gulp it down greedily.

"Can fix thaa," I try again. "I k'n."

"Nothing's broke," another of Tony's frat brothers says. I was introduced to him earlier. James, from the rowing squad.

"Th' noise..."

"TURN IT UP!" James shouts over his shoulder, and the cheering drowns out my objection.

"Air," I gulp. "Please?"

"All right let's go."

I'm lifted and passed towards the partially-open window. It's embarrassing how easily they can manhandle me, but I'm grateful nonetheless. The cold breeze strikes my face like a punch and I'm giggling and I have no idea why.

"I got the kid another drink," someone says. Another plastic cup is in my hand.

I'm sitting with my back against the wall, and the not-really-music continues its assault. My chest aches and nausea spikes in time with the beat. A tympanic membrane overlaid with an ultrafine copper mesh. I want paper and a pen so that I can take notes, but it's too hot in here.

"Woah, hey, kid...Don't take off your shirt."

"Leave him alone, he can do whatever he wants. He's a graduate student, right?"

"Studen'", I agree.

"He's like, what, fifteen?"

"The teachers suck up to the little freak like he's Hawking or something."

I should've invited Michael to this party, even though the music is too loud and the world is kind of spinny and the room is too hot. He doesn't go to parties. This is the first party I've been invited to; I'm not sure that I like it, but it feels nice to be asked. A sudden tremor shoots up my spine, and the liquid in my plastic cup sloshes over the lip while I concentrate on breathing.

"Damned kid's gonna graduate before I do."

"Don't worry about it, man."

"Yeah. Yeah, okay. It's just that he's an arrogant little shit, y'know? Thinks he's better 'n the rest of us."

It's Randy speaking now, and I want to object, but I'm so tired. I lean back and close my eyes just for a moment...

And wake up to sunlight and the sound of mocking laughter.

I wince and struggle to sit up. The world swivels but I still blearily recognize Randy and three of his fraternity brothers' backs as they sprint away. They'd been carrying me, I realize.

Fresh cut grass presses against the bare skin of my legs and I stare stupidly at my socks. I know this place instinctively; I recognize the sounds, the echoes, the movement of the trees. The flavor of the air is familiar, even through the acidic taste of bile. Killian Court; the green field at the campus' center.

More giggles, hushed and embarrassed. A few students are making their way to the physics department entrance and I can feel the weight of their furtive glances as they pass by.

I hug my bare knees to my unclad chest and try not to cry.

❦ ❦ ❦

"So," I began in Doctor Fid's digitally modified voice, "If I were to agree, how would we proceed?"

"It's almost five AM," the Red Ghost—or rather, the hero's alter-ego Miguel Espinoza—groaned. Even over the phone's limited audio fidelity, I could hear him fumble his way to a seated position in his bed; from the sound, he'd put the call on speaker. "I promise that I will answer the phone if you call at a more reasonable hour."

"I wanted to speak at a time when I knew you to be alone."

"He's not alone," Elaine Goldman (Regrowth) commented sleepily. "But don't mind me...I'm still asleep right now. I must be dreaming this because no sane person would pick up the phone at five AM."

I laughed, but neither of the two heroes seemed to find the statement humorous.

"Should I call back in a few hours?" I asked, hesitantly.

"No," Miguel sighed. "We're awake now. What was the question again?"

"If I were to agree to help Titan, how would we proceed?"

"Doing what now?" Elaine asked.

"Repairing the neural damage from Titan's Chronic Traumatic Encephalopathy," I replied.

"Oh, my—I should have known! That poor man...I wasn't told about this!" she accused, and I heard Miguel yelp. Presumably, she'd poked at her lover in punishment. Regrowth would not, I was certain, be willing to assist in future tasks intended to harass Titan; she was the child of a psychiatrist and a neurosurgeon and her ingrained empathy towards those afflicted with a degenerative brain disease was sure to outstrip the personal enmity she felt towards her former team leader.

"His medical records are secret," Miguel defended. "I couldn't tell you. I'm sorry."

"But you told a supervillain?"

"I told a medical professional whose talents I was hoping to enlist," the Red Ghost corrected. "As the temporary commander for the Guardians, my medical proxy rights are limited....I couldn't say anything to you. But if a supervillain happened to reveal confidential information to you, then I can't be held responsible."

Which was likely why he'd put the conversation on speaker rather than simply slipping out of bed to take the call on his own.

"You're tricky," Elaine grumbled. "And I need coffee. I'm going to start a pot, I'll argue more later."

I waited until I'd heard the heroine leave before asking, "So, once more...How would we proceed?"

"You would need to document the procedure, then our insurers would create a panel to review your abstract and determine if an experimental procedure is warranted."

"That sounds quite time-consuming."

"Less so than you'd think. It's in the company's best interests to have Titan healthy and on the streets; they stand to lose a fair amount of money if he is forced to retire."

"A financial benefit?" I chuckled. "I was expecting an argument about the greater good for society as a whole."

"I'd be happy to make that argument, but they're an insurance company. To them, there is no greater good beyond numbers on a spreadsheet."

That was an unexpectedly cynical attitude, but I could empathize; my civilian persona had to deal with the board of directors' chairman, after all.

"And when the panel gives the go ahead?"

"Then you provide the data, instructions and all technology to a neutral third party, who will perform the actual procedure."

And so vanished my dream of hiding high explosives within Titan's gray matter. Ah, well. If worse came to worst, I could always simply spend the next few years re-concussing him.

"I'm not certain that I like the idea of giving my technology to a supposedly 'neutral' third party," I complained. "I can't think of many who would understand the nanotechnology well enough to react if something went wrong."

"Whoever is chosen would be able to contact you as an outside expert, if necessary."

"Even so...I'm beginning to think that it would be simpler to just kidnap him and perform the procedure myself."

"That's not amusing, Doctor."

"I wasn't joking. If the intent is to see Titan healed, an abduction and forced neurosurgery would be significantly more efficient."

"The goal is to see Titan healed and returned to his place as leader of the Guardians," Miguel replied, though his voice had gained that subtle intensity that I normally associated with his red-garbed alter-ego. "You may have gathered goodwill for your actions in Chile, but no one will trust him if you've gotten your gauntlets directly inside his skull. The team's backers will dismiss him in a heartbeat."

"Titan's return is your goal," I chuckled. "I'm less convinced."

"After Starnyx's death, you told me that you were trying to be less of a devil and I believed you...but Titan stood against you when you were still the Doctor Fid of old." I could hear the difference in his tone; Miguel was speaking wholly as the Red Ghost now. "He was a good man and I believe that he will be a good man again."

Titan had always been arrogant. He'd always been a bit of a bully, relying on his size and strength to intimidate many into submitting to his decisions. He had been flawed, even from the beginning! In a real sense, the former leader of the Guardians had been precisely the sort of hero that Doctor Fid had come out of retirement to punish.

If the purpose of punishment was to change Titan's behavior, then allowing his retirement and decline would be counterproductive; likewise, if the desired end was to dissuade other heroes from committing their own similar misdeeds. It was only if the objective were vengeance that such a fate could be justified.

On an emotional level, the idea of vengeance was appealing. On all other levels, however, I was forced to agree with the Red Ghost: objectively, the greater good for society would be better served if an emotionally stable Titan were returned to active duty.

"I'll begin work on my end," I said and then ended the call.

🙢 🙢 🙢

"You have the right to remain silent."

"You've gotta to believe me," Randy objects as the handcuffs were tightened. *"None of that is mine, I have no idea how any of that shit got in there!"*

"Anything you say can and will be used against you in a court of law," the uniformed officer continued, clearly exasperated. *"You have the right to an attorney. If you cannot afford an attorney, one will be provided for you."*

Synthesizing the moderately large amount of LSD that the police had found in a shoe-box under Randy's bed had taken almost a month. Twenty-nine days of pretending that I didn't remember what had happened that evening, that I didn't know that Randy and his friends had stripped me to my underwear and left me, barely conscious, in the courtyard at the center of MIT campus. Twenty-nine days of helping Randy with his homework and working as his lab partner.

Twenty-nine days of surreptitiously gathering fingerprints and samples of Randy's handwriting. Every little baggy is marked with damning fabricated evidence. As is the sales ledger that will eventually be found in his backpack.

Randy struggles to twist and face the policeman who is holding his wrists, "I don't do drugs! Ask anyone!"

A urine test will reveal trace amounts of marijuana, cocaine, LSD, and heroin. Randy always carries a water bottle with him when he shows up to class, and he made the mistake of leaving it untended while he was chatting up a pretty girl during o-chem lab.

"Do you understand the rights I just read to you?" The officer asks. "Maybe you still wanna talk?"

"I've never seen any of that stuff in my life," Randy repeats, eyes wide in confused panic. "It's not mine!"

The officer releases a long-suffering sigh, "Look, kid, we might be able to make a deal if you tell me who your supplier is."

"I'm being set up!"

"Okay then. Let's take a ride. C'mon."

Randy continues to complain as the officer walks him out, away from the surveillance equipment that I'd hidden in the room. I smile, satisfied, and set down my earphones. "Maybe you can't change the entire world," I remember my Dad telling me. "But you can fix your little part of it. Find a way to win."

One down, three to go.

❦ ❦ ❦

Clues found in the Ancient's painting led me to an old library where I found a nondescript ledger hidden under one of the stacks. On a purely academic level, the ledger was a remarkable find. A quick skim through the contents did not reveal any obvious clues; it was, however, an interesting read.

The Ancient may have been an irredeemable monster, but he'd been an academically rigorous monster who documented his thought processes, successes, and failures. While a few of the studies were horrifically depraved, the majority had been almost mundane: a curious (and completely amoral) mind exploring the intersections between magic and science. At the Ancient's last trial, the prosecuting attorney had submitted photo after photo of the ornate drainage systems in the villain's vivisection room; much less focus had been placed on the horticulture or materials science laboratories in the same compound.

Sadly, the ledger was incomplete; I would need to find the Ancient's hidden library to learn more. Fortunately, I had an idea where further information might be found.

❦ ❦ ❦

The previous night had been spent rescuing New Orleans families from flooding; hurricane season was still in full swing. I wasn't the only villain assisting in the rescue efforts this time—Don Voudon had recently escaped from prison again—and there were a half dozen heroes working as well. The Governor of Louisiana was loathe to spend money on repairing crumbling infrastructure, but at least he was quick to eliminate any legal obstacles that might prevent superpowered visitors from providing free support.

Blueshift had been there. I'd never actually met him before; by all accounts, he was deathly afraid of me. There were alternate dimension shenanigans involved and I'd never delved deep enough to uncover a complete explanation. From what I'd gathered, he was an immigrant from an alternate future dimension and the histories surrounding his world's Doctor Fid were sufficiently daunting that he avoided me like the plague.

But New Orleans was his town, and his Fidphobia was apparently insufficient to keep him from offering help to his people. When I offered assistance in towing a boat full of flood victims to safety, he'd been terse but polite.

And so it had been a tiring night, followed by a day at the office filled with interminably long teleconferences. I took a nap before donning the Mk 36b medium-duty armor and heading towards the night's target.

For more than a decade, Imperator Rex had been unchallenged in his reign over Chicago's underworld. The third most populous city in the United States and he'd been so fearsome that no other major supervillain dared operate in his territory. There were rumors that he was so powerful that even the mighty Valiant did not dare to face him.

That proved to be untrue; seven years ago, Imperator Rex attempted to rob the Smithsonian and Valiant had beat him like a drum. Imperator Rex had been entombed in a supermax prison ever since.

It always seemed odd that some villains were able to slip from their bonds with impunity, traipsing in and out of jail as though the walls and barbed wire were of no import, while others were caught and stayed caught. I would never have guessed that Imperator Rex would be in the latter category, but life sometimes had a way of surprising me in that fashion.

The Mk 36b bulleted through the night sky from Boston to Chicago to see if Whisper's hypothesis as to the location of the Chicago-based villain's lair was correct. Somewhere, Imperator Rex had hidden a significant trove of Ancient artifacts; I meant to find them.

I'd debated using the Mk 37 for this journey, but the fall of Imperator Rex must surely have precipitated the rise of other villains who'd have snapped up power and influence in the region, which in turn would have attracted professional heroes and unlicensed vigilantes to combat the chaos. The odds of Doctor Fid being drawn into an unexpected battle were greater in this city than in most others. A truce declared with one local authority might cause another to lash out; I had little understanding of the local politics and the likelihood that I might negotiate my way free of conflict was uncertain. Of all my functional armors, the Mk 36b was best suited for combat in an urban environment.

When in doubt, the capacity for violence would always

trump diplomatic skill.

Strangely, as I approached the city the only aerial surveillance that I was able to detect was the Federal Aviation Administration's radar systems. I couldn't help but feel embarrassed on the local heroes' and villains' behalf. Even without Imperator Rex's guidance, I would have expected at least some proactive warning measures! If they hadn't wanted to invest in one of Professor Paradigm's full-spectrum monitoring systems, they could at least have purchased a more generic model from Paragon Research. I'd long since developed technologies to overcome those devices, of course, but other lesser threats might have been identified.

Even with the middling stealth capabilities of the Mk 36b, I floated unchallenged into the city of Chicago. My target was downtown, in the Loop. I kept expecting a trap: for sirens to blare and floodlights to snap on. Sadly, there was no resistance from the city below. Just the normal traffic and activity one would expect from a city of this size.

Once upon a time, this region of Chicago had been perforated with a complex web of tunnels forty feet below the city, used to transport coal and other sundries. They were abandoned now, and some routes had been flooded. I dropped into the water with barely a splash and followed the Chicago River inland to the DuSable Bridge.

A block or so southwest, I knew, there was a truly wonderful steakhouse. In the guise of Terry Markham, I'd exploited their truly excellent ribeye to woo a potential employee away from the University of Chicago. Alas, they were surely closed by this hour. I was also reasonably certain that they did not have seats sufficiently reinforced to support the Mk 36b.

For now, I scanned the dark depths for an entrance. Supposedly, there was an open tunnel here that allowed water to flow south past the Field Museum. I'd never taken this path before and the records had been poorly kept, but the entryway was eventually located. Still, I detected no hint that my arrival had been noticed.

I drifted my way under Chicago.

The arched tunnels were oddly small—perhaps seven feet from floor to ceiling—and there were iron tracks still laid upon the ground. Pipes, now decayed, ran along the tunnel's apex. Whatever carts or trains had once been employed to carry mail and coal through these tunnels, they must have been low slung. Navigating these tunnels felt tight in the Mk 36b; the Mk 35 wouldn't have been able to fit at all.

The tunnel branched three ways, and then another three. I deployed microdrones to explore and map what passageways hadn't been closed off, but Whisper's research had already suggested which twists and turns I should follow. Deep beneath Grant Park, I began to slide west. I passed two tunnels that had been sealed by the city and later re-opened by criminals; the water level dropped as the tunnel followed an incline and I floated now through air. From here, the path was less obvious; effort had been made to disguise the route. If I'd had to rely solely upon flashlight and visible light, I would likely have been at a loss. Fortunately, my armor's built-in scanners were capable of far better. I located the hidden passageway and, still dripping, found myself at a locked door.

Beyond this door was a sub-basement originally connected to one of the city's most beautiful theaters. Construction (and graft) had seen entire sections of the building walled off and completely disconnected from the public's eye. According to Whisper's research, Chicago's most infamous supervillain had taken one such chamber to use as secure storage.

There were still no hints of surveillance or monitoring. This was simply unprofessional. A steel reinforced door and two admittedly-well-constructed deadbolt locks were all that stood between me and my goal. I could have simply battered my way through, but I picked the locks just to feel as though something useful had been accomplished.

And so I opened the door and was momentarily surprised when I stepped into what looked to be a living area; sonar and radar had both indicated an uninhabited storage locker. The loft-style room was well appointed with a cream carpeted floor, comfortable-looking furniture, a den, and a kitchen and dining area with hardwood flooring.

"I wasn't expecting company," said Imperator Rex as he closed the refrigerator door. "Would you like a drink, or should we proceed directly to your brutal murder?"

CHAPTER THIRTEEN

I'D BEEN OPERATING THE MK 36B IN BLACKOUT MODE to avoid detection while flying over Chicago, so I believed it possible that Imperator Rex hadn't recognized me. A thought was all that was needed for stars to fade into being within my armor and for the armor's seams to allow an angry red glow to escape. Instead of seeming a random armored infiltrator, I was now Doctor Fid.

The infamous Chicago crimelord, dressed casually in jeans and a black t-shirt, seemed unmoved. His only adornment appeared to be a gold chain from which hung a stylized charm shaped like a hammer.

"I'll take that drink," I said. "We should talk."

He grunted assent, re-opened the fridge and then tossed a can of cheap American beer to me. Behind my helm's faceplate, I grimaced; in the interests of diplomacy, however, I opened the can's top and extended a straw-like appendage from my forearm into the can.

Most of the truly strong superhumans had a tendency to look the part. Titan was nearly seven feet tall with a powerfully muscular build. Valiant was even taller and broader, a veritable god among men. Imperator Rex, on the other hand, was a slim man of average height and average build. He was an oddly unattractive fellow with dark hair and eyes, an olive complexion and a pencil-thin mustache; he was the sort of person who could disappear into a crowd, who could wander past in the grocery store line without attracting notice. Until one looked into his eyes. Imperator Rex had a quiet, malevolent confidence that was legitimately disturbing to behold. When he smiled, I imagined someone else's blood between his teeth.

"Thank you. If I'd known that you were out of prison," I began, "I would have called ahead."

"If you'd known that I was out of prison," he chuckled, grabbing a second can for himself but didn't open it, "then we would have had other difficulties, you 'n me."

"I hadn't heard even a rumor," I admired. "If your freedom was intended to be a secret, then you've succeeded admirably."

"You'll never hear a word. My people know how to keep their mouths shut." He bared his teeth in a self-satisfied smile.

If my hasty research was correct, then what he'd managed was truly remarkable; some unfortunate soul had been shipped off—and remained—in the black site prison, but that person could not be the supervillain before me. Imperator Rex had never set a foot in jail nor had he allowed a hint of this information to become public knowledge. Presumably, he'd lurked in the shadows and maintained an iron grip on his criminal empire this entire time.

As best as I could determine, the only opportunity for a body-double switch had been directly after the trial. Whoever was impersonating Imperator Rex must have been incredibly loyal to have upheld the ruse for so long.

"Impressive," I said, and he looked smug.

"So. Fid. Whatcha want to talk about?"

Reluctantly, I consumed a mouthful of my beer. "I would like to negotiate access to a few artifacts that I believe to be in your possession."

"You came here to steal from me, then. That's good," he smirked. "I thought you might be thinkin' of takin' me back in."

"I came here to look, not take," I lied. "And I'm not out to arrest anyone."

"Yeah? The talk shows seem to think that you oughta add a white cape to that getup."

"I'm no hero," I growled, reflexively triggering the command that increased the red glow that seeped from the junctions of my armor. The angry glare boiled forth, trailing wisps of plasma like smoke. "I am Doctor Fid!"

"And I'm unimpressed." He popped the tab on his beer and took a swig. "You're in my home. Back the hell off."

I lowered the intensity of my armor's display. "My apologies. I didn't intend any offense."

"Yeah. Cause offending me 'd be stupid, and I never got the impression that you were stupid." Again, he grinned viciously. "Crazy, maybe, but not stupid."

"There's no need for name-calling," I replied softly, gesturing with both hands to indicate calm. "I'm here to do business."

"Ok, sure. Sure, let's go with that." He took another swallow from his can. "You wanted to look at some stuff I own? Which stuff?"

"I wish to examine the artworks once owned by the Ancient."

"Huh." He set his can down on the kitchen counter. "You chasing fairy tales, now?"

"I am very good at puzzles and I have no interest in the Ancient's lost treasure. All I want is his library." Both of us knew that the Ancient's scavenger hunt was no fairy tale; I'd found hints already, and the answers might be found in objects that Imperator Rex had gathered years before. "If you let me inspect your collection, then I will give you the lion's share of whatever spoils I uncover."

"That sounds like a good deal," Imperator Rex said, stretching slowly. "But I'm goin' to have to decline."

I tilted my head, confused. "If you wish some payment up front, I'm certain that we can come to an accord."

"I have a better idea," he smiled. "How about this? You give me everything you've found, you try 'n convince me that you're not gonna tell anyone you saw me, 'n if you do a good job maybe I let you get the hell outa my city."

"That doesn't seem like an equitable arrangement." I was more surprised than angry; when last we'd met, he'd treated me like a respected peer. For a brief moment, I wondered if this were the impostor and the true Imperator Rex was imprisoned after all...but no. This man's maddening, predatory smirk could not have been duplicated.

"There's no 'equal' here," Imperator Rex spat, then visibly reigned his temper. "Here's the thing: I've been watching the news, 'n you've been saving people left 'n right 'n it started with a kid. So I figure, whoever's inside that star-covered tin can has a family now, 'n you've gone soft. No shame in that; it happened to some of my best men. But those guys don't work for me no more, 'n they definitely don't set terms."

"I showed up unannounced, and I think that we've gotten off on the wrong foot," I gritted out between clenched teeth. Fortunately, the Mk 36b's vocoder limited how much anger was transmitted aloud. "But I should warn you-"

"Naw, Fid, I'm warnin' you. You give me what I want, or maybe I find your family 'n do to them what I did to Governor Culver's!"

I stilled. "Is that your final offer?"

"Damned right," he replied, smiling as though he knew what was about to happen.

I summoned my scepter and the red gem at its handle blazed like a dying sun...but Imperator Rex was already moving, impossibly fast, and I wasn't in position to block his first punch. A flash of yellow-white energy erupted from his fist at the moment of impact on my solar plexus and I was blown backwards with enough force that the poured-concrete-and-rebar wall disintegrated, and bedrock fractured against the Mk 36b's back. I responded with a blast of kinetic energy aimed from my scepter; the superpowered gangster was driven to one knee but laughed mockingly nonetheless.

Even if I managed to guide this battle into the tunnels,

there were only forty feet of solid stone protecting the city above. Real estate values in downtown Chicago, I thought, were about to become volatile.

❧ ❧ ❧

From: Cherenkov
To: BlueEyedGirl
Subject: Serious question

Hey, I've been thinking…You said your brother isn't a hero. Is he some sort of government agent? Like, secret James Bond stuff?

From: BlueEyedGirl
To: Cherenkov
Subject: Re: Serious question

I don't want to answer any questions about that. Oh! I saw that you and Exbow stopped a robbery on your last patrol. Congratulations! No video this time, though. :(

From: Cherenkov
To: BlueEyedGirl
Subject: Re: Re: Serious question

Yeah, some jerks were holding up a liquor store while we were right outside. I miss the cameradrone too, but Majestic says I can't bring it. :/ Look, I'm not trying to break your brother's cover, I just need some help. He's with the Department of Metahuman Affairs, right?

From: BlueEyedGirl
To: Cherenkov
Subject: Re: Re: Re: Serious question

What sort of help do you need?

From: Cherenkov
To: BlueEyedGirl
Subject: Re: Re: Re: Re: Serious question

Can he find out who MID-01483775-22 is?

From: BlueEyedGirl
To: Cherenkov
Subject: Re: Re: Re: Re: Re: Serious question

That's Cloner's original license number from before he retired; he has a new ID now. What's going on?

```
From: Cherenkov
To: BlueEyedGirl
Subject: Re: Re: Re: Re: Re: Re: Serious question

I think I'm in trouble.
```

❦ ❦ ❦

There was blood in my mouth, coppery and sweet; even through the orichalcum breastplate, I'd felt that first blow. Honestly, I was impressed! I'd studied footage of Imperator Rex's past fights, but this was the first time that we'd come to blows. The forces involved were greater even than I'd anticipated, though I'd now readied myself. Balanced and stable, I began work recalibrating my armor's inertial dampening field.

Imperator Rex darted forward—arm cocked for a haymaker—and I simply shot the ground out from under him with a blast from my scepter; he stumbled forward into a straight left punch. It was a solid hit, delivered with enough force that it might have stopped a moving car. Glassware in the kitchen shattered from the shockwave alone, yet the slim villain rocked back—unhurt. I managed to get in another quick jab before he recovered, and he retaliated by grabbing my wrist and swinging me once more into the wall, face-first. Reflexively, I dismissed my scepter back into its subspace storage so that both my hands were now free.

The physics of this were all wrong; my opponent lacked

the mass necessary to be the fulcrum for such a move. For that matter, the speed with which he rocketed forward was greater than could have been managed if it were mere friction that held his feet to the ground. There were other forces at work, forces that I hadn't accounted for. My microdrones were ordered to take careful readings; I'd failed to accurately map his powers and was now paying the price.

No matter. Imperator Rex had failed to understand the resiliency of the Mk 36b, as well as that of the man within. In the moment after my faceplate struck stone, he relaxed his grip on my wrist.

I took advantage, triggering my flight systems to right myself and triggered a pre-programmed Wing-Tsun centerline punch and a simultaneous low front-kick to my opponent's knee. The experienced brawler negated the first attack but not the latter, and I capitalized by transitioning into a hooking blow to his floating ribs when he dropped his guard.

Imperator Rex darted back so quickly that he may as well have teleported.

I didn't bother re-summoning my scepter; the blasters built into the MK 36b weren't as powerful, but they were fast. I alternated plasma bolts from each hand, grand flashes of heat and light that crashed over Imperator Rex like a tidal wave. He raised both hands in a boxing guard to protect his face, leaning into the onslaught. The room behind him glowed with heat, fire spreading in a roar, but the Chicago-based supervillain just spat some blood from his lips and returned to the offensive.

I had, at least, managed to wipe that smug smile from his lips. He looked furious.

The Mk 36b's defenses were not as powerful as those of the Mk 35 heavy-combat armor, but I knew that I could take a fairly significant pounding. When Imperator Rex closed to throw immensely powerful hooks, I ignored him and chose instead to spray the living area with massive concussive blasts. His television? Vaporized. The kitchen? Rendered into shrapnel. I laughed and he cursed, his punches getting more and more wild.

I re-summoned the scepter and pressed the pommel against his chest. Imperator Rex had just enough time to widen his eyes before a massive kinetic-energy blast sparked and blew him up into the ceiling. When he struck bedrock, the earth shook.

❧ ❧ ❧

```
From: BlueEyedGirl
To: Cherenkov
Subject: Trouble?

Oh no! What's going on? How can I help?
```

```
From: Cherenkov
To: BlueEyedGirl
Subject: Re: Trouble?
```

I was updating some of my paperwork for my hero licensing thing, and I noticed some papers I didn't recognize. They got tossed in my folder because Cloner's old number was invalid, I guess. It was Cloner's memo, when he recommended me to Junior Shield, but it's not the memo that I saw. This is crazy, I have to get out of here. I'll send another message when I get home.

From: BlueEyedGirl
To: Cherenkov
Subject: Re: Re: Trouble?

Ok, I'll be waiting!

From: Cherenkov
To: BlueEyedGirl
Subject: Re: Re: Re: Trouble?

I think Cloner is involved in something shady, and I think he's planning on using me as part of his plan. I can't really make sense of this. If I get this to your brother, can he have the D.M.A. investigate? Maybe it's nothing, I don't know. But this is really freaking me out.

```
From: BlueEyedGirl
To: Cherenkov
Subject: Re: Re: Re: Re: Trouble?

Um. Ok, send me what you have. I'll make sure my
brother looks into this.
```

※ ※ ※

Both of us were hurting; fortunately, my armors all include a plethora of onboard medications, and I could use my neural tap to completely turn off most forms of physical pain. The sheer volume of medical alerts popping up, however, was daunting. Internal bleeding, broken ribs, muscle damage, concussion...my medical nanites were, once more, going to be working overtime after I finished punishing Imperator Rex for his hubris.

"Surrender," I growled. "I'll take the Ancient's artifacts, but you can keep your city and your miserable life."

"Screw you, tin man," he panted, grinning maliciously. "I'm just getting warmed up."

We traded blows quickly and strategically, a high-speed pugilistic chess-match. Imperator Rex was more physically powerful than I'd expected and had kept up his skills remarkably well for a man who'd been in hiding for so long. It was no wonder that he'd earned so terrifying a reputation; he would likely have been victorious over the Doctor Fid of seven years earlier. This battle, however, had already been decided. He was tiring, and the Mk 36b had sufficient power to continue for days. Furthermore, my combat algorithms had been studying his fighting style. If I wished, I could take a nap and let my armor's programming fight with my body as a passenger without any loss in effectiveness. The end result was inevitable.

Despite my initial worries that we would turn downtown Chicago into a warzone, the battle had remained primarily contained in the main chamber and the into the tunnels; Imperator Rex hadn't tried to bring the fight to the surface lest his freedom be revealed to the public. I was happy to oblige; my ability to fly in the open air might have been advantageous, but maintaining plausible deniability was an issue for me as well. And so, in narrow confines, we battered each other and left shattered stone in our wake.

"Time has passed you by," I mocked. "It's sad to see that you've come to this. You've spent far, far too long as shadow king of your little empire."

"And you've spent too long playing hero," he sneered. "You've forgotten the first rule about fightin' like a villain."

"And what might that be?" I asked, summoning my scepter to my hand once more.

"If the game ain't playing out the way you want," he grinned and tore the charm from his necklace, "cheat!"

A massive warhammer of wrought iron and aged ashwood appeared in his hands; a hero named Viking had borne such a weapon for a brief career with the California-based Paragons. From what information I'd hacked from their records, the hammer granted a massive increase in strength and energy to the wielder in exchange for a portion of the wielder's life. Imperator Rex would age a year for every minute that this battle continued...however long that turned out to be.

He shot forward and I brought up my scepter to deflect his swing, to no avail. The scepter's haft—framed in orichalcum and reinforced with a structural integrity field—fractured in my hand; shards sprayed around me, embedding into solid stone as easily as if the walls were made of wet clay. I reflexively retreated half a step, which was the only thing that saved my life when his backhand swing sliced through the air where my head had been only a fraction of a second earlier.

This fight, I realized with a sinking feeling in the pit of my stomach, could have been over before Imperator Rex had aged a month.

I fled deeper into the tunnels and Imperator Rex tore after me, mad laughter trailing in his wake.

He swung at me twice more, gouging great divots out of the tunnel walls when I successfully dodged. There would be no surviving a direct hit. Even if the thicker orichalcum breastplate withstood the damage, the Mk 36b's inertial dampening system was insufficient and I would be shaken into paste within the armor. My only advantage was the darkness and that microdrones had mapped this section of tunnel well enough that I could keep ahead of the monstrously strong, hammer swinging supervillain.

Every strike that missed me demolished a section of wall. The shockwaves were visible, gravel and debris quaking along the tunnel floor, and no doubt shook the the city forty feet above. And then we came to a dead end and he paused, savoring the moment.

"You had a good run, tin man," he gloated, "but it ends now. You shouldn't have come to my town."

This was the villain who had terrified a nation. This, now, was the Imperator Rex of old. But I was Doctor Fid, and he had me trapped exactly where I wanted him.

"And you shouldn't have said anything about my family," I growled in return.

He smirked and drew back the great warhammer for one final blow, but I was faster: with both hands, I aimed a massive kinetic-energy blast at the wall to his left. For a moment he looked amused that I had missed, and I thought that I'd made a mistake in my calculations. And then the dam cracked, and Lake Michigan flooded into the tunnel in an icy deluge. The wall of water struck with the force of an oncoming train and the inevitability of an avalanche.

I hadn't forgotten the first rule, after all.

Surprise cost him his grip on his glowing hammer and also his only source of light; I dimmed my armor and, navigating by sonar, shot forward to catch his ankle and keep him from running. We were flushed into a second chamber and in a fraction of a second, we were both of us submerged. The Mk 36b had an enclosed recirculating air supply that could survive the vacuum of space. Imperator Rex was not so lucky.

From the moment our battle had begun, I'd been studying his power; Imperator Rex was a powerhouse who was physically stronger even than Titan, but strength alone hadn't been able to explain the force of his blows nor the speed with which he moved. There'd been a telekinetic aspect to his metahuman abilities, a kinetic energy multiplying field limited to affect only the surface of a solid object that he touched. With a punch, he could thrust more power into the blow at the moment of impact. When he ran, he could push off the ground with more force than raw strength would allow.

Floating in blackness, however, there was no direct contact with a solid surface for him to influence.

He struggled and kicked, a flailing ogre with monstrous strength. I let him go, then caught him again and spun him in place. According to my research, many people drown only feet from the water's surface because they become disoriented and swim in the wrong direction. I witnessed that now. The frantic supervillain's fingers found the floor and he dug at it, carving out handfuls of concrete and stone in search of air. In that cold inky blackness, I floated just out of his reach, poking and tugging to keep Imperator Rex disoriented as his last breath slowly deserted him.

He'd fought the most powerful heroes in human history and lived to tell the tale. He'd clawed his way into legend, earned respect akin to that of a monarch among criminals. For a brief, shining moment he'd thought that he'd managed to bring low even the infamous Doctor Fid! And in an instant, the light faded. He was blind and helpless, eyes wide and lips pulled back in a panicked, desperate snarl.

He could sense my eyes upon him, I was sure. He knew that I was right there—right out of reach—but he didn't beg; it wasn't in his nature. To the very end, Imperator Rex swung punches at nothing, grasped at empty water, fought for every last second.

Until finally...horribly...he went still.

I could have saved him, I knew. I could have grabbed him and cruised back to a clear section of tunnel and performed CPR. Weakened and beaten, he wouldn't have been able to resist as I dragged him to the appropriate authorities. The Red Ghost would smile approvingly, and (once his treatment had been successful) even Titan would grudgingly offer his respect. I could be a hero in truth instead of play acting. The option was painfully tempting; Bobby's spirit would finally have been able to look down upon his big brother with pride.

But Doctor Fid wasn't a hero. Doctor Fid wasn't worthy.

I weighed the corpse down with a massive hunk of concrete, then navigated my way back through the dark, silent tunnels to take ownership of Imperator Rex's hoard before flooding damaged any of my plunder.

CHAPTER FOURTEEN

"THIS JUST IN," THE NEWS PROGRAM ANCHOR graveled; he was one of the old guard, a grizzled reporter who'd been associated with the network for so long that his name was synonymous with the nightly news. "One of Chicago's oldest and most historic theaters has been closed due to damage to its foundation, possibly related to the city's flooded access tunnels. The investigation continues…"

I remembered watching this reporter, long ago, reporting on a hostage situation in South America. He took risks to get dramatic camera angles as he explained the situation, but his voice was serious and calming. When the shooting had begun, he'd continued his report—giving an honest blow-by-blow report as soldiers rushed the terrorist's stronghold. With earnest fervor, he'd relayed the dangers that the hostages faced and the heroism of the rescuers. He'd projected a bearing of confidence throughout the entire ordeal, an aura of absolute certainty that the soldiers were performing the right actions for the right reasons. When the first rescuees were escorted from the airport, it had felt like a triumph of righteousness over the forces of evil.

There were still hints of that remembered gravitas in the anchor's voice, but there was now a disappointing practiced aspect to his delivery. I suspected that he would display the same solemn fervor when delivering a pleasant weather report as he would when announcing a political assassination.

The damage to Chicago's Loop district had been less severe than I'd worried; after the Great Chicago Flood a few decades back, floodgates and water-tight hatches had been installed and updated. A small handful of businesses had flooded basements or had power interrupted but the effects had not been widespread. Imperator Rex's body had yet to be discovered, so this was being reported as a casualty-free incident.

"It's still unknown what caused this near-catastrophe," the news anchor intoned, "but authorities have confirmed that there is evidence of metahuman involvement. The investigation continues, leaving the city to wonder if this was a one-time event or if it was merely the first stage in some greater plo-".

I grumbled in soft complaint and turned off the television. Water damage had destroyed much of the evidence, but the destruction Imperator Rex had wrought had been severe enough to leave indelible signs. The clues would be followed, and the body found within days.

There was no surviving evidence that would link the death to Doctor Fid, I was reasonably certain. Even so...the world would discover that a murder had occurred.

I'd spent four hours floating in a nutrient bath while my

medical nanites performed their repairs, but I was not yet ready to rest. In the kitchen, I gathered up a few essentials for a long night of research at one of my remote laboratories: fruit, caffeine-laden sodas, frozen pizza; in silence, I packed it all in a small bag.

"You're leaving?" Whisper asked, quietly. I hadn't heard her approach.

"Just for the night," I forced a comforting smile. "You and Nyx have the house to yourselves."

"Nyx will miss you," she murmured, blue-glowing eyes averted towards the ground. "You know, the first few weeks are important when socializing a puppy to a new environment."

"I'll be back in the morning," I said, and inwardly winced when part of me wondered if I was lying.

"You have work tomorrow." The delicate little android girl bent to stroke at her black furred companion's back. "We won't see you for long."

Nyx was looking up at me, wagging nervously with tail held low. What did she see in me, I wondered? Did she have some strange canine ability to sense that I was a killer? Could she smell the imaginary blood on my hands?

I looked away, searching the cupboard for canned chili to add to my bag. "It's only one night, Whisper. You'll be fine."

"Mm," she shook her head. "It's not fine. There's things going on with Cherenkov, with Cloner. I need to tell you-"

"Not tonight!" I closed the cabinet a bit louder than I'd intended; my ward/adopted sister and her dog both flinched. "I just…I need to get out of the house."

"We could come with you," Whisper said in a rush. "We could go to the cabin in Maine! It's pretty there, and quiet!"

"Sweetheart, I want-" My voice cracked, and I grimaced. "I should be alone."

"You're wrong," she insisted, tremulously. "I was alone for years after my Father died. It was terrible."

She sounded as though she wanted to cry, but synthetic tear ducts hadn't been designed into her current body; I'd hoped that she'd never need them. My chest hurt and a new wave of guilt flushed over me and I dared not look at her directly.

"I'm sorry," I told her. "You didn't deserve that."

"Neither do you."

You're wrong, I sent, unable to speak aloud; she crossed the room to try and embrace me, but I flinched away and she flooded heartbreak to me over the neural link. I broke and sobbed for the both of us, scooping her up into a hug.

"I don't understand," she whimpered unsteadily against my shoulder, "You always say that you're a bad man. Why are you so broken up about doing a bad thing to another bad man? You've done other bad things and I still got hugs."

"Oh, sweetheart...I'm not guilty over what I did to Imperator Rex," I said, though I probably should be—I generally disapprove of torture and I could have found a cleaner way to end him. "But that's not why I'm-why I'm so upset."

"What, then?"

"Because on my way back from Chicago, I happened across an overturned transport vehicle and helped contain a dangerous chemical leak. I saved six people."

"But that's a heroic thing!"

"Yes," I nodded. "And I was a murderer pretending to be a hero. Just like Peregrine. Just like Sphinx. *Just like Bronze.*"

"...oh."

"I don't think I can maintain the charade any longer," I set Whisper back down and Nyx licked at her ankles, tail lashing now in hopeful play. "It seemed like a fun game at the beginning, but now...it feels too raw."

"It feels too real," my android sister amended softly. "So stop pretending. Be an actual hero."

"Being a hero is about more than just doing good things," I shook my head sadly. "People look up to heroes, they worship them; real heroes are worthy role-models. I can—have—saved entire planets, but it doesn't change what I am."

"Nothing can change what you *were*," Whisper corrected sagely. "What you want to be tomorrow? That, you get to choose."

I snorted incredulously, "Okay, clever girl, be honest: how many self-help books have you read since this conversation started?"

"A lot," she replied shyly. "But it's true, I think. The Red Ghost said you'd be a good hero."

"The Red Ghost is a fine man, but he doesn't know me as well as he thinks he does. The old Doctor Fid—the monstrous Fid—still lives inside my head. I let it out to fight Imperator Rex."

"And then you chained him back up as soon as he wasn't needed anymore." The little android knelt down to pet Nyx, who'd flopped out on top of one of her feet. She looked up at me with a sad smile, "Bobby thought you'd be a good hero."

"...That's a low blow, Whisper."

"I think you'd be a good hero, too."

I couldn't accept that—not so easily, so painlessly. The monster still strained at its bindings, and the feeling of numb acceptance as I watched Imperator Rex's struggles fade was still too fresh in my mind. I wasn't ready to believe that the choice Whisper wanted of me was one that I could make.

I unpacked my bag and stayed the night at home with family. Whatever I was, whoever I'd be...I wasn't alone.

※ ※ ※

Some think it odd that I, as the CEO of a growing biotech company, do not employ an executive assistant. I handle most of my organizational tasks myself, sort through my own documents and compile my own responses. When one has a surgically-installed neural link connected via quantum-tunnel to a vast farm of supercomputers designed specifically to respond to one's own mental commands, performing such work didn't take very much time at all. Since my employees were unaware of said neural link, however, they assumed that I was hard at work whenever my office door was closed.

My direct reports' employees did, however, often fill in for certain tasks on their own recognizance. As such, it was no surprise when my CTO's assistant knocked on my door. "Dr. Markham? Your three o'clock is here."

"Send him in," I replied, feigning calm.

And in strolled the Red Ghost, somehow relaxed and dignified even when wearing his crimson costume in a corporate environment.

On the off chance that he wasn't here to reveal my secret identity and have me arrested, I stepped around my desk to shake his hand. "Welcome!"

"Thank you," he grinned, and I saw no duplicity in his eyes. "I'm glad to see that you're recovering well."

"I've been getting a lot of fresh air lately," I replied. "My ward got a puppy, and that means more time out in the sun watching them play. It's been good for me, I think."

"I imagine it would be."

"While it's appreciated, I doubt that you came here simply to talk of my recovery." I returned to my own seat and waved for him to take the chair opposite me. He did, lifting his long cloak to drape over the back of the chair in a well-practiced motion. "It was my understanding that Titan pled no contest. Has that changed?"

"Not at all. No, I'm here on other business."

"Well, then...What can I do for you?"

"That is a bit of a long story," the Hispanic man sighed, "and I'd like to start by saying that this is not intended to affect your suit at all. That having been said...it has recently been revealed that Titan suffers from a medical condition that has affected his behavior, and certainly influenced the decisions he made while mishandling your rescue."

"I'm...sorry to hear that?"

"He's been diagnosed with Chronic Traumatic Encephalopathy; are you familiar with the condition?"

"Vaguely. It's a degenerative brain disease, usually associated with repeated head trauma. It used to be called 'Boxer's Dementia'?"

"Yes." Behind his mask, the Red Ghost's eyes closed in sympathy for the plight of his former team leader. I supposed that most heroes must fear such an illness; it isn't a safe profession that they've chosen for themselves.

Generally speaking, villains didn't worry about disease affecting their later years; their retirement plans usually involved incarceration or a shallow grave.

"The man has my sympathies, and I'll talk to my lawyer about dropping the lawsuit. If Titan is seeking treatment, then I'm satisfied."

"Titan's treatment is why I am here," the Ghost's expression turned serious. "Your company produces medical nanotechnology that is currently being applied towards inoperable cancers."

"Yes," I replied, chest puffing with a level of pride appropriate for a CEO's appreciation for his company's accomplishments. "...but I'm afraid that we're years away from being able to repair neurological issues."

Inside, I was practically slavering with anticipation; I'd begun to formulate a hypothesis as to why the Red Ghost was here, and if I was correct then the possibilities were marvelous.

"As it happens, a third party has already performed the research and programmed an appropriate regimen."

"That's not possible."

"I'm afraid that it is," he smiled apologetically. "When

Doctor Fid robbed your facility last year, he apparently escaped with samples of your nanotechnology. And according to the terms of the Technological Repatriation Act, your company has legal claim to any improvements made by a criminal third party."

"The Guardians captured some of Doctor Fid's Technology? That's wonderful!"

"We've managed to acquire it, yes." The Red Ghost shifted in his seat, looking slightly uncomfortable at having to let even the minor white lie of omission slip past. Heh. "I know that this is an imposition, but I would ask that you please have your team evaluate the procedures and provide a professional opinion as to whether or not this treatment could help improve Titan's medical condition."

Once upon a time, when I was very young, my Dad bought me a miniature lathe that was normally used for machining model railroad parts. I remembered touching the box and feeling the most remarkable sense of elation at the possibilities that lay before me. Before the wrapping was even opened, I had dozens of projects swirling through my mind. The Red Ghost's request elicited that same giddy feeling of hope and wonder.

"It wouldn't just help Titan; if this technology is what you say it is, it will help hundreds every month. What you're offering will save us years' worth of research and development." I tilted my head and hopefully hid my childish joy, "...and superheroes are, in certain circumstances, eligible for emergency treatments that bypass FDA and medical board evaluations. You want us to perform the treatment as well, don't you?"

"If you are willing."

"We'll need a contract limiting liability and also allowing us to use this for marketing purposes." I forced an apologetic frown, "I know it sounds mercenary, but it will help us cut through red tape later."

"That sounds reasonable; I'll have the lawyers begin their work immediately."

"Then I think that we have a deal." I stood up again to shake the Red Ghost's hand. "I'll put together a team and oversee their progress personally!"

Perhaps I'd get the opportunity to install those micro-explosive charges within Titan's skull after all.

※ ※ ※

Um. Terry? Whisper sent. **Are you busy?**

Yes, I replied mentally. **But I can take a break.**

I was in my ocean-floor manufacturing facility designing prototypes for what would (I hoped) eventually become the Mk 38 armor. The late and unlamented Imperator Rex had left my medium-duty suit on its last legs; it would be easier to build a new version from scratch than it would be to repair the Mk 36b.

And so, the Mk 38 was slowly taking shape with orichalcum plates recycled from its predecessor. Recent brawls had reinforced the lesson that I dared not rest upon my laurels; with refined forcefields and upgraded inertial-dampening technology, the new suit would come close to equaling the defensive capabilities of the much-larger heavy-combat armor.

I started organizing and putting away my tools; the teleport platforms operated silently, but an alert was transmitted to my neural link whenever the teleport grid was in use. Whisper had come to join me. I heard her approach before I saw her; Judging from the excited sound of paws scrabbling on concrete, I guessed that she'd brought Nyx with her.

"Hey sweetheart," I called. "I'm almost done cleaning up!"

"Mm!" she replied, though she sounded distracted. The hallway had a viewing wall of integrity-field-enhanced twelve-inch thick plexiglass; even this deep, there was often enough aquatic life visible to attract my ward's attention. This location—hidden under a rock outcropping within a fissure—had been chosen more for security than for aesthetics. Over the years, the factory had expanded and burrowed into the surrounding walls, with automatons and production lines operating in quiet darkness. Still, there was a stark beauty to the environment and I'd added the viewing port even before Whisper had entered into my life. Her fascination with fish and other aquatic life had made visitations here a more regular occurrence.

This was, however, the first time that a puppy had been brought along. I hastily programmed my security drones to make sure that Nyx didn't wander too close to unsafe machinery. For now, the canine seemed quite content to follow at his android mistress' ankles; still, it would be better to be safe than sorry.

"I didn't mean to interrupt," Whisper apologized as she entered my preferred lab-space. "It could've waited."

"It's fine," I smiled, "I'm waiting on simulations anyway. What did you need?"

"Umm...Do you know how I used to spend time talking to Cherenkov online?"

"And you told him how to find Doctor Fid when I was on my way back from Lassiter's Den." I chuckled. "Which led to me putting the poor boy into a hospital. Yes, I do recall."

"Well, I've kept in touch with him." Whisper lowered her eyes bashfully. "I know he's a hero, but he's my friend."

"That's fine, Whisper." I reached down to let a black-furred puppy sniff at my fingers. "You're being careful that your communication is untraceable?"

"Mm!" She smiled proudly. "I sneaked a tiny virus into his systems; he thinks he's reading his real forum page but it's actually an encrypted simulation with my comments added in. Nothing I say is actually stored on his server."

"Clever girl," I praised, and she preened happily. "Just be careful about what you say to him, is all."

"Yeah, about that..."

I closed my eyes and started calculating pi in my head to calm my initial reaction. "Go on."

"It's not that bad!" she said defensively. "I just, um, was trying to be helpful since he's with the Junior Shield, and now he thinks that my big brother works for the Department of Metahuman Affairs."

"Interesting." That was, I decided, far more innocuous

than many of my initial fear-spawned scenarios. Given that the little android had felt compelled to join me in the underwater lab and speak in person, I was waiting for the second shoe to drop.

"He came to me with something that he thinks that the D.M.A. should be investigating," she said in a rush. "I told him you'd look into it."

That…did not sound as though it was likely to result in a catastrophic outcome. I exhaled slowly, relieved.

"I'd be happy to investigate something for your friend," I told her. "I have the means to access the D.M.A. database; if he requires an official response, I can insert records into their pipeline."

"Really?" she perked up. "Cuboid designed their firewalls, I haven't been able to get in."

"I had one of my false identities added to the employee rolls decades ago," I chuckled. "Sometimes, bribery works better than vulnerability testing."

She pouted, "That's cheating!"

"I just opened a route for you to access my fake-employee's virtual private network. You can use that to get into the D.M.A. main network."

"Ooooh." Her glowing blue eyes seemed to lose focus for a moment as she bent the majority of her attention towards conquering a new domain. "Thank you!"

"Be careful," I warned, still smiling indulgently. "That's my oldest false ID, I'd prefer if it wasn't compromised."

She rewarded me by rolling her eyes and huffing indignantly, so I lifted a wagging puppy to lick at her nose and she exploded into giggles. I set Nyx in her arms and her grin became incandescent. Serious thoughts were abandoned, and we adjourned to watch the ocean through the hallway's viewing port.

"So, what did your friend need for me to investigate?" I eventually remembered to ask.

"Oh! I can take care of it now that I can get into the D.M.A." She looked surprised and embarrassed. "It's, um, nothing."

For a creature who could near-instantaneously consume every book on prevarication that had ever been published, Whisper was an adorably poor liar. She'd grow out of that eventually, I knew; her emotional developmental algorithms were remarkably complex.

"Why don't you tell me about it anyway? Maybe I can help," I prodded gently, then frowned when she looked ready to prevaricate further.

"Okay," she relented. "Some of Cloner's paperwork accidentally got mixed up with Cherenkov's. It was coded, but Corey figured out some of it and kind-of panicked. He thought Cloner brought him into the Junior Shield on false pretenses and was planning something illegal."

"Interesting," I said, and Whisper made the files available to me via neural link; I scanned through them quickly. "I take it that Cherenkov's assumption was incorrect?"

"Mm. Cherenkov misunderstood some of the coded message and thought Cloner was doing something bad, but he had it backwards," Whisper said mournfully. "Cloner thinks Cherenkov is leaking information to Doctor Fid and it's all my fault."

"...because you've been relaying information to me that you received from him." I pursed my lips grimly. If Cloner had suspected a data breach, isolating the source would have been a relatively simple matter. He could easily have revealed different stories to different people and then waited to see how Doctor Fid reacted.

And I'd jumped through the hoops Cloner had set up like a well-trained performing animal. The meeting with Cloner at Lassiter's Den had certainly been by design; he'd told me that he suspected a hack of his internal notification system, but he'd obviously been able to isolate the leak further to implicate the unfortunate Cherenkov.

More and more, I found myself being impressed by Cloner's skill at manipulation. At Lassiter's, he'd promised to suspend his scheming; was that pledge, I wondered, merely another calculated step pushing me towards some unknown end goal? Some of the notes in the file Cherenkov provided indicated action taken on later dates.

It also occurred to me that the fact that this file fell into Cherenkov's possession could just as well be part of a double bluff, a leak intended to make me overconfident that I was in control of the situation. More monitoring and study would be required before any direct action should be taken.

"I got Corey into so much trouble," Whisper mourned. "He's never going to forgive me."

It took me a moment to recognize Cherenkov's civilian name.

"Perhaps not," I chuckled, the outlines of a plan

beginning to form. "Your friend did the right thing in reaching out to the Department of Metahuman Affairs. We can use my virtual employee's account to set up and backdate an official investigation into Cloner's behavior. If Cherenkov is listed as a confidential informant..."

"...then any information he gave me would be part of the investigation. Cloner won't be able to get Corey in trouble!"

"Exactly. I'll take care of this one...I have a few ideas that I want to explore."

I may not have been ready to wage virtual war upon the leader of the New York Shield just yet but laying the groundwork for a possible counterattack only seemed prudent. Also, amusing.

※ ※ ※

```
From: G. Marcum <gregory.marcum@dma.gov>
To: Cherenkov <cherenkov@essee.com>
Subject: Department of Metahuman Affairs
Investigation C1337508-09
```

```
Thank you for bringing this issue to our attention.
We've reviewed the files you provided and have
associated them with an existing case; after a
thorough analysis, I would like to reassure you
that our analysts do not believe you to be in any
danger at this time. We will be monitoring the
situation closely and will keep you updated if
there is any indication that the circumstances have
changed. While we generally do not comment on an
```

active investigation, I would also like to reassure you that Cloner has not been directly implicated of any wrongdoing.

Our records indicate that your provisional license to act as a metahuman trainee asset was put into effect two weeks ago. If you are willing, we would like to advance your certification to an active state and ask that you remain as a member of the New York Junior Shield and return to your normal duties. We do not expect to require any further action on your part, but an informed pair of eyes on site may be helpful as our investigation moves forward.

If you have any further questions, you may contact me directly at this email address or call the Department of Metahuman Affairs hotline and refer to case C1337508-09. Again, thank you for your assistance.

- Agent Gregory Marcum, Lic:RDP-00655092-07

CHAPTER FIFTEEN

O NE OF MY LIGHT COMBAT DRONES, FULLY stealthed, floated motionless over the target of my observation. A swarm of microdrones explored below, carefully creeping through shadows and taking readings; vast amounts of data was being recorded for future analysis. The unassuming duplex was located in a lower-middle-class neighborhood; there was little foot traffic on the streets, for there were few stores or restaurants within easy walking distance. The roads were pitted with and cracked in disrepair, electrical and cable systems were spotty, and the traffic signals on the streets were outdated. To the temporary residents of the duplex, these traits were an advantage; the legacy systems were largely disconnected from the more modern hub, and thus this neighborhood was surprisingly resistant to passive surveillance methodology.

There was still no sign of Skullface himself, nor his second-in-command...but I'd found eight of Skullface's men.

The duplex had two double-wide garages and one van was parked in each. Penetrating sonar revealed that the remaining space in both garages had been re-purposed to hold free-standing shelving units, upon which weapons and bomb-making apparatus were neatly organized. The equipment was surprisingly mundane; none of it appeared to be Dr. Chaise's inventions, nor even knock-offs created by some other mad scientist. These were boring, mostly-untraceable military-grade munitions. Whatever havoc was planned, these eight intended to obfuscate their connection to a supervillain.

If I hadn't tracked their means of payment, I would have had no reason to guess that they were Skullface's minions.

Destroying this crew would have been a simple task. The mercenaries may have been professional and alert, but they certainly were not armed in a manner to defend against Doctor Fid. I could have rained destruction from the skies and they would have had barely enough time to curse in horror before their immolation.

Another option was to expand upon the existing surveillance and wait. Sooner or later, this crew would receive orders; when that occurred, I could trace the source of those orders back to their employer. Back to Skullface! If that could be managed, then finally this annoying game cat and skeletal mouse would come to an end.

Leaving the mercenaries *in situ* was a dangerous choice. No matter how many combat drones I hid in the region, no matter how extensive my microdrone surveillance…I could not reliably predict every possible threat that these armaments might pose. They took turns leaving the duplex in pairs—bristling with weapons concealed upon their persons—roaming the city for reasons unknown; if their orders arrived while they were wandering, Doctor Fid's ability to intervene would be limited.

Civilians within my territory would be at risk, but the opportunity to ferret out Skullface's location was too tempting an opportunity to ignore. My factory's production of surveillance microdrones was increased, and a nuanced observation algorithm was implemented; if there were any change in these criminals' status, I would be informed immediately.

❧ ❧ ❧

"This can't be serious," I laughed, genuinely taken aback. "Did someone make a mistake?"

"I'm afraid not, Dr. Markham." Andy—a relatively new hire from the legal department—replied. "The Board has a valid concern."

"Then they should have brought it to me."

"Traditionally...yes," he agreed, then frowned sympathetically, "but it's not a legal obligation."

My brows furrowed as I re-read the notice, hoping to find some nuance that rendered the resolution invalid. Sadly, the meaning was clear and the wording sufficiently simple that finding a loophole would be almost impossible.

"Can we make an argument that this is an operational matter and thus not within the Board's purview?" I asked, hopefully.

"We can make the argument," he shook his head doubtfully, "but it wouldn't be a slam-dunk. Legal matters and issues of community benefit are often considered high-level policy decisions. That's the Board's bread and butter."

This was my first time receiving a report directly from Andrew Pierson. He looked to be in his mid-fifties though well preserved. I imagined that his hair had once been blond but had long-since silvered, and he had the look of a man who'd spent a great deal of time smiling; his dimples could have been carved from granite. Andrew had dressed professionally for this meeting. Perhaps he'd suspected that he would be delivering bad news and hoped to make a good impression anyway.

A resolution had been issued declaring that funding for all humanitarian efforts needed to be approved by a full meeting of the Board. Even as the CEO, I would not be able to reassign any company staff to work on Titan's treatment without first receiving the Directors' blessing.

Not for the first time, I cursed my younger self's short-sightedness. AH Biotech had only been a means to an end then, and my pre-medical-nanite moderately-scarred brain still resistant to forming emotional bonds. When the investors who had helped form the company had insisted that no corporate executives be allowed on the board, I hadn't thought twice on the matter. I barely paid it any mind when the shares were diluted and restructured such that I lost my voting majority. I had, after all, poured inhuman efforts into gaining the skills necessary for the role of corporate executive. Arrogantly, I'd assumed that my intellect would allow me to guide the company so smoothly that the board would never have reason to doubt my leadership.

All false modesty aside, I had triumphed. AH Biotech had

rocketed from well-funded startup to publicly traded corporation to multinational concern in only a handful of years. We'd created marvels, and both our profit margin and our number of product lines continued to grow. The company was flourishing.

But I hadn't counted on Henry Collins and his cabal of activist investors who were slavishly devoted to short-term profits over long-term success.

"What about improper purpose?" I asked Andrew, though I saw the answer in his expression before I finished the sentence.

"It would be a hard sell," he confirmed. "I can spend some time looking up court cases that involve the Companies Act of 2006, but-"

"No, you're right." I let the paper fall to my desk. "This may be asinine, but it's not misconduct."

"Yes, sir."

"Call me Terry," I sighed tiredly. "I'm sorry for pressing you on this, it's not your fault."

"It's not a problem, Terry." He smiled and those aged dimples and laugh lines made his face light up. How he'd managed a long career in the field of law and still maintained so genuine a sense of joy, I had no idea. "It's what I was hired to do."

"Well, talk to our internal auditor and see if there's anything we can use; it's unlikely, but check anyway. I need to make some calls."

Andrew Pierson nodded and gathered his own papers before shaking my hand and seeing himself out the door.

Technically, any Director could request a meeting of the Board, but the Chairman would need to approve the request. Even if I managed to reach out to a majority of board members and convince them of the financial benefits of repairing the leader of the Guardians' degenerative brain disease, Henry Collins could simply refuse to schedule the meeting in a timely fashion.

It felt odd and decidedly unwelcome to be outmaneuvered by a man who didn't wear spandex or bench-press school-busses.

※ ※ ※

The Mk 38 medium-duty powered armor's maiden voyage began in the blackest depths; my ocean-floor manufacturing facility included a shielded moon pool, from which I could swim out to explore deeper trenches. The improved forcefields easily handled the massive pressures, and the icy cold of lightless brine was no match for the Mk 38's personal environmental controls. A nearby volcanically active region of ocean floor was located, and a few minutes spent floating in and out of hydrothermal vents in order to put the system through its paces, and then I rocketed upwards towards the surface.

With stealth systems engaged, I exploded into the night sky and settled into a long ballistic arc; this evening's target lay in Richmond, Virginia and I would have plenty of time to experiment with the flight systems during the journey.

I had, finally, determined what piece of artwork had been

Skullface's target when he attacked the Boston Museum of Fine Arts. All that violence and death had been theater, a bloody distraction to hide the theft of a small oceanscape thought to be an unsigned work by the famed nineteenth-century impressionist, Theodore Robinson.

I'd never seen the piece in person, but the insurers kept high definition photos in their record. Given the style and means used for authentication, it could very well have been a Robinson original. A tedious search through the records of previous owners, however, revealed another possibility: the work may have been painted by the Ancient himself...one of his early efforts to copy a past master's style.

I couldn't be certain, of course. The ownership records had been incomplete, and not all the relevant data had been digitized for me to steal. Perhaps in some musty basement, an unmarked box of forms contained the information needed to verify my hypothesis. That Skullface had sought out the work certainly supported my theory; it was certainly possible that he had access to resources that I did not.

But one thing was certain: Boston was my domain. Skullface may have found methods to scurry unseen near the borders, but Doctor Fid was attuned to the city's core and my city held secrets that Skullface could not possibly have known. The skeletal supervillain may have successfully drawn blood and caused terror in the heart of my territory, but he had failed to accomplish his desired goal. The impressionist painting that had been present in the Boston Museum of Fine Arts was a forgery, and the actual item—whether painted by Robinson or by the Ancient—had been stolen months earlier by one of the world's greatest thieves. And that thief lived in Richmond.

I soared onwards, toying with the aerodynamic effects of shaped force-fields to pass the time. Frictionless and aerodynamic contours allowed for efficient travel, but increasing drag and adding modulated ripples created haunting tones. If remaining undiscovered had not been a concern, I imagined that I could increase my speed and beat the air into a blazing trail of plasma as I passed, a roaring catastrophe pouring across the sky.

Simulations were begun immediately; I'd gotten tremendous benefit from my improved stealth technologies of late, but raw intimidation also had its place. I was still distracted by intriguing formulae and mathematical models when I arrived high above the state capital of Virginia. Fortunately, the Mk 38 armor knew my destination even if I were otherwise engaged.

Hovering unnoticed, I deployed a small swarm of microdrones to explore below. It was barely more than twenty minutes before my quarry's location was confirmed; I dropped from the sky and set down before a nondescript popup warehouse. The side door, I noted approvingly, was subtly obscured from any camera's or neighbor's view. I disabled stealth mode, let my traditional starfield-and-red display fade into existence, and knocked politely.

It was late, but it was only about thirty seconds before someone came to check the door; certain occupations tend to induce a nocturnal lifestyle. The Grey Cat's career certainly kept him most active during the evenings. My sensitive microphones caught quiet profanity when he recognized his late-night visitor through the security lens, but he quickly steadied himself and opened the door.

"Doctor Fid," the thief smiled pleasantly. He was a dangerously handsome man; slim and athletic, lightly tanned with features that hinted at some percentage of oriental ancestry despite his ice-blue eyes. When last I'd seen him, he'd worn his lustrous coal-black hair pulled back into a pony-tail but it was now cropped to medium length and swept back in an artfully unkempt manner. "Come in."

"Thank you." I stepped inside; the warehouse had been re-purposed to serve as a studio-style living area, a workshop, and a studio. In addition to his talents as a burglar, the Grey Cat was also a highly respected forger. Given the quality of the work he left behind, a significant percentage of his thefts had never been discovered. Certainly, the Boston Museum of Fine Arts had never realized that their un-signed Robinson had been replaced with a fake.

And neither had Skullface.

"So, to what do I owe this unexpected pleasure?" He waved me towards a sitting area.

This was one of the reasons that I'd never minded doing business with the Gray Cat. He was polite. His chairs were unlikely to support the weight of the Mk 38 powered armor, but he acted with complete trust that my technological mastery would protect his belongings. He was correct, of course; a careful application of anti-grav and force-fields, and I could sit comfortably without so much as scratching the upholstery.

Also, the odds that he would react with violence as had Imperator Rex were very low. The Gray Cat's preternaturally advanced sense of balance and coordination made him an exceptional thief, but that was not a power-set that would make one a threat to the likes of Doctor Fid.

"I was hoping to examine a work of art that may have passed through your hands," I said.

"Many of those in my line of work have been worried that you've gone white-cape," the thief laughed. "They're afraid they'll have to get honest work if the alternative is facing your tech. I told them they needn't worry; Doctor Fid would not come after the likes of us."

It was only because my sensors included heart-rate monitoring and breathing analysis that I was able to detect the relief behind his words. Visually, the change was imperceptible.

"So," he continued, "what piece of ill-gotten artwork has attracted your interest?"

"An unsigned work by Theodore Robinson that was taken from the Boston Museum of Fine Arts a little less than two years ago."

"I meant no offense," he was quick to apologize. "Working in your city, I mean. It seemed a small thing, below your interest."

"No offense was taken," I chuckled. "But don't worry, I only wish to study the original. I assume that your work was on commission; you need only point me towards your buyer."

"My clients expect a certain level of anonymity," he began, then quickly changed his tone when I went still as a statue and the stars displayed within the Mk 38 began to swirl: "But of course I'd be willing to make an exception for Doctor Fid! As it happens, this particular client never made his final payment; I have the work in question in storage."

"Excellent. Bring me to it so that I can perform my scans," I requested. "You will be compensated for your time."

"I'd prefer not to advertise my storage facility's location," he smiled in a placating manner. "I can bring it to you. Shall we say tomorrow evening?"

"You keep a climate-controlled storage space in Prince George County and your passcode is one-one-two-four-one-nine-seven-zero. Tonight would be preferable."

"Well." The Gray Cat's smile faltered, but he nodded his acquiescence; I was certain that he immediately understood that being forced to take a pleasant evening drive was a small price to pay for the insult of operating in Doctor Fid's domain without permission. "I suppose that I'll get my car keys."

And forty-six minutes later, I discovered key information regarding the location of the Ancient's hidden treasure.

🙣 🙣 🙣

A thin smile graced Henry Collins' lips as I entered the restaurant. As always, the man's couture was immaculate; his charcoal-gray three-piece suit was perfectly fitted and looked to have been recently pressed. It was a deliberate choice, I knew. He chose his outfits for effect, another weapon within his arsenal to establish dominance over his victims. There was not a fleck of lint upon his suit, not a scratch on the face of his expensive gold wristwatch, and not a gray hair out of place on his head. His skin-care regimen must have been astounding; his skin was as smooth as that of an infant, and pale like a creature untouched by the sun.

My own attire was professional, but I'd discarded my tie and left my shirt's top button undone. I wasn't trying to compete; Dr. Terry Markham was to be portrayed as a working CEO, fresh from meetings and labor.

I'd arrived on time, but Henry had chosen to seat himself early and had already begun his meal. Again, a not-particularly-subtle method of oozing dominance. I chose not to acknowledge the insult directly but instead flagged down a waiter's attention as I took my seat.

"Terrance. I'm glad that you agreed to this meeting."

"Henry," I acknowledged, looking over the menu. "I think that we both know I didn't have much of a choice."

An expression of smug conceit flickered across his features but was quickly replaced by his default dull and emotionless mien. It was only with significant effort that I was able to conceal my own amusement at his reaction.

We didn't speak until after the waiter had taken my order.

"So," I began with a sigh, "what do you want this time?"

"The same thing I always want," he replied. "For you to align the company's priorities with your stockholders' interests."

"If you're expecting to blackmail me into doing your bidding, you're going to have to be more specific," I grimaced. "I wouldn't want to accidentally do what's right for the company instead of what's right for you personally, after all."

"It's not personal." A frown of admonishment touched the corners of his lips. "I represent A.H. Biotech's shareholders, Terrance."

"You represent eight percent of our shareholders," I scoffed.

"A registered blockholder with eight percent ownership lobbied on my behalf," Henry Collins corrected, his expression one of fond recollection. "But in the end, I was confirmed by majority vote."

"I own more than three times as many shares as your voting bloc."

"Yes," he chuckled. "However—according to AHBT's articles of incorporation—executive staff have no voting rights. Technically speaking, I'm your proxy; I suppose it would be more accurate to say that I represent approximately thirty-five percent of shareholders, then."

It required Herculean effort to restrain a growl.

If Henry and his supporters ever succeeded in having me removed as CEO then I would regain my voting rights, but he and his supporters had enjoyed years to build up political support among the shareholders. Simply owning the large volume of shares would not guarantee me any significant influence over the company, and Henry knew it.

I took a deep breath and slowly exhaled. "All right, then. I'll ask again: what do you want?"

"I want for you to close down Blue Seas. If you do that, I'll make sure the Board votes in favor of your new vanity project."

The Blue Seas venture used colonies of genetically engineered bacteria to metabolize plastic debris within the ocean into harvest-able, sell-able chemicals; the enterprise wasn't profitable yet...but it would be eventually. I could think of only one reason that Henry would want to abandon the business unit before it had begun to earn revenue.

"You want us to sell our hardware and license the process to another company," I frowned. "Vanaheim Petrochemical is one of the major investors behind your voting bloc, aren't they?"

"As it happens, I believe that Vanaheim Petrochemical is readying a bid. It's a win-win scenario: A.H. Biotech gains licensing fees and has costly liabilities stripped from their balance sheet. Vanaheim Petrochemicals gets some good publicity and another profitable product line." His expression was predatory. "I think that it would be in A.H. Biotech's best interests to accept the offer, don't you?"

Theoretically, Vanaheim Petrochemical was well placed to take advantage of the deal. They had a large fleet of ships and would be able to expand operations more quickly than our own efforts had been able. On the other hand...their goal would be raw profit and I could already envision some of the harmful, polluting and destructive methods they would use to optimize the process, publicity be damned. Blue Seas was originated as a humanitarian and environmental movement; that goal would be lost before the ink on the contract dried. Licensing the technology to an outside business with more maritime experience may have been a decent idea but that particular customer would be a poor choice.

"No," I shook my head. "No, I don't think that A.H. Biotech is going to do that."

The slim man was unperturbed. "Last time we played this game, you needed to pull a remarkably impressive rabbit out of your hat in order to get your way. You can't do that every time, Terrance. Learn to play ball, life will become easier for you."

"The last time we played," I countered, "the rules were different."

"How so?"

I smiled wryly, "Somehow, I'd gotten it into my head that you were the villain in our little drama, and that meant that I was the plucky hero who had to struggle and outwit you to defeat your fiendish schemes. But you're not a villain. You're just a sad, selfish, hollow creature in a well-tailored suit. And if you're not a villain, then I don't have to play the hero's role.

"In which case, I'm just a very wealthy man who has a few dozen Senators and Congressmen on speed-dial. Also, Meredith Ellison. Do you remember her? She had an inoperable tumor, and saving her was one of A.H. Biotech's 'vanity projects'."

"I think I recall," Henry Collins replied wanly, seeming a bit more pale than usual.

"It turns out that she's the Secretary of the Interior's niece; Vanaheim Petrochemical is currently waiting on approval for four off-shore drilling projects, aren't they? I only ask because Secretary Brand and his family are coming by my house this weekend and it may come up in conversation."

The gray-haired man's jaw clenched. "This is beginning to feel very much like the blackmail you accused me of earlier."

"I will never ask anything of you other than to do your legal duty to act on behalf of all of A.H. Biotech's shareholders. If you think I'm pushing the company in the wrong direction? Fight me on it. I can take the hit and I'm willing to listen." I bared my teeth. "But if you try to manipulate my company to benefit your eight-percent at the expense of the other ninety-two, I promise you that I will use every tool at my disposal to ensure that every investor who supports you is going to have a bad day."

Henry Collins looked ill as he set down his silverware, and I waved down our waiter to get my meal packaged to go.

※ ※ ※

"I am Doctor Fid!" I boomed, my armor's volume raised loud enough to rattle windows. "Stand down immediately and your injuries will be minor."

For a moment, all was silent. And then the fully-automatic gunfire began.

I couldn't help but chuckle. Small arms, against Doctor Fid's towering Mk 35 heavy combat? Encased within this suit, I'd faced down the largest assembly of superheroes in modern history. The suit's strength had been matched against the mighty Valiant for twenty-two and a half minutes! Even after facing Skullface in his own domain, the Mk 35 had walked away under its own power. Skullface's mercenaries may as well have been throwing cotton-balls.

A surface to air missile might be able to scratch the electrostatic veneer from an orichalcum plate but mere copper-jacketed lead was no threat at all. Bullets spattered off the Mk 35's starfield surface, and I strode straight through the duplex's wall to confront the armed criminals.

I hadn't detected any communication from Skullface nor from Doctor Chaise; that avenue of investigation was lost to me. My sensors had, however, indicated that these mercenaries had been working non-stop at re-tasking their stockpiled explosives. These were not bombs designed to breach a fortified stronghold, nor were they intended to defend against a superpowered assault. These devices—flechettes and ball bearings shaped around a relatively small charge—were suitable for only one purpose: to cause mass casualties among unarmored civilians.

Skullface's minions had already created more than a hundred such implements before I'd decided to intervene; whatever they had been preparing for, the results would have been a horror. And so, laughing with vicious cheer, I waded through the duplex's wreckage to swat one gunman after another into the ground. Bones snapped and blood sprayed, but the damage was carefully non-lethal. The police were already en route and I wanted these mercenaries incarcerated: a very public warning to those who had accepted Skullface's employment.

If Terry Markham wasn't required to rigidly follow the

hero's role when confronting the chairman of the A.H. Biotech's board of directors, then perhaps Doctor Fid needn't be constrained to a scheming supervillain's path when opposing Skullface.

It was time for a more overt approach.

CHAPTER SIXTEEN

Sadly, Skullface chose not to cooperate with my desire for a more direct confrontation. Several mercenary cells—small units given specific tasks but little in the way of information—had been located and the criminals arrested (or hospitalized and arrested), and yet their employer's location still eluded me. I'd even 'accidentally' allowed one minion to escape so that I could surreptitiously monitor her; thus far, no contact had been made.

It was an annoying scenario, but I took solace in the certainty that whatever plans had been in store, the sudden spike in incarcerations would surely have been a disruption.

And even if I were unable to locate Skullface, it was plausible that sufficiently-tantalizing bait might draw the villain out.

Under cover of darkness, a swarm of utility drones and I performed detailed scans of an island off the east coast of Nova Scotia. Behind the Mk 38's star-field faceplate, I indulged in a smug smile; my calculations had been correct.

The Ancient had hidden tiny clues in the works that he'd

left behind; little discrepancies in technique or components that were indecipherable when taken individually but began to suggest a pattern when combined. I have no doubt that he'd intended for this pattern to be discovered via magical means, but my science and math had managed the task equally well. A picture had begun to emerge: an intensely complex geometric diagram.

The Ancient had published a monograph on the use of images for meditative purposes and I was immediately struck by the hidden illustration's similarity to a Buddhist mandala. The paper had stressed the importance of radial symmetry in such illustrations, but the diagram that I'd modeled from so many pieces of the Ancient's belongings was subtly flawed. At first I thought this a limitation of the artist's materials. Eventually, I realized that the blemishes were, in fact, the message.

The Ancient had fancied himself both scientist and wizard; for a practitioner of the mystic arts, I wondered, would understanding have been an instinctive thing? Attaining a deep trance state while contemplating the complicated drawing, until the solution was revealed by one's subconscious? I had no idea; my own analysis relied upon complex mathematical models, cryptographic methods, and steganographic techniques. One flaw led to another, and when laid upon a map they all pointed here: to a small and uninhabited island. And now, my sensors indicated that the island hid a system of caves below its surface.

There was, I was sure, some secret entrance. Some mystic password that my research had missed, some illusion to be disrupted. Given time, I was certain that I would have been able to identify and bypass that hurdle...but I was done with subtlety. My warstaff was summoned into my hand, and I poured a roaring jet of plasma upon the island's beach. Winds were whipped into a frenzy and the night sky was set alight by the fiery assault; molten rock spattered across the sand, crackling and hissing when thrown into nearby waters. And then I was through.

The newly-formed pit's walls had been melted to glass and were still dimly glowing as I descended. A swarm of microdrones explored ahead, and the networked devices' sonar and lidar readings were quickly compiled into a three-dimensional model that was overlayed across my vision by the time my feet touched the hidden tunnel's floor. Little light touched these walls save for the dull-red glow emitted from the Mk 38's seams and the trickle of starlight from within its surface, but so much sensory data was being poured into my brain via my neural tap that it was several seconds before I noticed the lack of visual input. A pair of construction drones were ordered to drop down the shaft and join me; they, at least, had floodlights installed.

The path undulated slightly, limiting my view in either direction. I dismissed my warstaff back to its subspace storage and chose a route in which to begin my investigation: Westward, towards the center of the island.

The tunnel's surface had a matte grey finish which caught the light emitted from my floating cylindrical utility drones but did not cast much in the way of reflection. Although sensor readings confirmed my suspicions that these tunnels were not naturally formed, I could detect no toolmarks upon the smooth stone walls. I imagined that, if I took the time to drill cores from the surrounding material, I would find stress fractures within the basalt that could not be explained by any natural process; the Ancient had written a monograph on geomancy and the evidence seemed to match the predictions in his text.

I recalled my visit to Chicago and had just a moment to feel a strange sense of deja vu, and then the flood of black-scaled bipedal lizard things fell upon me.

There'd been no warning, not even a hint of movement: just a twist of shadow and then there was a chaos of glowing red eyes and long fangs dripping with poison. Grinning wildly behind Doctor Fid's emotionless mask, I summoned my warstaff once more and stepped into the fray.

Years before, Bobby and I had watched images of Chimera and her compatriots battling monsters like these. Then, I'd been taken aback by the creatures' sinuous savagery. The video had not captured the half of it; even now, encased within the powerful Mk 38, I was impressed. They were inhumanly strong and moved with vicious coordination and speed. It was only reflexes honed by decades of nefarious deeds that kept me from being borne down in that initial assault.

A warning alarm blared within my skull; the poison from their fangs was fantastically caustic, and the design of my armor required that some plates had not been constructed of orichalcum; if I allowed too much venom to spill, the seals at some joints might be breached. And so I stepped back as I fought, falling into a violent rhythm. Dodge then strike, shift and parry. I used the curve of the tunnel to my advantage, forcing the creatures to crawl over each other to reach me rather than surrounding me as had been their original intention. My staff barked with power, each swing crackling with energy and every blow landing with the force of an oncoming truck. I shattered my enemies in waves but still they came. Claws scraped across my mask, and fangs strained to find purchase on my mask. I was jostled and poked, shoved and menaced and struck. My entire world was movement and danger.

I laughed and moved and killed until there was nothing left of me but the battle.

※ ※ ※

Standing before the University's budget advisory committee for the first time had been a bewildering experience. The first chair queried why they should fund my project, and I had waxed eloquent regarding the glory of discovery. They shifted uncomfortably, and I'd developed the distinct impression that they were considering asking me to step outside. But...I was the University's wunderkind, their teen-aged polymath pursuing studies in a half-dozen unrelated scientific fields! Given my burgeoning reputation, I was offered the benefit of the doubt; again, they questioned why this particular research should be subsidized...and I launched into an impassioned and poetic oration about the nobility inherent in the expansion of human understanding.

The board did not seem swayed.

I was fortunate that I'd included my minder—Michael, now a PhD. in his own right—within my team; he took pity on me and addressed the board directly. The research and subsequent academic papers, he explained, would attract future grants. He offered a series of simple justifications for his premises and the project was approved while I watched in open-mouthed confusion.

The moment of subsequent comprehension had been dizzying: I had made a mistake. I'd been so focused upon the truth of my answers (scientific inquiry is both noble and glorious!) that I'd failed to listen to the nuances of the questions being asked of me. Accurate content is insufficient if its context is inappropriate. In order to prosper in academia, I'd suddenly realized, I would need to be more aware of my surroundings.

As time passed and the string of successes behind me grew ever longer, it became increasingly difficult to remember that lesson.

❦ ❦ ❦

The black-scaled lizard-like monsters had driven me backwards through nearly a quarter-mile of tunnel, but I was unworried. I'd left behind a long trail of the dead and dying, and their numbers were beginning to thin. When the last hiss had been uttered, when the last glowing red eye dimmed, I would float over their corpses and claim my prize.

At first, I'd been somewhat concerned that the Ancient

might still be present within these caves, and that a more delicate confrontation lay before me. But no; these were mindless and brutal creatures with none of the malevolent guidance I'd seen hints of when watching television with Bobby. Hissing, rabid and dangerous guards, left behind by an absent master. Either I'd missed some valuable bit of intelligence—a command or sign that would have rendered this army quiescent, or else the Ancient had intended for his legacy only to fall into the hands of a powerful recipient. There were not many who could have weathered this torrent of violence.

The ferocious dance continued; my staff spun like the world's deadliest windmill to ward away grasping claws or splatters of venom. The sinuous creatures crawled over each other, long fangs bared eagerly as they sought to catch at me, to finally take me down. I used brief blasts of plasma or kinetic energy or sonic attacks to take them down, but dared not unleash too great a force within these hallowed halls; from what I'd read, geomancy was a tricky art to master and I had no desire to bring these walls down atop my conquest. And so I allowed the monstrous tide to push me back, until the tunnel ended in a great chamber with still water at its center, no doubt leading to an underwater tunnel that led to the open ocean.

With anti-grav enabled, I shot back so that I floated above the dark waters. With no solid ground upon which to stand, the creatures crowded at the stone floor's edge and I was able to strike at them with impunity. The warstaff was dismissed once more, and I summoned blasts of raw kinetic energy through my gauntlets. The hissing lizard-creatures were felled in waves, thrown back as though pounded by a giant, invisible fist. Their broken bodies piled along the large cavern's wall; my exhilarating, bloody task was nearing completion and I was victorious.

Once more, my sensors failed to offer any warning; there was only a hint of movement, a shifting shadow, and then pain. Purple-gray tentacles as thick as tree-trunks shot up from the depths and I was instantly engulfed. It was only instinct and clever programming that managed to reinforce the Mk 38 armor's structural integrity fields fast enough to prevent my leg from being twisted clean off my body.

❧ ❧ ❧

"Professor Markham?"

"Hm?" I don't look away from my blackboard. The formulae are correct but the proof is unfinished. The solution is near, though...I can feel it. The variables are sliding into place.

"Your office hours started at two, right?"

A quick brush with the eraser raises a cloud of chalk dust and I scribble notes; this one section will need further support, but for now it can be skipped. Another section has intriguing implications and will be relevant to other studies. And this can be simplified.

"Professor Markham...?"

Reluctantly, I set down the chalk and turn to face my visitor. "Yes?"

"I'm having trouble with a concept from yesterday's lecture. You spoke about high energy physics and multidimensional theory...?"

"Ah! Yes, I remember." My face heats with embarrassment; there had been many puzzled expressions in that room. The lecture had been intended to cover a different subject entirely, but an interesting theory had distracted me. I can only hope that I'd spent enough time on the actual course material before striking off on my unplanned tangent. It is nice to know that at least one student was more intrigued than confused. "Um. How can I help?"

"Some of the math was above my head, but you talked about probability distributions in and random outcomes, and I'm having trouble wrapping my head around how that matches to the actual examples we've seen."

"How so?"

"Well, um, y'know a bunch of heroes have traveled to different dimensions, right? And Professor Paradigm has that viewscreen?"

"Yes."

"Well, all the dimensions we've seen are pretty similar to this one. If everything's random, that doesn't make sense to me."

"That's an excellent point, and I definitely should've addressed it in class," I grin sheepishly. "The answer is that—even though there are an infinite number of possibilities—the dimensions aren't distributed randomly."

He looks befuddled rather than enlightened.

"Imagine that there's a beach covered in colored sand, spread out in all the colors of the rainbow," I suggest. "Red all the way on the north side of the beach, then orange, then yellow…all the way to violet on the south end of the beach."

"…Okay?"

"After a year of wind and tides and volleyball practice, some of the sand will get kicked around. The edges will be blurred, and *some colored grains have probably been tracked into completely different areas...but for the most part, the north section of the beach will still look red."*

"Okay, yeah, I think I get it."

"Since the beginning of time," I intone, feeling oddly melodramatic, *"every single particle in the Universe has undergone a massive number of interactions, guided by chance and natural forces. The probability of every particle moving in just the right way to end up where we are now is incalculable."*

"But it's an infinitely large beach," my student laughs in return, "and our dimension is a small blue grain of sand."

"Exactly!" I clap reflexively, then cough as I'm engulfed in another cloud of chalk. *"We know that the beach should theoretically have all the colors in the rainbow, but if we look around? All we're likely to find is shades of blue."*

When I was first offered a tenured position, I'd thought teaching to be a necessary evil: an unwanted chore to be endured if I wanted to stay at the University and continue my research. I'm certain that my early students had been just as miserable as I was. Pupils like this one had changed my mind.

Successfully imparting a lesson was intensely gratifying.

✥ ✥ ✥

I floated towards the antechamber, feeling smug in my triumph. Sadly, it seemed as though my right leg would be unsalvageable; a prosthetic would need to be jury-rigged to serve while a proper replacement was being cloned.

The giant squid, on the other hand, had certainly learned

its lesson.

The central room was the size of a small warehouse and was filled with well-organized shelves and display cabinets. The collection of precious metals and gems was astounding, as well as a remarkable array of eastern and western historical artifacts. Taking a proper inventory of this trove would, however, be an effort left to another time. For now, I summoned more drones to bring a shipping container or two on-site and to begin packing my plunder away for storage.

A greater treasure captured my attention: a bookshelf filled with leather-bound laboratory notebooks. These, too, would need to be bundled and transported to a secure location for future perusal...but there was no resisting the urge to open the first book, to explore the Ancient's early theories and methodologies. These books were all handwritten, careful and thoughtful and professional as only a rigorous academic could manage. The knowledge hidden within these tomes would, no doubt, prove invaluable...but more than that, these books represented a window into the Ancient's mind.

I'd kept such journals, once; they'd infested my shelves during my time at MIT. More than a mere recounting of my studies, those notebooks had been a log of my intellectual growth, of my thought process as new discoveries coalesced. I often regretted those books' immolation. I hadn't been precisely sane so soon after Bobby's death, and I'd believed that becoming Fid would require destroying Terry.

Terry Markham and Doctor Fid had eventually formed an easy alliance, but that had been much later: after Bronze's death, after Terry Markham's shadow had returned to academia for five years, and after a chance conversation with a fellow professor's son had kindled my desire to reclaim Doctor Fid's mask.

I hadn't prevaricated when answering Stanley Morrow and Pamela Green's questions on KNN CapeWatch. The Doctor Fid of those first few horrifically violent years may as well have been a different creature from the Doctor Fid who'd emerged from half a decade's hibernation. The armor's grim motif—a reflection-less starscape, so perfectly rendered that I looked to be a man-shaped portal into deep space, with three-dimensional form hinted at only by the angry red glow that bled from the armor's seems—remained the same, but the man within the armor had been reshaped: molded by time and choice into something new.

Some aspects of the old Fid remained, such as the grim pleasure I took in knowing what would come next. With this library as bait, I needn't spend another moment seeking out Skullface. He would come to me.

I pored through the Ancient's first journal, enjoying the afterglow of my victory.

A decision would also need to be made as to the disposition of the Ancient's corpse, but that choice didn't seem particularly pressing; the villain had been dead by his own hand for at least two decades. The botulinum toxin in his wine-glass was still detectable by my sensors. By means unknown, this section of the cave system had been kept cool, dry and vermin free; the Ancient's remains were desiccated but otherwise undamaged.

The laboratory notebook was proving to be a riveting read; this was the work of a focused, passionate young man who was working to reconcile the strict logic of science with the erratic behavior of observed supernatural phenomena. The initial experiments had been simple but rigorously applied, with notes in the margins describing even the most minute discrepancies between test cycles.

There were patterns here, interesting sequences whose implications could not possibly have been understood by someone who didn't have a high understanding of the mathematics that model interdimensional instability. Already, ideas for experimentation were beginning to percolate through my consciousness.

I paused; one of my exploring microdrones had made a discovery that had eluded my own cursory examination. The Ancient's almost-mummified corpse was holding a hand-written letter. The laboratory notebook was set aside so that I could take up the Ancient's last testament.

"There is no magic," the letter read.

Behind my starfield mask, I smiled.

CHAPTER SEVENTEEN

AS EXPECTED, THE ANCIENT HAD BEEN A GENIUS OF the highest caliber. His early work was rigorously well-supported, and his insights clever and innovative. The first few laboratory journals went into excruciating detail covering not only what experiments were being performed, but to also defend each decision and explain why certain investigations were prioritized. Most interesting was that they also spent a significant amount of page-space discussing the ethics of certain practices, and actively forgoing any questionable research.

The man who'd penned these first journals had not been a villain, he'd been an academic who had discovered a natural talent for sorcery by mere accident. A chance reading of an ancient text for an anthropology class had resulted in unexpected phenomena, and the young scientist had dedicated himself towards discovering more. He'd been filled with lofty goals and excitement at the challenge that lay before him.

I kept reading, intrigued.

The shift in demeanor was subtle, but it was simple to

determine when the change began: several years into his study, the Ancient had begun experimenting with summoning rituals. His original intent had merely been to study the ripples in the interdimensional boundaries when contact was made, but the Ancient's curiosity had exceeded his wisdom. Deals had been struck, and the slow drift towards amorality had begun. Either the extradimensional entities had a directly corrosive effect upon the Ancient's principles, or else he'd sold some part of himself that no human should do without.

If I'd kept up my own journals, I imagined that the same pattern would have been present during the period in which I'd begun performing self-induced brain surgeries. With every slice, it had become easier to justify the next operation, to cut away at parts of my brain that interfered with my chosen avocation. A tiny burn here to keep me from hesitating before attacking a downed opponent, a minor excision there to eliminate empathetic response. I'd reversed much of the damage when Bronze had died and before I'd boxed Doctor Fid into storage, but neural scarring remained. It was not until relatively recently—when I'd stolen medical nanites from A.H. Biotech and suffused my body with the reprogrammed microscopic machines—that the gray haze in my brain had truly receded.

I was still uncertain if anything resembling redemption could ever be attained by a creature like myself, but it was objectively true that my current moral state was improved. I'd saved Whisper. I'd saved dozens of planets from the Legion.

I'd saved a kitten named Mason.

Would only one more surgery have been the tipping point? One more course of psychoactive narcotics? How close had I come to the precipice? Never before had I actually felt grateful for the alcoholism-induced liver-damage that had taken Bronze's life. I still occasionally had pleasant dreams that involved my hands about his throat, but I supposed that, in the end, his premature passing had served a purpose. Doctor Fid slumbered for five years and then was resurrected as a new creature.

I read on.

Making a complete study of these journals would take years, but there was much to be gleaned from even a superficial examination. The Ancient had been obsessed with the study of akashic identity—the ephemeral gestalt of body and brain and spirit that marked a creature as being unique. The Ancient had hypothesized that this marker represented an individual's soul but had (at least as far as I'd read so far) been unable to establish a conclusive proof. He had, however, experimentally verified that there was some strange tie between akashic records and the membrane that separated dimensions. Much of the information within the manuals was useless to me—a man with no native talent for magecraft. But the Ancient had been studying the intersection of science and magic, and even the more mundane theories were intriguing. Already I was beginning to see opportunities for experimentation.

Ethical experimentation, with pre-programmed safeguards to incinerate me if ever I began following the path that led to the studies in laboratory journal number twenty-one.

※ ※ ※

Whisper had found her way into my office, a tiny black labrador trailing behind like an obedient duckling. She'd sat down on the floor to play with Nyx, whispering soft affirmations while I devoured the laboratory journals, occasionally pausing to take notes or perform complex calculations. The Ancient had been brilliant and his knowledge of the biological sciences far outstripped my own...but my scientific focuses were different. He'd faithfully recorded his observations but had failed to identify patterns that only a premier-level mathematician or physicist would notice. My heart was racing with exhilaration and, if I'd had a mirror, I was certain that I'd have been embarrassed by my giddy expression. But Whisper looked heartbreakingly sad. Pensive.

With journal and notes set aside, I moved to kneel at her side and my temporary prosthetic clicked loudly. She didn't look up to meet my eyes so I waited and reached towards Nyx. The little black dog sniffed at my hand and wagged uncertainly; I'd never been unkind to him and I fed him as often as not...but he was Whisper's puppy. In his little canine brain, I supposed that I must have been the biggest and scariest dog in his pack; what a perceptive little creature! His body language fairly screamed eager hopefulness.

I used my neural link to make a note in my virtual

calendar: increase playtime with Whisper and Nyx, and pat the dog gently atop his head.

"I don't want to be a bad girl," Whisper volunteered suddenly.

"We've had this conversation before," I answered, surprised. "I don't want you to be a bad girl. You're a good girl, and I love you the way you are."

"I know." She fidgeted, one hand resting on Nyx's neck as though for support. "But it's more complicated than that."

"How so?"

"You ask me to help you. And I do."

"Oh, sweetheart-"

"It makes me happy! I love you, and it makes me happy." The little android nibbled at her lower lip nervously. "But sometimes it makes me scared, too."

"I don't want you to be scared."

"I got to help you save the planet! Lots of planets!" She grinned briefly up at me briefly then again lowered her gaze. "I helped you find information about people."

"Bad people, for the most part," I commented.

"Mm! But not always. And...um...an artificially intelligent android like me might have supplied armor plates and parts for use in the armor and weapons for a person like you."

She had to speak in hypotheticals in order to avoid triggering safeguards installed by her supervillain father/creator; Whisper had inherited sole control over the orichalcum foundry left behind by Apotheosis but was also obligated to protect it. So long as we spoke as though discussing imaginary scenarios, the young AI could do as she wished. If, on the other hand, ever we directly confirmed that I knew that the foundry was operational...Whisper would be forced to conceal that knowledge by any means at her disposal. In the past, she'd done so by hacking my brain via my neural link and interrupting my short-term memory.

"A man like me would probably be very grateful to his adorable little sister," I replied; given a choice, I preferred sophistry over neural disruption.

"You've been doing good things with your armor. You stopped all those fires and saved lots of people from accidents and things. And that makes me happy," she trailed off.

"...but you're afraid of what Doctor Fid may do with the armor in the future," I finished sadly. "I'm so sorry, sweetheart. I'll disassemble the Mk 35, the Mk 36 and the Mk 38 immediately."

"No!" Whisper looked up at me and I was certain that (had the capability been installed) her eyes would have been filled with tears. "Then you'd get hurt and it'd be my fault. That would be even worse!"

"Then what can I do?" I asked, helplessly.

"You told me you could be a bad man who does good things."

"I did, yes." The corners of my lips quirked upwards, hesitantly. Continuing my philanthropic activities would be no hardship at all! If that was all she needed, then I was confident that I could erase the worry from her heart.

"I thought that'd be enough," she said, and her troubled expression soured my optimism. "But there's something you didn't say."

My brows furrowed. "And what's that?"

"You didn't say that you'd *only* do good things."

"Oh," I replied, and the word tasted like ash.

"If you tell me..." she offered, her synthetic voice sounding very small and young. "If you tell me, I'll believe you."

"I know you would," I nodded sadly. "And I wouldn't promise it if I didn't mean it."

"...you're not going to promise, are you?"

"I can't."

Nyx sensed his mistress' distress and licked at her fingers comfortingly, his ears and little tail held low. Whisper's own expression was tortured as she whimpered, "You would've promised Bobby."

Doctor Fid had endured a long and painful career. I'd been beaten near to death dozens of times, pummeled and mutilated and crushed and twisted in ways that beggar the imagination. And yet, I wasn't certain that I'd ever been skewered quite so adeptly.

"You're probably right," I grimaced, eyes burning with unshed tears. "But I would have been lying to him, and lying to myself. I'm hoping that I'm a better big brother now."

She crawled into my arms and I hugged her tight; we comforted each other, even though we both knew that nothing had truly been resolved.

"I'm still afraid," Whisper eventually murmured.

"As am I," I chuckled painfully. "I can't make the promise you want to hear, but I can promise I'll try."

"Maybe that'll be good enough," Whisper replied, but she

didn't sound convinced.

I wasn't convinced, either.

❦ ❦ ❦

With Whisper (and Nyx) visiting her friend Dinah, the house felt far too quiet. I'd lived alone on that property for more than a decade before Whisper came into my life; how had I failed to notice how oppressively silent the halls were?

Fortunately, an alert notified me that my new appendages had finished growing. The teleport platform hidden in my office allowed me to escape the mute prison and find my way to the medical facility in the Appalachian mountains instead.

Even though only one leg had been ruined in the battle against the Ancient's squidmonster, I'd decided that the other might as well be amputated as well. It would, after all, be easier to maintain even wear upon the new parts if the replacements were performed symmetrically. I'd already programmed my surgical automatons to perform the operation, so it was merely an issue of scheduling the procedure. And there was no time like the present: I'd arranged for a vacation day from the office and would be able to spend twenty-four hours floating in a recovery tank while the nanites in my bloodstream worked to make final adjustments and repairs.

Feeling heartbroken and confused about my conversation with Whisper had no effect upon my choice to spend the next day in a drugged coma. The opportunity was only a happy coincidence.

※ ※ ※

"You're not a hero," the Red Ghost graveled angrily, the eyes of his cowl narrowed to slits.

"This is true," I agreed, ensconced within the Mk 38 and floating lower to settle on the ground; the Ghost had summoned me to the now familiar abandoned warehouse near the docks, and I'd arrived as soon as could be managed. "Why did you want to talk? Is there a problem with scheduling Titan's treatment?"

"You're not going to try and defend yourself?" The hero spat, ignoring my question, with an expression twisted between fury and puzzled betrayal.

I was equally bewildered. "Defend what?"

The tension in his shoulders made me grateful for the impulse to scan for weapons and reinforcements before I'd dropped from the sky; we'd formed a tentative partnership, he and I, but at that moment I worried that this meeting would end in blows. That the Red Ghost had left behind his more powerful armaments was a positive sign, but he was a tremendously resourceful opponent.

I silently increased my shields' intensity in preparation against a surprise attack...just in case.

"Cloner, Blueshift, Valiant...they all came to me and asked if I thought you were still a villain." He closed his hands into trembling fists. His Chilango accent was more pronounced when he was enraged. "I defended you, damn it!"

"I've never lied to you about what I am. Not even once!" When I was wearing my armor—when I was Doctor Fid—my instinct was usually to inflict violence upon the source of any undesired emotion. And I certainly did not enjoy confusion. Nevertheless, I unsummoned the warstaff that had somehow found its way into my hand and dismissed the energy that had been building in my gauntlets. My occasional nemesis was seething, barely rational; I'd rarely seen him in such a state, and it was disturbing to think that I was the unintentional cause. Causing intentional emotional harm to an opponent was one thing. Doing so by accident was unconscionable.

"You let all of us believe that you'd changed!" the Red Ghost declared, glaring as though he'd gained a new superpower to inflict judgment upon me.

"If you didn't bring me here to talk about Titan's treatment," I snapped defensively, "then I have no idea what we're even talking about."

There was a long, tense silence before the Red Ghost bit out, "I was asked to assist in an investigation in Chicago. I think you know what I discovered".

Ah. "You found Imperator Rex."

"I found Imperator Rex's killer."

My fury dissipated and was replaced with curiosity; I hadn't thought that I'd left any evidence behind. At the moment, however, I doubted that my accuser would feel comfortable setting aside his animosity to explain his forensic techniques.

"What would you have me say?" I asked softly.

"I want you to give me a reason—any reason—why I shouldn't see you arrested!"

"I'll provide two reasons. First...I made every attempt to avoid conflict and was acting in self-defense. Second, while I have some level of respect for you as an opponent..." The stars within my armor began to swirl. "...I would resist arrest. Vigorously."

Some of the indignation slipped from his demeanor. "The battle started in Imperator Rex's living quarters; it looked as though you'd surprised him there."

His sense of betrayal made more sense, now. The Red Ghost had examined the evidence and concluded that I'd traveled to Chicago with the intent to commit cold-blooded, pre-meditated murder; that would not be a sin that he would easily forgive. An unintended fatality, however...that, he would treat differently: as a tragedy rather than a contemptible decision. For my own part, I saw it less as an unfortunate turn of events, and more as an inevitable consequence. In either case, it was gratifying to realize that the Red Ghost seemed quick to take me at my word.

Both of us often failed to reveal our whole truths. We chose our words carefully, we manipulated and twisted each sentence to our own advantage...but we didn't lie outright. It was a strange relationship, but it was almost like trust.

"I hadn't been expecting violence at all," I reassured. "I was negotiating access to view a few works of art in his possession."

The scarlet-clad hero paused and gave me a considering stare, eyes unfocused as though attempting to peer at the man behind the distant stars contained in my mask. "The Ancient's lost treasure is a myth," he eventually smirked. "I wouldn't have thought Doctor Fid to chase after fairy tales."

I hadn't realized that the legend had been known to the heroic community at all, but I'd forgotten that Cloner had been a long-time patron at Lassiter's Den; who knew how much gossip Cloner had gathered and spread to other spandex-clad do-gooders? I imagined that the Red Ghost had researched some of the items that Skullface had gathered and recognized the connection.

"No myth," I conceded, rewarding the Red Ghost's rather impressive logical leap with honesty. "I found the Ancient's remains. When I've completed my research, I intend on donating the majority of the recovered artifacts to the Boston Museum of Fine Arts."

Not the gold and silver bullion, of course. I was certain that a more productive use would eventually be found for those riches.

The Red Ghost chuckled wryly and rolled his eyes. "I should have known."

"I wasn't certain when I began my search," I admitted, moderately embarrassed.

"And yet, you found it. Hundreds of seekers before you, and you unburied a legend in only a few months' time."

"There are certain tasks at which I excel."

"I'm sorry," he said abruptly. "For the accusation, earlier."

"It wasn't unwarranted."

"It was...unkind. Truthfully, I'd come here hoping that I'd

misinterpreted the evidence."

In retrospect, that seemed obvious. The Red Ghost had no weapons that could possibly have overcome my defenses and my scanners did not detect any other reinforcements near enough to impede my retreat. Had violence erupted, the Red Ghost would have had no choice save to escape to the safety of his mist form until I'd flown away. And yet, he'd stated that he would see me arrested.

The realization struck like lightning.

"You've discovered my civilian identity," I said, and my armor's vocoder stripped the weary resignation from my voice.

He startled then relaxed when no attack seemed imminent. "Yes. I have."

There was a long moment of silence as I considered the ramifications. A quick scan of the Internet using my neural tap saw no hint of negative press at AH Biotech, nor did a scan of my home's security cameras reveal any approaching police. However the Ghost intended to use his information, the information hadn't been made public yet.

I rather liked the Red Ghost, but sudden and complete annihilation was still tempting. I was, unfortunately, very certain that the meticulous crimefighter before me had taken precautions to discourage that option. If I chose that bloody path, he would surely have engineered a pre-planned means for my identity to be revealed in a catastrophic manner.

I found myself already missing my too-quiet house and the endless meetings at AH Biotech, barbecues with my CTO, and bringing my adopted sister to the park to play with Nyx.

The Ghost could take all of that away with a word. It was a sobering feeling. Was this what he'd felt when I had stood across from his home and woken him with a phone call? When I'd revealed Doctor Fid to be hiding in the shadows in the park where his nephews played? If so, I'd failed to gloat sufficiently; it must have been terrifying to the Red Ghost and I'd barely noticed. In my defense, I'd been drunk. Next time, I would be certain to bask more thoroughly in the thrill of victory. If ever there was to be a next time.

I resisted the urge to contact Whisper mentally; wherever she was, she deserved at least a few more moments of peace and happiness.

"How'd you know." he asked suddenly, "that I'd figured it out?"

"We've fought many times, you and I." Behind my black starfield mask, I felt a wry smile touch the corners of my lips. "You've never seemed the sort to bluff; you said you'd see me arrested but brought no means to defeat Doctor Fid. The threat would only have teeth if you thought you could reach me outside my armor."

"Hm. I should have been more careful. I didn't intend the grand revelation just yet."

"Hoping to catch me unawares?"

"Honestly?" he grinned. "I was hoping to wake you up with a surprise phone call, the way that you did to me months ago. Turnabout is fair play."

That didn't sound like the actions of an enemy. Tit for tat is a game played by equals; against a more dedicated adversary, permanent solutions would be a wiser choice. For a moment, I felt something approaching hope...but that sensation faded as I realized that the sword of Damocles dangled overhead. If ever I stepped out of line, I would risk the destruction of a great many relationships that I'd come to value.

And perhaps that would be for the best. With choice ripped from my hands, I could be the creature Whisper wanted me to be! I could be Terry Markham, her brother and guardian. Fid's bloody crusade could finally come to an end.

The mission would be over. Rage warred with relief, and I was genuinely uncertain which emotion would struggle to primacy.

"When did you make your discovery?" I asked, still reeling.

"I had suspicions after my cross-dimensional jaunt, but I didn't know for certain until after you stepped in to protect Cherenkov."

The Red Ghost had visited my house twice since he'd returned from that other world, and I hadn't noticed a hint of wariness or misgivings. His acting abilities were impressive; he'd fooled even the scanners that I'd had watching for microexpressions and unconscious biological tells.

I was still pondering what connection he'd found when he tilted his head curiously, "Do you prefer 'Greg' or 'Gregory'?"

Exhilaration and disappointment pounded through me like a physical wave, crushing the breath from my lungs. If not for my armor's pre-programmed body-language control algorithms, I would have slumped in place.

"I prefer Doctor Fid," I managed to reply, dizzily.

The Red Ghost—a former forensic accountant and one of the most competent investigators I'd ever faced—had uncovered the wrong identity!

"As you wish," he chuckled, oblivious to the jarring shift in my mood.

I could imagine how it must have played out: In that other world, he'd met an adult Robert Markham—an alternate version of my deceased brother—and heard my fraternal analog's last name being spoken aloud. Given that the Red Ghost claimed to have been in close contact with Valiant, it was likely that my disclosure in Chile had provided a timeline for the Ghost to begin his inquiry.

"Were there any problems scheduling Titan's treatment?" I asked, as though nervously changing the subject.

The investigation would have spanned through mountains of old records to find information about the villain attack that had claimed the other world's Fid...except that I had been exhaustive in my efforts to make minor changes to old newspaper and police records; instead of finding Terry Markham, the hero had followed the breadcrumbs and found my oldest false identity instead: Gregory Marcum, who'd been known as a reclusive inventor more than three decades prior and who had made a small fortune selling inventions to oil companies. Who'd disappeared for five years after Bobby's death when Fid was at his maniacal worst.

Who'd resurfaced about the same time that Doctor Fid came out of retirement, and had acquired a job with the Department of Metahuman Affairs, and maintained that career for more than sixteen years...

"No," the crimson garbed hero replied. "Everything looks to be proceeding smoothly. The slowest part seems to be working through the insurance paperwork."

I'd written remarkably complex automated scripts to maintain that identity. Correspondences, occasional social media posts, the day to day workload required of an off-site data analyst...It was possible that an artificial intelligence like Whisper or Cuboid might uncover the ruse but no human observer would see the patterns. I'd made too many changes over the years and intervened manually when necessary.

"One of the many advantages of villainy: no paperwork to file."

Even better was that there were many in the main office who would swear that they've met Gregory Marcum, even though the man had never existed.

(Simple social manipulation technique: "Hey, this is Greg from Records; I know I haven't seen you since the Christmas party, but I need a favor..." If the message is ended with personal information—such as asking after the target's son and remarking about how time flies—it is quite easy to convince someone that the fictional interaction at the Christmas party had been a friendly one. Over time, the target will invent a memory.)

"There are advantages to standing on my side of the line," the Red Ghost eventually replied, a strange note of intensity and yearning in his voice. "You might find that you enjoyed it. In the long run, I think that you'd be welcomed."

Gregory Marcum had decades worth of history, begun long before Fid was even an idea; it was no wonder that the

Red Ghost had been fooled. I hadn't intended for that persona to be a decoy identity, but I'm not certain that I could have done better if the effort had been planned.

Doctor Fid and Terry Markham were both safe. AH Biotech was safe. Whisper was safe.

(Cherenkov would likely be viewed with suspicion for the rest of his heroic career. Ah, well.)

"There's still a part of me that is a monster," I warned. "I try to keep it chained, but don't forget who and what I am."

"You're the man who defended the entire planet single-handed, who helped Valiant rescue a school-full of children, and who is working to repair my former team-leader's sanity."

"And saved a kitten," I added, defeated.

"If you're not a hero, then what are you?"

What was I? Exhausted and confused. Without any better answer to offer, I offered a polite farewell and launched back into the night.

※ ※ ※

In science and math, I found my place of calm. Clarity. Also, the rationale behind the Ancient's final missive became clear.

In the early days—the first journals, when curiosity and high ideals drove every decision—the Ancient had envisioned magic to be part science but also part art. A sorcerer, he felt, trained to focus his instinctive understanding of the flow of supernatural forces. Scholarship provided an outline, but nuanced intuition formed the structure of a supernatural working. He'd spent a lifetime exploring this link, making suppositions and rigorously testing his theories. Year after year, he'd stretched himself to his limit and beyond in search of perfecting his understanding.

I identified the pattern first: He'd had his observations backwards. It wasn't that his instincts improved; instead, it was forces from outside our dimension that were gaining greater influence over his subconscious mind. The 'sorcery' that he'd come to revere was not the mastery of preternatural forces omnipresent in our world...it was merely another power caused by the interdimensional ripples set off by the Legion scientists centuries ago. A connection to dimensions so different from our own that there were no words that could adequately define the otherworldly laws of physics.

No language could suffice save for math. Fortunately, mathematics was a language at which I excelled.

I lacked the inborn ability to sense the forces that the Ancient had studied, and no machine could mimic the effect that the gestalt of mind and body and spirit had upon the ephemeral membranes between dimensions. There was, provably, something unique about the fields created by a complex brain. Something beyond the electrical impulses and chemical reactions. Some took this as evidence of the existence of a soul, but I preferred the label that the Ancient had settled upon: akashic identity. A pattern that was distinct and unique for every higher organism in the multiverse.

Superhuman powers were tied to individuals by some quirk of interdimensional forces, localized alterations of the laws of physics. A nigh-infinite array of influences somehow molded to shape when filtered from foreign worlds through an akashic field and into our reality. It was marvelous. It was extraordinary.

It was something that could be quantified. And—with the benefit of access to the Ancient's meticulous notes and exhaustive observations—there were certain effects that I could emulate.

In the future, I had many avenues of study to look forward to. For now, though, there was only one effect that required immediate attention. And with that effort completed, it would be time to lure Skullface into a final confrontation.

※ ※ ※

"Welcome to KNN CapeWatch, I'm Stanley Morrow."

"And I'm Pamela Green."

"Today, we have interesting news regarding one of the more enigmatic figures in the superpowered community: Doctor Fid."

"As our regular viewers will remember, Stanley and I interviewed the notorious supervillain not so very long ago. And I, for one, ended that interview with more new questions than I'd received in answers."

"As did I, Pam. As did I."

"In that interview, we touched upon the Doctor's long and violent history…and also upon the recent change in his behavior. In the time since, Doctor Fid has traveled the world rescuing people in need."

"Most visible, of course, was his cooperative effort alongside Valiant."

"More quietly, Doctor Fid has been providing robotic assistance in the efforts to rebuild the Museum of Fine Arts in his hometown of Boston."

"It's hard to believe that this is the same man who terrorized the eastern seaboard for more than a decade."

"Very true, Stanley. It seems almost as though he's a different person."

"Still frighteningly powerful, of course."

"Of course."

"The museum is reopening in two weeks, and Doctor Fid has announced that he's going to donate a new exhibit consisting of art and artifacts gathered from another villain's lair."

"The Ancient!"

"Our younger viewers may not recall how horrifying a villain the Ancient had been. He'd kidnapped hundreds for his vile, inhuman experiments…and very few of that number were ever rescued."

"Disgusting."

"Very much so. Still, the Ancient had acquired a large quantity of expensive and historically significant artifacts."

"It should be a beautiful exhibit."

"I expect that it will be."

"And that's not all. As a gesture of good faith—and to make sure that no one will ever misuse the knowledge that the Ancient had tortured so many to acquire—Doctor Fid intends to publicly cremate the Ancient's laboratory notebooks."

"It will be a private ceremony at a Rhode Island lighthouse on the cliffs, with only a few witnesses. A memorial to those taken and abused by the Ancient."

"Hopefully, the families of those who were lost will rest easy knowing that the Ancient's legacy has finally been destroyed."

"We can only hope, Pam. In other news, Blueshift was injured while battling Don Voudon in New Orleans today…"

❦ ❦ ❦

If Skullface wanted to rescue the Ancient's writings, he now had precise knowledge of when and where the books would be present. He would (rightfully) assume the event to be a trap but didn't have the option of letting the opportunity pass by. He'd invested too much in this scavenger hunt. It wasn't merely a question of losing resources…it was a matter of losing face. If he intended to maintain his position among the supervillainous elite, he dared not allow my actions to go unchallenged. His reputation would be irredeemably marred.

And besides…he coveted those laboratory journals. I wasn't a sorcerer, but even I could tell that the information contained within those leatherbound books would be a powerful boon to a worker of so-called 'magic'. Burning those tomes was going to feel delicious.

(I would keep my own digital scans, of course. There was

still science to be done.)

※ ※ ※

Terry? Whisper sent to me across the neural tap. **Are you coming home tonight?**

I was planning to, I admitted softly. Floating mid-air in the Mk 38, I was busy repairing a western-Pennsylvania bridge that had begun to fail; maintaining the fiction of heroism was still feasible. For now, at least.**If you prefer that I stay away for a few more days—**

No! Whisper objected. **I want you to come home.**

I thought that you might want more time to yourself. My heavy-combat drones—twelve feet of soaring destructive potential, reflection-less black pillars bristling with energy emitters and sensors—were a poor substitute for my construction automatons, but the latter devices were otherwise engaged. Still, the damaged section massed less than a thousand tons; the combat drones could stabilize that much weight while I restrung cables and welded replacement brackets into place.

Mm. she disagreed, and then shyly added: **Nyx misses you when you're not here.**

Oh, does she? I couldn't help but smile. **I miss Nyx, too. I'll come home soon.**

There were still sixteen cars stranded on the bridge; local heroes with the ability of flight were ferrying civilians to safety one at a time while I ensured that the structure did not collapse. My work would need to be re-evaluated and reinforced before traffic would be able to resume but this would, at least, buy sufficient time that no further lives would be lost.

I didn't mean to make you leave, Whisper said, sadly.

I know, sweetheart. I reconfigured my gauntlets' energy blasters to emit carefully regulated plasma, allowing me to spot weld thick i-beams with my grasp. There was a cacophony of screams and honking horns, but the bridge's shifting was minor. **It's not your fault.**

It kind-of is.

It absolutely is not, I countered. **You were being honest with me. You don't ever have to apologize for that.**

It's not your fault either. You were doing what I asked you to. What I told you was all right! Whisper insisted.

Then it's nobody's fault. The bridge still swayed, but there was no danger of further collapse. Ignoring the applause and cheers that I was unworthy of, I lifted further into the night sky. **Sometimes, life is cruel that way.**

Life isn't all that bad. Sometimes you get puppies!

And sometimes you get the best little sister in the world, I smiled, rocketing eastward with seven heavy-combat drones trailing behind me. **Who's going to grow up and be so good that the world won't need Doctor Fid anymore.**

Little sisters will always need their big brothers.

I wasn't certain that I could be the big brother that Whisper wanted. But I was grateful, nonetheless.

I'm on my way home, I told her. **Pick out a book!**

There was still so much to do. Deadlines loomed, and with them the chest-pounding hunger for resolution. Skullface would come! In days, our contest would be over. But an evening spent reading aloud to my android little sister would not be a night mis-spent.

Mm! she agreed cheerfully. **Oh, can we read the one about the porpoise named Ech—**

Echo? I finished, amused; we'd read that book twice already, but it remained one of her favorites. **Sure, we can read that one. Pull it from the shelf.**

There was no response, and my skull felt emptier than it had since I'd first allowed the adorable little A.I. access to my neural tap.

Whisper? Sweetheart, are you okay?

Silence.

CHAPTER EIGHTEEN

I DIDN'T FIGURE IT OUT UNTIL LATER. THAT THE weapons Skullface's mercenaries had stockpiled had been a misdirection; that the real danger had been their tendency to travel the city in pairs, seemingly without purpose or discernible pattern. I should have seen it! Once I'd started reading through the Ancient's texts, I should have made the connection. But my focus had been elsewhere, and all of my monitoring had failed to recognize the importance of the small ritual components that the mercenaries had placed around the city.

I'd been watching for hints of a physical attack. Body language, weapon usage, aggressive behavior; any of those would have raised alarms. A tendency to litter hadn't raised a red flag. Tiny leather bags of unsavory materials hidden within fast-food wrappers or crumpled tin cans had been surreptitiously dropped in precise locations...In flower pots, under mailboxes, hidden in tree stumps.

The significance had eluded me, even after I'd glossed over the Ancient's diagrams depicting the ornate magical circles that were used for the most powerful of sorceries. I understood the multidimensional math more thoroughly even then had the venerable supervillain, but still I'd failed to observe.

Every sentient being within that circle—within the greater Boston metropolitan area—was simply gone. According to the demands left burning in the night sky, they'd been taken by Skullface and held hostage against my good behavior. The scale of the abduction was astounding.

The 'spell' shouldn't have had any effect on Whisper. Her brain wasn't kept inside her skull! She was an artificial intelligence operating on a network of supercomputer connected via quantum tunnels. Half the world could have been consumed in thermonuclear fire and there should have been sufficient redundancy for her servers to maintain her identity. Her body (while adorable) was only supposed to be a remotely operated shell for her glorious, extraordinary psyche.

I'd always known that she was more than mere hardware. Whisper may have been born of technology, but she'd evolved into something far more magnificent. Why hadn't I checked to see how her akashic identity—her animus, her soul—had manifested? Self-identity was certain to have an effect, and she always thought of herself as a little girl first.

Whisper's core program was still operating on her server farms but had reverted to a pre-infantile state: a mindless and emotionless nucleus of vast potential, with no trace of the child who'd made faces at the fish through aquarium glass, or fell over in giggles the first time her friend Dinah's puppy licked at her nose. My sister was gone.

An alarm triggered in my skull and an autonomic-function algorithm forced me to start breathing again.

Whisper lay, doll-like and unresponsive, at the foot of a bookshelf so I carried her to her bed and tucked her under her covers and quietly read the first chapter of Echo the Porpoise. Nyx jumped up to curl up at her mistress' side, whimpering nervously with her tail curled right between her legs. I stroked at the puppy's back with trembling hands but had no reassurance for the little canine. I was hollow.

I'd been here before—

"Ow." Bobby looks bewildered, holding his chest. For the first time in my entire life I can't think. I can't calculate the angles, can't figure out what I did wrong. I'm holding my brother, shouting for help and feeling helpless and small. There is so much blood.

—but this was different. Whisper wasn't dead. She wasn't! She'd been taken, and I knew who had taken her. I would get her back.

(A small, screaming part of my mind recalled that the city had been empty as I'd rocketed overhead; there'd been no other bodies left behind, but Whisper was unique: a new form of life. Whatever Skullface had done, it had affected the little android differently than everyone else...and all the theory gleaned from the Ancient's tomes was of no use in understanding the consequences. I ended that thought-process with vicious fervor.)

There was no part of this that wasn't my fault. If I hadn't been playing at heroism, Skullface wouldn't have been so brazen. If I hadn't spent so much time and effort protecting AH Biotech and my civilian identity, I could have focused on ending the threat earlier. I could have done so much more if only I'd cared more about my little sister and less about keeping my humanity.

That wasn't a mistake I would make again.

It was Terry Markham who ensured that Nyx had food and water and was settled in Whisper's room, and it was Terry Markham who kissed his little sister's hairless brow goodnight. It was Doctor Fid who made his way to the teleportation platform hidden in my home office.

There was murder to be done and little to be gained by wasting time.

🙰 🙰 🙰

Skullface fancied himself a sorcerer, a mage of such prowess that he deserved to become heir to the Ancient's legacy. It was true that the skeletal menace had acquired an enviable level of power, but he didn't have a scientist's mind. He lacked sufficient imagination. As such, I imagined that he was completely nonplussed when Doctor Fid, encased within the recently upgraded Mk 35 heavy combat armor, burst into his artificially created subdimension. The Mk 38 and Mk 37, operated by automated systems, trailed behind. Reality screamed from the intrusion and the sky wept blood-red ichor that faded into mist before falling to the heat-scarred ground below.

"SKULLFACE!" I boomed, "I am here, and I have the

books! Show yourself!"

All three of my armors released their payload of microdrones; the strange physics here neutralized much of my scanning technology but every little bit of information would be of use.

As had been the case in my prior visit to one of Skullface's subdimensions, the space was vast and sickly. Yellow-brown atmosphere hung like a putrid fog and the dark sky above beat down upon me with pulses of cool malevolence. There were structures in the distance, barely visible through the haze; I accepted a metal-shod crate that the Mk 38 had been carrying and drifted in that direction. The Mk 37 and 38 initiated their cloaking systems and took different paths.

Last time, the area had been uninhabited save by Skullface and myself. This time, however, the world's pustulant surface seethed with alien life. Twisted creatures swam in glowing red pools and horrors wandered the wastelands. I paid them no mind.

There was only one monster here in dire need of slaying.

I floated on, pausing occasionally to roar my challenge. Here, in this place, I was certain that Skullface could hear my words. His delay in response was a show of power, a demonstration that he did not answer to an interloper! I understood his impulse to wait, to force me to stew in my own rage and helplessness...but it was the wrong choice. My drones were gathering more information with every unhindered second.

I'd yet to find any evidence of human presence. Nearly five million people had disappeared from the Boston area;

whatever Skullface had done to them, it was reassuring to know that he hadn't simply left them to their own devices in this vicious landscape. The death toll would have been horrific.

The worry, of course, was that the skeletal villain's alternate choice was even worse.

A column of shadow erupted amongst the distant buildings; the air positively thrummed with power, and tendrils of darkness spat through the air like ink-black lightning. The spectacle could only be a summons, and I increased my speed towards the display.

The great ebony pillar of energy had erupted at the center of an immense coliseum carved from a gray stone with the luster of marble. There were things watching from the stands, an eager audience with ill intent. I couldn't see them and my sensors revealed nothing; there was only movement and twisting mists. I could only feel the hateful audience's hunger, piercing my armor and stabbing at my heart.

But I was Doctor Fid and the cocktail of psychoactive drugs coursing through my system was a mix that I hadn't indulged in for more than twenty years. My heart was stone and I was calm as I settled to the ground, waiting patiently.

The pillar of eldritch forces guttered and died, revealing a fifteen-foot-tall skeletal monster settled upon a menacing throne of iron and rust: Skullface, wrapped in the power of his domain. When last we'd fought, he'd augmented his height to twice that of the mighty Mk 35. The villain had been monstrously strong and durable but the greater bulk had cost him speed, a fact that I'd capitalized upon throughout the battle. This time, he'd chosen to match the Mk 35's approximate dimensions. He'd upgraded his armor, too, since our last conflict; it was still a grotesque spike-laden gothic horror constructed of an unknown gray metal, but it looked thicker and the runes etched upon its surface blazed like a dying star.

Behind his throne was a giant purple crystal, pulsing like a great heart. In this place, Skullface was an entity of power, but the crystal's presence dwarfed him. Though it glowed only dimly, it was painful to look upon.

Microdrones immediately began ultrasonic scans.

"Doctor Fid," Skullface graveled, "You were foolish to come here."

"Your attack on my home was an invitation. It would have been impolite to stay away."

"You've brought my books?" He gestured at the crate that I'd carried with me.

"I came prepared to bargain. But first, a gift. This was the second time that you waited until I was gone before moving upon my territory." A trophy was withdrawn from a smaller secondary storage compartment in one of the Mk 35's thighs—a human spinal column, still covered in gore—and tossed to the ground at his feet; it landed with an unpleasant, wet clatter. "I thought you might be lacking one of these."

"You play a dangerous game, Doctor." There was warning in his tone, but also confusion; this confrontation was not playing out the way he'd expected. With millions of lives—millions of MY PEOPLE—at risk, Skullface had expected deference. The conflicted anti-hero I'd pretended at being would have been thoroughly cowed.

But I'd had plenty of time to reprogram my brain and excise that version of Doctor Fid, and I'd used some of that time to think. The kidnapping of Boston's populace had been an escalation the likes of which the world had not seen in half a century. The act was a statement of power, yes, but also a declaration of war! The world's heroes—and many villains—would rise against him in an unstoppable force. The decision only made sense if Skullface had truly believed that he was approaching his endgame: that (with the Ancient's manuals in his possession) he would somehow become invincible.

I saw now that there was more to his plan...an outside force that had driven Skullface to this excess. I may have appeared in this realm uninvited, but I was certain that he'd planned on bringing me here irregardless. For him to have prepared this stadium and the horrific throne, I sensed that he was trying to impress the observers. This was theater! It wasn't enough that he defeat me; he needed to be seen accomplishing the task. The entities in the stands were watching me but they were watching Skullface as well. There was power at stake; power enough that Skullface was willing to risk everything for a chance to bring Doctor Fid low.

The Ancient had mentioned enduring a similar ritual in his journals. Doctor Fid was no one's supplicant, and I did not intend to follow his script.

"That backbone belonged to Dr. Chaise," I informed the seething villain. "I'm afraid he doesn't need it anymore."

While Skullface had chosen to hire mercenaries from out of town to avoid attracting my attention, he hadn't been sufficiently careful to verify that none of his people had had family in Boston. It had taken only minutes to talk Chaise's location out of one ex-minion who'd been imprisoned in upstate New York. I'd done my bloody work and then used information peeled from the unfortunate madman to build the portal that brought me to this subdimension.

And besides, Chaise had nearly killed Regrowth. The Red Ghost might not appreciate a psychotic scientist's slaughter as an engagement gift, but he probably wouldn't object too loudly.

It was difficult to read emotions from a skeleton. From his body language, however, I imagined that Skullface had realized what I'd done: I'd offered a direct challenge, taken something of value from his domain in the same manner that he'd taken something from mine. Skullface no longer had the option of simply declaring victory if I handed over the Ancient's lore. The observing horrors would expect more.

"So," the towering villain's skeletal hands gathered into fists that shook with rage as he looked down upon the spine from what had once been his most trusted subordinate, "You're no hero after all."

"I am Doctor Fid," I replied grimly, feeling the truth lock into my soul. The label of 'hero' or 'villain' no longer mattered—not in the face of rage so cold that it felt like ice burning in my veins. I was beyond them. "I will be whatever the mission demands."

"And what's your mission?" He'd regained his bluster; his tone dripped with mocking scorn.

"To take back what is mine," I gestured to the crystal (a

stasis crystal, my drones had confirmed) behind him. "And to prove once and for all that you don't deserve the Ancient's legacy."

I dared not admit aloud that the size of the stasis crystal was daunting. I'd read about such things: mystical constructs intended as prisons. A physical representation of subspace storage similar to that which I used to hide my warstaff when it was not in use; even small crystals were, supposedly, difficult to create. The amount of skill and power necessary to forge a stasis crystal large enough to house an entire city's worth of population was astounding.

Fortunately, time didn't exist in subspace; if the sorcerer had done his work well, the abductees would be returned having endured less than a heartbeat's duration of discomfort. It was an odd thing to be hoping for skill and artistry from a man that I fully intended to murder.

"You said you came here to bargain," he scoffed. "Those mission goals don't sound like you intend to negotiate."

He was hoping to catch me in a lie, I knew; according to the Ancient's writings, the entities that moved among the stadium seats were entertained by misdirection but enraged by deceit. Being caught in a falsehood might encourage them to support one side or the other in the inevitable violence. I wasn't certain how these creatures from far-flung dimensions might augment Skullface's powers and I had little desire to find out.

"I said that I came prepared to bargain," I corrected. "And I am willing. I offer truce between us!"

His growl was feral and flame poured from his eye

sockets; I doubted that he expected me to be so knowledgeable about the watchers, but the Ancient had written about his dealings with extra-dimensional creatures. To the observing entities—eldritch beings in constant conflict—even a temporary armistice was a valuable commodity. To Skullface, on the other hand, peace would be of no benefit. If he accepted, our conflict would be concluded...but he would not gain the resources that he had hoped and sacrificed for. "I refuse!"

"If there cannot be peace, then I have nothing else to offer," I declared gravely, as though disappointed by the answer I knew would be given. And then triggered the Ancient's handwritten ledgers to self-immolate.

"NO!" In a flash, he'd charged forwards...but it was too late. The skeletal villain reached into the ash, heedless of the heat still radiating from the crate's melted, glowing shell. "What did you do?!?"

"Initiated hostilities," I laughed, summoning my warstaff and spinning it easily. "Your move."

He roared and hellfire streamed from his open jaws, but I was already moving. I dodged to the side then shot forward, shifting my grip and swinging the staff like a massive baseball bat. Skullface was ready for me; he'd summoned weapons of his own and my attack glanced off a shield's edge.

The next few passes were spent taking each other's measure; he'd chosen a double-edged arming sword to accompany his heater-style shield and was blisteringly fast in its use. The blade left ink-black trails of ghostly force in the wake of every swing, humming with power and promising a painful death if I misstepped. For my own part, the Mk 35's onboard combat algorithms enhanced my reaction speed until I could keep time with the strikes. My staff was a whirling windmill of parries and counterattacks, intended more to harry and enrage than to damage.

And then we both began to add non-physical attacks to our repertoire. Balefire clashed with plasma and masers were deflected by a mystically-enhanced shield's surface. The coliseum's gray stone floor shook, developing blackened scars and vicious chips as we circled.

Even my most sensitive microphones could detect no voices, but I somehow knew that the things in the bleachers were howling with excitement and blood-lust. I bellowed back at them, delivering a kinetic-energy blast through my orichalcum-framed warstaff that caught Skullface under the chin and threw him back into the stadium wall with earth shattering force. He was already back on his feet—lifted by crimson tendrils of mystical force—when I shot forward to capitalize; his sword swung in a horizontal arc that might have ended the battle if I hadn't shifted backwards in time.

The blade had cut through my forcefield as though it were nonexistent; I suspected that it would have done the same to my armor and flesh as well. No matter. It was simply a question of taking more readings and remodulating my shields until I'd found a functional model. I offloaded my body's movement to the Mk 35's combat algorithms so that I could concentrate on analysis.

The red coils of energy settled around Skullface's limbs,

appearing to guide his movements as he resumed the offensive: a mystic equivalent to my armor's programming. And so we fought, so-called 'magic' versus science, a frenzy of powerful blows and swift blocks while preparing for the next stage of combat.

I had just finished making adjustments to my defenses when Skullface spat an incantation that tore at my spirit to witness. Gravity twisted; for a moment I weighed less than a feather, and then suddenly more than a battleship. Inertial-displacement systems strained to resist the shifting forces but the response was too late: the ground spread open its maw. I could only roar in impotent rage as the earth crashed around me like a tsunami of granite and cobble.

≈ ≈ ≈

Bobby uses both hands to pile identical action figures into my grasp. "You play Cloner. I'm Bronze."

Bemused, I follow my brother to the rec room where he's used piles of books and laboratory apparatus to set up his battleground. It's good to see him more outgoing; in the first few weeks after our parents' car accident, he'd barely spoken at all. We'd spent much of that time traveling back and forth from my childhood home to my house in Massachusetts. Now that we've both moved to Boston permanently, he's begun to make friends at his new school. He still grieves but isolation doesn't suit him.

Mourning for Mom and Dad while being responsible for Bobby's welfare is a constant struggle. It feels like putting on a mask: masquerading as though strong, playing the role of caregiver and big brother…while every part of me wants to break down weeping. I'm only nineteen! Mom and Dad were supposed to be here when I accepted tenure. They were supposed to sit in the front row when my work on the Nobel prize winning astrophysics study is announced. They were supposed to love me, like I love them, forever.

But Bobby is setting up his toys, and sometimes he smiles and laughs. For his sake, I can pretend to do the same.

"So, Bronze, who are we fighting today?" I have one of the Cloners ask. I'm caching others in strategically useful locations on the makeshift map. Bobby has set up sections of high-ground where a combatant would have a clear view of the field, and ravines where individuals could take cover.

"We're fighting Chaos Overlord!" Bobby replies in a childish gruff voice that I'm sure he thinks sounds like his favorite hero.

"I thought he was dead?"

"He came back," Bobby wavers, losing his husky tone. "The bad guys always do."

My knowledge of current events isn't always accurate, but it is my understanding that Chaos Overlord has not, in fact, reappeared. But…Bobby is probably right; the heroes never found a body. Chaos Overlord probably will return, because he's a villain and villains cheat. I hate him and everyone like him. Villains **deserve** to be hated. If the gray-and-orange costumed super criminal can cheat death, why can't people who are infinitely more deserving? Why not our parents? It isn't fair.

Bobby is thinking similar thoughts; I can see it in his downcast eyes, the tremble of his lips.

"We'll catch him this time," I state through my Cloner figurine.

"He won't get away again."

I dare not tell Bobby, but right now I hate the heroes too. They let this happen. Chaos Overlord will come back, and eventually he'll be captured and eventually, he'll escape again. The heroes are just part of the cycle, and it's only people with brightly colored costumes and superpowers who get to play. Everyone else just gets run off the road by a drunk driver and their story ends. A sad-faced police officer knocks on their eldest son's door and tells him that he's afraid that he has bad news. Two lives end and two more are shattered and I hate everything except for my little brother.

"It's your turn," Bobby says, softly. He finds his Chaos Overlord figure and sets him up on top of a pile of textbooks.

"Okay," I fake-whisper. "I'll take high and low, you come up the middle."

Bronze and the Cloners creep towards their opponent, and then battle is joined.

※ ※ ※

I awakened slowly, which should have been an immediate warning that something had gone horribly wrong; every armor since the Mk 7 has included an onboard medical system that could pump adrenaline, amphetamines and any number of other chemicals into my system in order to shock me to awareness when needed. But I was drowsy and disoriented, and my throat felt as though I'd gargled shards of broken glass. An attempt to rub the weariness from my eyes, however, was unsuccessful.

My arms were trapped. Was the Mk 35 disabled?

A painfully hot breeze flooded over my face and a shiver of apprehension shot up my spine, jarring me back to full alertness. I blinked my eyes open and beheld Skullface, sitting once more upon his throne. The shattered remains of the Mk 35 lay at his side, and I was encased shoulder-deep within a stone prison.

"I recognize you," Skullface commented conversationally. "You're that CEO, the one who had my vase."

I strained ineffectually against my bonds. "The vase doesn't belong to you."

"It belongs to the Ancient's heir!"

"Precisely," I smiled, tasting blood between my teeth. "I think I'll keep it on my mantle."

Skullface stood from his throne and stepped towards me, and I saw now that he had shrunk from his oversized state to his mortal form; were I not buried in solid stone, we would have stood eye to empty eyesocket. I could hear flames crackling inside his empty chest. The eerie yellow-green flickering glow illuminated his bleached skull from below, and tendrils of smoke and fire occasionally licked upwards to caress the underside of his jaw.

"You are not the Ancient's heir," the creature growled.

"Am I not?" I chuckled. "I'm the only living soul who's read his journals."

Skullface reared back, angry flames roaring up his non-existent throat to pour from his jaws and eye sockets, and then struck me with an armored skeletal fist.

Stars filled my vision and I remembered my first evening camping in the Appalachian mountains. How small I'd felt beneath that endless sky, and how alive the night had seemed. I remembered the sound of the breeze coming through the trees in waves, from a gentle rustle building to a steady thrum, the entire canopy resonating until it drowned out even the drone of insects and birdsong and animal calls. I'd never taken Bobby camping; he would have loved it so much...

I spat tooth-shards at my assailant's feet and laughed. "The books are burned. Gone forever! If I am not the Ancient's heir, then no heir will ever be found."

Skullface punched me thrice more, powerful blows that made a ruin of my face. The last blow landed with a meaty thwack and I felt something shift under my left eye. He hadn't broken my jaw yet, though, so my laughter continued unabated.

"You live," the skeletal villain hissed, "only because I think that you are the sort of villain who would deny enlightenment to the rest of the world, but keep copies for yourself. Did you create copies before you destroyed those journals?"

"Of course I did. But they aren't for the likes of you." I stood corrected; my jaw had at least a hairline fracture and I heard it click oddly as I spoke. There was a wet and bubbly tone to my voice, too, that was unnerving. I couldn't help but giggle at the sound.

"I am the world's greatest living sorcerer!" Skullface snarled. "I've bargained with otherworldly beings beyond your comprehension. I traded my very flesh for knowledge and power!"

"None of that makes you worthy."

"Who do you think you are, to stand in judgment? You're just a man in a metal suit...I can see your tattered soul! You don't have even the slightest talent for magic."

The metal suit was a powerful tool, but the seeds of my less-wholesome persona had taken root in my soul long before the first armor had been constructed...fertilized by every childhood pain, every insult, every lonely moment, every loss, and every triumph. I closed my eyes, still chuckling softly to myself; all of me hurt, but I knew that Skullface's aspirations were undone.

"I am victorious!" the skeletal villain bellowed, and I knew that he was addressing the shifting things in the bleachers more than he was talking to me. "I have defeated my foe, and I have earned my prize!"

"And I am Doctor Fid!" I countered as loud as I could manage, and it sounded true even from Terry Markham's ravaged lips, with no vocoder or speaker to relay the decree. "You have won nothing!"

The explosive charges within my skull detonated.

CHAPTER NINETEEN

Disorientation is the wrong term. I shot towards the stars, fell into an endless chasm, and lay at eternal motionless rest…simultaneously. I was blind and saw all of creation, deaf and yet the whispers overwhelmed. The calm was terrifying, and something was missing, something I had no words for but still I ached for its return.

And then the moment passed and I was encased within the Mk 38, plummeting towards Skullface.

The warstaff's wreckage might be salvageable given sufficient time in a workshop; for now the smaller scepter felt comfortable in my hand. Lightning gathered at the pommel and one backswing slammed Skullface backwards as an explosion of dust and gravel heralded my arrival.

Sadly, some instinct had warned him of the blow; he'd shifted with the force of it and was barely injured. Still, his gaze shifted from the shattered corpse enclosed in stone to me, skeletal maw hanging open in disbelief.

I could not help but feel a moment's sadness for the loss of my first body; like Theseus' ship, every board and spar had been replaced...but there had been an emotional tie to my past, a persistent connection to the creature who I'd once been. Despite all the modifications that I'd made over the years, somehow, those had still been the arms that had hugged my parents and held Bobby when he was still an infant.

Perhaps when I was done with Skullface, I could scavenge a few spare parts for nostalgia's sake.

"How...a soul transfer?!" he scrambled to his feet, still in shock from watching my former body's bloody eruption. "But you aren't a mage!"

"In his heart of hearts, neither was the Ancient," I crowed. "He was a scientist! And I've had his journals for more than a week."

The urge to lecture was overwhelming: to explain how my methodology was superior to the means outlined in those leather-bound texts. How nanotechnology and the vast analytical capabilities of Whisper's server farm had allowed me to create so perfect a clone of Terry Markham that my memories could be pre-loaded into the new body, updated to the nanosecond before the prior body's expiration. That—unlike any so-called 'magical' method of akashic identity transfer—my process could be permanent without the need for constant energy input. In only a few days I had simulated and then improved upon a working that a sorcerer would have required a decade to master.

The Ancient would have appreciated the innovation. Skullface, on the other hand, would be baffled by the technicalities. I blasted him with a high-energy particle-beam on general principle.

His stance was stable as he was pushed backwards, his armored feet skidding across dust and rubble coated stone. Annoyingly, his armor was sufficient to ward off any damage.

I spun my scepter in one hand as though warming my wrist. "Shall we continue?"

Skullface leapt forward as though shot from a cannon, wreathed in yellow-green flame. There was no subtlety to his movements now, and very little skill: only rage and power. Rage and power still made for a credible threat; I pulsed my forcefield to its maximum and blocked his sword swing with the scepter's haft. His jaws opened wide and a vibrant stream of balefire poured over our crossed weapons, a wage of putrid, overwhelming heat that taxed even the Mk 38's environmental controls.

My current suit of armor was my most recent design and it was not as powerful as the oversized Mk 35 before it...but I had access to the accumulated sensor readings taken from the first stage of combat. My weapons and defenses were now far more well-tuned. The hellish fire spilled over the starfield surface of my armor, curled behind me and heated stone to a dull red glow. I waited until the deluge began to fade before countering with a second more-powerful stream of charged particles that snapped his jaws shut and threw him head over heels.

It was disturbing, how completely natural my new body felt; there was no discomfort, no hesitation. Neuron by altered neuron, even my reflexes had been completely reconstructed. Technically speaking, the new corpus was an upgrade—but it felt as though nothing had changed. If not for the now-charred carcass littering the amphitheater floor, it would have been easy to forget that Terry Markham had perished.

Onboard medical systems pumped adrenaline and amphetamines into my veins and the medical nanites continued their work to optimize pathways in my brain...to limit emotional response to that which was useful for the mission. The void of space was held within my armor's skin, a pulsing blood-red glow bled from the Mk 38's seams, and incandescent stars—distant and cold—offered judgment without comfort from within my being. I was wrath incarnate.

Doctor Fid lived.

Laughing gleefully, I followed the particle beam with three quick strikes from my scepter, each impact resounding like thunder. My skeletal opponent was driven back 'til he was braced against the towering stasis crystal at the coliseum's center. According to the Ancient's texts, such structures could not be breached by physical force; I tested this by pounding my opponent's skull against the pulsing purple surface with all of the Mk 38's considerable might.

Somehow, Skullface had lost his sword and shield; he grabbed my scepter with both hands and spat a word of power. The orichalcum core—that remarkable alloy discovered by Whisper's lost supervillain 'father' Apotheosis—burst into shrapnel, followed by a wave of light and energy that drove me into the sky. My opponent was wounded but not yet defeated.

With a joyous laugh, I dove back into combat.

※ ※ ※

Bobby is gone.

There's blood on my hands, more than I'd ever thought possible. The world smells of burnt nitrites, of carnage and shit and vomit and hate. My brother's heart isn't beating and I think that my own stopped, too. It feels like it...like my chest is compressed, tight and empty at the same time.

I breathe.

Automatic gunfire rattles; Bronze is focused on the insectoid supervillain who began this attack, and some of Locust's men have retaken their weapons and are rampaging as they try to escape. People are wailing, children scream and there's so much chaos that I couldn't follow it all if I wanted to.

Bobby's eyes are still turned towards the lobby across the street. To the very end, he'd stared uncomprehending at the place where his favorite hero had disappeared. He'd been confused but still hopeful at first, still waiting for his idol to come to save the day...and then his expression changed when he realized help wasn't coming. Not soon enough.

I'd brought my brother here. His birthday present: to meet a true superhero. It was supposed to be a surprise for both of them; Bobby is Bronze's biggest fan! Who wouldn't be thrilled to meet a kid with so much enthusiastic belief, so much joy? It was supposed to be a gift for everyone involved, for my little brother and for Paul Riley—Bronze's secret identity—both. It was supposed to be a present for me, too: I was going to get to watch Bobby's giddy smile.

Was. Bobby was *Bronze's* biggest fan. His eyes are unfocused, now. Unseeing.

Bronze is fighting Locust now but had come out of hiding far too late. He'd made that choice: to leave us in harm's way long enough to safeguard his alter-ego, Paul Riley. Bronze wasn't a hero, wasn't deserving of my brother's adoration. He was just a man who happened to have powers, just as flawed and unworthy as I.

Mom and Dad would have saved Bobby, I'm certain. I don't know how, but they would have! They'd given life to Bobby and me; Mom and Dad would have known what to do. What had I been thinking, taking Bobby in after the car accident? I'm just a skinny, pale youth who looks half a decade younger than my twenty-one years. A physicist, a mathematician, a professor. A freak. I should've known that I was destined to fail.

"Get up!"

A rough hand grabs my shoulder, pulling me away from Bobby. My brother's blood is still warm and slick on my hands, and Bobby's shirt slides from my grip when I try to resist. My captor is taller than me, stronger, and his grip is like iron. Something hard and sharp is pressed under my chin and I'm tugged back against a costumed man's chest like a human shield.

"All right, faggot! Move nice'n slow, maybe you get out of this alive."

Why on earth would I want that? I let Bobby die right in front of me. Also, I was at least moderately certain that I wasn't gay. The question as to my own sexuality had always seemed purely academic and there'd always been other subjects more worthy of study. I'm certainly observant enough to identify members of either gender who are aesthetically superior but that recognition never elicits any emotion other than an acknowledgment of my own deficiencies in comparison. The man pulling me along isn't making sense.

"Just keep moving," he growls into my ear then raises his voice to address the policemen who are pointing guns at me: "Let me go or I'll kill him right now!"

"Put the knife down!" one of the officers—the older one, the one on the left—orders. "Let the kid go!"

I don't have a knife, and Bobby is still by the concrete and wood-slab bench. The police aren't making any sense, either.

We're getting too far away from my brother, so I grab the thing at my neck and struggle with a renewed desperate ferocity. Heat blossoms in my fingers and in a line along my throat, but the surprised mercenary let me slip from his grasp. Gunfire erupts behind me as I stumble back to Bobby's side and drop to my knees.

The scent of freshly cut grass is still present under the acrid smoke and bile and death. I still smell salt on the air. The sky is a beautifully clear cerulean and the sun still shines.

Today is Bobby's birthday and his deathday. It isn't fair. It isn't right.

A hero would be able to make things right.

I think that maybe most of them aren't really heroes at all...that they're just people who pretend. If they didn't take willing part of this masquerade—if they didn't let children worship them—then I wouldn't have brought my brother to Virginia Beach at all! When horrors like this occur, it's the so-called 'heroes' fault as much as it is the villains'. Damn them.

At least the villains are honest. They don't profess to be anything other than what they are: monsters, freaks worthy only of *society's hate.*

Just like me, like Kenny Bryant and Louis Nguyen could see all those years ago.

I want to close Bobby's eyes but my hands are still covered in blood. So I kneel there, helpless, and finally begin to weep.

❧ ❧ ❧

With staff and scepter lost to me, I was reduced to fighting hand to hand; I dared not increase the distance between us—to hover above and launch energy blast after energy blast—lest he steal enough time to cast more complicated spells. Skullface may not have been worthy of being the Ancient's disciple but he was still a credible threat. He'd bartered with entities from far-flung dimensions, and (through ritual) could channel their power.

That was all that 'magic' was: the superpower to act as a conduit for beings that exist in alternate universes extraordinarily distant from our own. There was no ancient knowledge handed down from our ancestors, or arcane wisdom gleaned from secret texts; instead, there were only interdimensional beings that had learned to prey upon humans who believed in those moldy fairy tales.

It was a recent phenomenon; it wouldn't have been possible before the Legion scientists had done whatever they'd done halfway across the galaxy. Before they'd rung the dimension-separating membranes like a bell to make changes to the laws of physics, to give members of their own race the telepathic power that they'd intended to use to build an interstellar empire...and before they'd accidentally granted superpowers to the inhabitants of a few systems that happened to have the correct properties for quantum interactions to propagate. Before the Legion had unexpectedly created the superheroes and supervillains that had killed my little brother—and now, threatened my little sister.

In our home, Whisper's beloved puppy was curled against his mistress' side. She was still. The little android body was empty, and my opponent was to blame.

Battle-lust withered and rage exploded inside me like a physical force: a pressure at my center so intense that it felt as though my ribs were straining to contain it. Hate pulsed with the beat of my heart; I'd let this battle go on too long.

For their crimes, I'd thrown the Legion into such chaos that their empire would never recover. My plans for Skullface were far more visceral.

I rotated between Wing-Tsun chain punches to Fiore dei Liberi's late fourteenth century grappling method to Krav-Maga hammer-blows and elbow-strike techniques, advancing steadily and keeping my opponent off balance. No individual attack or counter was sufficient to cause damage but I remained in control and Skullface's temper continued to deteriorate. I felt no exultation, no pride...only grim conviction.

The unseeable things in the coliseum's seats moaned eagerly. They were too inhuman to truly care who was the victor in this battle. All they wanted was the spectacle: to witness skill and determination, drive and viciousness, power and control. I put on an exhibition, and I could see in Skullface's body language that he was aware that he had lost his audience's favor; he was shaking with rage and the first hints of fear. Both of us were pouring energy into every attack, great flashes of lightning and flame that threw shadows to the stadium walls.

In desperation, Skullface chanted a quick cantrip that called a howling pillar of balefire to erupt from beneath my feet; I'd been struck by similar attacks several times already in this battle, so my defenses had already been adjusted.

"Checkmate," I declared, and stepped through the flame to land a single straight punch to Skullface's missing nose.

Having unbreakable armor was of little use if an impulse could travel through the material to shatter the body encased in within. One of the most important innovations within Doctor Fid's feared powered armors, therefore, was the embedded inertial displacement systems. It was those mechanisms that allowed me to survive blows and falls and sudden movements that would liquefy an unprotected human being. The apparatus functioned by containing a carefully modulated energy field inside the armor's confines and measuring all the forces that were acting upon physical objects within that field. When an unexpected force—an impact, for example, or a sudden change in velocity or direction—occurred, the kinetic energy was shunted away to an artificially created subdimension. The apparatus had many possible uses; it was just such a device that I'd offered to the Red Ghost so that he could see to it that auto manufacturers would install a similar system.

With that final punch, I reversed the flow of stored kinetic energy: all the combined forces from a drop from low earth orbit, countless violent confrontations with heroes and villains alike, and seven thousand car accidents...all funneled through the surface of the Mk 38's knuckles.

A thunderous crack shattered the air; a shockwave pulsed the atmosphere into a sphere of plasma and the world went white. The cacophony was indescribable.

With the armor's defenses temporarily disabled, my arm was blown off clear at the shoulder and I was thrown back halfway to the coliseum wall. Medical alerts warred for my attention as burst organs and muscle tears were identified and prioritized. I relaxed, dizzy and lightheaded from sudden blood-loss; even Valiant would have been felled by that blow. The only remaining task, I thought, was to shatter the stasis crystal and return the population of Boston to their proper place. To wake Whisper up so that she could comfort her little black Labrador...

And then the dust settled and Skullface began to laugh. Somehow, he'd managed to raise a defense in time.

I strained to sit up, but the skeletal villain was there before I'd managed the feat: limping, with a broken jaw and shattered orbital socket, and his left arm flopping uselessly at his side...but alive. With his right hand, he grabbed at the Mk 38's faceplate and tore it away reveal the bleeding, injured man within. I was too sore, too damaged to resist.

"If you give me your copies of the Ancient's manuals," he slurred, "I'll make your death painless."

"You're an idiot," I wheezed, unable to keep from

chuckling, and the Mk 38 self-destructed in a glorious orange fireball.

After another strangely eternal moment of disorientation, I disabled the stealth systems on the Mk 37 light-combat armor while a singed Skullface slowly struggled to his feet. Empty space erupted into being within my armor's surface, cold and foreboding and emotionless.

"This suit doesn't have the raw might of the others," I admitted casually from my third body of the day, casually toying with the charm that hung from a necklace around my neck. "You're wounded but this would still be a challenging battle. But today, Doctor Fid is playing a villainous role...

"And if the game isn't playing out the way a villain originally hoped...villains cheat." I tugged at the charm and the massive warhammer once wielded by the superhero Viking (and more recently by the late and unlamented Imperator Rex) filled my hands.

An indescribable strength suffused my very being; I was wrapped in power like I'd never known, and my footstep echoed like a bass drum as I stepped forward towards my enemy. The air tasted of electricity and the horrors in the bandstands shrieked and peeled away into nothingness to escape the terrible power I held in my grasp.

There would be a cost, I knew. But for Whisper—and for all the people of Boston—I would pay it gladly.

Skullface tried to flee, then Skullface tried to fight. Finally, he tried to beg for his life. In the end, none of those solutions worked in his favor.

CHAPTER TWENTY

"I'M READY TO PROCEED," THE NEUROSURGEON announced.

I was in the observation booth under the guise of Terry Markham. The room was crowded and tense; the Boston Guardians sat as a group in quiet support, wearing their colorful superheroic uniforms while watching with varying expressions of concern, hope, and squeamishness. A priest was present, as well as a few medical experts and what I presumed were friends and family. And, of course, a representative of the insurance company that had authorized this scenario.

Titan was sedated on the operating room table, wrapped in blue and circled by medical personnel and equipment. His shaved head was exposed from the surgical tent, and his skull immobilized by a heavily reinforced pinion instrument.

Professor Paradigm had been flown in from California to assist in the first stage of the operation; the medical nanites that I'd supplied were not—could not be—as advanced as the versions flowing through my own veins. Some portions of the treatment were to be performed manually. With an expression of grave concentration, the graying west-coast based superheroic scientist manipulated a complex device intended to temporarily disable Titan's invulnerability so that the surgeon could operate.

The incision could not be seen directly from the observation booth, but I'd hacked the video cameras and had a few microdrones present to perform more detailed scans; I could monitor everything in real time. Truthfully, I wasn't particularly interested. My contribution to Titan's rehabilitation would come later.

And so we sat in solemn silence while the neurosurgeon and her nurses performed their labor. They were competent and they did not rush.

Aeon needed to leave the room three times. Veridian's expression was haunted but he barely moved throughout the entire procedure. The Red Ghost and Regrowth were holding hands, knuckles white with tension. The priest was comforting one of the other attendees, a young woman whose eyes were red and glassy.

It was three hours before the neurosurgeon was ready to inject the nanite slurry.

Willy Natchez, the Native-American microbiologist who AH Biotech had hired away from MIT only a year prior, had been chosen to assist. He'd been involved in the nanite program since he was still a post-doc, and had quickly become a well-respected member of his team. If there were no surprises, then William would not need to say a word. If there were questions or concerns, however, I had confidence that the young man would be able to represent the company in a professional manner.

I'd decided against adding hidden programming for the devices to eventually install subcranial explosives into Titan's gray matter. Having endured such an explosion first hand, I was reluctant to share the experience. That particular mode of termination felt oddly intimate, personal; it was mine now and no one else's.

There were no surprises; the microscopic machines would do their work. William offered the surgeon a grateful smile and retreated from the operating theater without a word.

When the neurosurgeon announced that the completed operation had been a success, no one cheered...but the release of tension was palpable. The young woman still talking to the priest burst into relieved tears.

After only a few weeks of recovery, the former leader of the Boston Guardian's concussion-induced Chronic Traumatic Encephalopathy would be a thing of the past. What the effect on his personality would be would take time to determine. I hoped that he would revert to the Titan of old: a dedicated, professional opponent. A proper leader for the superhero team stationed in Doctor Fid's domain. Red Ghost would certainly welcome Titan's return; the Ghost was competent enough, but he did not relish command.

"Thank you," the object of my reverie said, emotion rendering his Chilango accent more pronounced than usual. "Titan could have killed you during the kidnapping rescue, yet immediately you volunteered your company's resources to make this possible. You're a good man, Doctor Markham."

"Thank you for saying so," I chuckled, shaking his offered

hand. "But really, it's just enlightened self-interest. Boston will be safer when the Guardians are back at full force."

There had been some minor unrest since the citizens of Boston had been released from Skullface's stasis crystal; there'd been no riots, but the people were rightfully disturbed. There was anger and distrust, and the heroes were working harder than usual to ensure the public that they were protected.

The Ghost smiled and clapped me on the shoulder in a friendly manner, then returned to conversing with his fellow Guardians. With little else to do, I took my leave.

The hospital was a place of healing, and the creature roiling underneath Terry Markham's skin did not feel comfortable here.

※ ※ ※

There existed no reasonable means to attend in person, but I streamed audio and video from microdrones that had sneaked into the church and been spread throughout the estate where the reception was held. The wedding was lovely.

The service wasn't lavish, but the amount of care and affection that had gone into every aspect of the ceremony was readily apparent. Miguel (the Red Ghost) and Elaine (Regrowth) had written their own vows; they were so poignant that the bride's mother burst into tears. Members of both the Espinoza and Goldman families got along fabulously, all smiles and laughter and immediate friendship.

There was so much joy in that reception hall that it hurt to look upon.

As a wedding gift to Regrowth, one of my drones had delivered a 'To Go' bag with a sample of the painkiller she had jokingly stated that she wanted more of after our unsuccessful collaboration against Skullface (and the formula to reproduce it if she so desired). To the Red Ghost, I offered up several medical and safety technologies that his company could claim to have reverse engineered and thus offer to the public.

It wasn't certain that the Red Ghost would accept the gift. I hadn't acted with my usual care when tracking down and slaughtering Skullface's second in command; footage of Doctor Chaise's ruined corpse had made the rounds of the news programs, and Doctor Fid was feared once more.

Even though the first of the new replacement armors was complete, I'd been reluctant to seek out the Red Ghost to defend my actions. What justification could I offer? The way I'd killed Dr. Chaise hadn't been the act of a penitent man seeking redemption for past evils; it was a vicious, calculated choice made by a monster. That I'd been mad with grief and fear for Whisper was no exoneration. For some acts, there can be no excuse.

For a while, I thought, there'd been a seed of respect and friendship between the Red Ghost and Doctor Fid. That sprout had now withered, and whenever the hero and villain next met it would be as adversaries. In the end, this shift was likely for the best. I wished Miguel and his new wife every bit of happiness that they could squeeze from this world.

They deserved better than for Doctor Fid to hold any nonadversarial role in their lives.

❊ ❊ ❊

I'd deployed microdrones to infiltrate a New York hospital as well.

"You okay?" Cloner asked. This was one of his bodies that I hadn't seen before: willowy and slim with dirty-blond hair and piercing blue eyes. He was wearing his old costume, the one he'd used before his retirement. I'd once owned action-figures with that blue and gray color scheme.

"I'm fine," Cherenkov replied bravely. His bandages would need to be replaced soon; the wound on his chest was apparently still oozing and the gauze was developing a sickly yellow tone. "How's Exbow?"

"We got her out in time," Cloner smiled. "You saved her life."

"I'm glad."

"Yeah, me too. She's a good kid."

"She's the same age I am," the wounded young hero whined.

"You're a good kid, too."

"Whatever you say, old man." Cherenkov grinned and then winced as he shifted on the bed.

"It was a brave thing you did," Cloner praised. "No one would have blamed you if you hadn't leapt in right then."

"I would have blamed me," Cherenkov whispered.

For a while, both heroes were quiet.

"You familiar with John Wooden?" Cloner inquired suddenly.

"Huh? No...who's that?"

"He was a basketball coach out in California. I guess he was before your time, infant."

"Yeah, yeah..."

"He once said, 'The true test of a man's character is what he does when no one's watching'."

"Huh," Cherenkov replied, though he looked confused. "I like that. A basketball coach said that?"

"Yeah. All the philosophers played hoops back in the day." Cloner winked to let the patient know that he was kidding. "Y'know, you took a damn near impossible risk...you came out of nowhere."

"I had to or else it wouldn't've worked."

"I know. The point is...No one was watching you, 'n I think I know a bit more about your character now."

Cherenkov looked embarrassed. "Thanks."

"You'n I haven't been working close for a while. I know there're reasons for that but it's gonna stop now. What you did was stupid brave, so next time you gotta be smarter. Soon as the Doc says you're good, I'm bringing you in to train with the senior team."

"That'd be awesome! You mean it?"

"I mean it, kid. If you still want it when you graduate, there'll be a place for you in the New York Shield."

"Thank you!"

"You're a hero, kid. Don't ever doubt it."

Beneath those bandages were a series of burns and deep

cuts and two broken ribs, but no hint of pain could dim Cherenkov's broad, goofy grin.

Whisper would be overjoyed to discover that my machinations hadn't harmed her friend after all. And it was gratifying to see how much he'd matured from the image-obsessed teen who I'd hospitalized only a few months prior.

If ever Doctor Fid were again active in New York, facing young Cherenkov in battle would be a worthy endeavor.

❧ ❧ ❧

The Red Ghost was convinced that the man inside Doctor Fid's armor was a Department of Metahuman Affairs employee named Gregory Marcum...a false identity so old that the Ghost's first investigation had found no flaws. Given that the Red Ghost was now more likely to deepen his searching, I'd been slowly adding more details to the nonexistent agent's cover to lessen the likelihood that the mistake would be discovered. Nothing blatant was added, just little dribs and drabs of supplemental material—hints that would make the identity feel more real.

I was contemplating how to leave a physical trail when serendipity struck.

In exchange for free room, board and a moderate salary, the reclusive Agent Marcum was able to convince an out-of-work actor from Colorado to live in Marcum's house and perform his errands. Sooner or later, the actor would be caught on film and the Red Ghost would have a face to tie to the name of Gregory Marcum.

For all his childhood flaws, Kenny Bryant was by all accounts a decent actor. It would be interesting to see how the ruse eventually played out.

❧ ❧ ❧

Aaron's expression was grave and the beer in his hand had gone untouched for several minutes.

"Are you sure about this?" the CIO of AH Biotech asked.

"There will never be a better time," I replied. "Titan's treatment is generating a tremendous amount of good press, and I told you that Henry Collins' crew has been dealt with. We've got enough momentum that our stock price won't take a hit if we announce a re-org."

"This isn't just a re-organization that you're suggesting."

"No. But let me worry about the board. I'll make sure that the permanent appointment goes through."

"I'm not worried about the board," Aaron grimaced. "I'm worried about you."

I forced a chuckle that I hoped was reassuring, "I'm not going anywhere."

"You're my friend, Terry. You brought me in when the company was just a handful of ideas drawn on the back of napkins. You trusted me...so I need to know that this is what you really want."

"It's what I need," I said, and if my voice wavered then neither of us commented upon it. "And thank you. You've been with AH Biotech since the beginning. You know the business inside and out...That's why it has to be you."

"I'm honored, y'know."

"Don't be. You have no idea how much work is ahead of you."

"I think I have an idea," he chuckled softly then finally raised his drink to his lips.

"Then you accept?"

"You said it's what you need. Of course I do."

There was so much empathy, so much understanding in his expression that my heart clenched. I managed a smile, "Then let's make this official."

I shook his hand, then reached for my computer's mouse and clicked 'Send'.

❧ ❧ ❧

```
From: Terrance Markham
Tue 4/3, 1:43 PM
To: ahbt-all
```

First, I wanted to thank you all for the outpouring of support and sympathy that I've received in recent weeks. When this company was founded, it was done with high hopes…but I could never have imagined how wonderful a group of colleagues would be assembled. You all have made me proud to have been a part of AH Biotech's evolution.

The decision to retire has been a difficult one,

but I am confident that Aaron Schwartz will do an exemplary job as interim Chief Executive Officer; Aaron was one of our earliest hires and has been involved at every stage of our company's growth. He has the experience, leadership capabilities, customer focus and passion to lead AH Biotech through the next phase of expansion. I leave the company in good hands and look forward to watching your future success.

Announcements regarding the transition team will be made shortly…

≈ ≈ ≈

When the stasis crystal was shattered, the residents of Boston were instantaneously returned to the locations from which they'd been abducted. There had been a few injuries—people who tripped upon reappearance or discovered themselves suddenly mid-air due to movement of whatever they'd been standing or sitting on when the ritual was enacted—and quite a bit of confusion, but only one fatality that could directly be attributed to the mass abduction: a man who had been scheduled for a kidney transplant, but the donor organ had been granted to another recipient when the citizens of Boston disappeared.

For a few days, the entire city had seemed to be in shock. Quiet and withdrawn, the people hunkered down and reconnected with their friends and family. There was some hue and outcry—angry and scared people doing the sorts of things that angry and scared people do—but for the most part, the city had recovered smoothly. The lights were on, the streets were as safe as they ever were. The Boston Museum of Fine Arts re-opened on time. With the exception of the unfortunate victim of kidney failure, life resumed...for all but one.

Whisper slept.

The spell had not been designed with a unique creature like Whisper in mind. Instead of seizing her body, the spell had grabbed only her psyche: the part that made her a person. Her akashic identity. Her soul. And when the crystal fractured, that part of her did not return to the circuits and crystal matrices of the complex network of quantum computers that made up her physical brain.

My sister wasn't dead. I wouldn't allow it.

The first law of thermodynamics states that energy can neither be created nor destroyed...that it can only be transformed. The crystal had taken and later released something from Whisper. She still existed, a ghost without a shell. I was certain of it!

There was work to be done. New armors to be constructed, additional studies to be conducted, and more operations performed upon my brain to ensure that I was properly focused upon the task ahead. Now more than ever, I needed to be Doctor Fid.

Because Doctor Fid was going to find my sister and bring her home. Even if doing so meant burning all of creation to ash in the process.

DOCTOR FID WILL RETURN!

I hope that you enjoyed reading *Behind Distant Stars* as much as I enjoyed writing it. If so, please hop online and leave a review.

Reviews make sad authors into happy authors!

Also, I invite you to please connect with me via any of the following methods:

Twitter: http://twitter.com/davidhreiss
Facebook: http://facebook.com/davidhreiss
Author Web Page: https://www.davidhreiss.com

Readers who visit my author web page and join my mailing list will be notified of any promotions as well as be eligible for quarterly giveaways. They will also have the opportunity to read exclusive content and learn about upcoming releases.

ABOUT THE AUTHOR

While growing up, David was that weird kid with his nose in a book and his head in the clouds. He was the table-top role-playing game geek, the comic-book nerd, the storyteller and dreamer.

Fortunately, he hasn't changed much.

David Reiss is a software engineer by trade and long-time sci-fi and fantasy devotee by passion, and he resides in Silicon Valley with his partner of twenty-seven years. Until recently, the house was shared with a disturbingly spoiled cat named Freya.

Two new kittens have since taken over the home. The author is thoroughly smitten.

David's hobbies generally involve exploring the crafts and skills found in works of fiction. He's built replica lightsabers and forged medieval armor, programmed autonomous drones and brewed his own mead, started fires by rubbing two sticks together and started fires with lasers. Also, he has become equally mediocre at numerous martial arts, archery, sword fighting, paintball and lasertag.

Behind Distant Stars is David's second completed novel-length project and it certainly won't be his last—he's having far too much fun!

Printed in Poland
by Amazon Fulfillment
Poland Sp. z o.o., Wrocław